END OF EMPIRE

BOOK II

THE BULL
&
THE SWORD

NATHAN RICHARDS

"THIS BOOK IS DEDICATED TO MY
WONDERFUL WIFE.

WITHOUT HER, THIS STORY WOULD
ONLY LIVE IN MY MIND."
                    -THE AUTHOR.

P.S. THANK YOU READER FOR PICKING
UP BOOK 2, YOU WON'T BE DISSAPOINTED
THAT YOU DID.

THE EMPIRE 493 AF

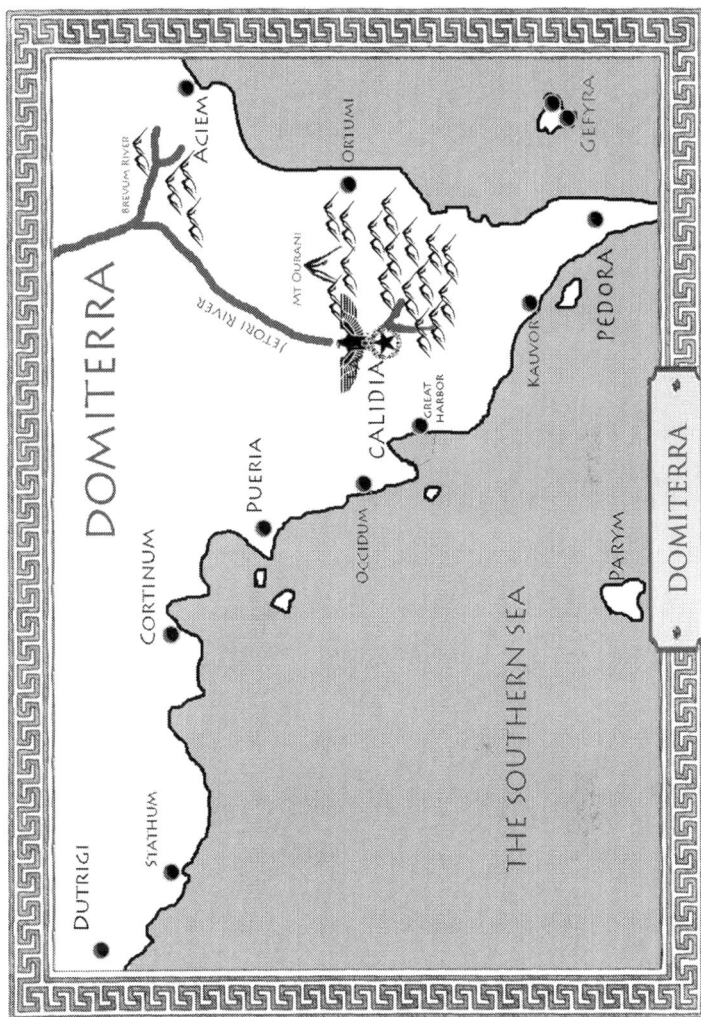

DOMITERRA

BREVUM RIVER
ACIEM
ORTUMI
GEFYRA

JETORI RIVER
MT OURANI
PEDORA
KAUVOR

DOMITERRA
CALIDIA
GREAT
HARBOR

PUERIA
OCCIDUM

CORTINUM

STATHIUM

DUTRIGI
PARYM

THE SOUTHERN SEA

DOMITERRA

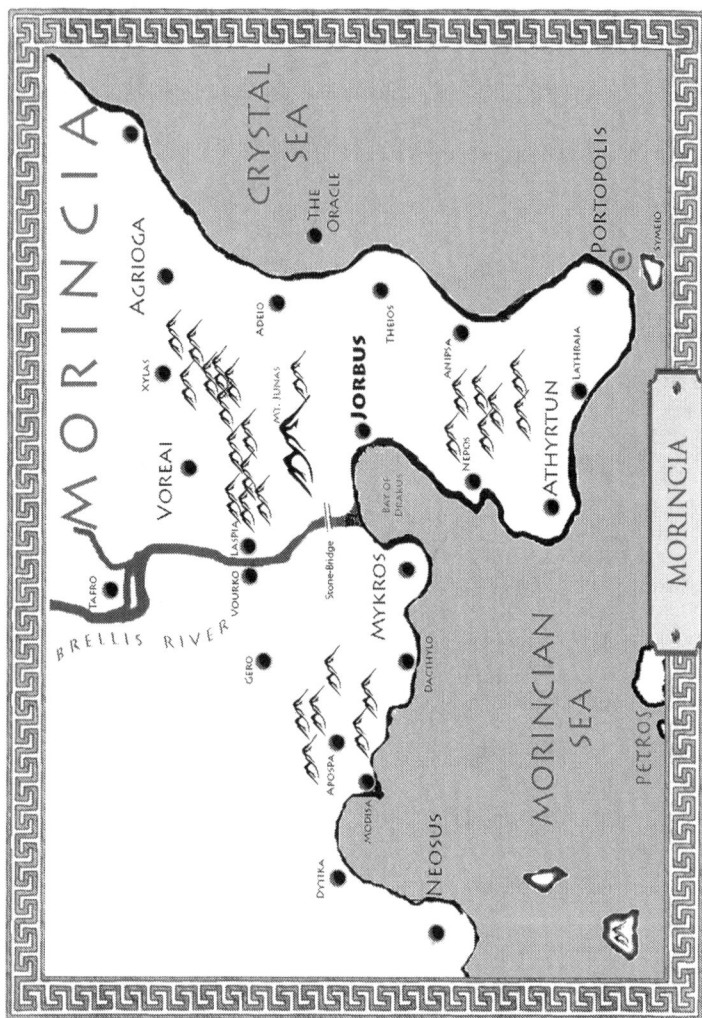

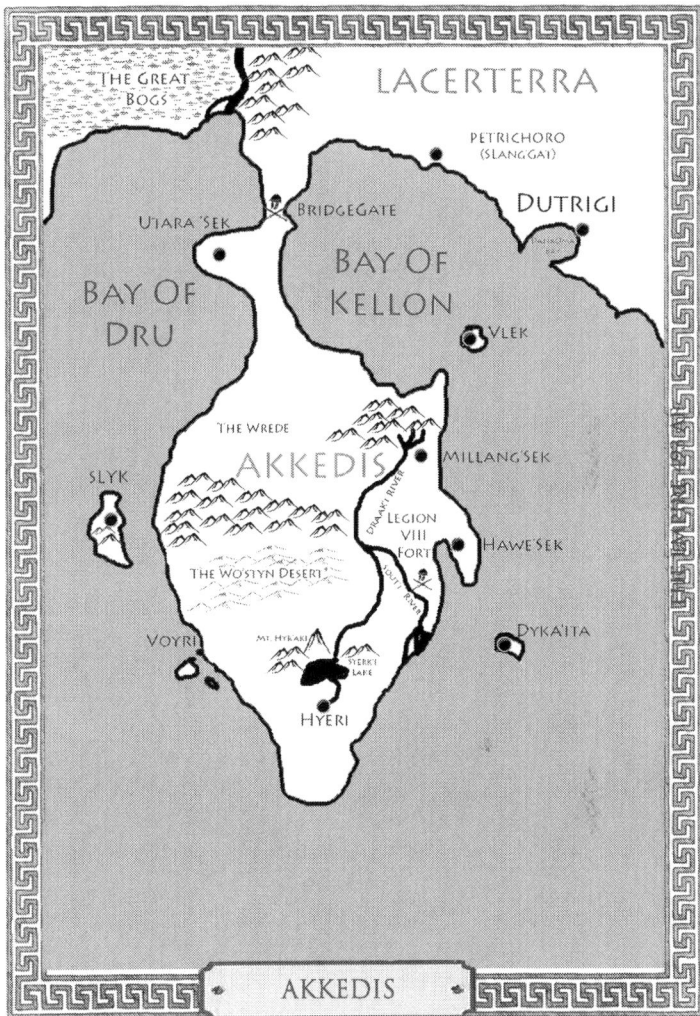

THE GREAT BOGS

LACERTERRA

PETRICHORO (SLANGGAI)

DUTRIGI

U'TARA 'SEK

BRIDGEGATE

BAY OF DRU

BAY OF KELLON

VLEK

THE WREDE

AKKEDIS

MILLANG SEK

SLYK

LEGION VIII FORT

HAWE SEK

DRAAKI RIVER

THE WO'STYN DESERT

DYKA'ITA

VOYRI

MT. HYKARI

SERKT LAKE

HYERI

AKKEDIS

PROLOGUE
THE OLD MAN

It was a peaceful, crisp morning as he lay in his bedding. The old man had awoken before sunrise, as most old men did, and for a very long time lay alone with his thoughts. As the sun rose, the breaking light of dawn filled countless drops of dew with glowing light. They sparkled like stars, stars the colors of which the world had never seen. It was a private spectacle that only he was witnessing, and he was in silent awe as it unfolded. Soon, the world was bright with daylight, and the young men in the camp began to stir and wake as well.

Cassius was the first up, and he went to relieve himself off in the bramble somewhere, and to gather some supplies for the trip. Jaimus was up next, and he rolled up his own bedding and began to break down the camp. The third boy, Marcus, continued to slumber, apparently a heavy sleeper like most adolescents. Perhaps he was the smart one, albeit lazy, resting while he still could. Soon, everyone was awake, stretching and shaking out the night's rest that had crept into their joints and bones. This was much harder for the old man to do, for his ancient joints stiffened terrible after nights like this. He was too old to be sleeping in the dirt like a youth, far too old.

Embarrassingly, the young travellers didn't have anything for breakfast, their meager supplies having dwindled to nothing recently. From his worn leather sack, the old man pulled out four squares of hardtack. Placing them each in a small bowl, he poured some wine over each to soften the near inedible biscuit. He broke a corner piece of off each one, mumbled a prayer to the Gods, and threw each chunk into the nearby bushes. It was an old superstition, but he had been doing it most of his life, so why take any chances by stopping. It was supposed to start the day with good luck, and if the Gods didn't appear to claim their offering, some birds probably would.

"Here, my friends." He handed the bowls out, to young men that accepted them gratefully. "A good way to start the day, date bread. I do not mind sharing, since you let me share your campsite last night. The fire was exactly what I needed to keep the chill away. I need to go feed and water my mule, Kaeso. Would one of you mind helping me get water from the cistern by the road?"

Two of the boys jumped up, Jaimus and Marcus, while Cassius didn't bother moving.

"I will get the water." Marcus said, grabbing the nearby cooking pot they had used the night before. Jaimus offered to feed the animal and was instructed in where the oats were kept in the wagon. Cassius stayed and finished packing and cinching up his travel bag. The blonde boy said nothing to the old man.

"You and your friends can take turns riding in the cart." The man offered, studying the boy with a scrupulous eye as he worked. "Kaeso is a strong beast, but can only pull two people on that cart at a time."

"I will walk." The boy said, slinging his pack on over his cloak. "A soldier needs to march. It is good training."

"Ah, of course." The man said. "No need to wait, might as well start now. But believe me, there will be no shortage of marching in the Legions."

"You were a legionary, then?" Cassius asked, nonchalantly. He was trying to get the man to admit to this in order to score a clue into his past, and who he might be from the man's story the night before.

The old man smiled. "Is it not common knowledge that legionaries march? Did you yourself not just say that?"

Cassius looked away, frustrated. He kicked sandy soil over the bright white ash from the dead fire. A gray plume rose from the disturbance, and a gentle breeze filtering up from the coast below stirred the cloud into nothingness.

Wiping his beard gently, the old man rocked back and forth to gather the momentum needed to rise to his feet. He let out a groan as his knees and back straightened. Throwing his worn leather satchel over his shoulder made a dull, hollow clinking sound. A final stretch of the arms, and he started towards his cart. Cassius was a step behind.

Kaeso was munching his own breakfast, and gave a happy snort as he saw his owner emerge onto the roadway. He patted the mule on the head, and stowed his belongings under the tarp. With empty water skins in hand, he went to the cistern to fill them. It was made of stone, old stone covered with moss and lichen. The spring that fed it bubbled water up and out of an old lead pipe that came out of the arched backsplash. The boys followed suit. Most of the campsites along the coastal road had popped up because of these cisterns. Where a cistern was built long ago, so followed a campsite. This particular one looked ancient.

"Feel free to stow your packs in the back of the wagon." The man offered. "One of you may ride on the top with me at a time. You can decide when and how you rotate. Shall we set out?" None of the boys wanted to be the first to sit down, and they forced Marcus to take the first shift. The other boys did not give up their packs, preferring to carry them like real men, like soldiers. The old man wondered if they would make it more than a few hours before wanting to discard them into the wagon.

The cart lurched as Kaeso pulled, and they were on their way south, towards the heart of the Calidia. The walk was silent, just the rumble of the cart down the dirt road and the occasional bray or snort from the mule. The sun was just above the treetops, and it was bright white and blinding. The woods were fully awake and alive if you were looking for it.

"Where is the Legion you are going to join? Occidum?" The man finally asked.

No one said anything for a long time.

"Do you not know?" The man asked as a follow up.

"We were going to walk the Coast Road until we found a fort, and then would join up there." Jaimus said.

"Ah. Then you do not know how much farther you have to go. That means our time together may end around the next bend. Perhaps a Legion has a castra just past those trees?" The old man laughed.

Marcus, sitting next to the old man looked at him, asked with a stammer: "T-That story you told us last night, is it real? I mean…w-were you there?"

"Yes. It is real. And yes, I was there." He responded, a smile on his face.

"Do you think maybe you could tell us the rest of it?" Marcus asked.

"I was planning on it." The man said, adjusting his straw hat to keep the sun from his eyes.

"Now I mean, while we are travelling?" Marcus added shyly.

The man laughed. "Are you sure you

want to hear it now? Last night you three didn't even want me to start it."

"Please," Marcus said. "Like you said, we don't know how much longer we will be travelling with you, and I want to hear the end of it all. I want to know…" He stopped.

"You want to know who I am?" He nodded to the boy.

All three youths were looking at him expectantly.

"Very well, my new friends." He uncorked his water skin and took a long pull, preparing his throat for the recanting. "Where did we leave off?"

"The Emperor was ill, and Macien was Dictator in his place." Marcus said. "The Enforcer Adypatus was searching for who it was that killed the Consul."

"Silious and that general of his were making plans to start the Civil War." Jaimus added. "And Macien declared him a traitor, and the Imperial Guardsman was captured, and Torbock started his mission, and then…"

"Yes, yes, yes. Now I remember." The man nodded to himself and smiled. "If I repeat anything, or skip over anything I apologize. It was all so very, very long ago. Sometimes I forget what people know or don't know. I do think it's time to introduce a few new players in this story, however."

"New people? Are any of them you?"

"Well, we will see. But I promise you

this… You will know which one I am not right away." And he chuckled to himself. The Boys looked perplexed a bit by this.

"You'll understand in a moment." He waved away their concern. "Have you ever heard of Atheltiades?"

The boys said nothing. The man sighed.

"It's a shame that his story is not better known. We will start with him, for he is quite important in the rest of the tale. Yes, let's start with him." He took a deep breath and began to tell that tale once more.

PART III

PRECIPICE
&
PROVOCATIONS

"NO MAN EVER STEPS IN THE SAME
RIVER TWICE, FOR IT'S NOT THE SAME
RIVER AND HE'S NOT THE SAME MAN."
— HERACLITUS

THE BULL & THE SWORD

I

ATHELTIADES

The morning sun washed the world in a golden-orange glow. A cool flow of air had moved in from the not too distant coast, making it a pleasantly brisk start to the day. Atheltiades stood on the stone ramparts of the Old Wall of the inner city, watching the expanse of Dutrigi come to life below. Just on the fringe of the sprawl, past the last of the buildings, a sea of grass and wheat could be seen. The young commander imagined what this view would have looked like so many generations ago, when General Niko Dutrigius had established the settlement as a fortress. The stone walls that he stood on now were the original walls of the massive fort, and below his feet would have been the start of the golden sea of grass. The oaks had been clear-cut as far as the eye could see, to provide lumber for construction, as well as to maximize visualization of enemy approaches.

These walls had never failed. These walls had always protected the soldiers that garrisoned it. In the same fashion, the soldiers inside were the ones that always held the walls and insured that they never failed. Ever since

Dutrigius took his elite soldiers and headed west to fight the Saurians, the Dutrigians had been the premier fighting force in the Calidian Empire. Descended from these soldiers, and growing up in such a dangerous and tumultuous environment, the offspring that turned this fort into an Imperial city grew up strong. They carried on the ancient tradition of their founders, and were the pinnacle of military strength in the known world.

The Saurian threat had long ago been removed from Domiterra and from their original lands of the adjacent Lacerterra. The Millangor capital of Slang'gat had been conquered, and all the green-skins had been driven into the Akkedan peninsula. Slang'gat had long ago been converted to a human city, being renamed Petrichoro. Despite a promising start to a campaign into the Akkedan peninsula, to eliminate not only the remaining Millangor threat, but to bring the fight to the red-skinned Hyerians. The momentum of the war stopped with the death of the grizzled old general. Dutrigius had been the motor that had given them so much success, and when he died, so did hopes of finishing the conquest of Akkedis and the destruction of the Saurian threat.

But this was all ancient history. Dutrigius, the bull, was long dead. The Emperors, seated far away in Calidia, were never able to support a successful campaign into Akkedis again. For hundreds of years, the situation had remained stagnant. The fort of Bridgegate was constructed on the narrowest point of the land bridge that connected the Akkedan peninsula with Lacerterra and Domiterra. The Saurians co-occupied the peninsula, being kept in check by Dutrigian forces working out of Bridgegate. Boundaries had been drawn in Akkedis, with the green-skinned Millangor occupying the north, and the red-skinned Hyerians occupying the south. The only thing stronger than their hatred for humans was their hatred for one another.

Cramming, confining these two Saurian species in an area so close to each other had done more for keeping them in check than any human force had done since the days when Dutrigius walked the earth. Tearing themselves apart with border disputes and raiding had kept their strength down.

Years and years of ineptitude from the government in Calidia were now making the situation in Akkedis extremely volatile. The Empire had decided that they could ally with the Millangor, deeming them a necessary evil. Through this political union, the Empire gets a steady flow of raw materials and ore, and a foothold in the heart of Akkedis. The Millangor get an apparent boost in their security.

The Empire has even become lax in its restriction on Saurians moving back into Domiterra. It made his stomach churn to think about it. Thousands had died over hundreds of years keeping those beasts out of our lands, and now they were throwing away those sacrifices like they were sawdust on a carpenter's floor. The hatred between Saurian and man was too deep to be washed away so quickly, and any attempt at an alliance was futile. The hatred between Saurian and Dutrigian was even deeper, and that would never go away.

The Empire had made it very clear that the forces of Dutrigi were to take no part in the military stationing in the Akkedis, or any military maneuvers within that theater. Insulting as that was, it was the best the Imperial Council could do to insure that no incidents were provoked that might damage the fragile alliance they had recently forged. If anything would cause such an incident, it would probably occur due to Millangors and Dutrigians working closely together.

So the Empire had sent a single, solitary legion to fortify the border between the north and the south. They originally had stationed more soldiers in Millang'Sek, the green-skin's new capital, but those troops had been recalled due to conflict with Homitha. The Imperial Navy had supplied vessels to patrol the Bay of Kellon, but it was a meager force, and Hyerian and Millangor pirates alike were constantly outmaneuvering, outfoxing, or outright outfighting the small armada.

The biggest blunder of this alliance however was how the Hyerians had reacted to it, and the lack of decisiveness from Calidia to deal with it. Like a cornered beast, the Hyerians had become ultra aggressive with the incursion of Legionaries on their northern boundary. They militarized at an alarming rate, and had done a lot of scabbard rattling and shield pounding along the border. It was only a matter of time before they became desperate enough to cross the Sout'I river and attack the Calidians and Millangor alike. Doubtless, they would try to continue north, and attempt to overrun Bridgegate and flood into Domiterra.

What the Empire did in Akkedis was their business. If they didn't want Dutrigi down their, that was fine. But if their policies and ineptitude allowed the Hyerians to invade the mainland, then it was an issue. Dutrigian forces still controlled Bridgegate, as was the ancient tradition. The fort had never fallen, just as an enemy had never taken the city of Dutrigi itself. If the Hyerians came close to even attempting to pass through Bridgegate by force, entire Dutrigian army would mobilize and crush them. They would most likely follow the enemy into Akkedis and eliminate them entirely; with or without the blessing of Calidia.

The army had been hit pretty hard in the recent war with Homitha. Emperor Kantaur had rallied the Dutrigians and used them in the fighting on Luctantum. Their very presence, the rows of Crimson cloaks and bronze helmets, round apsis shields with the image of a bull, had instilled fear in the Homithans. The Dutrigians had never lost a battle in the entire campaign; but they had suffered heavy loses, and now they were at home, replenishing their ranks, bringing a new generation of soldiers into the army.

Commander Atheltiades was the one who was in charge of their training. It had been his responsibility to get these young men ready for battle. Most had been training their entire lives to be soldiers, and these last few weeks had been fine-tuning, introducing them to actual military life and real time drilling. He shifted his crimson cloak on his shoulders, allowing the cool breeze to funnel in and it sent a shiver down his spine. Running his fingers through his jet black hair several times, he slicked it back enough to be able to place his helm on his head. His Dutrigian style helmet, which was a distinct variation of the Morincian style, was made of steel, but was gilded in bronze to honor the ancient traditions of the uniform.

Atop his helm was his horsehair crest, alternating sections of black and white denoting his rank as a Commander. The white was so brilliant, the black so dark, that the contrast was striking. There was no doubt that the crest was freshly made, betraying that he was only recently lifted to the rank. Some of the veteran commanders crests were so worn and faded, that it was almost impossible to see the design without much scrutiny. Only time would make his crest fade, and only time would make his temperament and skill match the tarnish and use of that crest.

His eyes continued to gaze down upon the city. The responsibility that he felt overwhelmed him; a responsibility to it's current residents, to it's past residents, and its future residents. He knew that behind him, on the grounds, the newest recruits were lined up in perfect rows, as his Captains patrolled the ranks, inspecting them in the manner they did every morning. Every nuance of their dress and their stance was open to scrutiny. They were a decent group of men, good soldiers so far from what he could tell, and their inspections always went well. The captains however had a duty to dehumanize them, and some of the offenses were very far fetched. Nonetheless, people always were disciplined during morning inspection.

Motion caught his eye, and his vision instinctively darted to the right, where the motion had came from. A red cloaked figured sidled up along side him, not speaking or announcing his presence. The design on the crest of the helmet he held in the crook of his arm gave away his rank as that of a *Polemarch*. The position of Polemarch was essentially equivalent to that of a Calidian Legate. The man's battered armor, patched cloak, and scarred skin gave away his experience level as that of a grizzled veteran. The man's facial features gave away the fact that it was

Atheltiades' father. The two men stood like statues for a few moments longer.

"Polemarch Atheicles," Atheltiades spoke first, not looking at the other man "Gods give strength, what brings you to see me this morning?"

"I just wanted to see how my new recruits are doing," The older man said in a gruff voice, sliding his helmet onto his head. "And to check up on their new Commander." The Polemarch placed a firm, yet comforting hand on his son's shoulder.

"The recruits should be fine. The training is almost complete, and soon they will be able to join the ranks and fill spots in the line." Atheltiades responded, still not looking at his father.

"I understand you begin The March this morning." The old man's voice had a hint of sternness in it, fortified with pride. His gaze wandered from his son to the distant horizon. "This is the single most important part of the training of our men, my son. When I was a Drill Commander, this was my favorite phase of the training."

The young commander turned his eyes to his father, whose face was almost entirely occluded by his helm. But he could see his father's eye, and recognized the shimmer in it.

"The March retraces the conquests of Dutrigius and our ancestors. When the Old Bull built the walls of the fortress we stand on now, everything below us and beyond us was Saurian territory. When he started his campaigning, every step between here and Bridgegate was paid for in sweat and blood. When you follow his route, you show these young men the sites of the battles, the monuments to the dead along the way. When you camp in Petrichoro, you will show them the site of the siege that lasted for almost a year. You will show them the field where the Millangors finally sally-forthed after the rain broke, and where they were finally broken and were forced to retreat down the neck of Akkedis, and out of Lacerterra forever." He tilted his head slightly, revealing a severe grimace set on his mouth.

"And when you complete the march to Bridgegate, you will tell them of the importance of that fort, how we hold it with our lives and our family's honor. And you will tell them how when we hold that fort, we are guarding the honor and the sacrifices of our ancestors, who spilled their blood and the blood of the enemy to take every inch of the March you just finished." The old officer turned and looked into the eyes of his son.

"I am very proud of you, Atheltiades." The glimmer in his eyes began to swell. "You honor me, you honor our family, and you honor all who have worn the red cloak and the image of the bull on their shield."

"All that I am is because of you, father." Atheltiades responded humbly.

"The world is changing. Warfare is changing. Dutrigi has not changed, that is what gives us our strength. Cavalry, ranged weapons, cohort style rank and file. All have been developed to give an advantage over a force that is strong and resolute like ours. Our history and our pride is what makes us invincible. The ancient Morincian style of the hoplite and the Phalanx is still being used by us because *it works*. We have perfected it. Even the old Morincian city-states have changed to meet this new world we live in. We have not. Perhaps we never will. It is your duty as the Drill Commander to instill these traditions and ways into this next crop of recruits." The old man turned his entire body to face his son, and then turned his head to look down on the rows of new recruits, clad in their crimson cloaks.

"These men are in your capable hands, and you will guide them well." The father turned to face his son, the blank expression on his face, usually rigid and betraying no emotion, had a hint of earnestness and sadness about it. It was as if he had something that he wanted to say, but something told him that he could not. Atheltiades had an idea of what it might be.

"Some of the other officers, father, said that Lord General Kruegius rides back to Dutrigi." He paused a moment, his calm tone shifting to a more urgent one. "In haste, he rides. And he has resigned as Master of Foot, and Macien of Jorbus allowed him to leave."

The father didn't say anything to this, but also did not look away, nor deny it.

Atheltiades continued. "Some say that the Oracle has spoken of a coming war, and not of one with Homitha. Is that why Kruegius has ridden home?"

His father gave a slow nod.

"As I said, strange things are underfoot in the world." Atheicles almost whispered. "Initial reports from Kruegius, his staff, and his field scouts have come to the conclusion that something will happen, relatively soon. Even the Gods are trying to warn us. Prophecies have come up, yes. But one in particular has stood out. The Divination Council has translated it. Kruegius has had it distributed to his senior officers." He reached into his cloak, and pulled out a scroll, one bound with simple twine. The quality of the paper was marginal, meaning it was a mass produced copy. The rolled parchment was extended to Atheltiades in a deliberate gesture.

"For me to have?" The young officer said, startled.

"It is my copy. I have no need for it any longer." The father said. "You take this with you on The March. I command you not to open it until you arrive at Bridgegate."

"Father," Atheltiades began to protest. "If a war is coming, I must be with the army, The March will take..."

"Silence!" His father bellowed, loud

enough for the troops below to look up. Some of them immediately began to get admonished by the Captains for their breaking rank and file. "You will do as you are commanded. The March is your place. You are the Drill Commander, your responsibility is to our future troops, and as a subordinate officer, it is your responsibility to follow commands."

Atheltiades immediately straightened his stance and rolled his shoulders back, as any one would do while being addressed by their father or a superior officer, or a combination of the two.

"You will leave immediately for The March as planned." A firm hand reached out and grasped his forearm in embrace. He reciprocated the hand shake. His fathers voice shifted to something a little more gentler. "I am proud of you son. Dismissed." His father turned without another word. Atheltiades watched him walk away, down the rampart. He had a sinking feeling it would be the last time he would ever see him.

II

DIMIDIUS TORBOCK

Torbock was tired, road weary from travelling hard. He was used to this type of life, this type of travel; he didn't know how Polemistius was dealing with it. Although, being an Imperial diplomat probably required it's fair-share of traveling like this. The Sentinel's crotch and backside were a swamp of sweat, as was his undershirt. The sun would be setting soon, and it was the hottest time of the day. Trees were scarce on this stretch of the Coast Road, and shade and wind blocks were non-existent. We should rest soon, he thought. We have orders to make good time, but we need to rest.

Jacean trotted a few steps behind on Torbock's left, and Polemistius rode to Torbock's right. They made no attempt to hide who they were. Any man, woman or child would see the trio, and be able to spot two Sentinels and a nobleman. Torbock had requested that they ride discreetly, three unremarkable highwaymen travelling along the roads, but Polemistius had overruled him. "We are Calidian citizens, and we have a right to walk our lands without fear for our lives," he had said. "No one would dare touch us."

Torbock grimaced as he had recalled that conversation. It had been wrong on so many levels. First off, Polemistius was the only citizen out of the three. Dimidius and Jacean would not be citizens until after their service had been completed. Secondly, Polemistius was out of his mind to think that raiders, thieves, rebels, or even just someone who was mean and hungry wouldn't touch him because of his ring. That ring, with this small of an escort, would draw miscreants like moths to a flame. But, begrudgingly, Torbock had trudged along.

They had already passed through Occidum and taken care of their business with the 2nd Legion that was camping there. After delivering the scrolls and dispatches, they had spent the night in the fort, with some cavalrymen that Torbock had fought alongside during his time on Luctantum. Polemistius had dined and slept with the command staff. The city of Pueria was close, but they would not make it until well after dark. They would need to rest soon, to feed and water the horses, and let the beasts rest while they themselves caught some sleep. They would pass through Pueria tomorrow, and then be on their way to Cortinum. The rest of their journey, of their mission after that was daunting.

Torbock puckered his mouth and then frowned, his long rough stubble undulated around his face as he did so. He had always spoken honestly with Jacean, for it was a cornerstone of the relationship between page and Sentinel, between partners. Trust and good communication, they were key. However, he had not been able to communicate the entirety of their mission to his young companion. Tonight he would. If for no reason other than it being unavoidable, then for the reason he needed to tell the boy before Polemistius did. That would create more trouble than it was worth. Jacean would be infuriated that Torbock hadn't told him, and he would have found out from a political haggler.

He hadn't told the boy yet because… well, it was hard to. Jacean had grown up in Lacerterra, close to Dutrigi. His father had been a Dutrigian military officer, who had been maimed on a campaign against Hyerian pirates or something like that. Torbock didn't know the whole story, and neither did Jacean. Torbock had met the man once, just before he died. Xizmontia Monodius had been a good man from how briefly he had known him. Forced to retire from his wounds, the senior Monodius had settled in to a farm with his family. When the Hyerian raiders came to the Monodius homestead, the small band of Sentinels and farm-folk had prepared defenses. The fighting had been brief but intense. Many very good people fell that day, including the old soldier Xizmontia.

As he lay dying, he whispered something to Torbock. The Sentinel had never told another soul what the man had told him, and he probably never would. It was a heavy burden, one that Xizmontia carried to the afterlife. Jacean hadn't been back to Lacerterra since. Not only would he need to explain that they would be returning to these lands, but he would then have to inform the kid that they would be marching into Akkedis! Jacean had been through enough in his young life to have a strong hatred for the Saurians. And more than likely, a strong fear of them. But the code of the Sentinel was about upholding the laws without bias, to execute orders without question, and to not let your emotions or fears rule you. One had to face down his fears to be successful in this line of work.

Torbock had to do the same, and have the conversation with his partner tonight. He beckoned for his counterpart to join him, and the young man brought his mount along side. "We will camp tonight. We will not make Pueria in time." Torbock only gave the boy a cursory glance. His eyes immediately fell upon the boy's faded red focale scarf around his neck. Torbock knew that the garment had been his fathers, part of his military cloak that the boys mother had repurposed for him. The sight of the cloth made him think of that day again, and think about the upcoming inevitable conversation. His eyes darted away, back to the road ahead.

"Yes, sir." Jacean Monodius responded respectfully. "I shall gather enough firewood for a cooking and warming fire, Torbock. You will allow a fire tonight?"

Torbock shifted for a moment, almost smiling. That had sounded more of a statement than a question, as if his apprentice was telling Torbock that they will be having a fire. He thought of saying no, but realized he would be doing so out of spite. There was no reason not to have a fire. Bandits would find them without one just the same.

"Yes," He said evenly. "We will have a fire. And I will take first watch, once we have made camp and taken care of the horses."

Polemistius chimed in from the other side. "Are we going to eat more of that amazingly awful gruel again? I may just eat my saddle instead. At least it will be salted. Can't you Sentinel types sustain yourselves off the land for long periods of time? Go kill some rabbits, or take down a buck. Venison would be much welcomed. And maybe a woman, too, while your out. Not to eat, but you know what I mean. Tomorrow in Pueria, we will stop and get provisions. Meat, bread, cheese, and snatch. Won't take more than an hour. Total. I promise. Will we stop to camp soon, my ass is chapping in a bad way..."

The man didn't take a breath or pause. A diplomat must be able to talk, Torbock guessed. That was his job, and he was doing it. Just like

the two Sentinels had a job to do and they were
doing it right now. He raised his hand and
pointed to a scrubby brush area under a copse of
bay trees. "We will break for camp there. I doubt
we will find a better spot in this area. You will
assist Sentinel Jacean with gathering firewood
and watering the horses."

"*The fuck I will.*" Polemistius scoffed.
"That is your job. I have dispatched to review
from our last stop. That is my job, to stay up on
current events."

Torbock frowned. He really didn't like
this diplomat. But, it was his mission to escort
the man safely, and that is what he would do.

*   *   *

The fire snapped and crackled as the men
huddled close to it, waiting for their meal to
warm. The night air was cooler, but it was not a
cold night. The thicket of chaparral brush that
surrounded their small campsite kept the wind
out. It was starting to blow from the sea, the
tops of the nearby trees swaying to and fro.
Jacean was running an oiled rag over his armor
and blades, while Torbock stoked the fire with a
stick. Polemistius had isolated himself several
feet away, using the firelight to read scrolls he
had removed from his bag.

"Jacean." Torbock spoke, almost
remorsefully. The boy looked up at him, still
working the rag into his gear. He said nothing as
he waited for his partner to speak.

"We must talk about this mission, about the whole journey." Torbock said, returning his gaze to the sparking fire. Jacean nodded, swallowed, and Torbock could tell the boy had an inkling of what was coming.

"We are to escort Vicaro Polemistius through Dutrigi, through Bridgegate, and down into Akkedis." He said it all at once, preferring to let the full force of his words hit at once. It was better that way.

The boy nodded slowly, and continued to oil his kit, vigorously now. "Yes sir." He said to his armor as he focused on his task. "I will go where we are sent." He picked up his sword, unsheathed the weapon, and began to run a whetstone along the blade. The sound of the sharpening and the crackling of the fire were the only sounds heard in the camp for a long time.

III

TARAES KANTAUR

The wagon rumbled and jolted slightly as it bounded down the roadway, always heading towards the sunrise. Her children slept in a jumble across from her, with their cousin. It was a warm morning, and the heat became trapped inside the tightly sealed cabin of the wagon. A thin, wispy palla adorned her shoulders and wrapped her head, allowing some concealment from prying eyes that got too close, but also allowing her to hold onto some normalcy from her life of just a few days prior. Kanion, along with a few other of Macien's own personal guard, had secretly escorted her and the children to this carriage, and they had departed in the very early hours of the morning. So far, there had been no incident.

Macien had been very sure that her life, and more importantly, the life of her children, had been in grave danger. She still internally resisted the command to be exiled from her husband, from her life in the palace, and from her titles. But not as much as before. She knew deep down that staying behind was foolish, that it would do nothing to help Greeth, or Macien for that matter. In fact, her staying would distract and endanger her brother and his associates.

She still felt pangs of guilt in her side when she thought about leaving behind Greeth, which was quite often. She thought of him laying on a slab, no longer breathing, cold to touch, with no one by his side. She welled with agony. Deep down, she knew that she would never see him again. She had said goodbye before being swept away in the night, and she had said all that she could to him. It wasn't enough, but it was all she could convey at the time. Some things don't need to be said to be understood, and Greeth knew how much she loved him. She didn't need to tell him everything.

The wagon hit a larger bump, and she was jostled into the present, back into her current situation. Her eyes fell to the children. They huddled together under a thick blue wool cloak, mouths parted and breathing gently. She wanted to touch them, to hold them, but she resisted. She settled instead for watching them sleep. The children had not slept much so far, and her even less. She was tired, but her instincts of being a parent forced her to remain awake. She knew that the heavily armed, heavily trained, highly capable men that escorted this wagon would die before they let anything happen to Taraes and the children. She knew that the anonymity of their journey

lowered the danger even more. But she still
needed to be awake, to be here for the little ones.

She sighed as her fingers found the knife
that was hidden beneath the folds of her chiton.
Chances were very slim that anyone would
make it into the cabin of the wagon if it came to
a raid or attack. Chances were even slimmer that
if even one man did make it in, that she would
be able to use the knife as it was intended to be
used. If it came down to it, the small blade
would probably be used as a mercy on the
children and herself. No. She couldn't do that.
Never. Her children were her entire world now,
the only thing in this life that made sense. Even
if she knew that putting a blade to them would
be far, far more merciful that anything a bandit,
or rebel, or traitor could muster up, she didn't
think she could do it. She knew she couldn't.
She was a coward then? Her fingertips
disengaged from the steel, and her empty hands
made her thoughts on the subject empty as well.

She closed her eyes and took a deep
breath, trying to escape back to a simpler time,
only a few days ago, when such evil thoughts
had never been formed before. The wax tablet
that she carried with her had fallen off the
bench, and she reached down and retrieved it.
Unclasping the lid, she opened it, revealing a
creamy yellow colored sheet of wax on either
side of the hinge. Thumbing her stylus, she
hesitated before she scratched into the smooth,
unmarred surface of the tablet. She slowly, with

pressure and precision, began to carve into the wax. She worked the stylus more like a scalpel than a pen. She was not writing, but drawing. She had always been an artist, and this particular tablet that she carried was for drawing, not note-taking. Paper and charcoal were her preferred medium, however that was not practical in this situation.

The shape of an ear took place, and with a deliberate sweeping, a rigid jaw line sprang to life from the bottom of the ear. Then, continuing the line with only a slight pause, the chin and lower lip appeared. She had made these lines hundreds of times. The speed and consistency in which she reproduced them was testament to that. She smudged the lines away, and repeated the image again. It was the face of her father that she drew. It was how she felt she could keep his memory alive. Over and over again, she drew his face. She preferred to draw him clean-shaven, his close cropped beard that he normally wore in his later life was omitted. This was the father she remembered from her early childhood.

The old Duke had looked like Macien, but different. His features were bolder, more robust. His jaw line was stronger, his brow more defined. And he had a cheerful disposition, something that Macien tended to lack. Her brother was always so serious. Her father had been Jovial. Aedien had been a man like no other, and he was the benchmark of how she judged all men that she met throughout her life. No one had ever come close to the warmth that this man had exuded. Perhaps Kanion's charisma came closest, but it still wasn't the same. She drew the face again. She could never get the eyes quite right. It was impossible to capture the fire and life that those eyes had held.

As her father lay dying, he had requested that Taraes be the one to make his effigy. Taraes had laughed at this, although she hadn't found it funny. Your body went through some strange emotional displays when grieving. She realized that she was experiencing this now once again for Greeth. She shuddered as she continued to carve out her fathers face in the honey-golden wax. She had laughed when he father had asked that of her. Surely the best artists in Morincia could make him a worthy effigy, one that immortalized him for who knows how long. His father had laughed back. "Let them try," He smiled as he had spoke. "They don't know me like you do, and to be honest, most aren't as good as people tell them they are…"

She drew his eye on the wax, quick and without thought. The lines flowed from her hands onto the surface, and the eye sprang back into existence. The sparkle, the little flash of life that Aedien's eyes always conveyed was there for a split second. But it was a cheap imitation, and it soon lost its substance, and just became a series of scratches in wax. Angrily, she smudged away the face, slammed the tablet shut, and threw it on the bench beside her. The thought that she might have to start doing these drawings for Greeth crept into her mind, and she shut them out.

Outside the window, through the translucent curtain, she watched the landscape roll beside her. Mossy trees and ferns, lichen covered boulders, and clumping grasses. They were close to the Ortumi, to the coastal creeks and marshes that hugged the eastern edge of the Ouranian mountain range. They would be along the shores of the Morincian Sea soon, along the Sunrise Road. Morincia was close, however Jorbus was still far. Stonebridge wasn't to be seen for a while yet.

As she was staring at a small waterfall that filled a shady pool alongside the road, the cabin door to her right slowly opened. Kanion swung in like a slow motion ape, hand clasped high above the head of the door, grasping an unseen rope or handle. Silently, he landed inside, with good footing, and let the door click shut behind him. He nodded towards the children, and gave her a grin. She nodded back, but did not return the smile.

"Empress," He said coyly. "I just wanted to let you know that we will be stopping soon to set up a camp for the evening. I apologize for not stopping in the last few days, but we needed to put some distance between us and Calidia."

"And any threats that enemies in the city might send after us?" She added, flatly.

"Precisely, your grace." He winked. "The beasts need some real rest though. And I'm not talking about myself, Tycho, or Andronikos. I mean the horses."

He smiled again, and once again she didn't reciprocate. Maybe she was just tired, maybe she was just overwhelmed.

"What of the bandits?" She asked.

"They are a real threat, my lady." He acknowledged. "Usually military garb is enough to deter them, but since we are travelling incognito…" He grabbed a fistful of his faded brown riding cloak. "…We lose that advantage. And this carriage will make a nice juicy pigeon of a target."

"Great news, Cassius." She used his personal name without any thought. She had known this man for most of her life, and formality went the wayside with him. "You really know exactly what to say to a woman in distress."

He gave her his best smile, and then put a dignified air on his face. "My lady, you have nothing to fear. Tycho and Andronikos are almost as good at what they do as I am, that's why I picked them for this mission. We would all die before we let anyone harm a hair on the head of the children or your own scalp. And trust me…" he ran a finger along that jagged cheek scar of his "…Many, many people have tried to kill us before, and we are still her. Rest assured, your highness." He double tapped the pommel of his sword, bowed, and then shot out the door. In one motion he clambered up to the upper deck of the carriage, his sandaled feet visible for a heartbeat in the window.

Taraes allowed herself to crack a smile after he was gone. It was reassuring having Kanion here. She knew that as long as he was close, she would be safe.

IV

ATHELTIADES

The group of men were nearing the end of their march for the day. The sun was getting low in the sky, the sandy, grassy plain they were crossing was beginning to darken as the daylight waned. It was time to start making camp. The wind came strong off the sea, the air sucking inland as the earth cooled. Commander Atheltiades gave the order to halt. With little direction, the camp was made just about as quickly and efficiently as possible. The warming fires were lit, and dinner was being prepared.

The men were permitted to stow weapons and helmets close by, in neat identical rows, but were required to keep on the rest of their panoply. That was the ancient way, the way of the Hoplite. Modern Morincian Hoplites and Imperial Legionaries might not follow this custom, but a Dutrigian always did. To live in ones armor was as natural as growing a beard. It was just there, on you, nothing special about it.

As the men began their evening routine, Atheltiades closed his eyes and reverently gave a prayer to the Gods by smoke and firelight. He prayed his thanks to Lucidus, who had seen them safely through the day. Night was approaching, and Lucidus would no longer rule. He prayed to the Shaardon as he approached, to watch over his men through the night. Laera, goddess of the moon, received prayers to have her remain bright tonight, so better to see any threat that may try to approach them. And he made his prayer to Merseus, God of war, the red god. He prayed to Merseus to allow him to be brave in any fight, to win glory for himself, for his family, and for his people. Merseus, God of War, for whom the Dutrigians wore their red cloaks.

Then, he made a personal prayer to the God Telos, the God of Lifetimes. He prayed for his father, Atheicles. He asked Telos not to take his fathers life, not yet. He asked his father be allowed to live to an old age, to see his grandsons take their place in the army. It was selfish to wish for your father to grow old, to dissuade his chances of dignity and dying with glory on the battlefield. He felt guilty for asking such a request, and also felt ashamed for putting his previous prayers in jeopardy. Surely to ask such a thing of the Gods would shame himself, mar his deeds and his past prayers, so that they are made null and void by the scorned deities.

Atheltiades began to pace between the fires, helm stuck in the crook of his arm, red cloak flowing. All the eyes of the camp were on him. Breath sharply went into his nose, and out his mouth.

"We undertake the March as the final rite

of your upbringing to tie everything you have been taught together." Atheltiades hollered in his best speaking voice. "When we march, we march the path our ancestors took. Every step between Dutrigi and Bridgegate, every step we take on the March, was paid for in blood. The blood of your ancestors fertilized this very soil, along with the blood of the enemy. When we sleep tonight, on this sandy dirt, know that beneath you, not that far down, will be bones. That is the past. That is what we are here to remember. Also, we are here to understand the future. You will know what has happened here, and from that you will understand why you will fight in the future!"

Despite this being a very passionate and moving subject, his audience displayed no emotion. He continued. "I must recant the tale of our founding, a I have every night on this trek, and that you have probably heard since infancy. We are proud of our origins, for they give us strength over all adversaries. Every step on this journey gives new insight to our history, and brings it into perspective." He paused, licked his lips, and was cognizant of the paper folded into his cloak pocket. The paper his father had given him with the prophecy written upon it. It took tremendous willpower not to open it, to disobey his father and read it. He let it fall from his mind.

"Soon after the Forging, the newly found Empire was burgeoning, and it needed to grow.

The untamed west was ripe for exploration and conquest. As the young Empire began to stretch and flourish, the western frontier was a wild, dangerous place. However, western expansion was as inevitable as it was difficult, and as necessary as it was perilous. Like anything that grows, The Empire required food and space, and like anything that grows strong, it required challenge and strife. The western lands had no shortage of these things to offer.

"From the western borders and beyond, tales of strange and exotic animals, creatures, beasts, people and monsters made there way back east. Some of these were just tales, with little truth behind them, and some were very true indeed. Some were frightening; some were magical, some awe-inspiring, some even preposterous and bizarre. That being said, none were more frightening or real as the Saurians.

"A savage race of green-skinned lizard-like people, The Saurians were destined to become the main enemy of the Empire, and the main monster in the stories told to children as the shadows came out. The 'Green Skinned' Saurians, or Millangors as they would become known as, inhabited the coast and lands above what would become known as the Bay of Kellon. Later, a second race would be discovered in the southern part of the Akkedis Peninsula. This second race, the 'Red Skinned' Hyerians, would prove to be even more vile and brutal than the Millangor.

"As mankind began to sprawl into Saurian land, tensions grew between the Saurians and the Empire, and it did not take long for it to turn hostile. After several incidents of aggression from both sides, the situation became a full-scale conflict. With the settlers and farmers scattered and disorganized, with only a single legion in the area already spread thin, the angered Millangors easily dominated the struggle. Crops were burned, settlements were razed, whole families and communities were slaughtered. Smoke and blood filled the west. Hope seemed lost to those on the fringe, and the threat of a Saurian Invasion into the Empire itself was on the lips of all. That was before the Empire sent reinforcements. That was before General Dutrigius.

"A young general at the outbreak of the Saurian Border Conflict, Niko Dutrigius was an unlikely candidate to lead the campaign to spread Imperial dominance in the West. That being said, he was the youngest son of the Duke of Morincia and the brother of the Archon of Jorbus. He was raised to be a leader of men, a military officer, and a politician, but the City-States held no place for him. However, his youth and inexperience as a General gave many doubt. Patrolling the Dry Mountains outside The Eastern Shield, and participating in campaigns against Duracee rebellions hardly qualified the man to be a talented and accomplished leader. He wasn't even in the

Imperial Military, just a Commander in the Morincian Phalanxes. Being from Morincia, what business did he have in the West? He was an unlikely candidate indeed. But Dutrigius aspired towards this, and as history would show, he rarely did not get what he desired. A born General and a soldier, he needed to lead and fight, and the west was where the glory was. Setting out for the capital, he meant to personally persuade the Emperor to let him lead an army westward.

"Convincing the Emperor to give him command was not as difficult as it would have been for most men. Dutrigius was a strong man, with confidence and charisma, and he was a remarkable and moving orator. When all was said and done, he not only swayed the Emperor, but most of the Imperial High Military that he would win in the West. The command was officially his, and he had the full support of the Empire. Returning to Jorbus for the last time in his life, he hand selected four thousand of the best hoplites in all of Morincia to be his personal force. He travelled to all the City-States on a recruitment tour, looking for the best men available.

"During this process, while walking the training grounds inside an Athyrtun barracks, a soldier exclaimed 'Sir, is this an auction yard? Are you buying cattle to feed to the Saurians?' Dutrigius laughed at this. 'Cattle? If men are cattle to these Saurians, then I'm in the market for the *bulls*. Its time they learned that we have horns.' That man became one of his most trusted Captains. Having picked his force, he outfitted his men with crimson cloaks, a color that none of the City-States wore, a color that was exclusively worn by the Priests of Merseus, God of War. On the shields, an apsis of a bull was panted, which would from that point on be the symbol of Dutrigius and his men. They left their homes, many for the last time, to fight in a land they had never seen before.

"Striking west, they rendezvoused with two Imperial Legions, which folded into his command. A trail of settlers, fortune seekers and merchants followed close behind. His plan was a simple one. Punch deeper into Saurian territory than ever before, find a suitable place to build a fortress, and have that fortress become the base of all future operations in the west. Once they passed Cortinum, they began searching for the best location to build this "Western Shield."

"Construction began that spring, along the coast of the Bay of Kellon, next to an inlet called Dankoma bay. That fort, the epicenter and home of his campaign, still stands today as the Citadel of Dutrigi, behind the Old Walls. It grew into a city, the city we call home, the city that we protect and fight for. We are all descended from those original four thousand troops that Dutrigius hand selected, the best that Morincia had to offer to the Empire. We still wear the read cloaks; we still have the bull emblazoned on our shields. We still to this day are locked in combat with the Saurians, since the General died before he could see his campaign completed. Kruegius is our leader, and he still had the title of 'Lord General,' same as Dutrigius. We uphold this tradition, and we are the fiercest fighters in the world. Even the Homithans, who faced us in Luctantum, cower at the sight of our crimson cloaks and bronze helmets lined up across from them.

"They say that warfare has changed, that our style is outdated and no longer relevant. I say *let it* change. We have no need to do such things. Warfare changes to try and find a way to beat *us*. Because we are the best, and cannot be beaten, they need to find new ways to give them any advantage possible. Let them try, I say. We will still stand, as we always have. The red line will always hold!"

He threw a first up to the nights sky, towards the heavens above. Everyone else in the camp did the same. Atheltiades let out a guttural roar, and the young men and soldiers around him echoed it back a thousand times louder. His face was a mask of pride and aggression, but in the depths of his mind, he thought of his father

V

PUBLIUS NEUMON

The myriad of campfires burning across
the ravine of the Sout'I River seemed to not burn
as brightly tonight. In fact, over his last few
sentry shifts, Publius had noticed the number of
fires slowly dwindling. At first he thought
perhaps he was just getting accustomed to the
intimidating number of fires. But now, he was
certain they were burning less and less. Maybe
the Hyerians were running out of fuel and
needed to consolidate their warming and
cooking fires. If that were the case, maybe the
enemy would become desperate, and finally
ford across this damned river, march across this
Gods forsaken terrain, and kill them all.

He swallowed hard, and retightened his
grip on his spear. It was well past midnight, and
still warm. Despite the balmy climate, Publius
always wrapped his cloak tight around his
body. It made him feel Calidian, to be wrapped
in a material of his homeland, and helped keep
away the alien environment. The warm wind
didn't penetrate his thick military cloak, and
that pleased him.

His thoughts returned to the fires across

the canyon, and the wicked beings that sat around them. This army of Saurians had been camped across from them for a long time. The commanders all claimed that based on the size of the force they saw, it might well be the entire Hyerian army. The entire Hyerian army would overrun this fortress in short time. Not even the best-defended fortress or position could hold out forever. And the few thousand Calidian men stationed within these wooden palisades would fall before the tens of thousands Hyerian berserkers in short time. What were they waiting for? Why hadn't they charged yet? It had been weeks. This invading army could have mopped up the 8th, and marched halfway to the throat of Akkedis by now, well on their way to take the entire peninsula back.

Maybe they had abandoned the cause? That might explain the dwindling number of fires across the river, on the border. Maybe this whole maneuver had been a genital measuring contest, some chest beating and sword rattling. Maybe they were back in their houses, drinking whatever it was Hyerians drank, and playing with their little lizard children. Maybe all this worry, all this gut-rotting fear, had been for nothing. The fires across the canyon still burned in great number, and he knew that any hope of that happening was false hope. Things were coming to a head between the Millangor and the Hyerians, and he was stuck between them.

By the time this was all done, the borders

in Akkedis will be redrawn one way or another.
Perhaps the Hyerians had stalled, fearing
retribution from the Empire for the imminent act
of obliterating the 8th, so they have not done so
yet. Whatever the cause of the reprieve,
Neumon was grateful but at the same time
anxious. If he was to be slain in battle, in a
foreign land, by a creature, while protecting a
fort that protected other creatures, then so be it.
The sooner the better, if it was inevitable and
unavoidable. The waiting was getting to him.

He closed his eyes, feeling the warm
wind fan his face, and a trickle of sweat beaded
down his temple, beneath his cheek guard. His
hair was matted and moist beneath his helm,
coarse with salt. He had scoured his helmet to a
brilliant shine just yesterday, and he will have to
do it again in the near future. The humidity
from the river below tarnished armor and
weapons incredibly fast. The Sout'l, or as it
translated to Calidian, The Salty River, divided
the north from the south. The minerals in the
water were the source of Akkedan Bronze, and
also was the reason the bones of the Saurians
were so strong.

That metal was one of the reasons the
Empire took such a keen interest in the lands of
Akkedis. Akkedan Bronze was a valuable
element, and the strength and resiliency of the
skeletal system of the Saurians made them great
laborers. The bronze was a key ingredient in the
alloy Boldranium, and that made it very

valuable indeed. Not as strong but lighter than Rigidium, it was a very coveted material used in metallurgy, weaponry, and armor. It was funny to him that he was here, to die for a metal that didn't adorn his own body.

The Gods work in mysterious ways. And they have a fucking perverted sense of humor. A wind shift brought the faint smells of the army across the river, but only trace amounts of the odor on the breeze.

VI

ADYPATUS EVENTUS

Tuek Sicarius. The name went through his mind over and over again. It was the only link he had to this case, the only living link that was. The two dead Imperial Guards were, no pun intended, a dead-end. No way to prove they were involved with anything, even with that third sword. It solidified his theory, but no one would buy it, not now. The Sibyl would die before admitting she had been bribed, and even if she did admit to falsifying the prophecy, it had no direct connection to the murders. Just another convenient coincidence.

Tuek Sicarius. He rolled the name on the tongue of his mind as he rolled his cup of wine in his hand. The name of the assassin he was looking for. Besides himself and Flaccus, Sicarius was probably the only man that could trace the attacks back to Silious. And that made all three of them targets. Eventus knew he had to find the man before the Imperial Guard did, otherwise he'd have to watch over his shoulder the rest of his life. Gods, if they knew he was on to them, at least his paranoia would be a short, like his life.

Tuek Sicarius. He knew he had heard the name before. A few years ago, during a particularly messy underground turf war, he remember an assassin being used to take out a gang. The entire gang, member by member, and saving the boss for last. Rumor had it that it had been this Tuek. But he had never met him, only heard of him here and there, rumors, whispers. His reputation preceded him. Honestly, Eventus was surprised that he had bungled the job, even if it was to kill the leader of the Empire. Either way, he needed to be found. And for that, he needed help. If this guy didn't want to be found, it was going to be hard to find him.

Yesterday he had met with Mustella, who had given him the name he was looking for. He had taken that name today, without Flaccus knowing, to Argentis. It was time to cash in that big favor he had been sitting on. One of them, at least. If anyone had a chance of finding this guy, it would be some with resources like Argentis. Cometa apparently had some connections as well, so at today's meeting he would give him the name as well. Perhaps Cometa had already come across some information that would be useful.

The corner bar that Eventus sat in was decent enough. The food looked edible, and the wine was good, slightly chilled. Two large stone countertops intersected in a corner, and each had several large holes cut into them. Inside these recessed holes were large cauldrons, which simmered and boiled whatever food the patron ordered. It was far too hot for anyone to use those, and behind the bar, a giant stacked clay oven was burning. It was Enthaki in origin, but the city of Calidia had a way of taking things from other cultures and making them better. The oven pumped out smoke, and each tier of the device had some sort of meat or vegetable in it.

The old gray bearded Enthaki man knew exactly what was in each of the many grottos, and the fare within was Calidian style, although spiced with foreign scents and the aroma was intoxicating. Eventus felt himself actually get hungry. As he waited to get the old mans attention, he looked around the shop. Yellow and cobalt blue awnings hung above as a tent, and ribbons of every color hung amongst the poles, different widths and lengths each one. *Enthaki prayer flags,* he realized. They tie them to their ceilings, in hopes of attracting their God's attention or some rubbish. Most were old and faded, tattered, and could use replacement. Maybe they never replaced them, maybe that was bad luck. He peered across the shop, through an opening between cloth and some of the other patrons. He could see the Corvus Nest, lonely and dilapidated. No one really had ever gone in or came out of the place while he had been watching. That was good. Or bad, depending how you looked at it. Easy to remember a face if you notice something unusual they did; *Hey, I remember that guy, he was the only guy that walked into that building.*

He sighed. He didn't like waiting like this, and he didn't like leaving Flaccus hanging in the wind, but he needed to make sure the meeting was safe, from a far away vantage point. At least he had a drink, and was about to get some decent looking food. The shop owner spoke only a little Domitian, heavy accented, but passable. Eventus tried to interject with some of the Enthaki that he knew, but as he soon discovered, his vocabulary in food related areas was lacking. He mostly knew the words for drinks and sexual perversions. The shop owner, who was named Kahlobo he discovered, made him a plate. Flatbread, with pickled vegetables, braised meat, and a yogurt sauce. A chopped green herb was sprinkled on top, with a healthy dose of a bright red powder.

Eventus picked it up, folded it, and tilted his head to take a bite. It wasn't what he ordered, but it was good. He couldn't tell what kind of meat it was, but it was good. Once he had finished, he ordered a final cup of wine.

Kahlobo shook his head. "No wine." He said.

"Why the hell not?" Eventus asked.

The Enthaki reached underneath the counter, and pulled out a liquid filled skin. Uncorking it, he squirted a fair amount into two cups. He slid one across to Eventus, and took the other for himself.

"This is more good, friend." Kahlobo said, hefting his cup up and waited for his customer to do the same. Eventus looked into the cup. It was a silky, almost lumpy whitish-gray semi thick drink. Eventus thought it looked like semen that had been mixed with old milk. He sniffed, and it made his eyes water. Strong stuff.

"Tor'sahd" The keeper said, slugging down his cup.

"Salute." And Eventus took his too. His mouth roiled. It tasted putrid, it burned, it clung to the crevices of his mouth, and it felt like hot wax going down his throat. Then, his belly warmed up to his throat, and a taste of vanilla and almonds resonated in his mouth. Eventus looked at Kahlobo, and nodded approvingly.

"Is more good, yes?" the shopkeeper said.

"It is good, I will give you that. What is in it?" Eventus asked.

"Al-co-hol." The man responded without hesitation.

"Yes I know, but what…" Eventus started, but then movement caught his eye. Across the way, Flaccus was entering the Corvus Nest. He was right on time. Eventus was going to sit here and make sure no one had followed the young man. Being where he was gave him a great view of the whole panorama. Eventus waited for the better part of a quarter hour, but saw nothing. He slid 4 or 5 Denarii onto the countertop, and started for the meeting. Kahlobo protested that he was paying too much, but Eventus insisted. As he trooped towards the

Corvus, he suddenly froze. Part of the street that he could only see as he got closer revealed a man in a cloak, leaning against a wall. He looked very inconspicuous. So inconspicuous, that he stuck out. A quick scan to the other end of the block revealed another man that could have been the first guys brother. Shit. They looked military. He quickly ducked behind a cart that was parked in the middle of the wide street, and thought of his options.

Flaccus was inside, probably with Cometa. One of them, maybe both, had been trailed. They were in danger, that was for sure. He had to warn them. As soon as he went inside, these goons might storm in and slit their throats. Or, catch them on the way out. Leaving wasn't an option. As much as it went against his survival instincts, he needed to get inside and warn those two. He deeply inhaled, and casually strolled out from behind the cart. Each step he took towards the building made him more anxious, and he wanted to run as fast as he could to the inside. But he forced himself to walk, and made sure not to look at the two men that he was sure were watching him out of the corner of their eyes. His heart raced, and once inside, he moved quickly. The big man Brudo saw him approach and tightened up. He then recognized him, and gave him a courteous nod. Eventus scanned the room, and found Flaccus sitting alone at a table. His young partner hadn't even seen him come in.

"Cometa." Adypatus had a frantic tinge to his voice. "Has he come in?"

Brudo said nothing.

"Come on man, it's important." And he reached for his coin purse. He pulled out his Enforcer medallion, and a few sestertii spilled out as well.

"No. Not since the last time he was here with you." The big man said, fingering the coins into his palm. Eventus felt his heart quicken.

"Shit." Eventus began towards Flaccus. "You may have trouble coming behind me." At that, Brudo dropped what he was doing, and fished out a club from under the bar. He gave Eventus a knowing nod.

"Flaccus!" He shouted, and his partner, who had already noticed him, jumped to his feet. He could sense the danger that Eventus was projecting. "You were followed. Cometa is not here. We need to get out of here right now."

Flaccus looked confused, and then started towards the door.

"We need to go out the back, they are watching the front." And the men started towards the old loading doors. They had long ago been sealed, nailed shut. Eventus began to look for another door, when Flaccus opened a shuttered window. The light that came into the cave like room was white and blinding. They stuck their heads through, and realized that the loading dock had long ago fallen apart, only the rotten pilings remained. A single beam below them looked like it wrapped around the building, proving enough footing for them to use. Eventus gestured with a head tilt, and Flaccus started through the window. His sword smacked Eventus in the chin as he clambered through the opening. Once he was through, Eventus followed. The footing was slippery, and the water beneath looked deep and muddy. This part of the river had been dredged long ago for boats. A slip meant they would get wet for sure. In a pinch, wet was better than bloody. They both shimmied along the beam, until they reached the corner of the building. Flaccus peered down the small alley between the Corvus Nest and the adjacent building they had approached. He didn't see any movement. Looking down at the water, he realized they were a lot farther from the shore than he would have imagined. Eventus thought briefly about going down to the network of pilings and posts that supported the building, and climbing around under there, maybe finding a way out or hiding out until it was safe.

Flaccus instead, jumped to the next building. *That works even better,* he thought. Once they were both over, they casually walked on the dock towards the rear door. Locked. Unoccupied. The next building in the line was too far away to jump to. Eventus returned his attention to the door. Judging from the bolts on the large double doors, it had a cross bar holding it closed. Eventus pulled out his pugio, and slid it into the gap between the doors. It was tight, but he got it in. He worked the knife upwards until he felt the crossbar. He tried to lift it, but it was heavy and he didn't have the leverage. Multiple times he tried ramming the blade upwards, harder each time. Each time he failed to undo the crossbar. He felt Flaccus tap him on the shoulder. Whirling around, he saw his partner had his gladius drawn. Flaccus jammed the longer blade in at a sharp upward angle, digging the tip into the heavy wooden lock. He hammered it in deeper with his palm, and then removed his own pugio, flipped it around pommel up, and pounded it against the pommel of his sword. A few beats later, the sword was torn from his hands, and slammed to the ground with tremendous speed. The door creaked open. Flaccus retrieved his sword and replaced it.

Both Enforcers made their way to the front of the warehouse, and each found a crack to peer through. The two thugs that had been casing the place had moved right out front of the Corvus Nest. And they had been joined by two more.

"Do you think they got Cometa?" Flaccus rasped out, his voice a strained whisper.

"I don't know." Eventus conceded. "The fact that he didn't show today doesn't bode well. Unless he realized he's being followed, and had to call the thing off. Wherever Cometa is now, we can't help him. We need to leave."

"Shouldn't we wait here until *they* leave?" Flaccus said startled.

"It wont take them long to realize we aren't coming out." Eventus said. "And then they will send someone in. They will figure out pretty quickly where we went, and then they will find us. If we walk out of here now, casual like, they won't bat an eye. The longer we wait, the more suspicious it will seem."

"But we are so close, they will recognize us for certain." Flaccus offered.

"Then we must blend in." And Eventus grabbed a sack that was lying on a pile by the door. It must have been filled with… onions? He hefted it up and dropped it on his partners shoulder. Eventus picked up a few rolls of colorful cloth fabric and put them on his own shoulder. They strolled out the front entrance, faces obscured by their cargo, and even locked the door behind them. The four ruffians never looked twice at them. They walked down the street, and passed the place where Eventus had just patronized. Walking up to the counter, Eventus tossed the colorful cloth down with a thud. This took Kahlobo aback, he was slightly startled.

"Prayer flags" Eventus said, pointing to the tatters on the ceiling.

"And onions." Flaccus added, dropping the sack down next to the cloth. He then pointed towards the clay oven as an after thought, mimicking Eventus.

Kahlobo held his mouth ajar, not saying or acknowledging anything.

"Tor'sahd" Eventus said, waving as they walked away.

VII

ANTONEUS COMETA

His head throbbed, pounded at him as he awoke. Stiffness in his neck from his head being slouched to the side for so long made him not want to move. Pain shot through his arms, his wrists were burning and his hands stung and tingled at the same time. The wound on his side was aching, and felt wet like it was leaking again. He tried to open his eyes, but was only half successful. One did not open, and it felt as if it was crusted with blood. Probably from the new wound to his head. He started remembering what had happened. Strolling, careless, he was ambushed, smacked over the head with a sword pommel. And now he was awakening in a strange room. His hands were manacled, and he hung from them by a chain, toes dragging on the stone floor.

The room was hot, and his body sweltered with beading sweat. The snapping and crackling sounds of a fire came from behind him. It was a very hot fire, like the ones he and his father kept for blacksmithing. A quick precursory glance of the room showed it to be small, built of stone, with few pieces of furniture. A thick slab table, rough and distressed, was tucked against the wall, beside an equally rough and thick arched door. That was all he could see in front of him, and if he were able to swing around, he would see a fire pit and a bellows, as well as a barrel filled with dirty water.

Cometa was certain that he was underground. The walls, despite being stone and in the same room as a cranking fire, seemed cool and saturated. The lack of windows that he could see hinted at that as well. Plus, a single root was working its way through a crack just below the ceiling on the wall to his left. A secret underground chamber, with some manacles and a fire all set up. This wasn't looking too good for him. He groaned, and once again his throat was dry and his thirst was great. Maybe this was all a misunderstanding. Maybe someone was trying to scare him. Maybe some foreign agent was kidnapping him because of his rank and wanted intelligence on the palace. Maybe... No, it was worthless. He knew why he was hanging where he was. The Guard. The same people in the Imperial Guard that were responsible for the assassinations had caught him, and they were going to torture him.

They would torture him until they were sure he had told them everything he knew. They would torture him until he confessed the names of everyone he had told about his suspicions and his findings. Then, they would kill him and he would disappear from the world like he had never existed. He groaned again, but did not feel bad for himself. He would never tell them everything. He would die before that would happen. He would… eventually break like everyman who had ever been tortured by the guard. Most men thought they were made of something that wouldn't break or bend under pain and interrogation. Most men folded, most men cried, most men wanted death to end it.

Some torturers used some excruciating techniques to get the results they desired. Cometa had rarely seen them do their work, but it was something that was often talked about. One particular incident that he had inadvertently participated in during his time in the Legions came to mind, and it made him shudder to recall it. A Homithan sympathizer had been ferretted out among the staff members. His title or rank or role he never knew, it wasn't important, but apparently traditional interrogation methods had failed on this man.

The story that he had heard was that during the process, he kept telling the Interrogators that they were 'being fed a line of shit,' and that 'he wasn't going to take the Empire's shit any longer.' Finally, they had decided to take it to the next level and in the style that any maniacal person who believes their craft is an art form would do. They tied his limbs together, put a wedging device that kept his mouth propped open, and tied his head back so that it remained upright. The man gave the appearance that he was howling up at the moon. Then, they lowered him into the latrine pit.

The man stayed down there for at least a full day and night. Long enough for the five thousand men to use it at least once. The confession soon followed. Antoneus cringed thinking what might be in store for him. The fire seemed particularly ominous. Burning flesh was something he had smelled far too often, and the thought made him sick to his stomach. Blades would be extremely ironic, and if this torturer was an aspiring artist like the latrine fellows, it seemed very likely that he might be carved up.

Perhaps trying to find a way out of the situation would be time better spent. Dwelling on what was to come only demoralized him that much more. He craned his head upwards, and as he did, a wave of pain went through his skull and strained his neck. The manacle chain was run through an iron ring, not hung on a hook unfortunately. That dashed any hopes he had of finding some impossible reserve of strength and energy to try and unhook himself. He slowly started spinning himself around, and as he did, he felt like his wrists were going to tear off. He saw the barrel of water, saw the fire, and the metal handles that stuck out of the coals. Most of the shaft of the tools that were in the fire glowed orange-white. His throat swallowed, but no liquid was in there to move.

Banging came from behind as the door mechanism was operated, and the door swung inward with a creak. Cometa spun himself back around, and saw a single man walking through the door, carrying a sack of some kind. The man was young, but had an older look to him. Early hair loss and pocking on his face made him look aged, but he had the unmistakable vitality of youth to his edges and his walk.

"Good, you are finally awake." The man said pleasantly, as he dropped his bag onto the wooden table. The sounds of metal crashing against metal echoed through the small room it thudded down. "I was hoping we could talk."

Cometa said nothing. This only widened the man's smile.

"No one wants to talk at the start of these things." The man said over his shoulder as he walked back through the open door and grabbed a low-backed chair and carried it into the room. He made a dismissive gesture to some unseen individuals farther outside the room, and then shut the door behind himself. "No one talks. It's not a conversation if only one of us is talking, soldier, is it?"

The man reached into his bag, pulled out a cup, and filled it with water from a skin flask. He then scooted the chair closer to Cometa, sat, and took a sip. "Everyone always talks at the end. Everyone. I wish we could forgo all these un-pleasantries and just talk. It would be better for me, and trust me, much, *much* better for you. Do you remember the old saying that approaching armies are asked by a garrisoned force within a city or a fort?"

Cometa knew what it was, most soldiers did. But he would not be enticed to talk. Not yet at least, not this early.

"Blood or water." The man spread his hands apart, as if grasping a large stone, or helmet in his hands. "Blood." He shook one hand. "Or water." He shook the other as he spoke. "It is a simple question. 'What are your intentions here? Are you hostile, or are you a friend just looking to water your forces?' So now I ask you, Antoneus Cometa; Blood or water?"

Cometa looked at the man, but didn't say a word, his face a stone.

"You can talk to me now, and have this water. Or remain silent, and then there will be blood." The man gestured towards him with the proffered cup, and then pointed towards his bag of accouterments on the table. Cometa's stomach turned as he spoke, his heart raced, and he felt desperate. The man had made an ultimatum, and needed an answer right away. His hope was fleeting as he remained silent. Tightened jaw muscles kept his mouth shut, and he had to fight some serious temptation to start talking. He remained silent still.

"Pity." The man took a gulp from his cup as he rose, and dashed the remaining water against the wall. As he unbuckled the straps on his bag, Cometa saw that it was actually a rolled up canvas. As it unfurled, light glistened off of dozens of very sharp, very painful looking instruments.

"My superior tells me that you are a traitor to the Empire. That you were involved in helping assassins get into the palace." The torturer tested the edge of a scalpel gingerly with a thumb. "That you made us all in the Guard look very bad."

The man tssked to himself as he continued to examine his kit, collecting supplies. A jingling, tinkling sound came from his hands, and Cometa saw the man was carrying a handful of nails, maybe large needles. "If that is truly the case," He continued. "Then I take back what I said earlier, Antoneus."

Without hesitation and as naturally as scratching his own nose, the man evenly and quickly stabbed a needle into Cometa's armpit. The spot he jabbed it into caused a wave of agony to surge through his entire body, and he violently thrashed. The pain ebbed only slightly, but was still excruciating. Breaths frothed through his shut mouth and flared nostrils.

Getting another needle ready, the torturer continued. "I think I am going to enjoy this after all."

VIII

MIKUS DERRATA

Mikus sat cross-legged, his helmet resting opening up in his lap. With a scratch awl, he was engraving his name on the inside of the neck guard. The awl was old; the tip kept sharp, and the round wooden handle was highly polished from unknown years of use. Mikus had borrowed it from the tents designated tool kit, which belonged to the entire squad, but was mostly used by the orderlies. The orderlies were responsible for most repairs to the equipment of the squad, but a lot of the soldiers tended to their own gear and kit. He looked at his "M. Derrata" as he finished. Despite the fact that he was free-handing the engraving, he still wrote it in the traditional chiseled style of text, with no round edges. The "D" was made with three straight lines, etc.

It was nighttime, and the tent was still empty. Except for Tilo, who was already sleeping inside. Earlier, Mikus had said hello to the man before he had fallen asleep, but he said nothing in return. Mikus was beginning to believe that the man was a mute after all. And possibly deaf, as well. The rest of the squad was out, probably drinking and gambling. Mikus still didn't feel comfortable going out with them, didn't feel like he had earned the right to be equals with them yet. He looked down at his hands, and the traces of the blue dye were still visible. Under his nails, in his cuticles, and in the occasional crack and crevice of a joint or knuckle, the blue remained. That was how new he was and he was still trying to find his place in the unit.

Toratum was a good Decanus, and he was a likeable enough leader. The men of the squad were allowed their freedoms in downtime, but he expected full and unbridled participation in the daily drills. It was a fair deal, one that no one truly complained about. He knew that he was lucky to have the Decanus he did, after seeing some of the other ones in the century. Some were micro-managers, some far too lax, some far too strict.

The rest of the squad he was still trying to figure out. Phenton and Strasa were just plain dicks. He doubted that they would ever turn out to be the kind of guys that put up a tough front at first, but then warmed up to you. Something told him that they were just mean down to their bones. Perhaps that was a good quality for a soldier to have, when it came down to a really hard scrape. Time would tell. As far as camp life went, it was a challenge to deal with. Phenton had more or less tricked Marcus and himself into polishing his armor and kit on a regular basis. When Decanus Toratum found out, he

admonished Phenton and punished him with
latrine duty. Phenton had taken it personal,
claiming that Mikus had ratted him out. The
next morning, Mikus had discovered his own
cloak was soaking wet with urine.

Titus Vinius seemed to be the most
welcoming of the group, and a genuinely
pleasant man. Mikus had played dice with
Vinius *one* time, and had lost a good portion of
his pay for that month. Since then, Mikus
steered clear of dice. Vinius always offered
though, and his charisma almost made him
jump into the game every time he asked. Mikus
suspected that he was a very strong man, and
had witnessed one or two things that confirmed
his suspicions. A gentle giant, much in the spirit
of Marcus. If it came to a fight, Mikus had a
hunch that Vinius would be a great man to have
by your side.

Adamas Ferro was a man that had
welcomed them at first, but then treated them
with indifference. It wasn't like the man held
them in contempt or anything like that, but a
feeling that they hadn't proved themselves only
entitled them to pleasant introductions.
Anything past that they needed to earn from
this man. He seemed decent enough, but there
was an edge to him that Mikus noticed. The man
conveyed to the world he was a professional
soldier, without having anything that shouted it.
Scars were one of the telltales. This man had
been through some serious battles. The eyes

were the other giveaway; piercing like
Phenton's, but without the odium. More
calculating than anything else, but still very
serious.

Marcus was his closet friend in the world
right now. The two men were usually glued at
the hip, doing most things together. Davus and
Dellon were in the same Cohort as them, and
Mikus had only seen them briefly since
completing their training. That left Marcus, and
they were becoming closer everyday. Marcus
was actually out trying to find the two Ganno
brothers to try and set up a time to grab some
drinks tomorrow. The need to catch up with
them was strong, but from what he understood,
the two brothers had landed in the same squad,
with a Decanus that was overbearing. They
might not have the same liberties with free-time
that his own squad was afforded.

So, Mikus found himself alone, sitting on
his bunk, tinkering with his gear that was
already in perfect working order. Soldiers took a
lot of pride in the appearance of their
equipment, and he had discovered that there
were two schools of thought in the matter. Some
liked their gear pristine, well polished, and
looking immaculate. Others liked their gear
looking worn, like they were veterans that had
seen fighting. It was a form of intimidation to
the enemy and a form of instilling esteem
amongst your fellow soldiers. Mikus had no
choice but to be of the first group, since he had

yet to engage in battle.

When all the squad's gear was lined up on their posts inside the tent, it was a smorgasbord of different pieces of armor; slightly different model helmets, different cuts of mail, etc. To the untrained eye, they looked near identical. Some had better gear than others, however. Mikus and Marcus had both been issued the latest model of helmet, and he found that some coveted it. Most verbal about this was Phenton. He had all but tried to steal the helmet from Mikus, but Mikus had refused. Phenton told him he would regret not giving it to him, but Mikus did not back down. Appius Phenton was a bully, and you couldn't give in to bullies he had discovered in his short life. It actually surprised him that the man wanted the helmet, since his gear was of the used, rough, veteran variety. But, the man still wanted it.

That was why he had just finished carving his name in it's collar. He placed the helmet back on his gear post, then replaced the awl exactly where he had found it. He didn't want to give the orderlies Fabian and Calvus any reason to have a gripe with him. Letting out a sigh, he reclined on his bunk, and intertwined his fingers behind his head. Tomorrow morning they had early drill and maneuvers with the entire century. To this point, the only drilling had been with just his squad. He had learned the foundation of what he needed to during basic training, but he had learned some pretty important stuff while training with the squad. They showed him the little tricks and nuances that had kept them alive through the war so far. He began to get a feel for each member's abilities, and he was able to see why each of them had survived to date. Some were ferocious fighters, some were self preserving and clever. They each had their strengths and each had their own survival mechanisms.

Mikus felt as though he contributed nothing to the squad. He was clumsy with the weapons, awkward with the formations, and off when it came to shield positions. But he was getting better. Each time he made a mistake, he felt ashamed. He could feel palpable disappointment amongst his squad-mates. He could feel their frustration, and as with Phenton, he could feel resentment and disdain. Marcus appeared to be much better at getting it than he was. That made him even more frustrated. Tomorrow, drilling with the whole century, all eighty men, was a daunting thought. What if he looked like a fool in front of all of them?

He rolled to his side, and looked at the wooden planks that made up the tent floor. His thoughts drifted to home. Not to the Brass Mule, or his Aunt and Uncle, but to the days on the farm. He thought of Manius, of Marcia, and his parents. He longed to see his brother and sister again. He wondered if Mani ever felt this way, or if he was easily assimilated into his own squad. Was his brother even still alive? And what of Marcia? She was married to that officer from the Cortinum Phalanx, and was probably living in the city, mingling with the Golden Class like she always dreamed of. Perhaps she would of heard about his disappearance from Lucia and Jerichus and wonder where he was, if he himself was even still alive. She didn't know if both her brothers were dead or alive.

Maybe one day soon he would write to her, and to Manius. He didn't know why he hadn't yet. Perhaps fear that Jerichus would find out where he was, and drag him back to the mule and punish him for running away and for stealing the Foronian. That was childish, Jerichus had no sway over him any longer. He had taken the Sacramentum, and he belonged to the Empire now. Perhaps one day, Marcia would find herself in the capital on some trip or visit, and would go to the Catalogos to read the names, and in the sea of stitching on the banners, would find him. It was an unlikely scenario, but one that filled him with pride in a strange way.

What was he doing just laying here by himself? He needed to make an attempt to fit into this squad, especially since they would be fighting together soon, and if the Gods allow, for a long time to come. Shooting up from his bunk with determination, he walked outside to try and find Marcus and the rest of his squad.

It was dark out, but fires throughout the camp gave a glow along the tops of the tents.

The pop and crackle of fires, the laughter and buzz of men telling tales to one another, and the occasional shout made sure the camp was not silent. Just outside the tent, Fabian was tending to the squads two mules. These mules carried the tent, extra supplies, and everything the squad would need that the legionaries themselves did not carry. The young man saw Mikus approach and nodded at him. Fabian wasn't much older than himself, but he had the appearance of a man much younger than he actually was. His growth was slightly stunted, thin framed, and his face was smooth without the need of a razor. The limp that plagued him was visible as he worked his way around the mules.

"Excuse me, Fabian…" Mikus said as the orderly turned his back to continue his work.

"Y-Y-Yes, Sir." Fabian stuttered back. "How can I h-help you?"

"Please, call me Mikus." He said.

"M-Mikus? Yes sir." He responded.

"I was hoping you could tell me where the other men have gone?" Mikus asked.

Fabian set down a brush that he had in his hand, and took a step closer to Mikus. "Most go over to the h-halls. Each Cohort has one. Others go to different t-t-tents to drink and dice. Sometimes, they go into the t-t-town, but the L-L-Legate has forbidden it recen-recently."

"Do you know where they are tonight?" He asked.

Fabian nodded, but said nothing.

"Do you think you could tell me?" Mikus pressed.

"Y-Yes." And he pointed to the right. "Toratum will be with the other D-Decanus' in that tent. Strasa and P-Ph-P-Phenton will be in the hall. Vinius, who knows. Ferro will most likely still be at the hall. Tilo is inside, and Ami-A-A-Ami-" he swallowed. "Marcus went to the 4th Century's site."

"Thank you, Fabian." Mikus said. "I think I will go and find them. Before I go, is there anything I can help you with?"

The boy looked away, ashamed. "No, Mikus. This is my j-job. I cannot fight, so I do this. You fight, and I do not expec-c-ct you to do my duties. Thank you though."

And with that, Mikus headed towards the hall. On his way he passed by lots of groups of half-drunk, singing, yelling, fighting men. Before he got close to the hall, still weaving his way through the masses, he came across the path of Strasa and Phenton as they were returning to the tent. Strasa carried a skin of wine, and in his other hand he barehanded a hunk of roasted meat. The grease shimmered on his fingers as the light from a nearby fire played on them. His eyes twinkled even more, glazed with the drunkenness of the evening. Phenton's own eyes shone, but since he appeared more sober. The intensity that those eyes shone with was attributed to hatred. The deep blue gaze of his locked onto Mikus like an eagle swooping down on a fish it had spotted in a lake below.

"Well, well Quel. Look who it is... our new friend." Appius Phenton said, making no attempt whatsoever to veil how he felt towards Mikus. He seethed loathing with every word.

Quel Strasa chuckled, as he tore another bite of flesh from his fistful of greasy meat.

"Good evening." Mikus said meekly. "I was just heading out to find you and the rest of the squad."

"Well, no one wants you out with them." Phenton snapped back. "And since we are going back to the tent, don't go there either."

Mikus cracked his mouth to speak, but no words came to mind. He felt flushed, with both anger and shame. He had done nothing to this man, but this man hated him. Why?

"I'm sorry guys, we seem to have gotten off on the wrong foot. If I have ever done anything to offend you, I apologize." Mikus offered.

"You were born, that's what you did." Phenton said. "Un-born yourself, and maybe we can be friends."

"Yeah, un-born yourself. To death..." Strasa chimed in, drinking from his wine skin.

"Very well, you said earlier that you resented me for taking the spot of your old squad mate. I'm sorry, but I meant no disrespect to the departed. I merely..."Mikus was cut-off.

"The man whose place you took,

Vauhnus, was a good soldier. But I hated him as a man." Phenton spat. "You are a terrible soldier, and I hate you as a man even more. At least he offered something to the squad. Perhaps you should become an orderly with that retard Fabian instead of a soldier."

Mikus balled his fists, clenched and unclenched them. He took a breath, and told himself to relax. This was exactly the kind of response the man was looking for, and told himself not to give in. He lowered his head, and started to walk past them, leaving the confrontation before it escalated.

"Hey!" Phenton grabbed his arm as he walked past. "Are you walking away from me, you pussy! I don't want a coward in line with me when we go to battle. If you break now, you'll break then, and get us all killed."

Quel dropped the skin and the scraps of meat in his fist, and reached for a dagger. "A coward, is he Appius? I can't stand a coward. Maybe it's our duty to toughen him up, for the greater good?" and he unsheathed a dagger. "Maybe we should give him a cut somewhere to make him brave?"

Mikus shook his arm free with a violent jerk. His brain told him to walk away, to leave while he could. But, he couldn't. He had to stand up to these two, even if that meant taking his lumps. He squared up to Phenton, and as he did out of the corner of his eye, he saw the blade that Strasa held falter slightly. Phenton stood slightly taller as Mikus stepped closer.

"If we are going to fight, it might as well be now. I don't want to, but you seem determined. Let's get this over with." Mikus said, not moving, but staring.

"This is the Legions, boy." Phenton responded in a rasping voice, veins bulging in his neck and on his forehead. "We play for keeps, and when we fight, we do it to kill."

Mikus felt a pressure above his naval, and then a pricking sensation. He didn't need to look down to know Phenton had a knife drawn on his belly. Mikus swallowed, but still didn't want to back down. His mind flashed to the execution they had all witnessed, for fratricide, and realized that this must be bluff. Options ran through his mind, but not many. A quick strike was his only hope, but was he faster than the already drawn blade?

"Is there a problem, here my friends?" The voice came from behind. Marcus stepped into the light, his bulky frame looming over them. "Why do you two have your blades drawn at Mikus here? If you want a fight, why don't you sheath those weapons, and fight like real men, with honor. If you still have any, that is."

Not a good time to goad them on, Marcus. But any help is appreciated.

"You stay out of this, you Boldran wannabe." Phenton said through his teeth. "I'm trying to teach this worm a lesson."

"Yeah, stay out of this…" Strasa said, his voice sounding more confident than his body language did.

"Drop the blades, and we can talk about this…" Marcus said.

Phenton was looking at the big man, not Mikus, and Mikus knew this was his best opportunity. With his left hand he grabbed Phenton's wrist that held the dagger, and with his right, he punched the man in the eye. His tormentor's head snapped back, and the man swore. Marcus then brought a mighty fist down onto the shoulder of Strasa, and that crumpled him to the grass. Phenton staggered backwards, holding his eye and snarling like a wounded beast. Strasa struggled to get to his knees, gasping. Marcus lifted him up very roughly, and set him on his feet.

"You are lucky your bodyguard showed up, Derrata." Phenton raged. "Next time, you wont be so lucky. This isn't over." He uncovered his eye, which had already swelled almost to the point of full occlusion. Gingerly, he touched it as he walked away, back to the tent. Strasa followed him, not saying a word, but audibly struggling to breath.

"Thank you, Marcus." Mikus patted his friend on the shoulder. "I appreciate it."

"You are my friend, Mikus." He smiled a wide smile. "And my squad mate. It is what we do for one another."

IX
ATHELTIADES

The sun had not yet completely risen as they crested the cliff. They had started out in darkness this morning, for today was the last day of the March. The sea below them that came into view was washed in a ruby-rose colored light, and the sunrise was a golden brown. It was a truly beautiful morning. The flat sliver of land they saw below was the neck of the Akkedan peninsula, the land bridge that connected it to the continent. Flocks of birds and *v's* of fowl flew below them as they looked down on their destination. Without preamble, they started down the road that followed the rocky hillside to the flats below. They had no horse or donkey with them; beasts did not do well in Akkedis. In fact, horses didn't do well around any Saurian. It was some sort of primal instinct against a dangerous predator, and they usually threw riders, became inconsolable, or bolted.

The walk was steep and winding. They were on a footpath now, having abandoned the main road. Single file, like a red snake, the Dutrigians made their way down the trail. The earth of the trail and the cut-bank was an orange brown, being decomposed granite. The occasional skeletal tree was blotted amongst the sparse chaparral that made up the flora of the area. Wispy bay trees, tortured and windblown, provided the only canopy. The acrid aroma of feet trampling over their dry, fallen leaves filled the air, mixing with the tang of the coast. The sun glistened off their highly polished Bronze helms and armor.

It was late morning by the time they reached the bottom by the sea, and began to walk down the neck. Although the land had looked flat from high above, almost like a sandbar emerging from the water, it was rather far above the sea. The thin piece of land, which was flanked on either side by the Bay of Dru and the Bay of Kellon, was essentially a jetty, about 20 feet above the water. The further they marched, the narrower the land became. Erosion by the waves of the sea caused the ever shrinking and narrowing strip of land to have shear cliffs on either side. Occasionally, there was a gentle sloping beach beneath them, but mostly it was rock and boulder. Relentless barrages of waves crashed on either side of them, the water getting rougher as the day went on. White sea foam would occasionally geyser on one side or the other as particularly large waves hit the rocks below just right.

Barking of seals could be heard nearby, but the animals were never seen. The men weren't on a leisure nature hike, and weren't interested in peering down in the water. Ahead was their objective; Bridgegate. The fortress at the end of the March and the edge of the Empire. They would soon be sworn in, and become official Dutrigian Soldiers. Culmination and anticipation was in the air, and it didn't feel like anxiety or excitement, but had more a feeling like determination.

The group approached a single, schoolmarm Eucalyptus tree, growing out of a rock scree. Atheltiades called a halt for the midday meal. Under the shade of the lone tree, which had been the only tree they had seen on the neck, the men sat and took out their rations. Many had sweat dripping down their brows, hair plastered from wearing their helms. They were conditioned well, and it was warm, but the young Commander guessed nerves had a lot to do with the extra sweat. Huge strips of shredded bark and long slender leaves made a nice cushion for the men to rest on. As they sat or moved about, the duff crackled and the unique menthol aroma became pungent in he air. He reached down a picked up a few of the trees discarded seedpods. The little brown, semi spheres looked like shriveled and dried citrus halves. Absently, he thumbed them and tossed them to the ground. Holding the last one for all to see, he stood. All eyes were on him.

"This very tree," Atheltiades looked upwards into the canopy. "This tree is a sign that we are entering a land that is not our home.

These trees are rare in Domiterra, but are prevalent in Akkedis. Keep that in mind. We are on the edge, the brink of the wild. South of here, men, we are reviled and hated. Our very presence, our very existence, puts our lives in danger beyond *this* point. Remember that when you take your oaths this evening. You are the last line of defense against everything south of this land bridge. We keep the Empire safe, we keep our families safe. All of you will spend some time at Bridgegate in your career, for that is your duty. When we get there, you will see how important this is. Just like this tree, Akkedis still spreads into our lands, even with our vigilance. But trees can be chopped down, and roads can be blocked.

"The government in Calidia has forgotten what a real threat the Saurians are. They don't remember like we remember. It's inconvenient for them to do so. There may come a day when this Empire no longer supports you, no longer supports this fortress we are about to arrive at. They have forgotten the atrocities the Millangor have done because it suits them now. They have forgotten the sacrifices that Dutrigi has made for centuries because it's easy to do so. Our ancestors fought and died in endless strife against the enemies of Calidia. The Saurians and us have been locked in warfare since the moment Dutrigius headed west. The Empire has also used us in other conflicts because we are the best. When the Empire could not destroy the

Vaus, the called upon the might of Dutrigi. We took their stronghold of Trimontis, and now, our cousins occupy that land. The Rams of Trimontis were once Bulls of Dutrigi, just like you and I. They are the closest people in the entire Empire to our own people.

When fighting Homitha, they used us. They have used us in Enthaki, in Duracee, in the Petros Rebellion. They use us because we are the best. But they do not allow us to fight our true enemy, for they have forgotten. Never forget, *never,* who the real enemy is. The Saurians, *green* or *red,* are the true enemy of Dutrigi, of the Empire, and of all mankind."

*   *   *

As they approached Bridgegate, it was midafternoon and the sun was glaring. Bronze helmets glinted, shields and breastplates glowed, and bare spearheads sparkled as they marched. The stone walls of the fort, the towers and the battlements rose from the earth the closer they got. Crimson flags snapped in the breeze, and the purple flag of Calidia flew above them all. The stone was a washed, honey gold, fading to near white from generations of exposure to the open elements. The fortress looked stout, well built, but plain. The shape was a square, with the far southern wall being the tallest. It was hard to appreciate the height of the walls until the group approached nearer. Upon the battlements patrolled red-cloaked

Dutrigians, dwarfed in size by the massive stone structures. Atheltiades guessed that the walls were at their shortest point, about 10 meters tall. Two massive stone spires rose in the far corners, looking south into Akkedis. They approached the rear gate, which was closed currently. The gate was actually a drawbridge, and was near as tall as the wall it was currently recessed into. When lowered, the drawbridge would span the gap of a ditch along the base of the walls, one that was nearly as deep as it was wide. The ditch was filled with iron spikes that were rusting away in the soupy seawater that ebbed and flowed into the channel like a moat.

On the north side of this ditch, the side they were approaching, a small tent city was popping up. Merchants and travelers who were hoping to be allowed through to continue their journeys were waiting for their chance to do so. Since this was the only point they could enter Akkedis, they were at the mercy of the Dutrigians within. If they kept the drawbridge closed, then this group needed to make camp until it was opened again. Atheltiades guessed a similar camp was forming on the other side of Bridgegate as well, people waiting to be allowed back into the mainland. Judging by the size of the tent camp forming up, the gate had been closed for a long while. Recently, the Imperial Government had given orders to the Dutrigians to allow a free flow of trade in and out of the peninsula, but that hadn't gone over very well.

Citing safety and security concerns, they often closed the bridges, and thoroughly searched through those that travelled through. The Empire's thirst for goods from Akkedis was very strong, and the route was used frequently by those trying to turn a profit.

Although the Empire was officially in a truce with the Millangors, and had extended amnesty to those who were willing to travel into Domiterra, no Saurian was allowed through the fort. No exceptions. That was the Dutrigian rule. If the Empire wanted to deal with that, then they could come down here and man the gates with Imperial troops. As long as Dutrigians operated the fort, no Saurians would ever come through.

The merchants and travellers in the site were lively as the force marched through, down the roadway that bisected the tent encampment. Atheltiades was at the head of the group, his black and white crest sticking out like the moon in the night's sky. Just behind him, a standard rose high in the sky, being held by the bearer. The Eagle on top glistened, the red Dutrigian Vexillum flapping in the wind. People of all different walks of life were milling about, some cooking food, some showing each other the goods that they carried, or playing games. A few approached the soldiers, trying to get them to take a look at silks or weaves that they thought they might like. The soldiers didn't even acknowledge them, continued past with the determination that marked their discipline.

Foamy salt water surged through the trench below him as Atheltiades came to a halt. He gave the dangerous defense below a cursory glance, with the jagged pieces of rusting iron jutting up like teeth from a goblin shark… or a Saurian. A massive stone footing was in front of him, a landing for the drawbridge to rest upon when it was lowered. He looked up, above the wooden planks of the bridge, and found several sentries staring back at him. One shouted a challenge down to him.

"I am Commander Atheltiades." He shouted up at them. "I am the Drill Commander in charge of these recruits. They have completed their training, and have arrived here to take their oaths."

"Welcome, brothers." An unseen man shouted from above. Silence filled the air for several moments. With a lurch and a groan, the bridge began to slowly lower. Chains and cranks made mechanical sounds that echoed through the area as the gate lumbered sluggishly yet deliberately downward. This created a buzz amongst the merchants; they believed that this was their opportunity to get through the fort and onto the other side.

"Defensive perimeter." Atheltiades ordered casually yet decisively. The soldiers behind him immediately broke rank, and formed a convex line around the stone footing of the drawbridge. The bull-adorned shields interlocked with a finality that anyone could understand. Wickedly sharp spears protruded through the wall with such uniformity, it was intimidating. The message to the campers was clear: *do not come near us.* And they all got the message, dismayed as they understood they would not be moving forward today.

The bridge made contact with the stone so softly, it barely made a sound. The well oiled Boldranium chains that raised and lowered the gate were heavy and still. Out of the newly revealed doorway, which happened to be much smaller than the massive drawbridge was, came a troupe of red-cloaked soldiers. They had their spears down, and their shields up, and leading them was a Captain. The all white crest atop his gleaming helmet denoted his rank. Atheltiades ruminated that he wore that same crest not that long ago, but now this man would formally be obligated to call him sir.

"Sir." The Captain saluted, as if on queue. "Welcome to Bridgegate. The Polemarch is away, but the garrison Commander has been notified of your arrival. I am Captain Alexios, I will personally escort you and your men inside."

"Well met, Captain. Thank you." And Atheltiades gave back the customary salute to a subordinate. He then turned to his men. "Let's move! Inside! Go! Go!" And he stood stationary as two lines of men ran past him at a quick pace. Alexios and he then gradually made their way across. Without any command, the drawbridge started it's ascent the moment they stepped off. Atheltiades found himself in a grassy square, surrounded on all four sides by walls.

The hollowness of the fortress was surprising to those that had never been through the bridge before. You would expect to see a small city filling the space inside, but it was only grass, a road that cut through the middle of it, and a few olive and fruit trees. The real fort was within the walls. The walls were so thick because there was a veritable urban center within them. Deep inside these walls that towered over him, he knew there was a garrison, barracks, temples, kitchens, stores, latrines, and everything else a base would need to house a guard force and to hold out during a siege.

Alexios bid him to follow towards a man door on their left. He ordered for his men to stay in place, and then made his way to the entry. They climbed a maze of stairs, wound their way through hallways, until Alexios brought him to what he thought he remembered was *the keep*, but it was hard to tell. Inside, going over documents at a desk, was a middle aged man in full military kit. His helmet was on the desk, faded black and white checkered crest indicating that this was the Commander. The man looked up as Atheltiades approached, his own helm in the crook of his arm. Alexios saluted promptly.

"Sir," The Captain snapped. "This is Drill Commander Atheltiades. He has just arrived from the March. He has brought forty recruits to take the oath."

The Commander rose from his seat. He was tall, broad shouldered, with dark hair and light blue eyes. He appraised the new officer that had just arrived in his fort with a scrupulous eye. Slowly, he nodded at him, as equally ranked officers do.

"Welcome to Bridgegate, Commander." The man's voice was deep, like he was performing in a play. "I am Commander Lysander, in charge of the fortress until the return of Polemarch Rhodenikos. We expect him back in a few days time; he went to the Fortress of South Pass on a certain diplomatic matter. Until his return, please feel free to be the guests of our own fortress. We could us the extra man power, to help sort through the baggage trains forming up outside the gates."

"Thank you, Lysander." Atheltiades returned the nod. "My men and I will be more than willing to help you with whatever you need while we are here. Will we be waiting for Polemarch Rhodenikos to return prior to my men taking the oath?"

Lysander's face was a blank wall. "Of Course. It is customary."

"Very well." Atheltiades frowned, but tried not to show it. The longer they stayed here, the more it delayed his return to Dutrigi, to his father. At least he had arrived, and his mind drifted to the scroll his father had given him.

Now he could finally read it, he had kept his word.

"I will give you a tour of the facility, it has probably been a long time since you served here, however not much has changed." Lysander grabbed his helmet, and gestured towards the door. Atheltiades followed the man, as he unconsciously rubbed the pressed paper that was in its hiding spot within it's cloak.

X

DANQUIN ELKNAUT

His breath was almost as ragged as his horse's when they skidded to a halt. The reigns of his beast were in his left hand, and his spatha sword was bared in his right. His spear had been lost earlier in the drill, so he was down to just his long blade. He wore the scaled mail shirt that usually was reserved for cavalry officers, and his ornate steel and bronze helm shimmered in the daylight. The leather shoulder armor and skirt was a brilliant white, which contrasted with his blue tunic and clothing. A devious grin flashed across Danquin's face, as he watched his *Turma* thunder across the hillside, looping back around towards his position. They moved magnificently.

The last few days, the new members of his squad had begun to seamlessly integrate themselves in with his veterans. They were almost up to full strength since the Imperial government passed a decree, allowing non Golden Glass citizens with the wealth to finance their own horse and kit, to enlist into the cavalry. It had been Consul Macien's idea apparently, that bleeding heart Morincian, but, a good military man. A possible 'middle class' may be born from this maneuver, and that concerned Elknaut. Those concerns must be addressed another day. He was training, with a much larger unit than he had been in command of previously, and for that he was grateful.

Digging his heels into his horse, Polyneices, his old animal partner began to run. He and this horse had been through a lot of battles together, and the beast was in its prime. A fearless warhorse was the most valuable thing in the world to a cavalryman. When Danquin had been unseated in the Battle of Payk'Ar, he feared that he had lost Polyneices. When the fighting had stopped, his mount was found with the rest of his unit, still in formation. The gray horse was a special thing indeed.

Even having started from a complete stop, with the other horses closing in, his horse was starting to pull away from his pursuers. His grin widened. They had been training like this for hours, taking turns running down certain members designated as the enemy. It was his turn to be the rabbit, and they had yet to come close. He slid his weapon back into it's sheath, pulled hard on the reigns, and brought his horse to a stop. The other cavalry men saw this, and started to slow as they approached their Lieutenant. Danquin removed his helmet, and ran a hand through his sweat soaked mop of hair. His men had grins as well, partially due to being pleased they were riding, and partially due to disappointment from not being able to catch their officer, mixed with admiration.

"Great riding, men!" Danquin exclaimed as they formed up around him. "Your maneuvers are getting better and better every day. Those Homithans won't stand a chance." Danquin gestured over his shoulder, onto a distant hill. "And, as you can see, our own wingmen have been watching with regard. The 13th is the best trained and on track to become the paramount *Turma* in the 2nd Legion. Be proud, men. The more we train like this, the less we bleed against the enemy."

The men all nodded in agreement, exhaustion showing on their faces. A few squinted as the sweat burned into their eyes.

"Decurions!" Elknaut shouted. "See that your men get their mounts fed and watered, and then let's all grab some chow for ourselves. Stow your kits and lets meet in 2 hours for dinner. Dismissed!" He smiled as his men trotted past him. Uncorking a skin that was hung from the saddle, he took a long pull of the now lukewarm water. His eyes went to the men that had been watching from the hilltop. They were gone. Recapping his skin, he started towards the stables himself.

*   *   *

His armor and kit stowed, Danquin walked through the stables in a sweat stained tunic and *bracae* trousers. He had logged the training hours for each member, and tabulated the feed and water for the supply master's records. Rumbling in his own stomach made it clear that he was overdue for a meal of his *own.* A stable boy approached him earnestly, a frantic look on his young face. Danquin himself stiffened up and rose a bit as the lad clearly had something urgent to say. The Lieutenant felt a danger approaching, and his hairs stood up on end.

"Sir, some officers are here to see you!" The boy chimed before Danquin could say a thing. "With legionaries, in full armor!"

Danquin felt even worse about this situation now, his instincts screaming at him.

"Thank you." He said almost distantly, swallowed a lump in his throat, and began to walk to the main entrance of the stables. As it came into view, he saw his Wing Commander was there, talking to two Tribunes who were escorted by a half dozen legionaries. His Wing Commander, Mikus Serepitus, looked irate and desperate as he faced off against the officers. It appeared that they were arguing about something or another. Danquin walked purposefully towards the group, putting up a hand in salute.

One of the Tribunes spun on his heels and lifted his chin as the Lieutenant approached.

"Lt. Danquin Elknaut?" the young officer inquired.

"Yes, Sir." Danquin gave a slight bow. "That is I, sir."

"The Legate and the General request your presence in the assembly tent immediately." The Tribune said, in a way that suggested he had no other option but to go with them right this second. The Legionaries emphasized that with the casual resting of their hands on their swords.

"Yes, Sir." Elknaut said, his head pounding in alarm. He then shifted to Commander Serepitus. "Sir, will you make sure my men are fed? They are expecting me at the mess hall." He didn't need to add that he should tell them what had happened to their Lieutenant. Serepitus said nothing, but gave a slow nod back.

"Let's go, Lieutenant." The Tribune said forcefully, his voice devoid of any sympathy.

As they walked down the streets of the camp, Danquin did not say a word, or ask a single question. He knew it would have been a waste, his escort would have offered nothing on the subject. His mind reeled as he tried to think of what this was all about. It had to have been a misunderstanding; he was being treated like a criminal. He could think of nothing he had done to be deserving of handling like this. Soon, he would have his answer, as he walked into the assembly hall.

General Titus Validus sat on his high chair, thumbing through scrolls that were piled in front of him on a table. His purple cloak hung from a hook out of arms reach, and his guards flanked him, one on either side. Tucked off in a corner, also going through papers, but with much more fervor, was Legate Acadius. The Tribune announced their arrival, and quickly departed after being handed a scroll from an aide, off on another urgent task. Danquin just stood there, in the middle of the room, for what felt like minutes until the General spoke. When Validus did speak, he read from a scroll.

"Lt. Danquin Elknaut." He traced his finger along the paper as he read. "13th Turma, 1st wing, 2nd Legion. You are on this list."

Danquin's heart quickened as the General spoke with such nonchalance. What list was this? Why was this a bad thing?

"By decree of Consul Macien, who speaks on behalf of Emperor Kantaur, you are hereby stripped of all titles and command. You will be escorted to Calidia to stand before a tribunal that will be inquiring into your loyalty and in regards to suspicion of *treason*." The General said with no remorse as he read the words.

Danquin was in shock. Treason? This had to have been a mistake, a mix-up of paperwork, an error, or a lie. He felt his entire future, his career, come crumbling down. All the hard work he had put in for this Legion in the past, the sacrifices he had made for the Empire, and the sweat and blood he had poured into his reputation was instantly made void. Everything was negated with a single sentence.

"A mistake, sir!" he blurted out without thinking. He opened his mouth to speak again, but the courage faded, and discipline took over. Dissent died in his throat as an escaping of breath. His mouth shut, and he stood at attention, straightening up.

"To imply that the Imperial Government makes mistakes like this, *Lieutenant*, seems to make me think you *are* a traitor." The General said coldly.

Legate Acadius walked into the picture, slowly rummaging through a few scrolls. "General, sir, may I explain to the Lieutenant what the circumstances are? We owe him that much."

"Very well, Legate. It wont make much difference now." The General said, turning his attention away from Elknaut.

"Thank you, sir." And Acadius gave Danquin his full attention. "Lt. Elknaut, several days ago, an Imperial agent delivered some scrolls directly to the General and myself. Consul Macien has decreed that anyone likely of harboring sympathies for Duke Silious of Akritus is to be removed from their position until further notice. A sensitive situation with the Duke of Frigiterra is unfolding, and the Imperial Council wants to remove any potential threats to the stability of the Legions. This is happening right now across the entire military, not just the 2nd Legion, and not just you. It will be temporary, and once you are found innocent of any wrongdoing, which I'm sure you will be, you will have your post returned. In the mean time, your name is on a proscription list that the Consul himself compiled. Apparently, you share enough blood with the Silious family to meet the qualifications to make the list. I apologize for any inconvenience this causes you personally. I will tell you that although I see some validity to this maneuver, it is causing havoc with my command structure. I'm losing several very good officers, yourself included."

Danquin felt his stomach drop. That was it? He was distantly related to Dahqual Silious, several generations' worth of blood apart, and his career was over. His men would get a new leader, maybe even be broken up. The training, the war… it was all over. His father would be humiliated. His son's all being stripped of command for suspicion of treason. Surely his brothers were being treated the same. Elknaut wanted to say, to tell these men that he was more closely related to the Emperor himself than Duke Silious. But it would do no good. He was not in a position to bargain, not in a position to refuse this order.

"However, Lord General, I ask that this man be spared." The Legate said, surprising even himself. "I have in my possession here, written letters of commendation from multiple officers in the Legion. The Lieutenant is a model officer, and we should not cast him away without taking these files into account. I have spoken personally with his Wing Commander, who also protests this move against the Lieutenant."

"Orders from Calidia are orders we *must* follow, Legate." Validus snapped.

"Yes, Sir." Acadius responded. "But you wear the purple cloak, sir. The Emperor trusts in you to make the best decisions in favor of the Empire. You share his Imperium. And I promise you this. Keeping the Lieutenant in his post is in the best interest of the Empire, and of this legion."

"Orders have been issued, ones that are easy to follow, and hard to break. Why would keeping this one man, out of all the rest on that list, be of any interest for us?" The General asked, annoyed.

"Instincts, Sir." The Legate said. "This order from the capital has already stripped me of some very good officers. I need to keep *some* of them to ensure order is kept. Give me this man, Sir. I swear it to the Gods above that I will take full responsibility if any retribution comes back from this."

The General chortled and shook his head. Silence filled the air again for a long while. He placed a fist to his mouth, as the wheels behind his eyes were in full motion.

"Very well, Acadius." The General shifted in his seat. "This man will be spared, his name stricken from our copy of the proscription list."

Elknaut felt a flush go through his body. Elation swelled within himself.

"The Lieutenant must speak his oath once again, in front of myself and all that are present. Then he may retake his post." The General resigned, indifferently.

"That is fair enough." Acadius said, giving a look to Elknaut. His eyes searched the young Lieutenant for approval. Danquin was an unreadable statue. He felt his fear melt away, and became replaced with anger and a resolute defiance. This was his opportunity to return to his calling, but he couldn't take it. Not like this. He had done nothing wrong, and the shame of being wrongly stripped of his command was nothing compared to the shame of having to retake your oath. He raised his chin, and balled his fists.

"No." He said. The Legate and the General looked at him incredulously. "No." He said again, more confidently. "I already have spoken the oath. I have not broken it. I have done nothing by the Imperial law that would require me to resay the Sacramentum. That would bring dishonor upon my family. I am no criminal."

The General's face grew hot with rage, and just when Elknaut felt like he had blown his only chance, Validus Spoke.

"You are correct, Lt. Elknaut." The General said in a flat voice. A smile then cracked on his face. "You have done nothing that would

require you to renew your oath. It takes courage
and confidence to do what you just did. Perhaps
the instincts of the Legate are correct in this
matter. You are dismissed to your regular post.
Gods give us all strength."

XI

DIMIDIUS TORBOCK

Cortinum was a large city, old but well
maintained. It had wide streets, fountains, trees,
well manicured plants, painted buildings. It was
a smaller, *cleaner* version of Calidia. It did not
lack the bustling feeling that Calidia had, for this
was a very busy city as well. It did not lack the
diversity, for this city was a melting pot of
cultures, maybe even more than the capital. It
did however lack the grime and the seediness of
Calidia. Most of the stone was a gray in color,
rather than the travertine and limestone that
made up most of its parent city. Green banners
flew from most every building, emerald green
being the color of the *'free city'*.

The occasional Guard walked down the
street, draped in green, griffin emblazoned on
the apsis of his *hoplon* shield. The Cortinum City
Guard was made up entirely from the ranks of
their Phalanx, the small military force that the
city was allotted through *the Forging*. Cortinum
had been the first real city founded in the west
during the era of Morincian Expansionism.
Therefore, under the law, they were allowed an
army. Like most Morincian cities, they were

utilized as a police force, upholding the local laws and keeping the peace.

Something about the city felt very right to Torbock, yet also very wrong at the same time. It had been a while since he had actually been inside the city, so perhaps the mood was somber due to the grieving for Selygo. People wore green as a source of city pride, but it was swathed with black as a sign or mourning.

Occasionally in the crowd of people walking down the streets, they passed Anurai. This was slightly startling, seeing these frogmen walk down the street without escort. Even more concerning was the Saurians. The free city was a sanctuary city, allowing Saurians to walk freely about without fear of retribution from officials. That didn't mean common folk wouldn't do anything to them, but if they did, it was not allowed under the law. Two Millangor walked past Torbock, Jacean, and Vicaro, dressed like common men. Torbock's hand reflexively settled on his sword as they passed by. It still made him jumpy. He had yet to see a red-skinned Hyerian, and in fact, doubted if any were in the city at all. Recent history had shown a softening of relations between the Millangor and Mankind. No such thing had happened between the Hyerians and Men. Even if the law allowed them to enter the city, the people would not allow it.

The city was very busy, and the trio seemed to be going against the flow of the majority of foot traffic. Carts and wagons rumbled down the cobbled roads, pushing more and more people to the edges of the streets. Being around this many people made Torbock feel a bit anxious. Polemistius had insisted that they stay in the city for the evening, much to Torbock's protests. They had a very time sensitive mission to accomplish, and this was adding the better part of a half a day to their completion. Torbock wanted to deliver his dispatches, and put miles between themselves and this city, closer to their final destination.

　　　One thing that Torbock really found unsettling was the lack of walls in the city. Cortinum lacked any defensive structures... no perimeter walls, no fortified strongholds, no sentry posts. A Legion was stationed nearby in a castra style fort. That was all the defense the city had allowed. They felt that walls didn't jibe with their message of freedom and inclusiveness, that it would deter people from coming within. *Yeah,* mused Torbock, *large groups of people with weapons and ill intentions might not flock within all at once.*

　　　The sterile and clean paint didn't seem too off-putting, but what was foreign was the lack of graffiti anywhere in the city. No drawings of genitals, no swear words, no colorful descriptive words about politicians and their wives. Also, all the statues were pristine... someone had the job of making sure they stayed sparkling. Despite the façade, the city did have a grimy underbelly, one that emerged and briefly reared its head here and there if you knew where to look.

Tucked off the main roads, down alleyways, beggars were hidden but present. They flocked to the free city, looking for handouts and the famous generosity that Cortinum was renowned for. Also, Torbock saw in the faces of many people the side effects of abuse on their bodies; too much alcohol, too many drugs, too much sexuality. Unkempt grooming, sleepless eyes, disheveled clothing that they tried to straighten out, but failed was everywhere. The glazed look of smoke-moss users, the puffy face of hard drinkers, the tweak motions of laudanum junkies. If you were looking, you could spot them.

They passed a massive statue in the middle of a plaza. It was a statue of an Ikaran, his wings spread wide, and a sword pointed to the sky. The mythical bird-man wore Morincian style armor, including a full helm. It was a reproduction of an ancient sculpture that had been recovered from the Ikaran ruins in the mountains north of Tycalus. The original was in a museum inside this city somewhere. The statue was awe-inspiring as they passed. The man they were escorting didn't even give it anything more than a once-over.

Polemistius lead them to the stoop of a clean looking building. The edifice was located midblock, sharing it's walls with it's neighbors.

It wasn't very wide, but went back quite a ways. Torbock glanced up into the second story window and saw the subtle symbol of Karia. *A brothel,* he thought dejectedly. *We will be staying in a brothel for the night.* Polemistius was bounding up the steps two at a time, and with an eager shove, pushed open the bronze double doors. He spread his arms wide like a priest as he entered, and although Torbock could not see his face, knew the diplomat was grinning from ear to ear. The man said something the Sentinel couldn't make out, and then a round of female laughter ensued. Torbock begrudgingly headed up the steps, for he still needed to make sure that this man was kept safe. Jacean followed, a bit more eagerly than his partner.

The inside was exquisitely decorated. As far as brothels go, this one was upscale. The walls were all painted a deep crimson, furniture and fixtures were gilded a gleaming gold. The couches were cushioned with red velvet, and atop them were seated some very beautiful women. Most were dressed very elegantly, in silken stolas, palas, and their hair up with a few curls flowing down. Gaudy jewelry was draped from their necks and ears, bangles stacked upon wrists and ankles. The room reeked of perfume, lavender and herbaceous oils. The overpowering aroma did a fair enough job of hiding the underlying odors of sweat and other bodily fluids.

Polemistius had taken a few moments

after they had stabled their mounts to hastily put on a toga before they had set out into the city. Torbock knew why now. Women flocked to him, some bringing wine for him to sip, others reaching out and caressing his face and shoulders. The Diplomat grinned from ear to ear, and winked at the two Sentinels as they stood in the threshold of the doorway. These women treated Golden Class men mush differently than common folk; the potential for a big payout was in it for them. Torbock and Jacean felt awkwardly out of place in their grungy riding clothes and weapons. A few of the ladies gave them cursory glances, hoping for a chance with the nobleman before they tried on his underlings.

Only one other man was in the room, sipping wine in the far corner, an ebony skinned Terdakian woman across his lap, whispering with a smile into his ear. Torbock could hear as he stepped into the room muffled sounds of passion coming from the rooms above. Having little experience in such establishments, he guessed this was just the lobby, the showroom. Business thankfully took place behind closed doors and out of sight. A fair-skinned, reddish-brown haired woman sauntered over towards the pair, and completely ignoring Torbock, went up to Jacean and took his hand. The young mans face flushed as a smile broke upon it.

"Hello." She said quietly, and with an accent that was heavy. Torbock guessed she was probably from the western barbarians, most likely Deklar. "My name is Nuala. How are you named?" She smiled a much-practiced smile, her expression innocent yet inviting. She seemed to be about the same age as his young partner.

"Well met, Nuala. I am Jacean Monodius," he gave a slight bow. "You, my dear, are the loveliest flower in this place."

"You are a very beautiful man." She responded, accent heavy.

"I will take that as a compliment." He gave a chuckle. "Shall we sit?"

Without a word or a gesture, she began to lead him towards an open couch close by. Jacean gave his mentor a pleading look. Torbock looked at the other man that had been on the couch with the Terdakian woman, and noticed they had moved on to another room. Couches lead to bedrooms, he mused.

"Do not leave the room, Jacean." Torbock said sternly, but a slight smile on his face. "We are on mission still."

"Yes sir." And the young man winked as he was dragged away towards the couch. Polemistius was gulping wine, purple streaks trickling down to his chin. One of the girls around him ran a finger up his neck to the corner of his mouth, gathering the dribble on her index finger. She then placed it in her mouth. Polemistius gave a rather annoying chuckle as she did so, and put his arm around her and another of the women. Taking a deep breath, Torbock apprised the rest of the building as he walked over to a single, poorly cushioned wooden chair. It was unquestionably the least comfortable looking seat in the establishment that he could see. He sat.

The place had tall ceilings, adorned with mosaics of the gods. A green Cortinum flag hung on the far wall behind what was an empty wine bar. Two bodyguards were standing in opposite corners, one by the front door and one by the stairwell in the rear. Both looked to be rather brutish, probably more for show and deterrence than anything else. Torbock didn't doubt that they could fight. The one closer to the door, a large bearded, bald Enthaki man with a big belly looked at the Sentinel scrupulously. The man's eyes appeared to be filled with resentment, although the rest of his body language was casual. Torbock didn't blame the man in the least, he would be concerned too if an armed man entered his arena of business. He gave the man a courteous nod, and the bouncer did not reciprocate. That was ok, he didn't want a friend, but was pleased to have a decent guard at the door. That would make his job of protecting the Ambassador that much easier.

One of the women gave a playful shriek as Vicaro Polemistius groped her behind. She gave him a playful slap back, and they all started to laugh. He shouted to the guard by the back stairwell, who nodded and then went down a nearby hallway. A few moments later, a new woman strode into the room. Torbock watched her enter, and he felt pressure in his chest, his heart flutter. She was gorgeous. He tried to look away, to stare at a wall as she appeared, but his heart raced and he needed to look at her. He could not look away. Her skin was olive colored, her hair jet black and softly curled. She wore an elegant silver *peplos* style dress, a white roped belt matching the corded hem of her garment. Long white laced gloves flowed up to her elbows, and a beautiful silver necklace adorned her graceful neck. She walked with poise and confidence, her chin slightly elevated, her shoulders relaxed. *She must be the Madame.*

Dimidius Torbock was immediately captivated by her, suddenly glad beyond words that the Ambassador had chosen to come here. She began to talk in a voice that Torbock could not hear to Polemistius, more likely than not discussing pricing for the night. The conversation was very brief, the man consenting to whatever terms this woman wanted. With a dismissive gesture to her, Polemistius rose, along with two of the women and they headed for the back. Just before they disappeared, the eager man turned about, gestured for a third woman whom had been left behind to join the group. As she hastily scurried after them with a giggle, they all vanished up the stairs. The woman then said something very discreetly to the bodyguard, and the guard nodded

subserviently back to her. It had probably been
some sort of warning about what might be
going on in that room tonight.

The woman then surveyed the room,
watching as another duo of men entered. She
gave them a beaming smile as they approached,
and immediately two more ladies suddenly
appeared behind her. She said something to
them with a graceful nod, and the two women
intercepted the newcomers and sat them on the
couch. Her stare then found its way to Torbock.
Eyes locked, and her smile from earlier faded
abruptly. She was frozen for a few moments,
and then began to slowly stride towards him.
Torbock felt embarrassment well up inside him,
and he began to fidget. Remembering his
manners, he rose as the woman approached. She
may be a Madame of a brothel, but she was still
a lady. And a beautiful lady at that. She
stopped a stride away from Torbock, and he
gave a nod without speaking a word. She slowly
extended the back of her gloved hand towards
him, and raised her chin as she angled her head
slightly to one side.

"Welcome, Sentinel." She said. Her voice
resonated through his head, and sent an
involuntary shiver down his spine. "My name is
Rania, and this is my establishment. Are you
here for business or pleasure? What can I do for
you?"

He reverently and gently grasped her
proffered hand, and upon touching it felt an

electric surge throughout his body, his core trembling. Never in his life, not even long ago with Pheona had he felt this connection. Something inside tugged on his heart.

"I am Dimidius Torbock." He said, the words coming out automatically and felt as if someone else was saying them. "It is a pleasure to meet you, Rania. You have a very nice place here." That sounded terrible, stupid.

"Thank you, sir." She smiled a wide smile. "I have put my heart and soul into this establishment."

Torbock only nodded at this. "Business." He blurted a few moments later.

Rania raised a dainty eyebrow, perplexed.

"I am here on business." He reiterated. "You asked if I was here for business or for…" He trailed off, slightly embarrassed and unable to say pleasure, for guiltily that was what was on his mind.

"With the nobleman?" she asked. "And with your partner", she gestured towards the couch, where Jacean and the girl sat conversing.

"Yes." He conceded. "We are escorting the man. That is all I can say, my lady."

"Fair enough." She said. "Just so you know, this room is for customers only. I'm sure you understand, sir. We cannot have random men loitering around, taking up space."

"I can not leave here, Madame." Torbock said. "I am on Imperial sanctioned business."

"Perhaps a little pleasure with your business?" She pressed.

Torbock's mouth opened, but no words came out. All the moisture had left his mouth, and found its way to his palms. "I cannot" he croaked, "I must remain… available. And vigilant."

"Sentinel Torbock," She exclaimed. "I assure you that your client is very safe, and very happy. I know his kind. He will be tired out and passed out drunk in several hours." She smiled. "I have several bodyguards watching the door and spread out amongst the building. Nothing happens to my patrons unless I order it. The man is as safe as can be. Also, he offered to pay for whatever services you and your partner wanted."

Torbock swallowed again, his stomach fluttering. His body was urging him, telling him to take the offer. But, he could not.

"I must decline, thank you though. Feel free to take the coin from the Ambassador anyways." He offered. "If that works for you, I wish to remain here."

"I will take his coin gladly." She almost laughed, her face even more beautiful as she did so. "But you must be a customer, and you cannot be one without getting something in return. How about a drink with me, in the garden? Tea if you refuse wine. It is beautiful back there this time of day." She reached down and took his hand, and slowly beckoned for him to follow. She sent another shiver down his spine as she did so, gooseflesh coursing along his arms and his neck.

"Jacean." He managed to mutter in protest.

"Your partner?" she asked. "He does not need to join us. He is in very good hands with Nuala. I can tell that she has a real liking for the young man."

They continued to walk towards that back, down a short hall, and through an open arched door. Torbock could see the verdant greenery before they even stepped outside. The garden was superb, an oasis in an urban environment. It was small, but gave an appearance of being much larger than it was. High walls encompassed it, plastered and painted, covered with climbing flowering vines. A pergola covered with an ancient wisteria was the centerpiece; a fountain was tucked in the corner, babbling as well. Poured benches that doubled as the front of planters encircled the quad, columns covered with creepers were here and there, as well as the occasional statue. A wonder replica of the famous statue of Karia by Molyeclicles was basking in the early evening sunshine, flowers along its base.

Rania lead Torbock to a bench under the pergola, a table already adorned with refreshments just to the front of it. They sat in the shade, and Rania poured them both wine. Torbock did not refuse. Then, they talked. The conversation was light in nature, introductions to one another's pasts and their current situations. They talked for hours, and the shadows grew longer.

"That was how I came to own this place." She finished a tale.

"You were once a slave, and now you have all this." He recanted back to her, amazed. "Cortinum allows women to own property and to run businesses without a male sponsor?"

"That is why I am here, in this city" She smiled. "I have no men in my life, none that I share it with." She grinned. Torbock smiled back, the wine doing wonders for his nerves. The more he talked with this woman, the more and more he became entranced by her. He had to tell her, it was suddenly the most important thing in the world to him, the only thing on his mind.

"Rania," he started, the words suddenly choked up in his throat. A expecting silence filled the garden, the trickling of the water feature and the calls of birds the exception. The words came then "I think you are…well, you are beautiful and…"

A loud crash from inside cut him off, and suddenly his mission returned to the front of his mind. With a jump, he was on his feet and heading back into the building, hand on the hilt of his sword. Quietly and quickly he entered the antechamber, to find a man sprawled on the floor, blood oozing from his nose. He wasn't completely unconscious, but also wasn't fully awake. Two other men were angrily shouting at the bouncers, as the big Enthaki that had been by the door forcibly scooped up the man on the floor, and tossed him outside. The ejected mans friends started shouting even more, and they were quickly ushered outside.

A woman sitting on a couch was rubbing the side of her face, and looked more annoyed and angry than she did hurt or frightened. Torbock could piece together what had happened fairly easily. These guards don't like when a guest happens to hit one of the women. He then relaxed as he realized the ambassador was not in danger. Rania appeared beside Torbock, nodding thanks towards the bouncers.

"Are you alright, Dahlea?" She asked. Torbock knew from his conversation with Rania that she knew all her girls on a personal level, and cared for each and every one of them.

"Yes, Madame Rania." The girl that was Dahlea said. "Gods curse that man, he was a *cinaede*, such a jerk." She daintily touched the corner of her mouth, and then checked her finger for traces of blood.

"I am glad you are unharmed. You may take the rest of the night off, my dear." Rania said sympathetically.

"Thank you Madame. I think I will be alright, though. He hit like an invalid. I will just powder up real quickly, my lady." Dahlea said, rising to head to a back room.

Rania nodded. Just then, a shirtless man carrying a sword came down the stairs, almost leaping into the room. Jacean was panting, his short cropped hair matted with sweat, his breathing ragged. His eyes widened as he saw his partner, and lowered his head shamefully. Torbock slowly shook his own, but a slender smile was on his face. Before he could say anything, Rania spoke.

"Master Sentinel," She spoke to Torbock. "I've provided your partner and Nuala with a room that shares a wall with your friend, Polemistius. He will be right next door if anything happens. My own guards will make sure that no one goes near either room. In the meantime, I've made arrangements for you two to have your filthy clothes laundered. They will be ready in the morning before you depart, no extra cost to your generous patron."

"Thank you, Madame. I will…" He started.

"I would very much like to continue our conversation." She cut him off.

"Yes, my lady." He replied.

"Shall we retire to my room?" She asked, but it wasn't much of a question, as she was already moving and leading him by the hand.

XII
MACIEN

He could see his breath as he walked, barely visible in the moonlight, but it was there when he looked. A clear, cold night. A good night for a stroll through the grounds. He had been inside all day long, writing dispatches, giving written orders, and reading intelligence sources that were flooding in from all over the Empire. He was exhausted, both mentally and physically, and needed to sleep. He couldn't sleep, there was far too much still to do. This walk around the grounds was his compromise. The blue cloak of Jorbus looked black in the darkness of the night, keeping him warm as the crisp air tried to get into his bones.

So much had happened in the last several days, it felt like months since the intruder had broken into the palace, the same night Selygo was murdered. *The days are long, and the nights seem even longer,* he thought. *I never wanted any of this. The entire situation is spinning out of control. Are we really on the brink of a civil war? A rebellion? What would you even call Silious and his rogue army? Restorationist? Was that a word? Reinstationaries?* He sighed. *What would they call themselves? Patriots? Liberators? Hopefully, no titles would ever form.* If the Gods truly loved this Empire, this rebellion would end before it started. Macien prayed that he had done the right things with the steps he had taken.

He had received a report today of troops amassing near Cruxium and a larger force headed south from Trekkus. This made it look like the Information that Dimidius Torbock had supplied was unfortunately accurate. A battle would take place soon in Lacerterra. Trimontis probably would be first in a series of systematic sieges towards the Capital. If it was Macien, in Silious' place, he would pass on trying to take Trimontis for now. That mountain city was a stronghold that could take a very long time to take and use up many resources in the process. It took the Empire generations to originally take the Vaus capital, and it was in large part due to tenacious fighting from the Dutrigians.

Perhaps the force that was gathering and staging at Cruxium would bypass the city of the Rams, and move on. Maybe Dutrigi? That would also be a very difficult battle to fight, but one that Silious would have to do sooner than later. If he and his forces marched past Dutrigi and tried to take Cortinum or even Calidia, he would be leaving their backside vulnerable to a mighty force. It would be either Trimontis or Dutrigi. Knowing that both of those forces would never jump to Silious' cause, and were inflexible warriors was a small comfort. He hoped they could contain this new enemy until

Macien could get the Legions mobilized and in the theater.

Shifting the Military focus completely away from Homitha would be disastrous. They had fought too long, sacrificed too much to concede anything to the Empire's enemy. They needed to keep a presence in Luctantum, even if the invasion force was temporarily being diverted to deal with Silious. The situation around the rest of the world was even more disheartening.

Rioting had started in Enthaki and civil revolt was a real concern. That meant the entire 11th legion would need to remain in the colonies over there to keep the peace. They would probably need reinforcements. Cylathian forces, under the Command of Homitha, had also been harassing the borders south of Enthaki, and they were probably the reason behind the rioting in the country.

A similar situation was brewing in Akkedis, with the Hyerian army camped along the border into Millangor lands. That was a delicate situation, and it would hopefully be resolved soon. He knew the 8th Legion camped along the borders and garrisoned in Millang'Sek were valuable over there, but they would be welcomed against Silious. Hopefully they would arrive in time, but more than that, he hoped he wouldn't need them.

The stability of the Crystal Sea was in jeopardy, which meant that Morincia was in jeopardy and Jorbus was in jeopardy. Duracee, the naval powerhouse of that region, was needed to qualm the uprising in Enthaki. Reports were trickling in about possible revolts planned in other cities in the area, and it was up to his brother Darien and uncle Kyberien to keep everything together. And he had just sent his sister and the heirs to the Empire back there. His head hurt thinking about it.

Hopefully the Silious insurgency was short-lived, and those officers that he had ordered be put before a tribunal to prove their loyalty could be reinstated to resume the campaign against Homitha. He wished that the Gods would send some sort of sign, tell him something to let him know he was doing the right thing. On the fringe of the city below, the 1st legion was preparing to mobilize. When they left, Macien would go with them. Then the war would be his only focus. Was it the right move, to head into the theater himself? If he died, who protect the Imperial Family? Who would stay behind to keep the city and the rest of the Empire running? Could he trust his Council? So many questions, so many probabilities.

He looked up to the full moon, and saw his breath puff around and make a haze in the moonbeams. Atop a tree, he saw motion. It was slight, but it was there. A bird. An Owl. The beast hooted, and his cry was answered with a plethora of similar hoots. As Macien looked around the tree line, he saw at least one owl in each tree, some had many. Dozens of them, all hooting, and all looking down at him. It sent a chill along his spine. If ever he needed a sign the Gods were watching him, this was it. His hand reached up and touched his broach.

The Owl was his sigil. It was also the eyes of Lucidus during the hours of Shaardon. This must be a good omen. It made him long for home, for Junæa. The silver moon made him wonder if back home, she was looking at the moon herself, wondering if Macien was doing the same. Then he thought of Mallea, her face jumping into his mind. He slammed his eyes shut in hopes of getting rid of her, but the tighter he squeezed, the more he thought of her. He felt her lips on his, felt her ribs as he moved his hand down along her side. The feeling of her bare heel digging in behind his knee was next, followed by memories from long, long ago. Shaking his head, he dismissed them.

The owls had grown silent. They were still there, but they said nothing, just observed.

"Tell me something, damn you." Macien pleaded to the Gods through the birds. "I need help." He admitted.

The owls remained quiet, so he continued his walk. Occasionally, he heard a distant hooting, or the sound of wings flying overhead.

XIII
MIKUS DERRATA

"I heard that there was some sort of conspiracy," Said Titus Vinius, ripping apart a piece of fluffy bread. "That's why they snatched up those Centurions and those other officers..." he pointed to no one in particular.

The squad was all sitting together at a long wooden table, along with the rest of the Century. It was midday meal, and the camp had the feeling that any meal in the mess hall could be the last before they received their marching orders. That meant no more fluffy bread, so the veterans told him. The food here was decent, nothing spectacular, but it was commonly joked that this slop was considered Imperial Palace quality compared to food eaten on the march.

"Why so soon before the campaign?" Asked Adamas Ferro. "Do you think they were going to desert? Treason?"

"Someone close to the Legate that I know told me it had to do with the camp treasury. Embezzlement or extortion of some kind." Vinius said, quietly.

"Who the hell do you know that's close to the Legate! Your such a blowhard, Titus." Phenton all but yelled. The bruising around his eye had faded to a greenish-yellow, with a touch of purple just on the top of his cheek. The hatred in his eyes when he looked at Derrata had not faded, however.

"I can't say, Phenton. It wouldn't be fair to him." Vinius said while chewing his food.

"You can't say," This came from Quel Strasa "Because he don't exist." Since the incident the other night, Strasa and Phenton had been even more distant from the rest of the squad, only joining in mandatory functions like training, inspections, and meals. That was all. Mikus had a terrible feeling that they were planning some sort of devious retaliation against him and Marcus. The rest of the squad had found out about the fight, and it had caused Mikus and Marcus to be regarded with more esteem and acceptance. He was sure that caused Phenton and Strasa to hate them even more.

"Treason." This came from Toratum. "I heard rumors of the Imperial government catching wind of a possible rebellion. They are suspected of being a part of it. Sounds like the thing is over. This is the last any of you will talk about it, unless you want your names added to the proscription list. That's an order."

No one said anything else on the matter.

"Great job this morning, training was a success." The squad leader said, breaking the silence. He looked at no one in particular as he talked, but focused on scooping up the remnants of sauce in his bowl with a heel of bread.

"Continue to show Derrata and Amintus what they can expect from the Homithans. You veterans know what its like, but until we get back on the field of battle, they have no way of knowing. Keep showing them, preparing them. Underestimating a foe, or not knowing what they are capable of, is a great way to get a *black eye.*" He looked at Phenton when he said that last, his serious mask dissolving to a mocking smile.

Phenton froze, and continued to stare down at his food, unmoving. A slight tremble was in his right arm. The rest of the squad stifled laughter; even Tilo cracked a grin but made no noise as usual. Mikus was stone faced; he did not need this kind of provocation. Marcus however, was jovial as usual, and actually chuckled out loud.

"Alright men, I have a meeting with the Optio. The afternoon is yours. Be ready to march at anytime, however. No blackout drunkenness…" he pointed toward Vinius. "…And no fighting." He patted Mikus on the shoulder. He carried his mess kit away to wash it, and was gone. Phenton and Strasa rose together once the Decanus left, and walked away without saying a word to anyone else.

"Those *two* do not like you *two* right now." Vinius said after a moment.

"We've known them a long time." Ferro said reassuringly. "They do this from time to time. They like to prey on those who aren't in positions to protect themselves. Now that you guys have stood up for yourselves, they are even bitterer. It will pass in time. All the same, I'd watch your backs. Phenton can be very vindictive."

"We will watch your backs, too." Added Vinius. "But they ain't dumb. If they try something, it's not going to be while we are around."

Tilo nodded to the group, stood, and went his own way, probably back to the tent for an afternoon nap.

"Let's talk about some Homithans, tell these kids some old war stories. And let's do it over dice…" Vinius said, rising to clean his own kit. The rest followed.

*   *   *

"Twenty four you slugs! Beat that!" Vinius bellowed, slapping the table with a large flat hand. "I stay!" The dice had jumped when he had banged the table, but everyone saw the roll as it came out of the cup. They had moved to the assembly hall, and were surrounded by other squads trying to pass away the day. The game they were playing "5 to 30", an old, classic dice game. It required 5 die, and a single player rolled all five at once. The goal was to get all sixes, or as high a number as possible, hence the 30. You could pick up the dice and reroll, but you had to leave at least one die behind each time, and all "1"s had to stay. Also, 3's and 4's were blank and added no value to the score. Vinius had just rolled three 6's, a 5, and a 1 on his first roll, and decided to stay. If everyone rolled over a 24, then Vinius would lose that round, be eliminated, and all the money he had put it the pot would go to the final winner. Each round eliminated the player with the lowest number, until only one was left.

The two other caveats to the game were this: If you rolled all 1's, you won that round automatically, and all other players had to double their ante for that round. The next was called the "dead mans throw", which was two 4's and three 3's. If any player rolled that, usually on their first roll, they automatically lost, and had to double their own ante. All other players got their ante back when that happened. Legend had it, some old Prince serving in the legions had gotten a knife in his back while playing dice one night, and that had been the throw he had made as the blade went in.

Next in line was Marcus, who placed the ivory dice into the leather cup, stirred and shook them, and then slammed the cup down onto the wooden table. The table rumbled as he did so, and then with a jolt snapped his cup up, revealing his hand. One 1, two 4's, a 5 and a 6. Picking up all but the 6, he rolled again. This time his new roll was two 6's, a 3, and a 2. He left the two 6's, which combined with his first 6 for a total of 18. He rolled his two dice, and was rewarded with a 2 and 3. Since the 3 didn't count for anything, he picked it up to roll again. If he rolled a 3 or 4, he would be on the hook for elimination, since Titus had rolled a 24. His total right now was 20. He needed a 5 or a 6. His lone die rattled in his cup as he shook it with one hand. He murmured prayers under his breath, a smile on his face, and then slammed the cup down.

Ever so slowly, he creaked the cup upwards, so only he could see the die. Building the suspense, his face blank, he lowered his cup to the table again. Everyone looked on expectantly, eyes wide with anticipation. Suddenly, the big mans blank face turned morose, shoulders slumped. Vinius smiled as he read the body language. Dejectedly, Marcus raised the cup, revealing a 5. The table broke out in cheers, Vinius angrily punching into the palm of his hand. Marcus laughed. Mikus joined in on the laughter with a chuckle, but restrained himself. It was his turn next, and rolling higher than a 24 was no simple task.

The cup slid from Marcus to Ferro (who had been eliminated the previous round), who then passed it to Mikus. The dice soon followed. One of the most grievous fouls a dice player could commit was to hand a player a loaded cup. You just didn't do it; a player always loaded his own dice. In some games, if you handed the cup full, you were eliminated, or had to pay a fine. With a chinking rattle, Mikus dropped the five dice into the leather cup. He reverently closed his eyes, gently swishing the pieces in the cup, round and round.

"Let's see if the Gods favor you, boy!" Vinius blurted. "Goddess Tyshae is a mistress of mine; with her, my luck never runs out!"

With a slam that rivaled the big man Marcus, Mikus brought the cup down hard. Without lifting it, he shook the dice up again while they were on the table, as if the cup was a brush and he was cleaning the wood. He took a deep breath, began to lift the cup up, and then… there was a bang as the doors to the hall slammed wide open. All eyes in the room turned to see what it was. Mikus kept his hand on the cup. A man in an Optio's cloak stood just a step or two inside from the door.

"All legionaries are to return to their tents immediately. Grab your kits and get in full gear, we are all to meet on the drill grounds for a briefing. The Legate has ordered mobilization, and we have begun breaking down the camp. We will be on the march this evening." The Optio barked, and then quickly left, on to make sure the message was passed on to others. The room was silent for a few moments and then sprang to life. Men jumped to their feet, and started picking up coin from tables. People shouted, some laughed, but everyone had been electrified by this announcement. The mood had changed to anticipation and excitement, as well as a healthy dose of nervous energy.

Mikus kept his hand on his cup, frozen.

Ferro began pulling his coin out from the pile, and so did Vinius. Marcus followed suite, but Mikus sat there, taken aback at how quickly the situation had changed. Ferro looked over at him, and casually said "Pick up the dice, we've got marching orders." His voice was cool, even, not excited or anxious like a lot of the energy in the room.

"What of my roll?" Mikus rebutted.

Ferro shook his head as the last of his coin clanked into his pocket.

"The game's over. Those are the rules, Derrata. Once an officer orders us to do something, the game ends right there. It's always been that way." He grasped Mikus on the shoulder, and pointed down to the cup.

"Best not to peek under there. Just shake 'em up before you lift that cup." Ferro offered his advice like an old sage.

Mikus hesitated, curiously staring at the leather cup. His muscles tensed in his grip, unsure if they were about to shake the cup of lift it. They were about to do something. Mikus licked his bottom lip, and Ferro keep his gaze locked on the young legionaries face.

"There's no such thing as what might've been, that's a waste of time." And with that last tidbit, Ferro turned away, leaving Mikus to his make his own decision.

Mikus took a deep breath, and then tilted the cup back.

Two 4's and three 3's stared back at him.

The dead man's throw.

*   *   *

The Legate stood in front of the legion, the sun high overhead. It had been one hour since the men had been in the hall, playing dice. Now the entire legion was in full marching kit, ready to mobilize on a moments notice. Aids and orderlies still packed tents and gear into the baggage train. The cohorts would lead out, the train following with an escort not far behind. Everything was happening much faster than Mikus had imagined it would. Say one thing for the Imperial Legions, they are efficient and effective.

"We have received orders directly from Consul Macien, who holds Imperium over all military operations." Legate Acadius started. "He has declared Duke Dahqual Silious IV a traitor to the Empire. Silious is being directed to peacefully turn himself in to stand before a Tribunal for treason. If he does not, then military action has been sanctioned against him and the forces he commands. We are part of a contingency force that is being sent west to participate in this action if it comes to that."

As the legate paused, no conversations could be heard, however glances and looks were shot back and forth between many soldiers. Acadius continued:

"I am sure that most of you are aware of certain officers that have been removed from their posts recently. To clarify and to stop rumors, their names were on a proscription list that was delivered to us along with these orders. The individuals are being sent to Calidia to stand before the same Tribunal we already mentioned due to the high probability they may be Silious sympathizers. These officers, many of them distinguished and fine men, are innocent until proven guilty. This is a precautionary step the Consul has taken. Have faith in what he is doing.

"Many of you have family in Frigiterra, or know men in the Frontier Army. If it does come to fighting, remember your oaths, and remember what you are all fighting for. I will do as I promised, and take care of you. All I ask is that you all follow my orders, no matter how difficult they may be. What we do, we do for all of Calidia. We leave in one half hour. Gods give strength. Dismissed."

XIV

NEROFIDES

From the window in his chambers, Archon Nerofides had a spectacular view of the Caldera of Petros. In fact, the room had four panoramic windows, each looking at the different cardinal directions from his island inside the rim. The crescent moon shape that made of the brunt of Petros was due east, wrapping to the north and south. Due west lay the smaller Temple Island, and beyond that was the larger island of Vygila. Two stout seawalls had been constructed between Vygila and the northern mainland, and Vygila and the southern tip of the main land. Small gates were built into these seawalls, allowing ships to enter or exit. The exterior of the main island of Petros was sheer cliff faces, with no safe place for ships to land. Inside the gates however, was a harbor like no other in the world. Not even Portopolis could compare.

Petros was a seafaring city-state, and even though Nerofides held the Morincian title of Archon, the title in his heart was Admiral. Morincia had always treated Petros as second rate, with Duracee being known as the real naval power in the region, and Petros lacking a

real land force. The Duracee were not true
Morincians, not like Petros. Long ago, Duracee
had traded their identity for renown in the
shipping lanes, their own culture being blown
away like the merchant ships they piloted. They
were whores, selling themselves for profits.
They were a mix of Enthaki, Homithan,
Calidian, and Morincian. It was disgusting that
they were allowed to keep their titles as
'Morincian.' Even Jorbus, the self-proclaimed
capital of Morincia had become so overrun with
Calidian culture, that it was almost
unrecognizable.

Petros was the last of the true Morincian
city-states. They had disobeyed the old King
Skiptro when he bent the knee at the Forging.
Only by force had they agreed to join the
Empire. Several times in their history, they had
rebelled against their overlords when they
disagreed with policy or leadership. They were
not afraid to say no, and they had opinions; that
was what a true Morincian City-State had been
founded on. They thought for themselves, and
when they disagreed with someone, they let that
person know.

Jorbus had been a bully in the past, using
the fist of the entire region to tame the small
island nation that Nerofides called home. And
now, Macien, son of Aedien, sat upon the Ebon
Throne in the Calidian Capital. *Figuratively* or
course, for that archaic symbol of leadership had
been abandoned generations ago. Nerofides ran

a contemplative hand over his graying, salt and pepper beard. Much had happened in the political realm in the last year or so. Opportunities that had not been open to him were suddenly popping up all over. Sometimes, great opportunities that only come once in a lifetime show up at the same time. Both are starkly different, and you may only choose one for once you do decide, the other option disappears forever.

He was looking east, towards the main island. The city of Petropolis, the largest city on Petros, was abuzz with activity. Although he could see no motion, he could hear the sounds of a thriving metropolis; ships in the docks, people living and building on the cliffs and the plateau above. Koronus, the island that his Palace was on, had a wonderful view of all his lands. It also provided a wonderful view of his ships. His fleet was a force to be reckoned with. Hundreds of ships, war vessels, filled with his finest sailors and marines. The yellow and teal colors of Petros flying in the wind, the sea-snake sigil emblazoned on each sail. It filled him with pride.

They would sail today. He would take his fleet, and they would sail towards the mainland. Not a single blow had been thrown yet, but a war had started. Behind him, on his desk, sat two scrolls. Both were very similar, yet drastically different. They both asked of him the same thing, but he had to choose one. When he made his decision, and obeyed one, the other just became a useless piece of paper. It would be up to him to decide which one he chose. Both claimed to offer the same thing upon completion of the task. Both were sealed by signet rings of well-respected families.

One promised to right wrongs that had been transgressed against his people by an oppressive sister state. The other was what he saw as a foreign tyrant that claimed dominion over his people through a treaty he had no part of claim in. That foreigner offered him future autonomy for his service. He trusted neither, and had bitter relations with both. Which would he choose?

One was sealed with blue wax and an image of an owl. The other had been sealed with orange wax and image of an eagle. The Owl and the Eagle. Two very different birds, he would have to choose.

XV
DAHQUAL SILIOUS

The scroll crumpled in his hand, and he mashed and twisted it in his shaking fists. He tore at it, trying to shred it, destroy it, but the paper was stout and he had already balled it up so it stayed whole. In frustration, he threw it against the wall of his tent. This made the messenger flinch. Dahqual wanted to beat the young man senseless for bringing him such foul news. The junior officers in his tent stood at attention during the time he had read the dispatch. The messenger had interrupted a strategic meeting to bring the urgent dispatch.

"How did he know to do this so quickly?" The Duke of Frigiterra said aloud to himself, sinking into his chair, face dour, a hand on his temple. Macien had declared him a traitor, stripped him of all titles, and requested that he peacefully turn himself over to stand before a tribunal. That made everything he did now completely illegal, no technicalities to hide behind any longer. He was like his ancestor Iroan Silious, rebelling against the regime that was weakening his Empire. Or even more accurate, Hastian II, returning to the throne by force to restore his the Bellatus Dynasty.

The other dispatches he had received were even more disconcerting. Some of his family had been detained, including his brother and uncle. Kruegius had fled the Capital, to return to Dutrigi. Did the Council have some sort of inkling to his campaign strategy? He never thought they would act on anything they suspected without hard evidence. This Macien had gall, that was certain. That prophecy that was sitting on his desk too made him wonder. It was not the one he had paid for of course, which made it even more disturbing.

He had no choice, that was clear. It did not matter anyways, for he had already put in motion plans that could not be undone. Now it felt that things were starting to feel very, very real and irrevocable. They needed to stay the course, and find a way to use this to their advantage.

"Messengers have been sent out to all the Prefects and Legions, carrying a similar communication to these?" Official Imperial announcements, though?" Silious asked the messenger. The man did not know.

"We need to stay ahead of these. I imagine I will receive the official notice of my orders to appear before the Tribunal shortly. You made good time getting here, soldier. Thank you. Report to the Dispatch tent, and await my orders. Once you get there, send a scribe here at once." Silious rose, hands clasped behind his back. The messenger saluted and disappeared.

"What is your next step, my Lord?" Lourede asked from a corner, standing by a brazier and a wooden dresser, shadows and light playing across his devious face.

"We continue on as planned." Silious stated. "We will rendezvous with General Victus as we arranged, and then start our campaign. All this other information is just a distraction. It will not change the outcome of our operation."

"Agreed, my lord." Lourede said in a placating tone. "But may I suggest taking some form of action against these dispatches?"

"I thought you were a seer, priest?" Silious said losing patience. "Couldn't you see that I am already doing just that!?"

"No disrespect was meant, my lord." Lourede maintained his soft tone. "What will you do?"

"I will write my own dispatches. I will send them west and I will send them north. I will even send them to the capital and overseas. I will denounce the Consul's own denouncement of myself. I will deny his claim to rule, and perpetuate my own. He has very shaky legal authority right now, and he will have none whatsoever when my dynasty is restored. I will play on the fears and anger of the people, and get them to hate him even more. I will send out agents to start revolts, to burn flags, to burn wicker men in the effigy of Macien and the

Emperor. In short, I will win over the nation even more by weakening the Consul's hold and strengthening my own love amongst the people." He spat, anger choking out his voice. "I will cut off all trade to the capital from my lands. Food trains will be interrupted. I will simultaneously cut off the common folk who support Macien, and then donate food to them after they believe their own government is responsible for their hunger. I will march to Calidia, and take that Ebon Throne to roaring applause of the masses."

XVI
ATHELTIADES

The Fortress of Bridgegate had changed little since he himself had served here for a short time. It was well garrisoned, well defended, and well provisioned. Commander Lysander had personally given Atheltiades a tour of the facilities and the fortifications. Thousands of spears and arrows and stones had been stored in caches along the battlements, generations upon generations adding to the supply. They could repel a large force for a long time if they needed to. Bridgegate was a tremendous source of pride among the Dutrigian people, and he felt pangs of shame for the brevity of his part in being stationed here.

After his own swearing in what seemed like many years ago, he had served several short months here. His reassignment had been quick, and he believed his father had pulled some strings to get him a better assignment, one more conducive to career advancement. Although his father had never mentioned it, and Atheltiades himself dared not broach the subject, it was all but apparent that was exactly what had happened.

But, he was here now, standing on these

ramparts, looking south in to the nest of his people's mortal enemy. Perhaps now that he was a Commander, he could request transfer to this posting. Maybe Lysander wanted a different posting of his own, bored with the monotony of his current job. Maybe he would ask him before he departed if that was something he would be interested in. For now, Atheltiades would fill in where he was needed until the Polemarch returned.

"What was the nature of Polemarch Rhodenikos diplomatic mission to South Pass?" Atheltiades said with passing interest to Lysander. The two men stood atop the rampart alone, cloaks flapping in the sea breeze, looking down on the caravan of carts that rumbled into the recently opened gates and into the Empire. From high above, the Dutrigians that were searching through the carts below looked like little red field mice, scurrying this way and that. His own men were down there, working beside the regular Bridgegate garrison force. The process of searching every cart made it very slow going, and the Dutrigians were very thorough.

"The Polemarch was meeting with the Commander in charge of the Imperial garrison force." Lysander said evenly, also watching the procession below, and not looking at his guest. "The Empire has taken over South Pass from Trimontis forces in recent history, and the he was hoping that they would allow Dutrigi to operate west of the fort on some raiding missions and scouting operations."

"West of South Pass?" Atheltiades questioned. "Isn't that barbarian land? Greld land?"

"It is Greld land, correct." Lysander said with concession in his tone. "However, we know for a fact that Millangor colonies have been set up along the Bay of Dru, past the Great Bogs."

Atheltiades said nothing, frowning, as he was slightly confused. What care did Dutrigi have of Saurians setting up colonies outside the Empire, in barbarian lands. That was none of their concern, and out of their jurisdiction. The gravity of what he just thought was not lost on him as he looked south of the spot they were standing. These lands were beyond the borders of the Empire, and his people wanted nothing more than to invade and purge these lands of Saurians.

"The Empire has forbade us from continuing our campaigns into Akkedis against the Millangor. They have declared them allies. We do a very good job of keeping them out of our own lands. However, nothing forbids us from pursuing them *outside* our lands, and outside the forbidden territory south of here. If Saurians are prospering elsewhere, and we have the means of dealing with them, then that is what we shall do. The Gods will it."

Part of Atheltiades understood that

statement completely. Another part, a weaker part, felt it was a bit over the top. If these Saurians were setting up colonies far away, fleeing the area of conflict, then perhaps they should be left alone. The first part of him chimed in, saying that maybe in a few generations, these colonies would become strong enough to wage war against his own descendants.

"We must ensure that these lands remain protected, Commander." Lysander stated, as if reading his counterparts thoughts. "Many of our own have fallen, and we must never forget their sacrifice."

"They will never be forgotten, Commander." Atheltiades consented. "We must all do our parts to keep Saurians from entering these lands again. Is targeting colonies that are moving farther away from our borders the best utilization of our forces, however?"

"Anytime we are given to kill Saurians, we must take it." Lysander snapped back. "They are fleeing because they fear Hyerian invasion from southern Akkedis. Deterring them from fleeing, perhaps we can keep them all packed in on that peninsula together and have them rip themselves apart. Then we can mop up the rest, and rid them from this world."

Atheltiades nodded to that. "What of the Red Skinned threat? Any update on their amassed force along the Sout'I?"

"No change that we-" A shout from

below cut off his response. Both Commanders looked down on the caravan that was streaming single file onto the drawbridge. Red cloaked sentries were swarming around one of the wagons, yelling orders. The driver was pulled down from his bench, violently tossed onto the hard packed dirt just south of the moat. He rolled once, and then came to a halt, sprawled on his belly, spear pointed between his shoulder blades. Piles of cloth were being haphazardly unloaded from the covered wagon, thrown onto the ground below. The Shouting intensified and the soldiers took a step back, spears leveled.

From the back of the wagon, a green skinned being appeared, arms spread high in the universal symbol of placation. It was a male Millangor, dressed not in military garb but a common wool tunic. His motions were slow, his body language screamed submission, and although from high above his words could not be heard, the tone of his speech was groveling. Taking a reluctant step forward, the Saurian continued to plead, now cupping his hands together. The first spear caught him on the right flank, and it caused him to stagger. The next thrust into his abdomen brought him to his knees. The beast roared, and the painful cries of the dying saurian mixed with other screams as well; human roars of hatred, and Saurian cries of despair. Multiple cries of despair.

As the Millangor was speared continually, its life soon draining away with its purplish blood, more beings were being hauled out of the wagon. A female Green Skin and her children. The mother roared as her two older children were forcefully pulled away from behind her. Kicking and screaming, they squealed like piglets as they were dragged. Making short work of it, the Dutrigians unceremoniously slit the throats of the younglings. Bellowing in pain and anger, the mother started to lurch forward, but was silenced and her momentum stopped as a half a dozen spears pierced her all at once. She died instantly.

Atheltiades said nothing, his face betraying no emotion as the corpses of the Saurians were cleared away to allow traffic to resume. The wagon had been pulled to the side, and was being searched more thoroughly, the driver being interrogated. No doubt he would claim he had no knowledge of his stowaways.

"These beasts are getting desperate and more bold." Commander Lysander stated. "The Hyerian threat, coupled with the amnesty the Imperial government is offering, is causing them to try this stunt more and more. Those who can't afford to take a ship try this. The ship is a much better gamble, with the Imperial Navy being stretched so thin in these waters. They are all trying to get into Cortinum, or other sanctuary cities the capital lets exist. It's a grievous sin against our people that such places endure."

The young Commander nodded to his

aged colleague. Even with Lord General Kruegius being the Duke of Lacerterra, and with eminent power over the Free City, he was powerless to change its policies. The Imperial government explicitly forbade him from rescinding the liberties the city had afforded itself.

"Your father is Atheicles, correct?" Lysander asked, catching Atheltiades off guard. He hadn't expected the conversation to so casually shift to a lighter subject.

"Yes, Atheicles is my father." Atheltiades said, no emotion, not even pride showing in his voice.

Lysander continued. "I served under your father many years ago, before the start of the Second Homithan War. He is a good man, and a good leader. You should be proud to be his son."

"I am. You pay him and my family honor. Thank you, Commander." Atheltiades said graciously. Just then, he remembered the note; the prophecy his father had given him, the one he had ordered him not to read until he arrived in Bridgegate.

"I will be returning to my duties now, Commander Atheltiades." Lysander said, already shifting away from the battlement. "If you need anything during your stay, do not hesitate to ask. I appreciate you and your men's help in assisting with our duties. Gods give strength."

"Gods give strength, Commander."
Atheltiades repeated, and watched the
Commander of the Fort leave. With anticipation,
he dug into his pockets, trying to fish out the
scroll as soon as he could. His fingers found the
smooth parchment, and he reverently pulled it
out, into the breezy air. A deep breath filled his
lungs, and then he unfurled the paper. The
paper had been moist from sweat, and creased
from being crushed inside his cloak for so long.
The words however, were clear as day. He
silently read the prophecy, eyes jumping from
side to side as he did. When he had finished, he
read it once more, this time more slowly and
meticulously.

"The land will crack with a fight
For they will not bend like the light
Shone through a crystal prism
When a cough creates a schism

The red shines through bright
When there is no chance of flight
Awash in orange, yellow and black
Silver in front, brown and grey to the back

A new friend born that was once a foe
An old friend will strike a fatal blow

Above the stars, but below the bird
A line once defined becomes blurred

Death will come upon a horse
But the red will stay the course
A calf will have to become a bull
What was almost empty becomes too full

Like blood from the mountain comes scree
To wash against the walls and to free
Half will go across the sea
The rest will arrive in Dutrigi"

Chills went up and down his spine as he read it. His father had read this very piece of paper, and realized what it meant, and sent him away. Anger flashed inside at the thought of his father doing such a thoughtless, careless act. How could he? Then sadness flooded in, as the gravity of what he read sank in. He looked south, deep into the heart of the Empires true enemy. The chills intensified.

XVII
ADYPATUS EVENTUS

"We need to tell someone!" Flaccus pleaded, a step behind Eventus as they made their way down the street. Eventus said nothing, just continued to weave through the crowd, determined to make good time across the city.

"Eventus, stop for a second. Let's talk." Flaccus reached out and clasped his shoulder, bringing them both to a halt. His partner had an expression on his face of deep concern. It was more than that; his eyes were saying something further. Fear. Flaccus was afraid. And if he was being honest with himself, Adypatus was a little fearful too.

"We can't tell anyone." Eventus reiterated, firmly yet calmly.

"Why not!" Flaccus protested. "They already know who we are, and they already know what we know. We need to tell more people, we need back up. If anything happens to us, then they win…"

"We don't know what they know." Eventus countered. "They may not know what we know, but they will know if we tell people what we know. We do know what they think we know, but they don't know that. You know?"

Eventus continued walking, more slowly now. He was frustrated by the situation, and afraid for his own life. That kind of stress was making him a poor communicator and an even poorer partner. But, he had never been a good partner in the first place; as he had explained to everyone well before this assignment started.

"We need to tell the Cohorts. Lt. Grattus can help us." Flaccus offered.

"No." Eventus rebuked. "We can't trust anyone, not until we have proof of what we know. It's too dangerous."

"We need to tell the palace, then." Flaccus exclaimed. "It is our duty to protect the Imperial family, and they are in jeopardy right now because the Imperial Guard has been compromised."

"That's a great idea, Flaccus." Eventus said sarcastically. "March into the vipers nest, wade through them and hope we make it to the other side. The Guard would have us skewered before we made it to the front gates, trust me."

"Cometa is missing, we need to find him." Flaccus desperately threw out.

"He is a grown man, and a trained soldier." Eventus countered. "If he isn't already dead, then he's on his own and fine. Either way, we can't do a thing for him."

"What are you going to do, then?" Flaccus was getting angry now. "The Guard is still after us, we need to find this assassin, and we need evidence that the Guard is corrupt.

How are you going to do that? What's your plan?"

"I do not have a plan." Eventus admitted with a remorseful sigh. "But I do have some leads. I know the name of the assassin, and I have contacts looking for him. That's our best possible mode of action right now."

"You know his name?" Flaccus asked, shocked. "Who is he?"

"Tuek Sicarius." Eventus said, looking around them suspiciously.

"Tuek Sicarius." Flaccus repeated back, the name slowly rolling off his tongue. "Are you certain that is the name? How did you get it?"

"It is the name and the man we are looking for." Eventus said. "We need to cross reference that name in the Cohorts records, see if anything comes up associated with it. Hopefully my contacts will have found something soon to help us. Once we check the records, we need to disappear for a while, avoid our normal routines and places. The Guard will be looking for us, and that will be where they find us, trust me."

"I will go to the records hall," Flaccus stated. "I will give the name to the aides and see what they can find. It will take a long time to do a search like that."

"Good." Eventus said curtly. "Grab whatever coin you have stashed away, and any items you will need. I'm going to go do the same. Let's meet by the statue of Iroan Silious, the one by the bridge on Imperial way, tonight at dusk. We will go from there."

"Sounds like a start." Flaccus said, but he hovered, more on his mind that he wanted to say. Eventus waited for more to come, but nothing was said. Flaccus bit his lip, and let out a long sigh. "Dusk. Silious statue." He said, with a slow nod.

"A nice touch of irony, that statue. Hopefully the message won't be lost on anyone that's following us." And Eventus let a smile crack his face. He embraced his partner's arm, and they went their separate ways.

*   *   *

Something was wrong at his apartment. Even as he approached, from a distance, he knew it was wrong. The small grill shop on the first floor was empty, no sign the cooking fires were burning, no people milling about. The place was subpar, that was why Eventus never patronized the establishment, but it usually had some customers, especially at this time of day. The rest of the street seemed normal enough, his building just seemed wrong. Verka was missing, that was the real concern. The doorman never left his post, not for more than a moment to relieve himself once or twice a day. Even then, he usually did it a step or two from where he normally sat.

The front door was closed. Grasping his dagger as he drew closer, Eventus scanned up and down the street for any signs of danger.

None materialized, but he knew that he was being watched. Reaching the front door, he gingerly pushed on the heavy wood, and it began to open with a very faint creak. It only opened about six inches before hitting some resistance. Eventus pushed harder, and the door budged only a little. Putting his shoulder into it with a heavy lean, he pumped his legs and heaved. The door opened about halfway, enough to get his head through. Carefully, he peeked inside. On the floor was the limp mass of Verka, acting as a doorstop.

Cursing, Eventus managed to slide and shimmy his way inside the lobby. A quick scanned revealed the room to be empty, besides himself and the doorman. He knelt and checked on the big Terdakian brute. He had a pulse, and he had breath. His face was swollen and bruising, blood caked on his mouth and nostrils. Eventus began to check the rest of the body. The big man wheezed and struggled to breath as the Enforcer poked and prodded. Broken ribs, a broken arm, and a few lacerations here and there. Possible internal damage to the organs from the beating, but relatively stable. He was on the loosing end of a fight that was for certain.

"Verka." Eventus said, patting his cheeks. "Verka. Wake up."

The big man groaned, stirred slightly, but did not awaken.

"Verka." Eventus rubbed the man's sternum with his knuckles. "Verka, its

Adypatus. What happened, my friend? Who did this to you?"

"Adypatus," The man whispered, eyes still closed.

"Yes, I am here my friend." Eventus said, cradling the large man's head. "Who did this? How did it happen?"

"They came for you." Verka struggled to speak. "Soldiers. Not dressed like them, but they were."

Eventus shivered, and then anger began to creep in. "Why did they do this?"

"I would not let them in." Verka opened his eyes, and tried to lift his head. The man set his head back down on the dusty stone floor. Eventus struggled to get the man to sit upright, and once he did, the doorman wobbled side to side. Eventus kneeled by his side to offer support and balance.

"I messed some of them up good, Adypatus." Verka managed a nasty grin, white teeth highlighted in red blood.

"That I do not doubt, my friend." Eventus responded, starting to rise to his feet. "What can you tell me about them?"

"They should have killed me…" Verka said, his voice wavering.

"Something must have kept them from doing so, especially if you roughed some of them up. What can you tell me about them?" Eventus reiterated.

The Terdakian rubbed his forehead and

groaned. "They came to the door. They asked for you, all business like. Six of them in all. I told them nothing. One tried to walk past me, so I grabbed him. Then they swarmed me. They all carried swords and daggers, but mostly used their fists. I got many punches in before I went down. Then they kicked, and that's all I really remember."

Eventus nodded grimly, and pulled out his skin of Wyrian wine, offering it to the beaten man. Verka did not refuse. "Stay here. I need to go up to my room. Do you know if they all left together?"

Verka shook his head, slowly and in apparent pain. "I do not know."

With a sigh, Eventus pulled out his pugio dagger once more, and slowly started up the steps to his room. He heard nothing. As he climbed, he saw nothing. When he got to his floor, nothing seemed out of place. Creeping down the hall, he didn't sense anything amiss. Then, he saw his apartment door was ajar. It wasn't cracked, but had been left open deliberately. As he approached, he routinely looked left and right at the various doors he passed, as well as over his shoulder to make sure someone wasn't about to knife him from behind.

Once he reached his room, he peered in very cautiously. The place had always been slightly a mess before, but from what he could see, it now looked destroyed. Maybe *ransacked* was a better word. With even, steady pressure he pushed the door open, dagger held up ready to strike. The room was empty, he was undoubtedly alone. No bad guys lurking in corners or behind doors. Most of the furniture was destroyed, laying in shattered pieces across the floor. All his clothes were tossed in heaps, most shredded to tatters. His mattress was gutted, ripped open in several long slashes and the eviscerated stuffing flung out in messy piles. They had searched everything thoroughly, looked in every nook and cranny. If they were hunting for something very particular, they must not of found it

Firstly, if they were looking for information on the case, there would be none here. The only things of any value that he kept in his apartment were his weapons and his saved coin. Eventus knew that to look for either would be futile, the intruders would have taken them out of spite. The only small consolation was that Cat was nowhere to be seen. Hopefully that little fluffy shithead had been gone before these goons came. The cracked shell that was the remains of his military chest showed that they had even taken his honor decorations.

A sinking feeling filled the pit of his stomach, and he suddenly wished that he hadn't given Verka that Wyrian Wine. He wanted a drink, and the intruders had smashed all the amphora and vessels, empty or full, on the floor. Dejectedly, with shoulders slumped, he turned to leave. There was nothing here for him, nothing to take that he could use in the following days. All it did was confirm that the Imperial Guard was...

A man was striding towards him, already inside the doorway. A garrote was in his hands, and if Eventus hadn't turned when he did, he was certain it would have very shortly been around his neck. The way this man was heading towards him, with determination and deliberateness, the weapon might still find its way there. Eventus reflexively took a step backwards, pugio shooting up in defense. As he did, he lost his balance as some debris shifted underfoot. He wobbled backwards, and then propelled himself forward into his attacker. Putting his own head down and weight forward, he collided with the man's chest.

The attacker caught the brunt of the Enforcer, and they stumbled backwards. Like a python snake, the intruder began to coil the wire in his hand around Eventus' neck, a sneer on his face revealing yellowing teeth. Before the man could tighten the garrote enough to do any damage, Eventus began stabbing into his soft tissue, the belly and up under the ribs. Wide-eyed and silent, the ruffian released his grip, and slid to the floor below.

Panting and standing over the dying man, like a hunter looming over wounded prey with blood already on his hands, Eventus nonchalantly slit the man's throat. The thought of questioning the doomed man flashed in his mind before he did, but a nice safe corpse was more appealing. The man wouldn't of had much to say anyways, he was sure. A cursory pat down of the freshly dead man revealed some coin, not much but better than nothing, and a military issued pugio, very similar to his own. Further investigation revealed an eagle tattoo on the man's right shoulder, in black ink, with a "VII" below it. Exposing the left shoulder showed another tattoo, a scorpion, this one in a purple outline. The alternate symbol of the Imperial Guard. Shit.

"Gods give strength." He muttered to himself, and also to the dead man sprawled across his floor. Wiping his dagger clean on a dry part of the shirt of the man he just killed, Eventus rose. He sheathed his weapon, and went on his way.

XVIII
DIMIDIUS TORBOCK

The coastal town of Stathum had been a quick stop for the trio. Once they had delivered the dispatches to the 7th Legion, they resupplied their kits and stores, and pushed on. Polemistius had complained little about the quick movement through the area, much to Torbock's surprise. Perhaps the diplomat had been worn out back in Cortinum, and would cease his griping for the rest of the journey. The Sentinel doubted it would last that long, but one was nothing without hope. Strangely enough, Torbock had experienced the opposite problem; he longed to *return* to that city.

Before he had set foot inside that establishment in Cortinum, the mission and his duty consumed him. Now, his mind was distracted with images and thoughts of Rania. Polemistius however, now appeared more focused on the mission at hand than ever before. Jacean also appeared to have in his mind on something distant as they rode, but that was nothing new for him. That girl Nuala had him smitten, just like Rania had captured his own attention. Jacean had a much harder time of hiding it though. Torbock was much better at keeping his face a mask.

Rania. He clutched at his reigns tighter as thought of her face. His body grew dull as he concentrated on the sensation of the little charm she had given him brushing against his chest. It gently swayed this way and that as the horse rocked him down the road. Rania had removed the charm from a fine bracelet she had worn, and slid it onto his Sentinel chain. When he put the chain back on, the little bobble had remained hidden behind his medallion. It was nice, secret reminder he had of her. That and the scarf that still carried her scent.

"You are thinking of her." Jacean said wryly. "It is written all over your face, Dimidius."

Torbock felt his checks grow flush. "I am thinking of our next stop, Jacean. As you should be doing." He was surprised at the defensive tone that his voice carried.

"Of course." The grin on Jacean's face widened as he spoke. "You are thinking only of Dutrigi."

"I admit," Torbock allowed. "I have thought of the lady from time to time since we left Cortinum. She was very kind to us. And she laundered your clothes, which I was *very* grateful for since the stench was becoming unbearable." He wrinkled his nose slightly. "You may need it done again soon, boy."

"That's why you think of her? Because

she cleaned our clothes?" Jacean asked for clarification on the matter, unconvinced.

"She cleaned *something* for you, alright! I'm sure clothes weren't involved at all…" Polemistius chimed in. "You bagged the Madame of the Compass Rose, that's no small feat my friend."

Inwardly, Torbock felt embarrassed and ashamed. He had wanted to do what they all thought he had done, but he couldn't bring himself to do it. She had wanted it, too. Respect had taken over, and he didn't want to ruin the wonderful feeling he was having just being cordial with Rania. Perhaps he would return to Cortinum soon in his travels, and they could start something official. Absently, the charm caressed his skin, and that made him content with whatever was to come.

"We have delivered all dispatches to the Imperial Legions that were given the assignment to notify." Torbock said, changing the subject. "The 7th was the posting of Silious' brother, Vaquin. His uncle the General Sequenius Silious was in camp, and both have been detained by Imperial decree. We have one more document to deliver to Dutrigi, and then we will set sail to Akkedis. The Island of Vlek will be our first stop. From there, a short jump to Millang'Sek. From this point on, Polemistius, it's your half of the mission, we will just be your escorts."

"Perfect. You do your jobs, and I will do mine." Vicaro Polemistius said, almost aggravated. "There's not much to talk about beyond that."

"Perhaps if you told us a little about your mission, we may assist you." Torbock started. "If we knew the plan, it would help us do our part. The more we know the better."

"Do not worry about it." The Diplomat said dismissively. "I have built a relationship and have a very good understanding with the Dutrigians as well as the Millangor. It is my job. I just need to phrase the request of the Consul into words these people can relate to."

"What has the Consul requested?" Torbock asked, not letting up on his prying.

"I said not to worry about it. It is my concern, not yours." He snapped back.

"With all due respect, Ambassador," Torbock said, irritation creeping into his normally even voice. "You don't exactly exude tact when you talk with us. How is that you are an Imperial Diplomat?"

"You, Sentinel, are a bit of an ambassador yourself, correct?" Vicaro said, unwrapping a piece of heavily peppered smoked cod that they had purchased in Stathum. He took a large bite of the fish, and continued to talk with his mouth full as he chewed. "You solve problems, settle disputes all around the Empire, right? You know the laws, you know the rules, and you know the customs. You know when words fail, and when steel talks. The first priority is to keep the steel sheathed and the words should be your

weapons. But, you read the situation, and
through experience, know when to act and how
to act. Sometimes, you just have to *gut*
somebody." He paused to nimbly pull a cluster
of bones from his mouth, and discarded them
with a flick of finger and thumb.

Torbock said nothing, knowing the
statement had been rhetorical, and the
monologue was to continue.

"Just like you, Torbock, I read the
situation and can read people. I know what to
say, when to say it, and who to say it to." He
took another chomp of his food. "The me you
see here, is the real me. Consider it a privilege
that I act the way I do around you. I have no
need to toady to you, and you respect honesty
above all else. How more honest can I be than to
be completely myself around you two? I happen
to be a vindictive, self-centered bastard when it
comes down to it, and I accept that. When I get
to Dutrigi, I will act how the Dutrigians expect
me to act; a groveling, weak bodied civilian,
with no military experience. That is how I am
perceived, and it does a world of good to fit into
someone's stereotype. They are a lot more
receptive to ideas when they feel intelligent and
think they have an accurate assessment on a
situation.

"In Akkedis, I need to be stern yet
respectful, however with an air of superiority,
for they regard that well. My mission over there
is easy; Get the Millangor King Strank'lakon,

whose name means '*Cracked Tusk*' in their language by the way, to consent to allow the 8th Legion to leave their post and return to Domiterra. Easy enough, considering that this Legion is the only thing keeping the Hyerian hordes from invading their lands, and is the one bargaining chip the Empire implanted to allow a very uneasy truce between our peoples. Any suggestions on how you can help with that? Either of you?"

After a long silence, Jacean spoke a response of one word: "Money."

Vicaro laughed. "Young man, for being so travelled around these lands, you are so naïve. The Saurians care not for money, not when their people are in such grave danger. We already have a stranglehold on their economy, and the precious resources they have and we want could make them very powerful one day. But we don't allow that, we stunt it. They want protection, and we gave them a legion to protect their border to the south. And now I must ask them to give that back. The Dutrigians to their north won't offer any aid, that is for certain. Coin means nothing to these Saurians at the moment."

Jacean said nothing, although his face darkened with shame at being dismissed so quickly. Perhaps the shame was for being so wrong to start with.

"How about you, Torbock? Any great ideas?" Vicaro asked in a tone that was far more haughty than inquisitive.

"Offer them inclusion." The Sentinel said, seriously.

Vicaro stopped chewing and cocked his head ever so slightly, surprised.

"Inclusion into what?" The Ambassador asked for clarification.

"The Empire." Torbock said without hesitation.

"Just like that?" Vicaro scoffed, his tone changing from interest to indifference seamlessly, like a trained negotiator, like a politician. There was still something in his voice, the slightest hint of defensiveness, that his stance was a charade. "Hundreds of years of hatred, bloodshed, war, massacres, just washed away with a friendly gesture. Neither side would go for it, too much history, and too much bad blood. Why would they want to be part of our Empire?"

"Safety, like you said." Torbock rebutted. "Inclusion was probably their goal by agreeing to this armistice. They even allow troops to be garrisoned close to their capital. They *want* the safety we can offer. They *want* inclusion. All these barbarian enemies that we have conquered over the centuries, they have all been absorbed into our society, and atrocities were committed in those wars too. Will we never be able to accept the Millangor because they aren't human? We've included races that weren't considered Calidian, and now you can't even tell them apart from everyone else. I say offer inclusion."

"Inclusion?" Vicaro said sideways through his mouth as he popped the last of the fish in to be masticated. "Interesting approach from a half-Homithan, half-Calidian former slave. Maybe that's just what *you* want, and you are projecting it on that entire race. I guess deep down, we all want to be included and accepted into something greater than ourselves."

"So, what are you going to offer the Millangor?" Torbock asked once more.

Vicaro was silent for a few moments, and then gave a diplomatic response.

"I will offer the terms that Consul Macien dispatched me to offer. When we set out on this mission, we had different tasks to accomplish. You two were travelling under the guise of being my escort. Macien told you the true purpose of the mission was to deliver those scrolls to the Legions, which among other documents included those proscription lists. Escorting me to Millang'Sek was just the diversion to deliver the information along the way. In actuality, my mission to Millang'Sek is the real mission. Once we are on that ship leaving Dutrigi, we are completely on our own in strange lands, and the success of the entire mission depends on getting to that meeting to treat with Strank'Lakon. This entire war may depend on it; we need to get more soldiers on the field against the enemy, for we are weakened and vulnerable."

"What terms are being offered?" Torbock asked a final time. "What if something unforeseen happens to you? If this mission is so amazingly important, and you are the only one that knows the moves, what do we do if you go missing?"

Polemistius had a look on his face like he had just gotten a whiff of something putrid. Composing himself, he looked right at Torbock; "You are a smart man, you'll figure something out."

XIX

TARAES KANTAUR

The evening sun washed the world in a brilliant golden hue. Shadows were a dark brown, and everything else was a fiery copper. They had travelled farther than expected today, and despite recommendations from her escorts, they did not stop to make camp earlier. She would lay eyes on her home city today. It had been such a long time since she had been to Jorbus, and she hadn't realized how much she had missed it until she had gotten close. The closer she got, the more she longed to see the city, be in the city. They had meandered through farmland and forests today, all very familiar to her. And now, they were cresting the final rise before the city came into view. She had caught the far west tip that jutted out on Dankoma bay, but that had just been a tease.

As they careened up the hill, and more of Mt Junas became visible, the expanse of the city below revealed itself. She smiled widely. The sight of the grayish white buildings intermixed with the lush green trees, the salty smell of the sea mixed with the richness of the mountain flora, it all brought back so many memories of

her youth. Simpler times, happier times, she
longed for them, cherished them. Even with her
children beside her, part of her still wished for
those days of innocence. She dismissed such
thoughts, brushed them aside and categorized
them as mere fond memories. It was a lifetime
ago.

She felt a tug on her side as her son
clambered up onto her lap, and headed towards
the window. The little blond boy grasped the
framed opening, shoving his way in front of his
mother's face, hogging the view for himself.
Qoara sat on the bench across from her mother,
alongside Raquel her cousin. Raquel was the
only child of Quel Secundus, and her mother,
Clodia, had been banished from the Imperial
Palace because of a scandal. Raquel was more or
less being raised by Linara and Taraes. The two
girls looked tired, and absently starred out the
window at the changing scenery. Greeth was
much more content and enthralled with what he
was seeing.

"We own this place too, mommy?" The
little boy asked eagerly, not taking his eyes
away from the emerging cityscape. For the
duration of the journey, he had asked that
question every time they so much as passed a
barn. Of all the places they had seen, this one
was the hardest to answer. The easy answer was
yes. But so much more went into it. Morincia
was part of the Empire, so yes the Imperial
family owned it. Her family in particular had

been its steward for centuries. But Morincia, and especially Jorbus, was more an idea, an ideal than it was a city. That was something that no one could own, but rather the other way around. Perhaps someday she could explain it better to her children.

"Yes." She smiled, gently rubbing his back. "This is all ours, my son."

"Daddy owns everything." He said proudly. "I love daddy. I wish he came with us."

A twang of pain shot into her heart as he longingly spoke those words. She missed her husband very much, and regretted abandoning him when he was most vulnerable. However, Macien had spoken the truth, and protecting her children was the most important thing right now. The danger swirling around the capital was too real to ignore. This had been the best course of action to take, to flee, to hide; to go home. At the very least, she would complete that promise she had made to her father. It was time to make that effigy, to bring to life that image of him that had been burned in her mind since his death. Perhaps such a thing would pacify them both, allow peace and rest for father and daughter, the living and the dead.

*   *   *

The Palace of the King, as it had been called since before the Forging, looked unchanged to her. In fact, it probably had changed little in the last five hundred years. It sat atop a spur ridge near the base of Mt. Junas, over looking the bay and the majority of the city below. Its outer walls stood tall, and draped along in intervals was the blue flag bearing the image of the owl of Jorbus. On top of the battlements flew the purple flag of the Empire, the golden eagle always flying high above the local apsis.

Large trunked, gnarled, ancient olive trees lined the road that approached the gates to the palace. As a child, she had climbed and played on these same trees, and couldn't help but smirk as her own children looked at them, the longing to do so written on their own faces. Earlier today, Kanion and the other escorts had changed back into their uniforms, proudly displaying their position as members of the Duke's Honor Guard. They rode in front of the carriage in full armor, giving proper chaperone to the Empress. Blue-clad hoplites that patrolled the city saluted as they passed, unaware but possibly having a suspicion of who sat inside the carriage.

With little challenge the coach was allowed to enter the walls of the old palace. It travelled through the main yard, down a gravelly road that brought it towards the formal entrance. A small retinue had hurriedly gathered on the wide steps to welcome the newest visitors. The horses came to a halt between the steps and a giant statue that was the centerpiece of the yard. It was an identical copy of the bronze sculpture of The Forging that sat in the vestibule to the Imperial Palace. This one however was outdoors and had developed a deep green patina, making it look even more ancient than its counterpart in Calidia. Neat, low hedgerows and landscaping encircled the statue's round base.

Here, in this palace, it looked more like a marring or a shackle than a source of pride or a trophy like in the Capital. They were identical, created for the purpose of solidifying the bond that brought the two former nations, two former kingdoms, and two distinct cultures together. Yet here, it seemed a reminder of subservience and loss of independence. She took her eyes from the statue and gazed upon her children and a warm feeling filled her. Perhaps sacrificing ones independence for the greater good was usually the right thing to do.

She scanned the guards, servants, slaves and aides that were filing in on the marble steps, scanning for familiar faces. She recognized some, but she was looking for a few in particular. Her eyes searched desperately for Darien, Kyberien, Junæa, her mother, her niece and nephew, her cousin Kallista, her friends Leto and Damara. She continued to search, even as Kanion walked in front of the window to open the door to the cabin. With a gentle smile and a hand held palm up, he beckoned for her to step out into the evening air. Ducking her head slightly, she emerged into the courtyard. Cheers erupted from the greeting party as it became clear that their Empress had returned to her childhood home. She took a step forward, still looking for her family in the crowd, waving a gentle ladylike wave to her people. Kanion helped heft the kids down out of the carriage behind her as Taraes took it all in.

Behind and beyond the palace in the distance, the three peaks of Mt Junas emerged, green and shadowed in the setting sun. It would be dark very soon. Birds cried in the near distance, gulls squawked farther away. It looked like home, it smelled like home, it sounded like home, but it did not feel like home. Her home was the Capital now; this had been the place she had grown up in, that's all. This was a visit. But still, it felt right to be here. Her heart needed this, she now understood.

A blur of motion caught the corner of her eye, as something came barreling at her from the left. At first she thought it might be a hound, or some sort of animal how quickly it moved. As the strong arm of Kanion swooped it up before it got too close to her, she realized it was a child. The curly mop of brown hair and the face made it apparent who the child was.

"Hey!" Kanion said loudly but playfully, holding the boy's collar as if he were a puppy being examined by its nape. "I remember you, lad. Do you remember me?"

The boy kicked his feet as they floated in

the air, ineffectually trying to writhe his way free. Even as he struggled, he had a grin on his face. "You're my dad's soldier. Is he here? Have you brought my father home?"

"No, little man. Your father is a busy man. And I have a name. I know yours, do you remember mine?" Kanion feigned insult towards the child.

The boy's mouth was shut tight, and he vigorously shook his head no.

"Very well, I will not let you down until you remember my name is Kanion, or…" The big man quickly stopped talking and let out a playful groan, as if he had spoiled some great secret.

"Kanion! Kanion! You're name is Kanion, I remembered!" The boy shouted, almost laughing.

"Very well, my little Dukeling…" And Kanion lowered the boy down to the gravel. "Aedien, do you remember your aunt Taraes?" He gestured towards the Empress, whom now had both of her children huddled in front of her, arms resting on their shoulders. Qoara stood shyly by her cousin Raquel, holding her hand for support.

"No." The boy innocently shook his head. "I don't know her. Who are these kids? Can we play?" He looked at Kanion for permission, as if he was his new guardian.

Taraes crouched down to the boy's eye level, her dress crunching into the dusty gravel road below. She did not mind, her clothes were filthy from her travels.

"Aedien," She said warmly. "It has been a while since I have seen you, I am your aunt Taraes. Your father Macien is my brother. These are my children, Qoara and Greeth. They are your cousins. And this is their cousin, Raquel." Greeth tried to hide behind his mom, but Qoara walked forward with Raquel and gave the boy a strong hug. Taraes giggled as she saw this, emotion welling inside her and escaping through laughter. A tear formed in the corner of her eye, but not enough to bother wiping away. She ushered Greeth forward, urging him to say hello. They were about the same age, and hopefully they would become great friends for life. But for now, they had to get past introductions.

"Greeth, do you remember your cousin? You met once when you very young." She asked her son. He shook his head no, but remained silent.

"Why don't you introduce yourself?" She suggested.

Like a small man, the blond boy raised up his chin, and extended his arm for a customary greeting. "Prince Greeth Secundus Kantaur. My dad is the Emperor of the world. Well met." The boy said, voice swollen with pride and a little nervousness.

The brown haired boy didn't take the extended hand, but waved instead. "I'm Aedien.

This is my dad's house. Do you want to go play in the garden? We have a maze! The girls can come too!"

The young prince dropped his hand to his side, and then looked at his mother. "We're gonna play!" He exclaimed.

"You two can play tomorrow. It is getting late, and we need to find some supper." His mother said regretfully.

"*I* already ate, *I'm* going to go play!" and Aedien spun around on his heels, about to run towards whatever he had in his mind. He made it all of two steps before colliding with a pair of legs. Junæa Actulus, Duchess of Morincia grabbed a wiggling arm as the little boy tried to skirt around the obstacle.

"You will stay with me, little Bug. Never run away from me like that again." The woman said sternly but with no trace of meanness in her voice. Amara was a step behind her, standing like a little lady. If Aedien was the spitting image of his father, she was a copy of her mother. The little guy protested, but was then placated.

"Empress Taraes." Junæa said with a respectful bow. "An unexpected yet not unwanted visit. It is good to see you again." The Duchess had a thin smile on her face, which did little to mask the weariness that he body exuded. She had dark bags under her eyes and worry marks creasing her face. Her skin looked a shade or two on the paler side of healthy, and her shoulders had a defeated slouch to them. They were all subtly there, but together they added up to paint the picture of a person that was under a great deal of stress and strife.

"Please, Sister," Taraes returned the bow. "You never need to call me that. We are family." And the two embraced in a deep hug. Once all the introductions were made and remade, the group headed inside for a meal and to get settled in.

*   *   *

Junæa poured them both wine from a very ornately decorated amphora, depicting some ancient scene from Morincian history in black and red and white. The liquid that filled the clear glass was dark, almost black, and depending on what angle the light played off of it, it either had a violet or crimson hint. It was delightful: robust and full-bodied, and had a subtly sweet taste and floral aroma. Taraes savored it as it went down.

"Theiosian Jasmine-wine." Junæa said, reading the expression on her sister-in-laws face. "The same family of vintners has been crafting this wine since well before any Calidian set foot in Foron. The best wines in the Empire come from Morincia."

"I fear my time in the capital has perverted my palate, sister. This may be the best wine I have ever tasted." Taraes set the glass down on the small table, and reclined in her couch. She was very tired, the travelling taking a toll on her body. Sleep was much desired, but she hadn't seen Junæa in a very long time. Her and the children had eaten a small meal of cold meats and fresh cheeses, along with soft breads and honey, butter, and fruit spreads. The children had all gone to bed, the girls retiring to the same chambers, and the two boys insisting on sleeping in the same room. Tycho and Andronikos would watch over them personally tonight. Kanion would undoubtedly show up early tomorrow morning, with no explanation of where he had gone the night before.

"Janis said she is making a special meal for you tomorrow, braised lamb with yogurt lemon potatoes, I believe. She said it is your favorite, at least it used to be." The Duchess took a long sip of wine. The Empress smiled.

"That will be much welcomed, it has been too long since I have tasted cooking like Janis'." Taraes took a small sip, and then settled into more serious conversation.

"Junæa, how are you doing?" She asked genuinely, concern in her voice. "You look like you are exhausted and under a great deal of strain. Is it anything I can help with?"

Her brother's wife stared into her glass as she swirled it about, and did not look her in the eye as she spoke. "I am well enough, Taraes. I am just so tired of... of it all." And she shook her head. "This war, it has taken so much. Macien has been gone for so long, I can't even remember

life with him home. His children do not know
him, I feel like *I* do not know him anymore. And
all these new things; Greeth being ill, Macien
being Dictator, the Consul being murdered and
the assassination attempts, and now this threat
from the west. Every time I receive a letter from
Macien or a dispatch from the capital, I cringe
before I open it. I haven't been able to sleep
since he left here; I worry all the time. I fear for
him, and I fear for our children, I fear for
everyone but myself." She finally looked up at
her sister-in-law, and a tear was welling in her
eye.

Junæa was very beautiful with traditional
Morincian features. Her was pulled back, with
elegantly curled bangs falling on either side of
her face. Despite the weariness in her face, her
beauty was still there. She had a sharp face, with
a somewhat hook nose, which added to her
beauty, not detracted from it.

"These are things we cannot control."
Taraes started. "We must…"

"I am so sorry." Junæa cut her off. "I am
complaining about something to you, and your
own husband is…" She stopped, not knowing
how to finish.

"It's ok. It is not a competition. We are
family, and we will be here for one another, no
matter what." Her own tears began to fill her
eyes. She wiped one away before it had a chance
to run down her cheek.

"Look at us," Junæa said, almost

laughing. "Two stereotypical upper class wives, in their Palaces, crying over their husbands."

Taraes chuckled at this also.

"We are both very tired, my sister." The Empress said. "Let's retire for the night, and start this heavy conversation again tomorrow morning."

"That sounds wonderful," Junæa said, rising to her feet and draining the last remnants of her cup.

Taraes stood herself, and pulled out a small scroll from a fold in her garment. She handed it to the Duchess, who took it gingerly.

"Kanion gave that to me earlier tonight. It is from my brother. I have a feeling that this letter has nothing within it to make you fearful." She smiled gently, and then hugged her sister-in-law goodnight. "We love you Junæa, Macien most of all. I will see you in the morning, sister."

XX

ANTONEUS COMETA

The water roused him from his semi-conscious state. It wasn't cold, but when it was thrown in his face, it shocked him enough to bring him back around. The water hadn't been clean to start with, but it mixed with the sweat, grime, and blood that was caked on his skin, and made dirty rivulets that ran down his face. As he gasped for air, the nasty water went into his mouth, and despite his thirst, it was fowl to taste and he spit and sputtered it out. He groggily opened his eyes, and saw his torturer standing before him, a slight devious smile on his face.

"Awake again. Good, you piece of scum. We have more to talk about. You haven't told me a thing I've wanted to hear yet." The man set down the wooden bucket, and walked over to his victim. As the water ran down over Cometa's chest and towards his abdomen, stinging sensations went through his body. It was excruciating. The pain brought back memories from what he had endured before he had passed out. How long had he been hanging here in this torture chamber? A day? A week? He was beyond thirst and beyond hunger; even pain was becoming a blur to him.

The needles. Those were the worst. The scalpels that had been filleting parts of his skin had been very cruel, but the needles had been the wickedest. Hundreds of times those metal spines had been inserted in all the wrong places. This man, whose name he did not know, was incredibly familiar with how to make those things find their mark. He was a gods-damn artist of pain, and he knew it. This vile person before him must have sold part of his soul to Passeus for the terrific knowledge in hurting and suffering.

Blurring was closing in on the edge of his vision, as his mind and body both tried to slip off to sweet sleep once again. A quick thrust of a needle into his cheek struck all notions of rest from his wind. With a stifled shout he became fully alert. Inside his mouth, the tip of the needle could be felt atop his tongue. He reflexively began to try and work the foreign object out by opening and closing his jaw and sweeping his tongue back and forth. The familiar metallic salt taste of his own blood filled his mouth.

With a deep breath he calmed himself, and reaffirmed that he would not say a word to this man. He also promised that he would make this man pay. And more importantly, since this man was following orders, he would make whoever had ordered this torture pay. This man though, although following orders, was taking too much pleasure in this. He would pay some way or another. His left shoulder stung as sweat and water dripped upon it from his head. The memory of this man slowly and methodically opening his skin and exposing the layers underneath came back. The exposed patch was sensitive to the slightest touch and movement. Still, he would not cry out, he would not talk.

"Who, traitor, are you working for? Who have you told about your plots? Who has helped you?" The man said, his tone even and mechanical, having asked these questions dozens upon dozens of times. Cometa hung his head, and focused on his breathing; in and out, in and out. He would say nothing to this man.

"I am impressed that you have held up this long, Cometa." The man said nonchalantly. "I pride myself on getting people to speak with methods I developed. Perhaps some more traditional, tried and true techniques are in order." He began to put on the thick leather blacksmith gloves. With his head dangling, Cometa watched from beneath his brow and out of the corner of his eye. Fear filled his stomach and chest, radiating through his entire body. The torturer casually walked over to the blazing hot fire that sweltered behind him, and removed an iron. It glowed a bright white and orange at the tip, which became red and then black down by the handle. The man held it like a Thylonian dueling sword, leveling the hooked tip at the hanging man's chest. Slowly and deliberately, he moved it towards his victim.

"I ensure you, Cometa, it is in your best interests to begin talking now." He said, inching the fiery metal closer to his prisoner. As it drew nearer, the smell of the iron burning the air gave the all too familiar odor of his youth. Almost a foot away, he could feel the heat emanating away from the tool. Clenching his jaw and shutting his eyes, a whimper escaped between gritted teeth as the burning sensation started. He knew that the piece hadn't touched him yet, that the radiant heat was enough to cause the pain he was feeling. His right pectoral, hallway between his nipple and collarbone started to burn and blister. He knew that it was about to get much more worse in a few moments.

Then it happened. A rippling, boiling sensation erupted on his flesh. The sizzle and crackle of his flesh burning filled his ears, drowned out only by his scream. He thrashed away, but the man drove the poker deeper. Then the torturer retracted his device, and still the burn continued to cook, snapping with clear fluid boiling and leaking out. Between heaving breaths, Cometa realized he had bitten his tongue and blood was dribbling out of his mouth and down his chin. The pain intensified with every second since the iron was removed, the fried nerves catching up with pain that tore through the body.

The iron went back into the fire. There was no shortage of them to choose from. Casually, the man came back into view, removing his gloves.

"Some interrogators," He used the more tasteful title for his kind. "Will start with a relentless strike of hot irons, one after another until the person almost passes out. I prefer to space them out, let each one sink in. If that doesn't get the results we are hoping for, I may speed things up a bit. If you talk now, another iron doesn't need to move from that fire."

Cometa said nothing, just focused on his breathing. He was going to kill this man, and kill whoever ordered this. That mantra ran through his mind as he breathed; in and out, in and out.

"Very well, if you still will not cooperate, then we shall continue with the persuasive procedures. I will be back in a moment, it's meal time." He took off his leather apron, and hung it on a hook. "In the meantime, take this little respite to enjoy your having both eyes and both testicles intact. I've seen what those hot irons do to those soft places, and believe me they rarely survive the experience. I'm not sure which one I will start with, the testicle or the eye, but unless you start talking, we will find time to get to one of each."

The man turned to open the door, when it exploded inward with tremendous force. He let out a girlish shriek and threw his hands up as the sudden motion startled him. A pair of armored men wearing blue cloaks stormed into the room, swords drawn and prepared to fight.

One of them grabbed the torturer by his collar and forcibly backed him against the stone wall, sword tip held to his abdomen. The torturer did not resist and complied with a showing of submission that was previously unthinkable of the man. The tables had turned, and apparently he was made of meek stuff after all. The other soldier strode over and checked Cometa, somewhat forcibly grabbing his face and examining it.

"He's alive." The man said, releasing his hold on Cometa's head much more gently than he had snatched it.

"You have no..." The torturer started to protest.

The soldier gave him a hard shove, pushing him back against the wall. Leveling the sword once again, this time at the man's throat, he told the man to shut up. Cometa recognized these men's uniforms as being in Consul Macien's Honor Guard. His head was spinning as he was trying to wrap his addled mind around an explanation. The other soldier went over and picked up a pair of pincers, and began to straighten and pry off the bent steel pegs that locked the iron manacles.

"This is Imperial Guard busi..." He was silenced this time by a loud smack as the flat of a gladius struck his cheek.

"Not another word, or I will gut you." The guard said. "Consul Macien has ordered this man to be brought to him at once. Whatever

orders you were following have been revoked."
The torturer nodded subserviently, and
slouched down against the wall. Cometa was
lowered down onto the shoulder of his liberator,
too weak to do anything but collapse into dead
weight. He closed his eyes, and sweet sleep
found him.

*   *   *

The medicus applied the salve to his burn
and wounds, and a chilling sensation crept into
his flesh. His head ached, and the lukewarm
broth he was given only made his hunger return
with a vengeance. He needed to sleep, he
needed to heal, but most of all he needed to do
his sworn duty. Attempting to rise feebly, a
gentle hand from the medicus kept him in place
and he plopped back down into the seat.

"Easy, son." The man warned. "You have
been through a lot, and you need to stay right
where you are."

"The Consul." Cometa spat. "I need to
speak to him as soon as possible. Right now."

"He is aware, having been the one who
sent for you in the first place. Obligations of
leadership are his priority right now, he will be
here as soon as possible." The old healer said,
soaking some bandages in a clear, yellowish
liquid.

"The Emperor..." Cometa wasn't sure
himself if he had said it as a statement or a
question.

"What of him? His condition has not changed. He still slumbers." The medicus said dismissively, continuing his tasks. "Are you sure you don't want some Laudanum? It will help with the pain, and make it easier for you to sleep." Again, Cometa refused. He needed to keep what wits he had about him, and not dull his already exhausted mind any more. Another sip of broth cause him pain in his shoulders as he moved the bowl to his lips. He felt like he had been a roasted chicken, one that the chef had pulled the wing out from the carcass, and then decided to put it back together again. The strain caused by hanging for however long he had been up on that chain had damaged his joints.

Through the already open door, two members of the Jorbus Honor Guard silently strode in. As they parted after entering, they revealed Consul Macien and Captain Baello walking just behind them. Macien had a concerned look on his face, while the Captain's face was much more cross.

"Gods, Cometa, what happened to you?!" Baello was the first to speak. The wounded Guardsman shifted his body weight, trying to prop himself up to speak to his superiors.

"Take it easy, Antoneus." This came from Macien. "The Medicus told me you need to rest, to gather your strength." The Medicus nodded as the Consul spoke. Macien sat on the stool the Medicus had used, positioned beside Cometa. "I feel like we just met under these circumstances, my friend. And I recall you being explicitly ordered to recuperate from your last injuries, being relieved of duty until you were healed."

"Sir, I must tell you of some things I have come across. I…" Cometa started, but Macien held up a hand for quiet.

"I will tell you first what I know, then the floor is all yours. And I expect answers. Time is of the essence, the 1st legion is finalizing its mobilization and we head out later today." Macien said. Cometa nodded.

"An Urban Enforcer came to the palace today, and told the gate Captain he had information that he could only trust to deliver directly to me. It took some persistence to get to me, but this Flaccus was very determined. The report that he told me was about how he and his partner had been investigating the Selygo assassination, and found a connection with that and the Palace intruder. Further investigation revealed possible treasonous actions by members of the Imperial Guard in both incidents. That's how you crossed path with them. Then they said you went missing, and he came here to inquire about your whereabouts. Captain Baello here tracked down that you had been placed under arrest for treason yourself." The Consul had a sympathetic look on his face as he spoke.

"No one knows who filed the arrest order, but apparently your interrogators and captors were under the impression that you were detained while deserting your post. They were also informed that you were suspected in aiding the assassins, and should be treated accordingly. We have people searching for some evidence of who said what, but we need to hear from you exactly what happened."

Cometa wasted no time retelling his story, as both his Captain and the Consul listened intently. When he had finished, they both exchanged glances with one another, and then with the wounded man.

"An incredible story. And some strong accusations. They were most likely torturing you to find out who else you had talked to, rather than killing you outright." Macien said.

"I find it hard to believe that members of the Imperial Guard, the most trusted unit in the Empire, could be bought and sold like that. To commit treason, to kill their own brothers…"

"It has happened all throughout the history of the Empire, Captain." Macien started. "Many Emperors found themselves on the wrong side of their own guards blades. Every unit has virtuous men and corrupt men. In this case, the corrupt happen to be very, very dangerous."

"You must investigate the entire Guard!" Cometa blurted. "None of us are safe, not you, your family, or the Emperor. Use your own men, like you are starting to do," he gestured to the Jorbus guards standing by the door. "You must protect the Imperial family! The Emperor, I beg you, move him somewhere, away from the Imperial Guard. Put your own people on sentry duty. I will watch him myself. I will…" The agitated Cometa shot upright, ready to spring into action.

"Slow down, Antoneus." Macien said placing hands on his shoulders, and Baello took a step forward, helping to restrain the man from rising.

"We can't pull the entire Guard out of service just because a handful may have been involved in an assassination gone bad. We need them right now. I promise you the Imperial family is safe. The Emperor will be watched over by the most trusted men we have. And I have moved him to a location that few know of. As for most of the Guard, they will be marching with us in the 1st. They can prove themselves on the field of battle against the enemy, if it comes to that. And you are coming with us, Cometa. I need good men like you beside me in what ever may come."

XXI
MACIEN

His armor felt like an old friend. He hadn't worn it since Luctantum, but when he put it on, he was a leader of men, a military man, and a soldier. Life was simpler in armor, it was the *toga* that complicated things. Political intrigue and maneuvers was not his strength. Now it had come to this, and it felt right. But it felt very wrong at the exact same time. He was leading an army, wearing his armor, against his *own* people. In war, it helped to separate yourself from your enemy, but it was hard to do that in a civil war. He hoped that it wouldn't come to that, but his instincts were telling him that it already had. His father's words echoed in his mind as he mounted his horse. *"Don't march your army unless you are prepared to use them."* He sighed; the old Duke had advice for every situation it seemed. Longing filled his heart as he wished he were here to advise him now. Deep down, he knew this was the only option, the right path. A flash of that memory came back, in that cave on the mountain, for only a brief moment. He shook it off.

Everything was in motion; there was no turning back. The Legions were moving into position, and the latest intelligence put Silious and his rebel army on the move as well, one step ahead. *Better than two steps ahead,* he mused. The Emperor was as safe as he could be, moved to a much more secure location, yet again. This was due to the insistence of Cometa, who was lumbering behind in a baggage train wagon, under the care of a several Medicii. The Imperial family was securely tucked away in Jorbus, far away from the western belligerents. The daily running of the Empire was left to very trusted and experienced people. The Imperial Mother Linara, and the Imperial Princess Mallea. They had a lifetime of exposure to how this government ran, and would do better than he could.

The people would never follow women, so his uncle Kyberien was summoned to serve as Master of Troops while Macien was gone. He would officially run things in his absence, just as a Master of Troops was supposed to do. He however, would just be advising the two women and helping guide them in their decision-making, with Macien's own military priorities taking maximum precedence. The sooner this war was ended, the sooner they could return to a normal government.

Then there was always Homitha. That lingering threat was ever-present in the back of his mind. Wasting time and energy with this civil revolt that was inevitably about to happen was detracting from the real enemy. It was

Macien's responsibility to end this insurrection as quickly and efficiently as possible, and get that invasion plan of Greeth's back on track for the Emperor.

In his hand, he held a scroll. It came with the latest intelligence that had been delivered to him just an hour ago. The other information that the courier on the frothing horse had brought was no great surprise. Silious and his army were headed along the course that he had suspected. Apparently, the rebel Duke had bypassed Trimontis, and was marching his force directly for Dutrigi. He only hoped that Kruegius had the foresight to hunker down until the relief Macien had sent would arrive. Or if it came to battle, the Dutrigians would humiliate this new enemy so soundly, it broke the entire rebellion before it started.

The scroll he held now, however, had yet to be read. It was sealed with orange wax, and had the Silious eagle, the signet ring of his family, pressed deep into it. So much value was placed on those rings, that Macien almost didn't want to give it any of its awe-inspiring power. The Silious family's *Pater Familias* had worn that same ring for hundreds of years, since even before they had been the Imperial family. The fact that he used it now, in the capacity of holding imperium over an army, made him a little sick. It was just a ring, but people put so much emphasis on symbolism. With the flick of a wrist, he slid a finger under the seal, and cracked it open, the eagle crumbling away with the wax. The note written within was short, and did not take long to read:

> *"Duke Macien,*
> *I have received your written request for me to surrender myself to Imperial custody in order to stand before a tribunal. I do not recognize your authority, so I must decline. I will retain all titles and rights bestowed upon me by the Emperor. This includes Prefect of Akritus, Duke of Frigiterra, and Commander of the Frontier Forces. I am currently in the process of ensuring that all my new subordinates recognize my right to rule over them. If you truly would like to speak with me, you may find me anywhere in my lands. Bring an army, and I will be forced to treat you as a traitor and act against you accordingly. In summary, if you want me, come and get me.*
>
> *Dahqual Aquilan Silious IV"*

Macien slowly closed the parchment, creased it, and handed it to a man to his right.

"Please deliver this to Secretary Amicus for filing. Thank you." He tried to hide the anger in his voice, but he was unsuccessful. Knowing he was being provoked didn't infuriate him, but the fact that he was being left no choice but to look like the aggressor did. If he did nothing, Silious would eventually take Dutrigi, claiming the city was disobeying the Emperor's bestowment of command upon him. And then Cortinum would fall, and then Trimontis. He would gather momentum and forces, and then truly be able to overpower his enemy; that enemy being Macien himself. Macien had to go on the offensive, sitting back and letting Silious look like the aggressor only gave the rebel the element of surprise and the upper hand.

He thought of symbolism as he put his helmet on his head. Although he would not wear it for the entire march, he would wear it as he gave the order to move out. That sort of visual instilled confidence in his men, as being seen as a leader ready and prepared for battle. As he looked west, towards the lands he would be marching into in order to quell a rebellion, motion caught his eye as a rider approached from behind. Mallea Kantaur was the last person he thought to see riding to the front of a legion. An escort of guards kept pace several strides behind. She quietly sidled up alongside Macien, not saying anything as she approached, not even a greeting.

"Princess." Macien said after a few moments. "I do not think it is wise for you come along on this campaign." Macien had only a trace or sarcasm in his voice, for he did not know her intentions for showing up just before they embarked.

"Macien, I have no intention of travelling with you or leaving the city. I only offer you a gift and wish to give you a proper send off before you leave." Her voice was smooth, yet slightly sad, and a bit remorseful.

"A send off?" Macien asked, skeptical.

"That is what a wife does for her husband."

"Or what the Imperial Family does for it's General." She said defensively. "Or what a friend does for a friend." Her voice softened. "Thank you for all that you have done. My mother and I will not let you down in this endeavor. End this thing as quickly as possible, but know that you have left Calidia in good hands. When you return to the city, I will thank you again. In the meantime, I offer you this."

She extended her hand, fist closed. When she opened her palm, a golden chain unfurled, with a ring dancing on the end of it. The signet ring of the Kantaur family, the Imperial seal dangled from her finger. The last time he had seen that had been on Greeth's hand as he lay in his coma. It had never felt right or seemed proper for him to take it. There had been no need. Mallea however, must have taken it before Greeth had been moved. She held it out for him to take, a gesture of his right to rule in her brother's place.

Timidly, he reached out towards the piece of jewelry. He remembered the Silious seal that he had just broken, and the symbolism put into that. With a sweeping motion, he scooped up the ring and chain, and placed it gently back into Mallea's hand. He then curled her fingers around it, and gave her hand a reassuring squeeze.

"That belongs to you and your family. You keep it. In fact, use it as your own seal for dispatches. I look forward to seeing that seal used again. Princess Mallea Kantaur needs something to give her some validity in the political realm." He smiled, and withdrew his hand. "Excuse me, my lady, but I have to get this Legion on the move."

A long, slow smile crept across her face, a shimmer in her eyes as she looked at him. "Gods give strength Consul Macien, please return safe an unharmed."

"That's the plan. You take care of yourself." He said to her, and with another smile, she departed. Macien took a few more deep breaths, alone, looking west. It was time to march; all he was doing was delaying it now, for no reason at all. Bringing his horse around to face his force, he took in the entirety of what he was commanding. The 1st legion, mobilized, to fight in the field, ready to move as soon as he gave the order. The Imperial Guard in purple, the rest of them in their signature black garb. The cavalry flanking on either side also wore black, and all were eagerly awaiting the marching orders.

Once he started this campaign, nothing else mattered. The world of the Palace and politics and government would be melt away to a memory. His military objectives would be top priority. Everything else would take care of itself. When they set out today, he would be Macien the general.

With a rasping sound, he drew his sword, held it high in the air, and then pointed it west. He made no sound himself, but the legion came to life, horns were blown, drums started, and men shouted. It had begun.

XXII
ADYPATUS EVENTUS

It was after dark, but the city was still busy. People were enjoying the nice weather that brought about a very agreeable evening. Eventus and Flaccus made their way through the jovial crowds, through the people that were meandering from food stalls to wine bars, sitting by fountains, or strolling on the steps and pathways between buildings. It was a strange juxtaposition, these unconcerned masses, ignorant of what was happening around them in the world, and the two Enforcers, who were very serious and in real danger, making their way through them. Torches and lanterns illuminated pockets of the street, leaving many corners and stretches emerged in darkness. A bright moon provided silver light to chase away the shadows.

"Will you tell me where we are going?" Flaccus asked, once again trying to keep up with the pace set by his partner. For a man approaching middle age, with a love for indulging in drinking, Eventus was in very good shape all things considered. His younger partner continued one step behind, Adypatus walking with speed and determination, staying on course to his destination.

"Yes. In a moment, when we are on quieter streets." Adypatus Eventus almost said dismissively, his mind occupied and his eyes searching for any apparent threats. After helping Verka get back on his feet, they tossed that Imperial Guard's body down the street into a heap of garbage that was piling up down an alleyway. Before leaving to continue his search, the doorman told him that just prior to the men showing up and giving him that beating, a youth had come, a message runner. The boy had a message for Eventus, and asked him to pass it along. The message was short; "The favor has been fulfilled."

Once he had heard that, Eventus felt his heart skip a beat. Argentis had come through; he had the assassin, Tuek Sicarius. After making sure Verka was okay, Eventus had taken off to get in contact with Argentis and his crew. A contact told him that Argentis was expecting him to collect his favor at a warehouse on the Jetori tonight. Eventus knew which warehouse it was, and went to meet with Flaccus at the statue of Silious. Now they were headed to that warehouse, to collect this Sicarius and hopefully find out who had hired him.

Flaccus had spent the day helping search the records for Sicarius, but it was wasted effort. It would take weeks for the aides to find anything solid, and by then, it would all be too late. It was coming to a head, and people would be dying before then. Speed was of the essence. If the Enforcers got to this assassin first, they might have a chance of getting out of this alive. If the Guard got to the assassin first, or to the pair of Enforcers first, they would all be dead. The information this captured mercenary had was the only chance they had of bringing this conspiracy to light, the only shield they had against the Guard.

Turning down a narrow street between two tall *insula,* the crowd thinned, and Flaccus began to walk shoulder to shoulder with his partner. With an expecting look on his face, he silently urged his partner to talk, to explain where they were going.

"I know someone who has Sicarius." Eventus admitted. "That's were we are going. It's our only option to get out of this mess and solve this case."

Flaccus froze on the spot. "Wait. What? You tracked him down? You got the assassin?" He asked incredulously.

Eventus continued to walk, slower now. They had made there way back down to the river.

"Yes. Remember I said I had contacts looking for him. Well, that panned out. I called in a favor from an influential associate, and he made good on it. That is where we are going right now." Eventus said.

"We... We need to get back up. We can't blow this." Flaccus sputtered back.

"No. We go it alone. This is a very delicate situation, Ronio." Eventus said. "My contact would like to avoid any further... *legal* entanglements."

"We still need to tell someone. This is far too important, Eventus. This is bigger than just you and me now. The stakes are raised tremendously." Flaccus stopped walking again, backup was the direction they came, not the way they were headed. Eventus took a few more steps himself before halting and facing his partner.

"Telling other people is dangerous. To them, and to us. If we tell people, tell people who are on our side, all we are doing is compromising them and placing them in harms way. If we tell people and it turns out they are not our friends, then our own lives are in that much more danger. We don't know whom we can trust. We rely on one another, and get through this. That's why we have partners." Eventus starred him down in the eyes. Flaccus broke the gaze first. "We can't tell anyone until we secure Sicarius. With his confession, we have a chance of exposing those that are after us." Eventus had to this point left out telling his partner about the ransacking of his apartment, and the killing of the intruder. He swallowed a hard lump. A leap of faith, a sign of trust to his partner, he needed to tell him.

"Earlier today, when we split up and I went back to my place, I found it had been raided. My building's doorman, who was beaten near to death, said the men who did it were soldiers. It was the Guard, they came for me." Eventus paused, letting it set in.

Flaccus was wide-eyed, an attentive look on his face.

"We know they've been following us," Eventus continued, "And when I was there, one of them had remained behind, tried to kill me."

"What?" Flaccus was shocked. "What happened?"

"Well," Eventus made a mockery of checking himself for holes. "I'm still here, but he's no longer alive. I'm sure they are following us now. And I'm sure these guys got to Cometa, maybe even got him to give us up. Somehow, they confirmed our identities and what we were looking into."

Flaccus had a flush on his cheeks, and Eventus knew right then that something was wrong.

"I went to the Palace." Flaccus said remorsefully. "I asked about Cometa, and informed his superiors he was missing. I even talked to Consul Macien, and warned him of the situation. When I left, they were looking for any information on Cometa they could find. This must have drawn attention of the conspirators, who found us again and… expedited their efforts to silence us."

A weight landed on the shoulders of Eventus, and weighed him down in dismay.

Betrayal and anger flashed inside him. *This is what I get for trusting someone again,* he thought. He took a deep breath, and let it out slowly. Surprisingly, acceptance washed over him and the anger was flushed out. Flaccus had only done what he felt was right, and that was honorable. Foolish, dumb even, but still honorable. Honor was something he had long ago grown out of, and truth be told he kind of missed it.

"It's okay, Flaccus." He said, genuinely. "Your intentions were good. Next time, let's talk about things like that before you make a unilateral decision, one that affects both of us." Immediately Eventus was hit with the hypocrisy of his words. Since they first met, Eventus had made nothing but unilateral decisions that affected both of them. He was doing it right now, dragging them into this thieves den without Flaccus having any clue what was going on.

"I can't ask you to do something I myself am not willing to do." Eventus took a deep breath, and scrunched his face up before talking. "We are headed into that warehouse right there." He pointed at a building a short ways down the street. "It's a warehouse owned and operated by a man named Argentis. Have you heard of him?"

Flaccus gave a slow nod.

"I have a… a *symbiotic* relationship with Argentis. We've known one another for many years, and from time to time we exchange favors." Eventus explained.

His partner began to talk, but Eventus held up a hand in protest.

"Let me finish Ronio, you owe me that much." Eventus took a breath. "I've never done anything illegal, and I've never taken money as a bribe. Everything I've ever done, every deal I've made, has been for the Goddess and for the greater good of this city and it's people. If I die today, I know I will have a clean conscience and will be judged fairly. So, I have nothing to be ashamed of."

Flaccus, his mouth still shut, nodded. "I know. I know all about you and Argentis. It's one of the first things that Lt. Grattus told me when I was assigned as your partner. After I was promoted, he told me to keep an eye on your dealings with some of the seedier residents of this city. If anything illegal came up, or anything that just felt wrong, I was to report directly to him."

Eventus felt like someone was ripping his heart down into his gut. His instincts had been right the entire time, but he had ignored them. This man, his supposed partner, was a spy. His superiors had thought low enough of him that they implanted someone to watch his every move, and report back to them if something wasn't on the up and up. The betrayal he felt earlier was nothing compared to what he was experiencing now. Anger wasn't part of the equation, just sadness and disappointment.

"You spied on me, Ronio. From the beginning?" He cleared his throat as he spoke. It was a pretty significant revelation to have dropped on him prior to going into this dangerous situation. He needed to focus on this meeting, this exchange, not have this wrecking havoc on his mind.

"I never reported back anything bad at all, I swear." Flaccus said. "And that's because I didn't see anything. But If I follow you into this place, with this know criminal organization, handing over an apprehended person, I will have to report this. I really like you Eventus, I do. I respect you and all that you do. But I can't lie, I can't break the oath that I made to the Goddess and the word I gave to my superiors."

"Our best chance at survival, at solving this case, is in that warehouse. We never would have caught this guy if it weren't for that criminal organization." Eventus rebutted. "Look, I appreciate your honesty, and if you can't bring yourself to follow me inside, fine. I'm going in, and I'm getting the answers we've been looking for."

"Why?" Flaccus protested. "What are we going to prove? Silious was behind all this; we don't need proof of that. Consul Macien has declared him a traitor and is marching with the 1st legion west to arrest him. If it's to save our own lives, then let us go to Urban Cohorts. They can protect us from these rogue Imperial Guard agents. We need to bring everyone we can in on this, to root out every last treasonous member of this conspiracy. We can't do that alone. Does solving this thing by yourself mean that much to you?"

"We can't wait. The Imperial Guard may have already beaten us to this damn warehouse. Every second we stand here arguing, is time lost forever." Eventus was growing angry, feeling like that last barb at him by Flaccus was personal. "It's my duty to apprehend this man, bring him back to the Hold, and get a confession. He will give us the name, and from there we track down the others. Then it's over."

"What if he's dead? What if he won't talk? Maybe he doesn't know who hired him, that's a common practice, you know." Flaccus shot back.

"Maybe he doesn't know a thing, true. Or, maybe he knows *everything*. Enforcers investigate, and this is an investigation. I'm going to investigate…" Eventus said.

"Enforcers enforce the laws. We don't do that by consorting with known criminals, Eventus." Flaccus fired back.

"Don't lecture me on being an Enforcer, boy. I didn't earn my Medallion by being a mole for the higher ups." Eventus lost his temper on that one, seething it through clenched teeth.

"I'm going to follow the rules, Eventus. I'm going to go back to the Cohorts Garrison, and bring some armed soldiers here. I will tell them exactly what is happening." He said defiantly.

"Good luck, then." Eventus responded.

"I'm going to say that you were investigating a lead on our case, and tracked the assassin down to this warehouse. You sent me for back up, considering the fact that there might be a large criminal element inside. And that's the truth." Flaccus gave him a nod, and extended his arm for an embrace. Eventus took it, and then clasped him on the shoulder.

"Gods give strength, Ronio." Eventus cracked a wry smile.

"Gods give strength, Adypatus." Flaccus said in farewell. "Keep it together until I get back." And with that, he began to run up hill, towards the garrison.

Maybe there was hope for him after all, thought Eventus. He just didn't know if that was meant in regards for himself of for his partner.

XXIII

DAHQUAL SILIOUS

The morning fog had burned off, but the smoke still hung in the distance like a haze, a memory of the mists of morning. Atop the hill, in full battle armor, upon his horse, Dahqual Silious sat, surrounded by his Eagle Guard and his top advisors. Behind him was a sizable portion of his army; below was a field, and beyond that were the outer walls of Dutrigi. His armor was exquisite; the deep black of pure rigidium, ornately decorated with trim of finely wrought copper orange Akkedan bronze. It resembled the traditional Morincian style favored by officers and leaders, but with much upgraded enhancements. These included segmented shoulder guards and knee armor, as well as mail in certain vulnerable areas. The Wyrian smiths he had paid a fortune to had produced a work of art.

His helmet, a full-face cover version of ironically enough, a Dutrigian design, was wedged in the crook of his arm. His orange cape matched the orange crest atop his helm, both fluttering slightly in the gentle breeze. The brunt of the army had arrived last night, and the

Dutrigians had been well aware of their approach before they ever left Cruxium. Now they were waiting.

This morning, they had sent an emissary out to ask their intentions. This junior officer was told to return back to the city with instructions that Kruegius himself must come to the parlay, as was the custom. If he sent another other than himself, that man would be killed on the spot. If he failed to appear within the hour, they would begin burning the fields and farms around the city. The entire countryside had been abandoned; the occupants more than likely all taking refuge inside the Old Walls of the Citadel. That way, they can't be used as hostages. They didn't have time to gather all their crops and livestock, and Silious had sent out foragers to replenish supplies.

The hill he sat upon was very familiar to him, although he was certain that this was the first time he had ever stood upon it. The slope below him, that led to the contours of the field below, he was very intimate with, although he may have only laid eyes on it once or twice in his life. A cacophony of noise from behind and beside him didn't distract him in the least. In fact, the hammering and pounding was somewhat soothing. It was the culmination of years of planning, of months of logistics and generations of anticipation.

Just behind Silious, planted firmly in the ground in a very precise spot, was his standard.

Atop the pole was the golden eagle, just like any Imperial legion. That had been his family's symbol, so it seemed fitting to keep it. The vexillum below was a field of orange with a black eagles head, encompassed in a black circle. That standard, and it's position, had everything in the world to do with the outcome of this battle. If it was off by inches, the window for error changed dramatically.

Wooden beams and torsion devices were quickly and precisely snapped into position, machines of warfare taking shape. His operators had built each one from raw materials years ago, assembled and disassembled them almost on a daily basis, and trained in their operation just as often. They could assemble, operate, and disassemble these engines as easily and naturally as a herding dog would steer a flock. They could make accurate adjustments on them as easily and naturally as a man would scratch a sudden itch.

Everything so far was going perfect. General Victus, who wore a full Wyrian suit of armor, stylized to look somewhat Calidian, was grinning. His visor was up, and all on the field saw his dark goateed face, and its content look. This was his element that they were in now, Silious was just a valued guest. The men would fight for Silious, but Victus had control of the tactics and strategy today. This operation was his by conception, and the Duke had to admire the precision and dedication the man had poured into the planning.

"So far, we're on course, General." Silious rasped, his voice dry from nerves and from the smoke that lingered around their position.

"Once everything is in place, we can begin. The fact that the Dutrigian Army hasn't shown any signs of facing us, that means we will have time to finish. We need them to sally forth and engage, not to turn this into a siege." The tone Victus used carried reproach. Silious made a mental note of that, to be dealt with later.

"They will take the field, just as I swore to you." Silious gave a subtle nod to the city that lay before them. "Leave that part to me."

"Very well." Victus conceded to his monarch of choice. "Much planning has gone into this day. If we follow the plan, Dutrigi will be a memory by sunset, and all the Empire and the world will know what we have done here today. The ruby of the Imperial forces, the Bulls, will be gone. We will have punched the biggest man in the arena right in the mouth, and everyone will know that we are the apex predators now."

"Let's hope so, Victus." Silious said seriously. "For your sake. I've put a tremendous amount of trust and faith in you. If it has been misplaced, you will regret it for the rest of your short life, and go to your grave knowing that your memory will be erased from the histories."

"My memory, my lord, will be a legacy

that will only be overshadowed by you and your ancestors amazing accomplishments. I ensure you, we will win today, and our debut in this war will set the tone for the rest of the fighting. Look…" Victus raised an armored hand towards the main gate of the Young Walls. The motion of the door raising was detracted from by the flash of crimson that appeared in stark contrast to the grass and stone of the landscape. A small group of riders on horseback were making their way towards Silious' position. Silious raised a hand, and his own group started down the hill, to meet in the middle.

As they drew closer to the retinue that approached, a mere three riders, Silious spied a wall of red clad men along the entirety of the wall. A crooked grin grew on his face; not only had they assembled the army, but they had a large audience. The Gods were good.

"You don't say a word, Victus. If you do, I will cut out your tongue myself. Do you understand?" Silious said, not bothering to look at his general, eyes fixed on the slowly approaching party. Victus didn't say a word in acknowledgement, remaining silent. "Good. Now, I think we've gone far enough. They can come the rest of the way to us."

Kruegius approached, bronze helmet on his head, the same as his two escorts. The Dutrigian armor and uniform had changed little since the city's founding. Just like the Dutrigian

Army itself, it embodied the sentiment of 'why change a good thing.'

The horsemen came to halt across from them, several paces between them. Silious was flank by a half dozen of his well armed and armored Eagle Guard. Kruegius had come unarmed apparently, his honor not allowing him to bring a weapon to a parlay. His guards carried spear and shield openly, swords sheathed on hips. The Duke of Lacerterra, former Master of Foot, and Lord General of the Dutrigian Army stared coldly at Silious. Silious returned the stare with a feigned smile.

"Aren't you supposed to ask 'blood or water' as is the standing and time honored tradition?" Silious broke the silence, condensation in his voice more than humor.

"That depends. Are you an invading army?" Kruegius asked.

"That depends, will you swear fealty to me as commanded by the Emperor when he gave me dominion over your forces?" Silious asked.

"Last I heard, Silious, you've been declared a traitor." Kruegius growled. "You have no legal authority here, and no imperium over those forces you march with. I am within my rights and would be doing my duty to the Empire to snuff you out right here."

"That order issued by Macien is not recognized by me and my forces as having any legality. I retain all titles unless the Emperor commands it. You should do the same, or you will be a traitor, Lord General. Then I will have no choice but to 'snuff you out' as you so eloquently put it." Silious had ice in his voice as he spoke.

"Macien is a Consul during the interim regime. He speaks on behalf of the Emperor. If he said you are a traitor, then you are a traitor to the Empire. I tried to get him to declare you a traitor from the first day he took command, but he wouldn't listen. The boy grew some stones, so I am more than happy to uphold his ruling." Kruegius flashed uncharacteristically white teeth when he grimaced through the narrow slit in his helmet.

"You refuse to recognize my authority, then?" Silious asked.

"I never recognized your authority, or your manhood." Kruegius shot back.

"I ask one more time. Let this end peacefully. Give me control of your army, and we will all leave here healthy and intact. That is the best option you have, Lord General; me on the other hand, I win either way." And Silious grinned right back at the man.

In Kruegius' defense, he never lost his calm. "As much as I would enjoy absolutely destroying you on the field of battle, Gods I would enjoy that, I'm afraid it won't be happening. The Empire is already sending reinforcements, and we can hold out a long while if you lay siege. So I'm afraid I must ask you to leave now. You will receive neither blood nor water."

Silious let out a loud laugh, and he slapped his helmet that was tucked under his arm. "That is rich, *neither blood nor water*. You are such a poetic orator, Kruegius, you truly missed your calling. Tell me, did you just come up with that or have you been waiting to use it since you discovered we were marching to your city?"

Kruegius just glared back at him, un-amused.

"Unfortunately, Kruegius, I have chosen blood already. And you will have no choice in the matter of whether or not your army faces us today. I'm sorry for all this pretense, but part of me truly wanted you to come to my side." Silious said. "It's a pity. I always respected you and your people. It's a shame we never got along."

"If you lay siege to this city, this city that has never been sacked, by man or Saurian, you are a fool. I hope you try, for everyone's sake. Let's end this little rebellion of yours before its gets anymore pathetic. History will remember you as a footnote, if at all. "

"While we are talking about history, I just want you to know that after we crush your forces today, I will honor the tradition of your once mighty people. You however, will be erased from the annals. No one will know Kruegius ever existed a generation from now." Silious had a flat look on his face, showing he meant every word he said.

"You will not be dictating any histories, worm. This parley is over." Kruegius said, starting to turn away.

"Kruegius, before you go, I believe I said that I wanted blood." Silious said, and then turned to his Eagle Guard. "Kill the other two, leave the *Lord General* alive."

With incredible speed that was attributed to years of disciplined training, the Dutrigians snapped to life. Shields went up, spears were leveled to thrust. Silious' men were faster. All three horses were hit with multiple projectiles, dropping them in death almost instantly. The riders, trying to scramble to their feet were killed by swinging swords as the Eagle Guard rode them down. Kruegius picked up a shield and a sword from his fallen men, and began to hold his ground. It was useless, the Eagle Guard encircled him. A deep shoulder slash, followed by a hamstrung wound to the back of his leg dropped him.

Two Eagle Guard dismounted, and casually strolled over to the struggling figure trying to rise to his feet. A gauntleted fist smashed into the front of his face, and a fountain of blood erupted. The blow knocked his helmet off, revealing his dark black curls. Another punch to his solar plexus left him gasping for air. Grabbing him under his armpits, they drug him towards Silious.

Casually, Silious looked down from his

horse. "Break both his legs, up high. And both his arms, too." Without another word, his men did as they had been ordered. Despite his best efforts not to, Kruegius screamed. Silious rode away from the group, eyes on the battlement of the city behind him. He could see the commotion, the reaction he was getting from what he was doing. Perfect, this was the only way he could coax them out now.

Now, for another show. Facing the wall, he raised his left hand high in the air as a signal. He then pointed it out to his side, down towards the ground close by himself. The entire time, he never took his eyes off of Dutrigi and the people within. He remained frozen like that for several moments, and then he heard it; a whirring sound, one that got louder as it approached. He felt the air rush past him, and the vibrations of the earth shaking as an object impacted next to him. Right where he had been pointing, right where he had ordered, a massive wooden missile landed, embedding itself deep in the earth. It was as thick as a man's leg, and even taller than your average person. That show of his weapon power should strike some doubt into those who thought of opposing him. He was planting the seeds of fear within their minds. Now he would goad them out, to face him in the field.

"Strip him naked and chain him to this post." Silious ordered. "Then piss on him so all these people can see. Leave him hanging, and then let's get ready for a battle."

XXIV
ADYPATUS EVENTUS

The man before him looked physically broken, yet still resolute and defiant in spirit. Tied to a wooden post that supported the roof and second story of this massive warehouse, was the man that Argentis claimed was Tuek Sicarius. His face was bruised and streaked with blood, similar to the rest of his naked body, but his eyes shone bright with contempt for all those who surrounded him. Dignity had not yet fled from this man, who sat against the post, hands bound behind it, and was sitting in a small puddle of what the Enforcer assumed was sweat, blood, and urine. The man looked Calidian, just as Cometa had suspected by his knife skills. He wore his dark hair short in the military style. As Eventus approached, he noticed a large scar where a Legion tattoo would have been on the man's shoulder.

"May I present to you the elusive Tuek Sicarius." Argentis said as Eventus drew closer. The crime boss was wiping his hands on a towel that was stained in blotches of orange-pink watered down blood. "The failed assassin you've been looking for."

"How do you know it is him?" Eventus

asked skeptically.

"Eventus, you wound me," Argentis spread his hands wide. He had a dozen or so men, nasty looking brutes, milling about the room. "I would never make such a blunder repaying a favor to an important friend like you. We tracked him down to a small inn by Great Harbor. He must have been waiting for a certain ship to come in. It was lucky we found him when we did, my reach doesn't extend across the sea...yet."

Eventus nodded. "Still, how did you find him?"

"I have a good network of people who keep an eye and an ear out for such things. I'd be lying if I told you locating him was very difficult. Capturing him proved to be a challenge, however. After a fight that killed several of my men, he escaped for a short time again. But, he is here now, my gift to you. All debts are repaid." Argentis had no pleasure in his voice or on his face when he spoke. "If you still cannot believe it, ask him yourself who he is."

The Enforcer had known enough men like Sicarius in his day to understand that he would never give up information about himself or his employer freely. There was an honor amongst mercenaries and assassins, an unwritten law that if you receive coin for a task, you never told who hired you. Until the interrogation started, then they usually cracked.

Once the pain and the threat of a terrible death outweighed whatever sum of money they had been paid, they talked. This one however, looked like he would be challenging. If he admitted to what he had done, he faced treason charges of the worst kind.

"What is your name?" Eventus thought he would at least try.

"Tuek Sicarius." The man admitted, iron in his voice. Eventus was slightly taken aback, and decided to press on.

"Were you the intruder that entered the palace recently?" He tried.

"Yes, I was." The man said with little hesitation.

"And who was your target?" Eventus said, crouching by the man.

"Macien." The answer was curt.

"Not the Emperor?" Eventus asked.

"No, just Macien, and whoever got in the way." The man locked eyes with Eventus, and it sent chills down the Enforcers spine. This man was a killer.

"Why are you so freely admitting to all this? What about your code of honor?" Eventus asked.

"I admit to it freely because you ask, and I did do it. I am bound by no code of honor, for my client never paid me for my services." The man explained. "In fact, he tried to kill me once he discovered I had failed."

"Who was your client? Who contacted

you?" Eventus felt his heart race. This was exactly what they needed. This Sicarius was freely talking and would point to whoever hired him. Case closed. This would be enough to launch an investigation into the Imperial Guard and ferret out the conspirators. Even if half of them were marching towards battle, they would still...

"I do not know his name, he never told me." The assassin admitted. Eventus now felt his stomach drop. Fear crept into his brain and his heart.

"Was it Duke Silious?" He asked desperately.

"No." Tuek shook his head.

"Someone working for him?" Eventus asked.

"I do not know for certain, but that seems very likely." Tuek said, indifferently.

Eventus ran his hands through his hair nervously, crouching next to this man, surrounded by all these gangsters. Was it all for nothing? "What can you tell me about the man who hired you? Anything, any detail will help. I know this fellow wronged you, and I promise that if you help me get him, you will get a pardon from the government."

"I don't want a pardon. If the Gods decide my fate is to die because I failed in my mission, then so be it." The man responded with determination. "However, I will tell you what I know because the man that hired me *did* wrong me. And he was a prick."

"What? Tell me." Eventus asked.

"He was Calidian, about your age, short black hair, muscular build. Deep set dark eyes." The man paused. "The most telling thing was he was missing his right ear, most of it that is."

Eventus nodded slowly. He felt a feeling of recognition within him, intuition tugging at him. For some reason, the missing right ear triggered something, but he couldn't remember what it meant. It wasn't recent, but he knew it was something, some connection that made perfect sense.

"If I brought the man before you, you could identify him?" Eventus asked.

"Yes." Tuek nodded.

"You would swear before the Goddess Dikasta what you have told me?" Eventus raised an eyebrow. "Even if it means your death?"

"Yes." Tuek nodded.

"A one eared man?" Argentis chimed in from the background. "Would you like me to start scouring the city for such a person? That might cost you several favors…"

Eventus sighed. He knew his time with Argentis was over. All debts had been paid, and Flaccus would be showing up here with a raiding party soon. Argentis might live, he might not, but their relationship was finished. Eventus was okay with this; it felt good to be liberated from such an insidious individual. No harm in keeping up the guise until he was out of the building, it was probably safer that way.

"Please do. This is the utmost importance, as you know." Eventus said, disappointed that the network Argentis used wouldn't be utilized in this endeavor; they might actually be very useful.

"Anything, my friend." And he smiled his wolfish smile. Argentis' days of using Eventus were over; he just didn't know it yet. Now, Eventus needed to get Tuek outside of here before that raiding party showed up and complicated things. Maybe the Cohorts that would be arriving soon would help escort this man to Hold, in case anyone tried anything between here and there.

"Could we get something to wrap him up in? Walking a naked man down the street at night might raise some suspicion and attract people we are hoping to avoid." Eventus said.

Without a word, Argentis gave a simple gesture to a lackey, who disappeared to do his bidding.

"While we are waiting, I have another question." Eventus said to Sicarius. "How did you get inside the palace undetected? You scaled the walls, ran across the grounds, and found some opening somewhere? At night, that place is buttoned up tighter than a wine barrel."

Tuek Sicarius turned to face him, craning his head up at the Enforcer. "The man who hired me took care of that. He told me the guards at the front gate would let me walk in, and they did. Then, I used a tunnel that brought me inside the palace. Once I was inside, he told me I was on my own." A cloak was thrown over him like a blanket.

"Wait…" Eventus started, but was cut off by a bang and a crash. The door to the warehouse was blown inward, exploding into shards. Argentis and his men around him sprang to life, pulling out weapons and immediately going on the defensive. Flaccus hadn't wasted anytime; the Cohorts shouldn't have gotten here this quickly.

Men started filing in. They were not Urban Guardsmen. They wore short cloaks and tunics, although glimpses of mail and armor could be seen under some of the garments. They carried military issued Gladii. Eventus felt his heart sink.

"Nobody fucking move!" A man stepping through the door bellowed. He was tall and wiry, head shaven, and was clearly in charge of these men. On the side of his face and under one eye was a fresh bruise, swollen and painful looking. Verka's handiwork, no doubt. As he spoke, everyone in the room froze. Banging from above indicated men were getting into position on the second floor mezzanine. Eventus glanced up and saw two men, holding a bundle of pila spears each. Less than ten men had just entered the room. Although they were very well trained men, they were outnumbered nearly two to one.

"I am here in my capacity as a member of the Imperial Guard! By my right, I demand you hand over the assassin and the Enforcer." The bald man ordered. "I will only ask once, if you fail to comply, everyone here dies, no exceptions."

"I will gladly comply to your demands," Argentis spoke, a dagger in one hand. "But myself, being a Golden Class citizen," he wagged his ring finger. "And you being on my property, I will require proof of your identity since to me you look like common street criminals. And also I must ask what these men, my guests, are charged with."

"You have no right to demand anything from us!" The lead intruder said. "But for clarification, the man tied to the post, Sicarius, is a hired assassin. He killed Consul Selygo, and killed members of our unit. The Enforcer Eventus is wanted for aiding him, and also for the murder of another Urban Enforcer."

"What?" Eventus said loud enough for everyone to hear.

Without a word, the bald man reached into a sack and pulled an object out, tossing it across the room. Eventus couldn't understand what he was seeing, as the thing bounced once, then rolled, and finally skidded to a halt several paces away. Then it made sense. The face was turned away from him, but he knew without a doubt that it was the head of Ronio Flaccus. His stomach churned.

"You found out he was a rat, so you killed him before you got here, right around the corner. Even left your own engraved gladius stuck in his headless body." The man said, a flat expression on his face. Eventus remembered that they had taken all his weapons from his room, including his gladius, which was engraved with his name.

"I will kill you for this." Eventus said, rage boiling in voice. He drew his dagger in a sign of defiance. A smile broke across the face of the Imperial Guardsmen that was in charge of this raid.

"Kill everyone but the Enforcer, those are our orders." He said in a calm, matter-of-fact voice. Then it all started. Men charged at one another, and it turned into a brawl. The gangsters wielded swords, daggers, clubs, cestuses, one even had a hatchet; they were all very effective. The Imperial guard all used Gladii and pugio, in military fashion. The two lines blended as they bashed into one another, forming a mass of swinging and hacking weapons and limbs. The bodies started to hit the floor.

A Pilum came down from above with such force that it went through the leg of a big Terdakian, pinning him to the wooden floor below. A quick swipe from a pugio opened his throat. The fighting was fierce, but it was looking like it would be over quickly. With spears raining down from above, and with the precision of the Imperial Guard below, the gangsters were loosing the fight.

Eventus saw the bald man, making his way towards him, cutting down a thug that stepped in his path. Eventus gripped his dagger, wanting nothing more than to kill that bastard. The fray kept him back though. He would wait until he got to him. His back was to the wall right now, literally.

He glanced down at Tuek, who was watching the fighting with passing interest. The man who was tied up had to have known that if this Imperial Guard faction won this skirmish, he was a dead man. Still, he sat there calmly, calculating. Eventus adjusted the grip on his dagger, took a step towards the man, and with a slash cuts the ropes that bound his hands. The man looked up at him with a blank face. Just then, Argentis approached from out of the corner of his eye.

"I have to ask another favor of you, my friend." The gang leader said. "Make sure that they all pay for this, every one of them. Up the stairs, there is another door to the outside, go now."

"If I do this favor for you," Eventus recoiled slightly as a pilum slammed into the floor a few strides away, having narrowly missed its quarry. "How will I collect the favor you will owe me?"

Argentis had an angry look on his face. "I think in a few moments, we will be even. Now go. Goodbye, Adypatus." And with that, he turned and ran towards the fight, dagger coiled and ready to strike. The criminal boss had a strong desire to live, but his honor didn't allow him to run from this one, not with his men dying like they were.

"Let's go, Sicarius. Up the stairs." The other man was already on his feet, cloak on, and heading towards the wooden steps behind them. The bald man saw them fleeing, and shouted orders for them to be pursued. When they reached the mezzanine, the two spear throwers had their backs turned, facing the fight down below. It looked as if they were both on their last throw.

Eventus, without much thought, instinctively ran and lowered his shoulder into the closest one. With a surprised whimper, the man was launched off the edge, his limbs flailing as he landed on the floor below with a hollow thud. Tuek dispatched the other with much more finesse, his cloak fluttering as he moved in. Grabbing the pilum that was about to be released with one hand, he pulled the soldiers pugio out with the other. He then stabbed it into the man's ribcage, spun him around and pushed the dying man hard into the wooden wall behind them. The old, weather beaten dry wood shattered as the man burst through, falling two stories down into the river below. Before the splash was even heard, Sicarius spun and hurdled the Pilum he still grasped in the direction of Eventus.

The Enforcer was so surprised by the unexpected action, that he didn't even flinch as the projectile whizzed right past his chest. The sound of it hitting flesh came from behind him, and Eventus turned to see an Imperial Guardsman that wasn't all the way up the stairwell yet, with the spear buried to it's shaft just below the man's neck. Eventus turned back to look at the assassin, who was gesturing towards the hole in the wall.

"They will be coming up both sets of stairs." Tuek said. "We need to jump, down into the river below."

His mind flashed to when he and Flaccus had to climb out the back of the Corvus Nest not too long ago. Flaccus was dead now… and he was going to be framed for that. He needed to bring these men to justice, for Flaccus and for everyone else. He needed to get Sicarius to the Hold.

"Thank you." Eventus said, nodding back to the dead man in the stairwell.

"You saved my life down there, we are even now." And with that, Tuek Sicarius jumped down to the river below. Eventus followed. He hit with a tremendous splash, and the cold, dark water enveloped him. The feel of the gravely mud bottom of the Jetori pressed against his backside as he bottomed out on the river floor. With a push, he made his way to the surface. Taking a deep breath as he breached, he quickly scanned his surroundings. Sicarius was nowhere to be seen, and Eventus didn't need to be an Enforcer to figure out that he didn't want to be found.

Shouting from the warehouse floated down to him as he began to swim down river. They had probably spotted him, and would be sending people to track him down. For the moment, he didn't care. It was a peaceful feeling to be swimming down the river that ran through his city, sometime around midnight, with a full moon shining silver in the clear night. It was probably the last peaceful moment he would have for a very long time, if ever. Silently, except for the gentle lapping of the water, he swam. He didn't know where he was going, so he just swam.

XXV
QUINTUS VICTUS

Silious had done his part. Now it was his own turn. The Duke of Frigiterra had given him a second chance, a chance to redeem himself and put himself back in the command of an army. He had given Victus free reign to dictate how this battle would go, put complete faith in his new, unprecedented stratagem. Silious had even made good on his promise to coax the enemy out to face them in the field. Before him, in formation were his legions. Beyond them was an army clad in red, with their backs to a stone wall. Between the two armies a single figure writhed on a post. Kruegius was still alive, torturously hanging from that scorpion bolt.

Seeing their leader being treated with such wonton disrespect, being defiled, and then left mutilated and in misery had stirred the Dutrigians into a frenzy. It hadn't taken long for them to get riled up enough to foolishly come out to fight. If it had been Victus, he would wait for reinforcements no matter what the enemy did. The Dutrigian sense of pride apparently overrode the survival mechanism that Victus himself held dear. Perhaps they felt they could truly win. They did, after all, have a superiority complex from everyone telling them what amazing warriors they all were. Victus had to give them the respect they were due.

The Dutrigians had for a long time been the benchmark for any fighting force. They fought under a set of rules that were obsolete, however. Any good force needed to adapt to dynamic changing situations, and these Dutrigians had always just put their head down and charged through rather than change. That will be their undoing. There was so much more to warfare than strength and courage. Math was a huge factor, perhaps the only factor that truly mattered at all. Numbers. Geometry. Victus was always seeing the math in a fight, and that served him well.

His long calculations and planning were about to pay out in dividends. The equation was still in front of him, and he could see the final answer. All variables had been accounted for, and the sums were clearly marked. The angles had all been planned out long ago, literally. The Dutrigians had no idea that they were about to be obliterated completely; they had no say in the matter.

Over a year ago, Duke Silious had sent prospectors to Dutrigi. These prospectors were experts in locating veins of Rigidium, a mineral that was prominent in the west. They claimed that they had developed a way of locating deposits based upon the surface topography of the region. Kruegius himself granted these entrepreneurs permission to survey the area in hopes of finding a mineable site. Of course, no such deposit was ever discovered, Rigidium is rarely found that far south. The surveyors' real reason for their mission was a great success though.

Through advancements in instruments and topographic mapping, they captured enough information to reconstruct the field that lay before Victus back in Frigiterra. Every slope, every ditch, every large rock, even the very hill that he was standing on right now had been duplicated. Looking down on it now, he felt like he had been here hundreds of times.

The standard that fluttered behind him, stuck in a very precise location, was the keystone of the entire operation. Every war machine they carried was positioned in predetermined places and turned in certain angles using the standard as a sighting. The engineers had used these weapons hundreds upon hundreds of times on the replicated hill they created back home. It was going to be a dance, a dance that was scripted in the mathematics of Euthagomedes. And it would mean the end of the Dutrigians.

The enemy was lined up across from them, not yet moving. Once they did, the predetermined maneuvers would begin. The wall of red-cloaked men was unwavering, standing still like statues. The glint off their bronze helms and their hoplon shields emblazoned with the Bull was somewhat distracting, but not terribly. They were arranged in a solid line, about a half mile wide, and 30-35 men deep; a massive phalanx of men that stood still like statues. Behind that first large line, stood a smaller reserve force of the most veteran warriors. On either side in blocks were the skirmishers, armed with slings and javelins. Flanking the army on the far ends were the cavalry. It's true, Dutrigians did not produce any real cavalry, so they needed to augment their forces with allied horsemen.

Generations ago, for some reason that no one exactly remembers, Equium pledged to provide the cavalry forces for the Dutrigian army. And Equium fielded some of the best horsemen in the world. Together, they made a mighty opponent. That was why this needed to go perfectly, and why this force needed to be culled from the theater before this war became extended. With Dutrigi a mere memory, the west would be safe, especially with the rest of the plans they had in store for the area.

An officer approached, and informed him that everything was in place perfectly. He told him to ready the flagman with the red flag. In front of his station, Legion 1 and Legion 2 were positioned, and on the opposite flanks of where they were adjacent to one another, each legion had a thick, fortified wedge. They were mirror images of one another, with only a slight gap between. Legion 3 was held in reserve, split into two blocks, a western force and an eastern force just in front of the war machines. The longbow archers were in position, protected just behind the wall that was Legion 1 and Legion 2, centered on the gap between the two units. A special contingent of heavy troops formed an immediate wall around these valuable troops as well. Cavalry remained behind the hill, out of sight. Everything was in place. It was time.

The Dutrigians more than likely felt that they had a favorable advantage in this battle, since it was on their home turf. They were intimately familiar with the terrain, and they would use that to their advantage. They preferred to maneuver in landscapes like this, with minimal obstacles. Plus, the city walls protected their rear. Granted, Victus and his troops were uphill, but no field of battle was absolutely perfect. Historically, when Dutrigi took to a field like this, their line was near impossible to break, and the strength of their line was one of their greatest strengths.

It was time to remove these advantages. Once the enemy started moving, he would make it so. And then, the anticipation ended. The order from the enemy came, and the phalanx locked shields, spears extended, and began to advance. Eerily silent and even more disturbingly gradual, the Dutrigians were moving towards his army.

"Raise the red flag!" Victus called. His voice quivered slightly as he barked the order, emotions running hot. It was time. Behind him, a soldier raised a simple square of red on a long, narrow pole. All down the line, each war machine's flagman imitated this with their own flag. Men barked orders, and parts began to move, units began to shift. The sound of torsion devices releasing, the twang of thick wood flexing, and the whir of projectiles filled the air. More orders were called, and adjustments were made with little thinking. Devices were reloaded, time and time again. In a matter of minutes, the red flag was ordered to be lowered, and the firing of the giant scorpions ceased. Not a single bolt had struck an enemy.

On the field below, dozens upon dozens of giant stakes, just like the one Kruegius hung from, were scattered along the battlefield. They made a virtual forest of bare wooden trees, one that had just sprung up out of nowhere. A giant triangle, one that pointed right to the middle of the Dutrigian line had formed. The figure of Kruegius was stuck inside this new forest, unscathed by the volley.

"There goes their continuous line. They will be forced to split in two, and funneled to meet our forces, which are stacked heavy on those sides." He was speaking to himself, more than to Silious. The Duke said nothing, just watched.

"Raise the white flag!" Victus said, and it set into motion another series of events. The smaller onagers in front of him sprung to life, raising themselves off the ground as they unloaded. These onagers didn't fire large stones into the enemy. If you didn't know better, you'd think they were firing dry, because nothing leapt out of them that one could see. In fact, they were scattering thousands of caltrops across the pole forest obstacle that they had just created. These spikes, sharp enough that they would pierce through the foot of whoever stepped on them, were an extra deterrent to keep the Dutrigians from attempting to make their way through the obstacle field.

The new barrier now protected the middle of legion 1 and Legion 2, and they started to shift even more towards the edges. Below, the heavy troops that protected the archers started to escort the bowmen down into the obstacle field. The longbow men now had more range and visibility against the enemy. Victus watched as the red army began to part as they hit the newly emergent wedge he had just thrown at them.

The longbow men began to snipe at the enemy. Every arrow they loosed, with incredible range and accuracy, dropped an enemy. They had received orders to target the officers first, but take any target that presented itself. From his vantage point, Victus saw crested helmets fall. The headdress of officers had always been a double-edged sword; your own men could find you with ease, but so could the enemy. And when the enemy had the accuracy to reach out and touch someone the way the Longbow archers could, it was a terrible disadvantage. The Dutrigians had never faced a foe as deadly and precise as a Wyrian archer armed with a longbow, and Victus beyond pleased that Silious had started training these men with the foreign weapon over a decade ago.

With renewed vigor and frustration, the Dutrigian lines, now split in two, picked up their speed. The sooner they clashed with the enemy line, they assumed, the sooner they would be safe from projectiles. The enemy skirmishers were trailing behind the hoplites now, and once the lines met, they would unload their volleys. The lines were about hundred yards from meeting one another, and that was the trigger point

"Blue flag!" Victus shouted. And almost as quickly as he had given the order, the scorpions sprang to life once again, turned and ranged for their next predetermined target area. That area just happened to be the Dutrigian front. The first volley fired, and it was devastating to the Dutrigians, smashing their front row and stalling their forward progress. They recovered with great composure, and were on the move once again when the second volley hit. Undeterred, they pressed on, even after the third and fourth volleys struck. Just before the fifth volley hit the tail end of their charge, the front crashed into the legions. The hedgehog formation of the phalanx immediately began to make progress against the legionaries.

Victus couldn't help but feel pained as he saw his vastly technologically superior force being overwhelmed by brute strength and brawn. The skirmishers began to unload on his soldiers, and momentum subtly shifted to the Dutrigians. He needed to put his cavalry in play, but he couldn't until the Equium forces made their move. The lines wavered slightly, but the red cloaks were still pushing his forces back. The enemy skirmishers had turned their focus to the longbow men that were centered in the obstacle field. If the infantry couldn't get to them, then ranged weapons could. The only problem with that was the range of the Longbow men was extraordinarily farther than a sling or javelin. Still, they pelted and few shots got lucky, but the heavy armored troops took the brunt of it.

Victus could do nothing but watch as the lines clashed, and his own line slowly was being overpowered. This was wrong. The backup strategy he had developed, the contingency plan, was to send Legion 3 to reinforce the two fronts. He did not want to do that. All the planning, the practice, the preparation would be for nothing. Just then, he saw it. Then he felt it.

The Equium cavalry entered the fight. Simultaneously both wings began to gallop into the fight, slowly picking up steam. The brown uniform and flags adorned with the horsehead apsis of their city became a blur of motion. Victus had positioned his cavalry far to the rear, in an apparent move to protect that side from attack or circumvention. The enemy cavalry knew that his own horsemen couldn't get down fast enough to stop them from doing lethal damage. They saw a window of opportunity and struck with lightening speed.

"Black flag! Black flag now!" Victus screamed. His heart pounded. Everything hung on this. If it worked, the battle was his. The slightest mistake, miscalculation, and the battle and the war were lost. This is what it all came down to. Flanking him, on either side, were twin sets of huge blocks covered with tarpaulins. When the black flags went up, the coverings were removed, each revealing a massive wooden framework. Men scrambled to pull down a giant lever on the backside of each one. Motion started in the corned of his eye, as a black shape emerged. Out of the frames came giant metal balls, each taller than a man. The black metal that shone on the outside was Rigidium for strength, but the core was lead for weight. Slowly, almost painfully, they began to roll down hill. They soon started picking up speed.

The Reapers were in play. They had been his brainchild, and this might be the only time in history they would ever be used. He held his breath. As each pair of balls made their way down, the chains that connected the sets together began to unfurl. Each pair was like a giant two headed snake, striking down hill. The balls did not hop or bounce; they were too heavy for that. They plowed through the soil, crushing anything underfoot. The thick chain of solid rigidium, which was attached to the pair of balls with heavy swivels, flapped and danced as it was pulled down hill. Slapping and banging, the chain flailed, and when it came down, it lacerated the earth, gouged it several feet deep.

It was perfect. So much energy, so much planning had gone into these Reapers. Countless times they had rolled down that replicated training ground back in Akritus. Each time, they needed to be rolled up the hill once more. But it was all worth it. Transporting these weapons south, prepositioning them in Cruxium and personally escorting them had been worth it. The spheres were maxed out in distance, the chain growing taught. The right flank's pair was moving slightly faster than the left flanks, but that had been accounted for.

When the reapers hit the horses, it was surreal. Hundreds upon hundreds of animal screams mixed with the screams of man to create a single, unrecognizable sound. That sound had never been heard before in history, and it would never be heard again. Nothing lived where there had once been so much life. The massive chain had cut down all the cavalry like wheat to scythe before the horsemen could reach his forces. He could see the chain as it made it's way through the mass, the bodies rising and dropping in a wave. Once the

reaper's made it through the other side of the
cavalry, he knew he had won the battle. They
had no horse.

"Orange flag!" Victus almost cheered.
"ORANGE FLAG!"

Moments later, the thunder of their own
cavalry shook the earth, as they descended on
the unprotected flanks and the skirmishers in
the rear. Immediately the two fronts of the
Dutrigian army formed defensive squares, but
all forward momentum had stopped. In perfect
symmetry, Victus watched the two squares get
attacked; the cavalry smashed the outer and rear
flanks, the Legions surged onto the front, and
the inner flanks were pressed against the
obstacle field, being peppered by the longbow
men. Scorpions and onagers surgically smashed
the interior of the formations. He watched as
Dutrigi died. It would take time, but there was
no way the Bulls would win this.

The enemy reserve force of veterans
began to move. They were the last hope of their
beleaguered comrades. It was true, if these
forces were permitted to enter the fight, they
might make a difference. But they never would.

"Green flag. And the purple flag." His
voice was much calmer than earlier, since he
was well aware that he had won the battle. It
was over. The heavy onagers, yet unused in this
fight, had been dialed in on the reserve force.
The unloaded massive projectiles, and when
they hit the mass of men, they took out swaths

that were three or four men wide. Shields shattered and so did bodies. The Scorpions had been repositioned as well, and they rapid fired their sharpened stakes into the ravaged force below. That had only been half the order; the reserve cavalry, which had been positioned even farther back than the initial force appeared, and headed towards the veterans. It was over.

It would be over two hours before the last Dutrigian soldier was killed on the battlefield. Killing men, slaughtering men, was hard tedious work. It was a testament to their strength and honor that no one surrendered. That meant that none lived. Except for Kruegius; Silious had planned for him to helplessly watch the entire battle unfold, to watch his entire army be obliterated.

"That was the Battle of Dutrigi, my lord." Victus said to his Duke, nodding in satisfaction.

"Well done, General Victus. I see that I was wise to select you for this task." Silious nodded back. "Let's take a tour of our newest city."

XXVI
ATHELTIADES

The panorama of watching the sun set from the top of the fort's walls was breathtaking. The orange ball was dipping behind the water to the west, turning the choppy sea into a field of sparkling gems. A breeze, warm and dry, was blowing from the south, making his red cloak dance. That was Akkedan air he was feeling, hot like the breath of the Saurian's that breathed it. The violet pink sky was getting darker as the sun began to disappear, looking like the Bay of Dru was swallowing it whole. He was alone with his thoughts, and his thoughts were running rampant.

Thoughts of his father were on his mind the most. Somehow, he knew his father was dead; he could feel the connection the man had to the world was severed. His mind tried to tell him that he was being ridiculous, that there was no way he could know these things. His heart however told him different. It hurt, was being wrenched. He knew a battle was coming, so it was a very real possibility the old Polemarch had died honorably. He did not doubt that if Atheicles were to die, it would be in some glorious manner. That made him proud. At the same time, he felt shamed for being sent here, to a safe posting, while the rest of the army was fighting.

The note his father had given him, the prophecy, was folded and sat next to his breast, close to his heart. That was another truth he would carry with him, the certainty of the battle he had avoided. He couldn't blame his father for insisting that he be rushed and stashed away in a safe place, far from the fight. Atheltiades had no children of his own, but he knew what love was. He loved his family. He loved his father, he loved his mother, and he had loved his brother. His father had experienced so much grief when his first son had been killed, that he probably couldn't have bore losing his other. If he could change places with any of them when it came to life over death, he would.

That, after all, was a human trait. It was universal. This brought him to the other dilemma he had been dwelling on for so long today: watching those Millangor Saurians be butchered without provocation. They had done nothing threatening; in fact they were refugees, trying to protect their family. Just like his own father had been trying to ensure his safety, to remove him from a combat zone, they were looking out for their children. They risked great danger to avoid great danger. Unfortunately for them, they lost the gamble. Those younglings screams, he could still hear them in his mind, the wail of the mother as she watched them die.

He was told his entire life that these Saurians were wild, savage beasts. But how different could they be if they displayed such human traits? His entire upbringing was based on having a hatred for those creatures, on the basis that they were a threat to his own way of life, his elder's way of life. Why did he feel so much sorrow for those he had watched die earlier? Would they feel the same if they saw Atheltiades murdered at the hands of the Millangor? Was it murder, or was it war? Surely those children would have grown up to become enemies that tried to kill his own children some day on some future battle site.

Perhaps it was time to forgive. Maybe holding on to all that hate, lifetimes upon lifetimes of suffering and pain, wasn't that great of a thing. Sure, it had been a wonderful motivator for war, but the war never ended. Coexistence had been tried before, but always failed. The blood and hate and anger always lingered just beneath the surface, and the fighting continued time and time again. Could two peoples, with such a history of violence against one another, ever live in peace? Did one need to be completely destroyed before the other would know peace? Maybe they needed to earn the peace, rather than just try and force it upon armies. He didn't even know what that meant, but to him, it sounded right.

Until then, he a duty to lead his men against whatever enemy threatened them.

The sun was just a sliver now, and the earliest, brightest stars began to appear in the heavens. This day was ending, and tomorrow would be something new. Looking up at the sky as the light died, he thought of his father. A weight of grief and guilt settled on his shoulders. It wasn't just that, but something else also rested on them now. Time would reveal what that was.

XXVII
DIMIDIUS TORBOCK

The trio had ridden until after dark. They knew Dutrigi was close, and if they arrived late at night, that was better than making camp and setting out again tomorrow. If they rode all the way to the city, they could get a real bed, and then find a ship in the morning to take them to Akkedis. Torbock was convinced they could make up for lost time. That had been the plan at least. Something had changed. Torbock could smell the smoke on the night wind long before he saw the light of the fires. They continued onward, cautious, curious and ready for anything. Polemistius had convinced himself it was probably a farm that was burning, maybe even set intentionally. He had failed to convert the others to get behind his theory.

The closer they got to the city, the more prominent the glow became. It looked like the sun was beginning to rise in the west, reversing the course it had just taken a few hours earlier. The sounds came next. Distant crashes, rumbles, and screams. Once they crested the next hill, it all came into view. Dutrigi was burning. Buildings within the walls were ablaze, outlining thick smoke that billowed into the dark sky. The fields surrounding the city looked like they were covered in the coals of a dying campfire. The fires turned night into day. And he could see the soldiers. They were everywhere, swarming like ants on the carcass of a dead animal.

It was a scene he had seen too many times before. The war had started. He felt a spasm in his chest, a twitch as his heart must have skipped a beat. Dankoma Bay shone orange with the glow of the fires. All the ships in harbor had been lit ablaze. He understood now that this part of their mission would never be accomplished; there was no longer a Dutrigian army to give these dispatches to. The piles of men being stacked next to giant bonfires and the distinct smell of burning human flesh was proof of that. The torched husks of the ships in the water meant they wouldn't be catching a ride from this port.

"We need to skirt around the city." Torbock said, breaking the spell of the moment. "Inland a bit, and then head for Petrichoro or down through Bridgegate. We will find no friends amongst this army."

"It looks and sounds like there is still fighting inside the city! The city still lives, the people are resisting, dying!" Jacean said. "As long as we are able, we must protect these people. As Sentinels, we have a duty to do harm to the enemies of the Empire!" Emotions ran high in the young man's voice, and Torbock felt a pang of guilt. This was the home city of Jacean's people, and he must have been feeling an extra desire to act. Torbock knew this would be difficult.

"Jacean, we must continue with our mission. Dutrigi is beyond our help. It has fallen. The only thing we can do now is to deliver the messages as we were ordered, to bring the help that will stop this madness." It was sterner and less empathetic than Torbock had wanted to sound. But it had to do. This indomitable force had been laid to waste, and that had shaken everyone.

Jacean visibly bared and gritted his teeth, nose scrunching in waves, temples pulsing. He would do as he was told, as hard as it was for him to do so. Some low banking smoke made it up the hill, through the tree line they were sitting in. The hot air it was carried in dried out Torbock's mouth and lungs, and made his eyes sting.

"Petrichoro has a small garrison force of Dutrigians. They will have ships, and…" Polemistius started.

"Silious would have taken Petrichoro already. If he hasn't, he will before we get there." Torbock realized this to be true as he said it. "We need to make the rest of the trip on land, through Bridgegate and down to Millang'Sek."

"Are you daft?" The Ambassador said,

turning his horse to shield himself from the smoke. "This is enemy territory now. We can't just scurry through unannounced. We would be seen as spies and killed if we are caught sneaking through. We are diplomats and they will treat us as such."

"We don't have another option." Torbock argued. "Even if we backtracked to Stathum or Cortinum, which would cost us days upon days, the seas will be no safer passage than the roads."

Polemistius scowled, more from the options laid before him, but also due to the smoke. "No. We will not try and slink by here in secrecy." He declared. "I am a member of the Golden Class and an official agent of the Imperial Government. They have no right to harass or detain me as I ride free through my lands. Silious wouldn't allow such a thing."

"Don't be a fool!" Torbock snapped. "You just said yourself that this is enemy territory. They don't recognize your authority at all, they are rebels, and you are bringing with you directions that will put enemies in the field against them. They will gut you and not think twice."

"We will see." Polemistius said. "You have been ordered to escort me, and I am riding down this road. If anyone challenges me, I will protest under diplomatic immunity. If they don't recognize it, as you claim, well then I have you two to keep me safe."

"We will not follow you down there,

Polemistius." Torbock shook his head, and his horse whinnied at the same time, as if agreeing with his rider. "This is suicide. Someone needs to continue the mission."

"I am the mission, Sentinel." Polemistius snapped. "You will follow me, and you will protect me." And with that, he started down hill along the well-travelled road. Torbock cursed, and held the reigns tight. Jacean started to move, but the elder Sentinel braced him with an arm across his breast. Jacean looked at him, defiantly.

"The mission comes first, Torbock. You always tell me that. In fact, you just told me that." The young man glared at him. "And that man is right, he is the mission."

"Are you so eager to die, my boy?" Torbock seethed through his own gritted teeth this time. "The diplomat's reckless abandon is endangering the mission. All three of us will die within moments of being spotted."

"But, we…" Jacean started.

"Listen to me!" Torbock raised his voice, anger flooding in. It wasn't anger at his partner; it was the situation the diplomat had put them in, and the lack of options. He watched as the man rode farther down the hill as he spoke. "I will go with Polemistius. You will travel north from here, and circumvent around to safely make your way to Bridgegate. If I am not there when you arrive, continue south to Millang'Sek, and treat with the Millangor King. That is our only hope."

"Treat with a Saurian King?" Jacean scoffed. "How do I do that? I'm not trained to… I'm not authorized to make… I don't speak…"

"Sentinels obey the laws of the Empire. We keep the people safe. And we obey our Emperor. The Emperor entrusts us with part of his power to give us the authority to do so. For generations, we have been the Emperor's hand. And when there's a time for it, we are his voice. You are a Sentinel, Jacean Monodius. When it comes to it, you will know what is right." Torbock clasped him on the shoulder.

"I am not a true Sentinel, not yet." His young partner responded.

"Yes, you are. I have nothing more to teach you." Torbock said.

"But the oath, the temple…" He began to protest.

"Not important." Torbock shook his head dismissively. "That is only a formality. What it takes to be a Sentinel is in here…" He gently tapped his own breast. "And in here." And he moved his fingers to his temple. "Now go. I must catch up with Polemistius. You know these lands well; travel safely and smartly. I will meet you at the fort, four days from now I'd wager." He winked, and Jacean gave a hesitant nod in return.

"Gods give strength, Sentinel Monodius." Torbock embraced his partner, and then rode hard down the road, his horse's feet clopping on the dry dirt. In his peripheral vision, he saw the image of his partner begin to head north. The road Torbock rode on was covered with tall oaks and bay trees, and a smaller hill lay between him and the city. It was dark where he was riding, the fires being blotted out by the terrain.

A few bends farther down the road, he came across Polemistius. He was still on horseback, but wasn't moving. A few carts and wagons, as well as other people on horseback were stopped in the road. Torches had been set up, and illuminated the area dimly. It was bright enough for Torbock to see the soldiers. A slight wave of fear flashed inside him as he recognized them for what they were. That was soon replaced with a heightened sense of awareness, and a cool acceptance that the die had been cast, this was his current situation, and this was the only thing that mattered right now.

There were at least ten soldiers he could see, probably more that he couldn't. They had made a roadblock to keep anyone from entering the battle area. Most people that had been forced to halt on the road were congregating, arguing with the troops or complaining to one another. One man, with a heavy Duracee accent, the best Torbock could tell, was vehemently protesting the situation to what appeared to be the leader of the soldiers. The armor they wore was what he had seen during his visit to Akritis and the rest of Frigiterra. It was a segmented armor, made of a dark Rigidium alloy. Grey tunics were worn where blue would have been on an Imperial legionary.

He casually sidled up next to Polemistius, who indifferently glanced over at him, none in the least surprised to see him appear.

"Where is the boy?" The Diplomat asked.

"I sent him away. No need for all of us to die here, we still have a mission to complete." Torbock said through the side of his mouth.

"No one will be dying, Sentinel." The man had a self-assured smile on his face. Just then, as the Duracee man that had been protesting with the commander reached a crescendo, a fist smashed into his nose with a crunch. The man went down with a flop onto his back. Dark blood erupted and leaked through the moaning man's hands that covered his new wound. A string of curses followed, which earned the down man a kick to the head. Then the blades came out. A gladius was stuck in the man's gut, and a pugio went into his neck.

Some screams came from the onlookers, some roars of defiance. The soldiers called for silence. A horse reared, and it's owner tried desperately to calm the beast. Torbock had seen this before, it has many names; bloodlust, battle frenzy, Merseus' madness. It had more titles, but the cause was the same. It was a breakdown in discipline due to the emotional release and group mentality following a battle. Many more non-combatants would fall victim to this

tonight, and not all of those that would be
victims meant they would be killed. This army
would do terrible things to slake its thirst and
it's needs.

"We need to get out of here." Polemistius
said, fear starting to show on his face. "We
should turn back up…"

"Everyone! Line up over here! Off your
horses, off your wagons, over here!" This came
from a tall man, older than most of the other
soldiers. His face was wrinkled and scarred,
weathered from a career of campaigning. The
veteran was walking down the line, forcibly
getting people to do his bidding.

"If we tried to run now, those men would
skewer us with pila before we barely got turned
around. Everyone is on edge." Torbock said.
"Dismount, stay calm." Torbock got off of his
own horse before the shouting soldier reached
them. Polemistius and the two horses were
between him and the soldier walking down the
line. With a deep breath, Torbock slowly
grasped his *spatha* sword, the handle perfectly
fitted for his hand, his hand a perfect match for
the pommel. With a deep breath, and the clarity
that he would probably die here, Torbock
prepared himself for what was to come.

He watched a pair of sandaled feet
approach Ambassador Polemistius from the gap
underneath the horses. Not far off, a woman
screamed and a loud snapping sound was
heard, like wood breaking. Commotion was

followed by angry voices and then the rabble was reduced to a murmur. While this was going on, the soldier that was by Polemistius was ordering him to go with the other civilians.

Go with him, don't make this more difficult, thought Torbock.

Of course, he couldn't hear him, and of course, he didn't follow the commands.

"I am a Golden Class citizen. You have no right to command me to do anything. I am also a member of the Imperial Government, an ambassador, who get's diplomatic immunity from any..." Polemistius stopped speaking as a loud, fleshy smack filled the air. Torbock watched the ambassador's sandaled feet stagger. With a faint rasp, he drew his sword, and walked around the back of the horse.

"I'm sorry your highness, I forgot that you were better than me!" The old veteran croaked in false subservience. "You're the reason we are out here fighting! Men like us who fight and die for you don't get any..." He froze as he saw Torbock appear baring steel. The man's eyes widened in surprise as the Sentinel steadily bore down on him. Torbock saw that the soldier's right eye had a slight droop to it, with a large, starfish shaped scar on the edge of it. He opened his mouth to say something, but all air was stopped from escaping through it as Torbock's sword opened his throat.

"Get behind the horses." Torbock ordered as he advanced forward, past Polemistius and towards the other soldiers. Most had their backs turned to him, as they tried to control the mass of people they were herding. Amazingly, they hadn't seen their comrade being slain. With swift determination, he sprung forward, hamstringing two men with a single sweeping arc of his sword, and then continuing on. He had a dagger out now, and jammed it up under the ribcage of a third, as a forth was killed with a downward hack to were his neck met his chest, the sword finding its way expertly between helmet and armor.

The frightened people cowered away, as two more soldiers charged after him, gladii drawn and ready for the kill. These men swung their infantry swords wildly, like they were smaller versions of his own cavalry sword. That's not how those swords had been designed to be used, and he expertly parried the sloppy attacks away. Kneeling and with an upward thrust, one of them received a sword up into the lower abdomen via the groin, opening the femoral artery at the same time. The other he killed by grabbing the man, and pulling him into an embrace, as if he had been a long lost family member. As he gave the man the hug and drew him closer, the man slid down the length of Torbock's leveled, outstretched blade. A jerk and a twist on the impaled blade killed him almost instantly.

Two pila struck the back of the dying man, thrown by his own squad mates. One glanced off, the other lodged into the meat under the armor. Torbock held his new shield of flesh for a few moments as he appraised the situation. It looked like there was a total of five men huddled together, weapons ready. The two that he had hamstrung were attempting to rise, but they wouldn't be a threat at the moment. Another volley of pila, this time four of them. None found Torbock. Slowly lowering his dead passenger, he scurried behind a wagon. Polemistius saw him, and scampered his direction, panting from fear and adrenaline.

"Five left." Torbock said to him. "I can't take another five, not with them on alert like this. Stay here, hide, run, do something. Continue with the mission, meet with Jacean at Bridgegate. Don't let my sacrifice be for nothing, Polemistius." And he handed the man his bloodied dagger. Breathing hard, the diplomat slumped to the ground, back against the wooden wagon. He was not a soldier, that was for certain.

"You don't need to apologize." Torbock said, his voice without humor.

"For what?" The diplomat wheezed.

"For this, for me dying for your stupidity." Torbock said, and rose to his feet from the crouch he had been in.

With wide eyes, the diplomat watched Torbock walk to the fight, to his own end. "Sorry." The man murmured.

A pilum whizzed past him as he started

his charge. Then another hit the dirt by his feet, not sticking but bouncing away ineffectually. Two soldiers charged at him, while two remained behind throwing spears. The fifth was missing; most likely he had headed back to the main force to get reinforcements. The two who rushed him used a coordinated attack, one going high, and one going low. Blocking the one who went low, he ducked the blow from the one who went high. He punched at one, and as he did, the other brought a pommel down on the back of Torbock's head. White light exploded in his vision, and he lost any advantage he had. He felt a sword slide along his side, cutting broadside along his flank.

A blind swing of his sword resulted in a loud clank as it ricocheted off of that segmented Rigidium chest armor. He fell to one knee, and blocked a downward swing that was targeted at his neck. Dizziness caused the scene around him to spin abnormally, and he couldn't have moved if he had wanted to as two more pila flew past him, one grazing his cloak. Death was closing in, and Torbock was attempting to stave it off a few moments more. Perhaps he could take one or two more of them out before they killed him. Hot, sharp pain erupted in his left lower leg as a pilum came to a lurch in his flesh. The pyramid shaped head had burst out the other side. A man screaming came from what seemed like two different directions at once, and he could have sworn he heard the sound of a horses thundering gallop.

He caught a glimpse of steel in torchlight, and focused on what was right in front of his face. Summoning a reserve of strength, he swung his sword up and away, catching the man in the crotch and the femoral artery in one long gash. As that man fell away in agony, Torbock felt his own sword get violently knocked from his grip. Then, a hand on his shoulder slammed him onto his back. A moment too late, he saw a gladius being raised and cocked ready to strike, aimed at his neck. Before he could react, his whole vision went red with blood.

It took him a moment to realize that it wasn't his blood. The spray had covered his face and blotted out his sight, and once he cleared his eyes, he saw what had happened. The enemy that had been poised to open Torbock's throat had just had his own opened, hacked near to the neck-bone from a gash to one side. As the dead man fell, Torbock began to get to his feet, knowing he still had more enemies to face. He did not expect to see what he did.

A rider sat upon a horse, holding a blooded sword, and none of the soldiers remained standing. It was Jacean. He must have rode down from behind the enemy position, taking them unawares and killing the last of them. Including the one that was a mere moment from killing his partner. Torbock tried to stand, but his wounds prevented it. Instead, sprawling out and propping himself up on the ground, as if he were reclining on a couch, he gave his friend a nod of thanks.

"I told you to ride away from here." He admonished.

"That's a strange way of giving thanks, Dimidius." Jacean said, dismounting his horse to help his former master. He patted the horse on the neck as he knelt down to look at the wounds. "I just saved your life, sir."

"You disobeyed an order. But thank you." Torbock winced as Jacean prodded and tugged at the pilum still stuck in his leg. Just then, a yell for help came from behind them. The shouting was coming from one of the hamstrung soldiers. Jacean strode over, blade already drawn, and silenced the man before his shouts carried to unwanted ears. The other man that had been wounded wasn't to be seen. That was when he glanced in the direction of Polemistius' hiding spot, and saw the studded caligae boots sticking out; soldier's boots. The man had crawled to where the diplomat had been weathering out the fight. Blood was pooling on the ground, the torchlight flickering off the dark creeping puddle.

With a silent point from Torbock, Jacean sprung into action towards the site. With sword held ready to strike, he rounded the back of the wagon, and then froze. Lowering his weapon, he reached down and pulled the dead soldiers into the open. Torbock saw a dozen wounds on the soldiers face, arms, and neck, anywhere that flesh was exposed. Jacean helped Polemistius get to his feet. The diplomat held the dagger that was drenched with blood in one hand, and with the others he held the crimson stained area of his own stomach. By the way he walked, and the way he grimaced, he could tell the blood was his own.

As Torbock watched the pair approach, someone unseen stepped close to him. Reaching for his weapon that he had spotted on the ground nearby, a voice spoke, "Easy friend, I am here to help." The voice sounded off, slightly muffled, as if the man had just coughed up phlegm into his mouth and was speaking through a kerchief. He could not yet see the man, but he felt at ease. A comfort flowed through his body, radiating out from his chest. The pain was there, but it was much more manageable. A pressure was felt on his leg as hands firmly descended upon him. When he saw the man who had spoken and said he was here to help, Torbock flinched, recoiled in surprise and shock.

One hand was bare skin; the other was wrapped in linen bandages. It appeared as if the entire right side of the man was covered in such a fashion, even most of his face. Memories of the colonies of those with the *Fleshrot* disease on Luctantum came to mind. They were covered like this as the disease slowly ate away at their bodies, consuming them until they withered and died. Jacean approached, setting down Polemistius with a thud, and then went over to the stranger that was prodding his partner. At first, the anger was visible on his face and in his gate, but as he got closer, Torbock watched his tone soften. The man offered no threat to his friend, he knew it was true.

"Boy," The man with the covered face locked eyes with Jacean. "From my wagon there, fetch my file and pincers. In that side compartment, above the back wheel."

"I'm no boy." Jacean said defiantly.

"You don't look like a girl." The man said back.

"I am a Sentinel." Jacean continued.

"Good for you. Sentinel boy, fetch them." The man reiterated. "We need to get on the move before reinforcements arrive. You two may have saved all these people, but it will be for nothing if we don't all get out of here. I need to remove this spear and get your partner loaded."

Jacean made his way to get the tools.

"They sent a runner back to the main force." Torbock grunted. "They will be here soon."

"Your partner slew the runner on his way down to here." The man said. "Your wounds seem manageable. You will heal quickly, I'm sure you always do. You might have a bruised brain, and the slash to your side isn't that deep. The pilum head went through the muscle, didn't hit the bone or any major vessels. Once we get that removed, we will get a move on."

"The other man, tend to him as well. He is an important ..." Torbock started.

"An Important man with a fatal abdominal wound." The man said only loud enough for Torbock to hear. "He will not bleed to death, but the wound will grow infected, and it will be a long, painful end."

Torbock nodded. Jacean appeared with the tools, and was directed to begin filing close to the wooden shaft. "The heads of these new pila have a softer metal shank. They're designed to bend after hitting their target. It's easy to file through, and once scored, can be bent until it snaps. Then, we will pull it the rest of the way through. As Jacean filed, the vibrations sent waves of pain through his leg and up into the rest of his body.

"That's good." The bandaged man used the pincers to secure the shank, using that point as a fulcrum, as Jacean bent the wooden shaft up and down. It snapped free. "Ok, Sentinel. Deep breath, this part will be painful. Hold his leg, boy." The man readjusted the pincers, now grasping just the shank just behind the sharpened, hardened pyramidal point. With a wet sound, the weapon head was pulled the rest of the way through the calf. Torbock writhed a little initially, but regained his composure.

"Done." The man said, applying a bandage to the leg wound. An image flashed in

Torbock's mind, a memory that he never had. He thought of a tomb, in a faraway land, with a corpse wrapped in linen like this man. Although he had never been to such a place, he was certain it was a tomb of a Cylathian king. His chest pained as the image faded from his mind.

"Alright boy," The man stood. "Let's get these two loaded into my wagon, and let's head north."

"We are…" Jacean started.

"You are going to travel with me. These two cannot ride a horse, and I'm sure you three won't get far with an invading army in the area. I will bring you to wherever you need to go, you have my word." The man said, no room for argument in his tone.

"Akkedis." Was the only response, this came from Torbock.

"I was heading that way, anyways. Now let's get going." The man said.

"Who are you? What is your name?" Jacean demanded.

"Kataris." The bandaged man replied. "Now, we need to get a move on."

PART IV

PROLIFERATION
&
POWER PLAYS

"BRAVE MEN ARE A CITY'S STRONGEST
TOWER OF DEFENSE"
- ALCAEUS

XXVIII
MIKUS DERRATA

He guessed that he was towards the front of the middle section of the long serpent of men that crept over the landscape. That was the logical answer, based on the fact that he was in the 3rd cohort out of six. However, he could not see the front or the rear of the marching army, so he could not be completely certain. The helmet and the kit of the man in front of him was all he had stared at for the majority of the last several days. They marched from before sun up until sunset. They erected the same camp every night, in a different location. Thousands of men, all stepping in file to the same destination was a singular experience. The sound of the boots marching in almost perfect unison, the vibrations in the ground, the cloud of dust trailing behind them; it was remarkable.

When the passed through farmland or through towns, they drew crowds. Some people cheered, some shouted encouragement, but most just stared. Perhaps some were looking for a familiar face, a loved one, a son, brother or father. The occasional woman would blow a kiss, and Mikus couldn't help but smile at that, even though he wasn't supposed to. A majority of the time was spent just putting one foot in front of the other, a mundane task if there ever was one. They marched in full armor, carried their shield and weapons, helmets on to defend them from the blaring sun. When the sun wasn't directly overhead, close to setting, they were allowed to hang their helmets off their chest, to begin cooling down.

Mikus constantly felt as though he had sand in his mouth, every time he chomped his jaw, granules crunched and ground between his teeth. Sweat and road dust made a sticky grim on his skin, and he felt the sting of the sun on the back of his neck and face. He had darkened significantly since he had joined the Legion, so he didn't burn to the point of his skin peeling off, but he always had that burned feeling. So he marched on, looking forward to the day ending so he could get some much needed rest. His eyes stung each day from the dust, sun, and perpetual lack of sleep.

Occasionally, the cavalry would thunder past the edges of the column, patrolling from the front to the baggage train, all the way back to the rearguard, and then to the front again. The likelihood of them encountering an enemy this close to the capital was unlikely, but you could never be too certain, apparently. Mikus found this reassuring, that his Legate took precautions such as this and kept his vigilance up.

By late afternoon on that day, the army was marching through Pueria. It felt strange to be returning to his hometown in such a fashion, so soon after leaving. Thinking back however, running away from this place felt like a lifetime ago. Perhaps it was, he felt like a different person altogether. His muscles had grown, his face had changed shape, and he had changed mentally and spiritually. Since he had taken the Sacramentum, he belonged to this Legion, to the Calidian Empire. If the Emperor, or Consul as was the case right now, ordered him to lay down his life, he had taken an oath to obey.

Marching down a street that he had walked on most of his life, looking at the familiar vistas that passed by was quite satisfying. He felt no longing for the life he had left behind, for the life he had left he did not want. Lamenting for the life before that, his life on the farm with his family that was gone, well that was a waste of time. He hadn't left that life behind, that life had left him long ago. He would keep an eye out for the roof of the Brass Mule as they marched through; just to make sure it was still there. The crowds of people that lined up along the road, and jammed themselves into side streets, upon roofs and balconies to watch the army pass through didn't cause Mikus to break his gaze from the man in front of him.

Surely, people he had known his entire life, friends and relatives, were watching the 2nd Legion today. In the slim chance that one of them spotted him, he wanted to make sure they saw a soldier, a man determined, and not a silly homesick boy searching for a familiar face from before he left. The chance that someone would spot him, or Dellan or Davus was small, but not out of the realm of possibility. Maybe then someone in his family would know what happened to the runaway boy called Mikus Derrata.

Just before the sun started to dip behind the sea, the Legion halted to make camp. With 5,000 plus soldiers that suddenly became construction workers, the massive project didn't take that long. They built the castra on the site of a previous one, which made the work easier. The old ditch was still outlined, and filled with loose dirt that was removed almost effortlessly with the army of shovels. A cache of sharpened stakes and logs were kept back in the city, stashed strategically by the Legion's during the last war. They erected the walls and battlements in near record time, the fastest they had on this march for certain. And just like that, in a matter of hours, the castra sprang to life. In the morning, it would disappear once again.

*   *   *

That night, Mikus stepped out away from his entire squad, even leaving Marcus without giving him a chance to come with him. He found Dellan and Davus, alone, sitting by a fire they had created for themselves. Apparently the homecoming had the same affect on them that it did on him. Quiet contemplation by himself had sounded appealing, but so did sharing his thoughts with another. He joined the circle without a word, sitting cross-legged in the dirt. Remembering their journey together, back when it had been just the three of them, wasn't hard to do with them sitting around a fire. The rest of the world melted away, drifted into a haze like the smoke from the fire.

For sometime, nothing was said. Dellan broke the silence.

"I'm sure I saw Kadtia today." He almost mumbled. "She was standing on a railing in front of that old laundry. You know, the one with the green roof?"

"Did she see you?" Davus asked, looking longingly at his brother, hoping that he had some sort of news about their sister, about their family.

"I don't think so." The younger brother said with remorse. "She was searching for us, I know it. She scanned the men like she was trying to pick us out."

"She probably figured it out." Davus said. "She was always the smartest of all of us."

"Do you think they miss us?" Dellan brought up.

"I'm sure they do. Mother and the girls, at least." Davus responded. "Father is probably too furious with us to miss us."

"Your father probably misses you the most." Mikus interjected. "He cares deeply for you, I always saw it. Sometimes I wished I had a father like him. If he is mad at you, it's probably because you ran away without talking to him."

The brothers both lowered their heads in silence, Davus poking at the fire with a stick.

"Did you see your Aunt and Uncle?" Dellan asked Mikus.

"No. I wasn't looking though. I didn't want to see anyone, you know?" Mikus said. Both boys shook their heads slowly, but Mikus didn't elaborate.

"I would have given one of my balls for a glimpse of Lorelei Menkenna, though." Davus said, and the boys chuckled. "I might even risk sneaking into town and try to find her. Maybe she would give a brave legionary some attention."

"I kissed her once, you know." Mikus said with a smile.

"Yes." Both the Ganno brothers said in unison, exasperation heavy in their voice. "You were both six name days old." Davus continued.

"Seven." Mikus corrected, with a playful tone. The others shook their head. They had been hearing that story for years and years.

"I wish we could go home tonight. Just for a few minutes if nothing else." Dellan blurted, almost as if he hadn't wanted to say it aloud.

"We can't." Davus shook his head. "We are all restricted to camp, Legate's orders. Otherwise, I think I would go too."

"Part of me would want to go to the Mule." Mikus said, surprising even himself as he said it. "Just to see the look on the face of Jerichus. And to knock him in the face with one hard punch."

The group turned silent again, and Mikus contemplated on what he had just said. He knew there would be time to do that later, when he got back from this war.

For now, under the backdrop of their childhood, the friends sat and spoke idly to one another. The conversation never breached any subject more serious than what they had already discussed. When it was time for Dav and Del's squad to take sentry duty, Mikus said farewell and retired to his own tent for the night. He had expected everyone to be asleep, but that was not the case.

Lively conversation was emitting from the tent, audible before he ever stepped inside. Everyone was awake. Even Tilo was still up, although he just lay on his bunk, eyes open. He wasn't talking, as was the norm. The group didn't even acknowledge him as walked over and began getting things ready for bed. Apparently everyone was gossiping about enemy troop movements. Every once in awhile, Mikus had to remind himself that the enemy everyone referred to was no longer the Homithan forces, but fellow Calidians. Rebels. Traitors. Maybe some of them were just like him, joining up to serve their country, and then were swept up in a war between politicians that he had never met. A private war for power, about to be fought with the forces of the Empire, himself included.

"I know for a fact that Silious and his army were just outside Dutrigi. That's where they are going to hit first. A contact I know in the staff verified it." Titus Vinius spouted, absolution in his voice.

"And leave the Rams of Trimontis between him and his home base?" This came from Quel Strasa. "To fight the Dutrigians, who would whoop anybody who takes the field against them?"

"Dutrigi has never fallen." Ferro said. "Not to a Saurian force, and not to man. Even the Imperial Legions would be hard pressed to take them out head on in a face-to-face duel. Seems foolish to me."

"It would seem bold to me." Vinius defended his argument. "Silious and his forces are relatively untested. Barbarians, sure they fight those, and a lot of his ranks are made up of old veteran's. But they have never taken the field together against another large force. What better message to send to validate your force than to do that against the Dutrigians. It sends a hell of a message to everyone in the Empire, in the world."

"Even if they do go to Dutrigi, that doesn't mean they will win. Kruegius and the Bulls may end this war before it even really starts." Ferro countered.

"Win or lose, I'm telling you, that's were this war starts. There is no love loss between Silious and Kruegius." Vinius folded his arms when he spoke, ending the conversation on his end.

"Aren't we heading to Cortinum?" Ferro asked no one in particular. "If the fight is going to be in Dutrigi, why aren't we headed there?"

"Because," this came from the Decanus. "The fight will be most likely be over before we get there. And the 7th, which is camped at Stathum, and the 9th, which is in Cortinum, are closer. If there is a siege, they will be the ones who break it. We will be the back up line of defense. Now everyone grab some sleep, we have another long day's march tomorrow. "

Mikus was asleep a few minutes later. Exhaustion had taken it's toll, and that overcame the thoughts that filled his mind.

XXIX
DAHQUAL SILIOUS

The sun was red that morning; *Quite poetic,* mused Dahqual. The smoke from the fires had turned it that color, the color of blood, the color of the Dutrigian Army. The fires that had consumed parts of the city, the fires that had been fueled by the bodies of the dead Dutrigians had done that. It was all very fitting. Silious rubbed at his eyes, they burned and watered from lack of sleep and from the smoke. He hadn't slept a wink the night before; he had been too occupied with occupying this city. Hunger pangs shot through his stomach, and he embraced them. The coarse stubble on his face and scalp made him anxious for a shave, to partake in his daily ritual.

Soon, he could dispense with that process, he smiled to himself. With this victory, he was a giant leap closer to reclaiming his rite to sit upon the Ebon Throne. A lot was owed to Victus, it was he who conceived the strategy that toppled the once formidable Dutrigian forces. The General's diligence, planning and vision had made this such an incredible, lopsided win for his side. The only thing that bothered Silious, that made him nervous, was how inflexible the plan had been. Everything hinged on very specific things happening at very specific times. Other future aspects of the campaign hung on very precise maneuvers as well, and that didn't sit well.

Obviously, if everything lined up, and he got results like this, then there was nothing to worry about. Predicting the future was difficult, and the future was dynamic. The strategy needed to be able to be altered accordingly. He readjusted his ornamental helmet from one crook of his arm to the other as he stepped over a dead soldier. His highly polished, black rigidium armor glistened in the bright red morning light. The orange cape that hung from his shoulders was marred with soot and charcoal from the night's fires.

Several buildings still burned, as he made his way through the city. Most of the population had held itself up within the Old Walls, the original site of Fort Dutrigius. They had laid siege to the citadel that was made up with the Old Walls when they had stormed the city. The city had fallen, and the population was already held up in a prison of sorts. As far as he was concerned, the surviving Dutrigian population could remain there until they starved. He had taken the city, he had destroyed the army, that was all that mattered. Let the women, children, and geriatrics remain in this convenient confinement; he had bigger game to hunt.

A glimpse of the skeletal remains of the

ships in the harbor, some protruding upwards like breaching whales, others capsized and aground. Wisps of smoke arose from some, although the sea had extinguished most of the embers already. He could see gulls perched atop some of the burned keels and ribs. With a sigh of admiration, he then turned and looked back in the direction of the battle the day prior. Large billows of black smoke, noxious looking and thick, choked upwards into the sky. Silious knew that those were the fires fueled by the bodies of the fallen enemy. They would burn for days, doubtless.

The entire army, down to the last man, had fought to the death. No survivors. Even Kruegius, whom he hoped would live to watch the entirety of his force get slaughtered, unfortunately didn't make it through the battle. Reports said that his own peltasts had killed him off with their slings. They thought it was better to murder their own leader than allow him to suffer through watching them all die. Bizarre people, these Dutrigians. Why they or any Morincians for that matter, were allowed to still field military forces in the modern Calidian Empire was beyond him. He was fixing that right now. And he would continue to do so.

He had ordered Kruegius and all the other high ranking officers of the enemy he could find to be crucified postmortem in front of the main gates to the Young Walls of the city. Kruegius had openly defied Dahqual's right to rule over this land, and now he was a message of defiance to his enemies. Word of the Dutrigian annihilation would reach every corner of the empire soon. That meant the ferocity of his forces would precede them no matter where they struck next.

Victus was out marshaling the forces to continue the march west. Silious had wanted a moment to walk through his very first city he had won through conquest alone. He could feel the eyes of his ancestors upon him, and he wondered if this was how they had felt when they subjugated people and cities of their own. He was going to create a new Empire, one that was larger than any the world had ever seen, and it started today. Despite his wish to be alone, his Eagle guard was several paces behind him wherever he went.

As he slowly strolled through the streets, with a slight coastal breeze blowing the smoke away from his face, he took it all in. Rounding a corner, the sight of Genieda Lourede standing in the middle of the street made him freeze. The priest strode over to him, a far too broad smile on his face.

"Emperor Silious." The man bowed slightly, hands clasped.

"I am not an Emperor, yet." Silious corrected, his tone irritated.

"The Gods say it is so." The priest said seriously. "Today is a great victory. The Dutrigians were a mighty threat to our people, and that threat has been removed. That is one less factor for us to worry about when the final battle comes, my lord Silious."

The Duke of Frigiterra gave a simple nod in acknowledgement. Screeching birds over head drew the attention of the priest, who watched swarms of ravens and buzzards flying over the city, making their way to the killing fields. Carrion birds, the eyes of Shaardon. Many priests used birds to divine things the Gods were trying to communicate to the mortal world. Studying the birds a moment longer, the squinting priest returned his gaze to Silious.

"My lord, I am bound to you by an unbreakable blood oath." Lourede stated. "Two separate tasks bind me to you until they are fulfilled. I have been sworn to give you military council based upon the will of the Gods. Now, they speak to me. They tell me that in your next battle, the Eagle must strike before the Owl. If not, the battle will be lost."

"Macien will be at the next battle?" Silious asked, eagerness in his voice.

"The Gods say it is so." Lourede said. "You must draw first blood."

Silious nodded, his thoughts distant.

"As for the second task that I am bound to you by, I have an update on that." Silious smiled as he spoke.

"What? How?" Silious spat, his heart beginning to race in excitement.

"During the battle, I felt the presence of

an Immortal, a strong Immortal presence. I explained to you that not all Immortals were snuffed out of the world, some escaped the smiting of the Gods." The priest explained. "We were close to one yesterday, but it is gone now. I have advised all soldiers to look for the mark I described to you amongst the dead. I am certain they will not find it, but it is better that they know what to look for."

"And you are certain you can extract one of these beings immortality, so that I may possess it for myself?" Silious felt foolish as the words escaped his lips, but at the same time he wanted nothing more in the whole world. He craved immortality more than he craved the Ebon Throne.

"I have done it before for others. I cannot lie to you, and you know it, my lord." The priest continued.

Silious did know that Lourede could not lie to him; after many trials and tests, he had discovered the man always told the truth.

"Explain to me again, what is keeping you from seizing this immortality for yourself, priest?" Silious asked.

"I serve the Gods faithfully. I do not fear death. I know I will be rewarded for my service once I pass over. This life is but a test before the real one, my lord." And with that, the priest nodded and turned away, leaving Silious alone. The Duke looked up to the sky, and watched the birds go about their flight paths. He had no idea how anything could be discerned from such things. If Silious became a God one day, he would communicate with mankind through his voice, not by birds and eviscerated animal guts.

XXX

TARAES KANTAUR

The Terraced Gardens were designed to instill peace and calm in those who entered them. It was soothing to be here once again for Taraes, and for a few moments she lost herself in what she saw. Perhaps the ancient architects had known the world was a chaotic, whirlwind of a place, and felt a need to create a slice of tranquility and serenity literally set in stone. This spot was a bastion for those who needed to reset themselves.

From the beach, snaking all the way up through the city and up into the woods of Mt. Junas, the park had been laid out. It followed the path of a creek, which flowed from a lake high in the mountains. By the time the creek reached where the park began, it was diverted through stone canals that flowed down dozens upon dozens of waterfalls as it cascaded from level to level. The Terraced Garden were just as the name described, and were made of huge stone bulkheads, stacked one atop of the other, all the way to the top. Each level was expertly manicured with beautiful flora, all fed and

watered from the creek that flowed through the
heart of it all.

If you wanted to stroll through shady
trees, some levels provided that. If you wanted
flowers, other ones were just that. If you wanted
to feel grass under your feet, those were in
abundance. Some walls had flowering vines
growing up or down them; others were bare
stonewalls, which were beautiful in their own
right. Statues and fountains were sporadically
and tastefully placed throughout the grounds.
When someone walked down the steps that
connected all the terraces, benches that
overlooked vista were placed through the park
to sit. Some of these seats looked over the park
itself, while others overlooked the cityscape of
Jorbus or the panorama of Drakus Bay. The
waters were turquoise and clear, and you could
see the white sand underneath, or the clumps of
coppery colored rocks here and there.

Empress Taraes Kantaur strolled down
some shallow and wide steps that brought her
down to the next level. The terrace that she was
stepping onto was short cut, lush green grass. A
gravel pathway cut through the center of he
space, parallel to the offset, asymmetrical
channel of the creek. The water flowed down
several shallow locks before disappearing over
the edge, down to the next level. Other than
that, this terrace was empty of anything else,
except for her and one other person. The man
was standing with his back to her, gazing out at

the water below and beyond.

The cerulean blue of his cloak shone brightly in the morning sun, and the fabric waved elegantly in the gentle sea breeze. He looked over his shoulder as she approached, having sensed someone drawing near to him. The man did a double take upon seeing her, and then rushed over to embrace her. Like a vice, his arms coiled around her as he picked her up off her feet and gave her a twirl. His face beamed, and they both laughed.

"The Empress is here! I heard she got in last night under a secret escort. I didn't believe it; such dirty rumors are always flying around! Sister! It is so good to see you!" Darien Aktulus exclaimed as he set her down. "I am sorry to hear of Greeth, Taraes. I pray to the Gods every day for his health. I heard the children are here, I can't wait to see them!"

Taraes smiled. Her brother had always been excitable and easily distracted. It was refreshing to know that even with all his new responsibilities and his changing role in this dynamic world, he remained his true nature.

"Darien, I have missed you." She said, clasping his hands together. "And I'm ashamed to admit, I didn't realize how much I did until just now. I didn't know how much I missed this place until I returned, if that make sense."

"It does." He nodded. "This place hasn't changed much since you left, that must be comforting to you. Have you seen Junæa and the children? Amara is getting tall, and Aedien is a little ember flung from Malleus' forge. Mother and Uncle aren't here right now, but I think Uncle will be back soon. He's taking care of a work strike of sorts with the Anurai."

"So I have heard." Taraes said, stepping beside her brother, both looking out over the water shoulder to shoulder. "And mother?"

"The elder Duchess Ariadne spends most of her time staying up on the family chateau." Darien kicked his head back towards Mt Junas behind them. "She comes down here about once a month, for various reasons. She doesn't stay long when she does. For the most part, she hikes and wanders all over the mountain during the day, and returns to that place to sleep. She said she's looking for something, but won't say what. I think she's becoming a witch like her ancestors were rumored to be, searching for ingredients to make potions. Maybe she's the Witch on the Mountain, like the stories we were told as children. She probably is just lonely, and likes to be close to father." He was referring to the family tomb, which was tunneled into part of the upper mountain.

If her mother would not come to her, she would need to go to Ariadne herself. While she was at it, she would visit father and take care of that effigy as she promised him she would. She dismissed that from her mind, and focused on her little brother. She looked at him, studied him while he looked out at sea, at the parade of ships coming and going out of the harbor. Darien had grown, aged into a young man. He was tall, taller than both her and Macien. His dark brown, almost black locks of hair were longer than she was used to seeing on a daily basis, but he wore it well. The soft features of his young face had sharpened only slightly since she had seen him last, but his skin showed the vitality of his age. No creases or lines had started to appear, as they were on Macien, Greeth, and everyone else her age.

Darien had grown into a very handsome man, and he took after their mother more than the old Duke with his features and complexion. She looked at his clothes, and noticed that they were cut and in a fashion that she wasn't used to seeing in the Imperial palace. The cerulean cloak that he wore was almost sheer, thin like silk. It was in stark contrast with the thick woolen military cloaks that had become very fashionable lately. His shoes were strapped with loads of very thin laces that travelled halfway up his leg. The tunic he wore was plain, but finely made. He was dressed like a rich youth aught to dress, she thought.

"How are you liking your role as provisional Archon?" She asked, curious how the situation was going. "I guess it's really Provisional Duke, if we are being realistic."

A feigned, insincere smile crept along his face and he looked at her cockeyed. "You mean how am I enjoying being a replacement Macien?

I am not our brother, and I will be the first to say it. Kyberien does most of the official decision-making, but he always explains and justifies them to me. He seeks council from me on some matters, but I think it's more for my confidence and self-esteem than anything else. I am trying though. I will do it for my people and for my family, but I do not excel at it and I do not relish it."

She understood what he meant, unsurprised by his revelation. Darien never had shown any interest in government life or politics. His passion had always been the arts; acting, singing, poetry, sculpture and painting. She would need to talk to Kyberien to get an accurate state of Morincian affairs and events. For a moment, she considered asking him of his love life, of his art, of his passions, but the moment seemed wrong. The young man seemed morose, contemplative.

"Sometimes, I need to get away from all the craziness that has been thrust upon me in this life. It can be overwhelming, especially for someone who lacks the skills and knack for it like I do." He took a deep breath. "That's why I come here. It's peaceful. The ships coming and going without end, heading for or coming from some exotic locale far from this place."

"Remember watching them as children, and trying to guess which ship came from what place around the world?" Taraes asked.

"Macien always seemed to know, or at

least he was confident with his answers." Darien stated. "I still wonder, sometimes, where they all are going to or coming from. How many men on those ships look up here and wish they could have a life like mine? Would they be surprised to know sometimes I dream of the freedom they have. The urge for me to throw on a hooded cloak, board one of these ships, and take off to see the world is overwhelming at times."

"Where would you go, Darien, if you could sail away to anywhere in the world right now?" She asked, curious.

Remaining quiet, staring at the sparkling bay, he didn't say anything for a long time. "Nowhere." He finally said. "Anywhere. Everywhere." Then he laughed. She wrapped an arm around him. "It is good to have you home, sister."

XXXI
NEROFIDES

The bow of the ship weaved up and down as it broke across the wavy surface of the sea. Salty spray erupted each time it hit a wave at the right time, splattering Admiral Nerofides as he leaned forward at the front of the ship. He loved it. He, like the rest of the people he commanded, was born to be on the sea. They were born to be mariners, they were born to be on warships. The creak and groan of wood and rope tightening and loosening as the ship rode the waves was familiar and comforting to the man. He grinned as his tongue darted out to lick the salty water speckling his face. Behind him, his marines stood ready. In front of him, a harbor came into view. It was time.

He and his men wore leather and linen armor, the only metal that adorned them were their helms and their swords. Metal rusted, and metal was heavy. A full panoply of armor acted like an anchor if you fell overboard, which was common in sea battles. Marines dressed light, to remain mobile and to stay afloat if they fell in the big drink. The Gods Dru and Kellon held just as much sway in a sea battle as the war God Merseus. This was their realm, and the men of

Petros would follow their rules.

Several transports carried land troops, heavy infantry hoplites to help secure the beachhead once they had taken the water. The marines would storm the land as well, but it was nice to have hoplites to help in the matter. The first mate of his command ship, the Salt Fang, shouted out that enemy vessels were in sight. No doubt that the enemy was taken completely aback by the Petros fleet appearing before them. In fact, they would probably be startled they were considered the enemy at all. No provocations had been made by either side; this was a complete surprise attack initiated by Petros. Like the sea snake emblazoned on their shields and their sails, they would administer a deadly, crippling strike without them knowing what was happening until it was too late.

"When we are in range, Captain Tykonos, give the order to launch our first volley." Nerofides snarled out, his voice dry and raspy. If a snake had a voice that man could hear, it would have been his voice. He gritted his teeth in anticipation of what was to come. For over a year, Petros had been ramping up for a conflict with someone. They had been down and out for a long while, since they were put down in the last rebellion. The rest of Morincia long ago had sacrificed it's freedom to a King, and then that King had submitted to another. Petros had never recognized either as it's master. That desire to remain free had been passed down through the generations since.

Revolts and rebellions had been commonplace over the years, and the Imperial government had usually given the task of quelling these events to Jorbus. The Owls had a navy, true, but nothing to match his own people. Duracee had time and time again aided the Dukes of Jorbus with these battles, since only they could rival the naval might of Petros. Duracee was not here now. They would be busy with problems of their own. Mainland Morincia lay ripe for the picking. The softhearted people of Jorbus didn't have what it took to put the threat his people posed down for good. Nerofides would not make that same mistake.

Silious and Macien had written him near identical letters. Both asked for his assistance in the war that was to come, the war that was here now. It took a little soul searching and some heavy praying to solidify that he was making the right decision. Macien had offered him autonomy, freedom from the Imperial yoke, and a full pardon for all past transgression. It had been tempting. Silious, who had ambitions for the Calidian throne, had made a somewhat more compelling offer; Full pardon, as well as being able to kill his old enemies and remain a dominant force in the Morincian sea. That had been all he needed to read. Better to settle old scores and make new friendships than try and befriend an old enemy.

The omens had been good before sailing,

and Dru and Kellon were pleased with his decision. Now, he was leading part of his force to Portopolis, the largest harbor and port in Morincia. Situated where it was geographically, the city made a wonderful trading post between the Morincian Sea and the Crystal Sea, between Enthaki and Morincia. As the island of Petros fell from favor since the Forging, Portopolis had been on the rise. They had been so self-assured of their superiority for so long, felt like they were safe from pirates and enemy attack. They even flew a sea turtle on their flag, if that wasn't a symbol for feeling armored and protected and safe, then he didn't know what was.

The ships that they started to scramble upon spotting Nerofides approach began to spill out the mouth of the Cothon. The walled double harbor was one of the modern wonders that made Portopolis so remarkable. Huge impregnable stone walls kept enemy ships out, and the warships station in the middle ring had their own entrance. They could button up their merchant fleet if there was a raid, and launch their warships out of a separate, isolated chamber. It offered much protection, true, but also gave them a feeling of superiority and a false sense of security. The sails, teal with the black image of the sea turtle began to catch a little wind and the ships picked up speed. Mostly these triremes were being powered by oars; a lot of which were probably powered by those frog-devil Anurai. Good, he hoped those abominations were on board. The pleasure of watching those creatures die, to burn, added to the flavor of this operation.

"Loose!" He roared, his voice coarse but loud.

Dozens of catapults unloaded in relative unison, some lagging behind. Objects streaked from his ships, arching high up into the sky, then crashing down with tremendous speed. Some hit the harbor, some hit the surface of the sea, and some hit the approaching ships. All exploded upon impact. A conflagration flared as they did, flames engulfing all they could see for a split second. The fires receded rapidly, but did not go out. They continued to burn whatever they had touched, wood, man, cloth, and even the water.

"Reload for another volley!" he shouted, pride filling his voice. It had worked wonderfully. He watched as the ships that had started their way burned, masts ablaze, sails already disintegrated. They were too far off to hear distinct sounds, but he thought he could hear screams carried on the wind. The naphtha they had acquired from the east was such a wonderful naval weapon. The supplier had been more than happy make sure Petros had enough to administer fiery justice against mutual enemies.

The next volleys went farther into the harbor, burning the trapped warships nestled deep within the previously unreachable inner harbor. He would burn this whole city down if he could. He cared not for Portopolis on the grand scale of things, it was a target of convenience, it was a message, and its loss would cripple Morincia for decades. The real prize was next. Once they mopped up this place, most of the fleet was headed west.

XXXII

DIMIDIUS TORBOCK

The gentle rumble was a pleasant way to awaken. He was rocking ever so slightly up and down, with a little side to side, as if he were lying on a boat travelling upon calm waters. The sound of grinding surfaces and animal footfalls was the only thing that gave away they were on land. Daylight emitted through pinholes and gaps in the awning that covered the back of the wagon. Dimidius wiped the last of the sleep from his eyes, stirring back to the land of the living. He felt rested, albeit drained of strength, but rested. Pain from his wounds returned as he began to stretch and move.

The cart he was in was fairly empty, the man who helped them must not of been a very successful merchant. Or, perhaps he was very good, and was simply returning back home after unloading a big supply of something or another. But wouldn't he bring more merchandise back? Torbock didn't know anything about a merchants life and routine. Beside him, and tucked a little deeper in the wagon, lay Vicaro Polemistius.

Asleep and breathing laboriously, the

ambassador looked sickly.

Trembles went through his supine body, his shoulders and head propped up on a bundle of rugs. Without touching the man, Torbock knew he was febrile. His dark hair was matted and wet, contrasting with now pale and sallow flesh. Tiny beads of sweat were welling up on his face, around his eyes and nose. He smelled foul, like decay, like putrefaction. Torbock, rather than disturb the man's fitful resting, began to check on his own wounds.

He peeled back the bandage that clung to his side, and saw the slash had been stitched with gut, and glistened with a viscous, greasy salve. Gingerly he touched the wound, and winced as he applied pressure. It was more a reflexive action, the pain wasn't terrible. He rolled the salve between his thumb and finger, and gave it a smell. It had potent botanicals in it, menthol the most pungent and overpowering of the ingredients. Bright white linen was wrapped nice and snug around his leg wound, and he didn't even bother to check on it. It showed no sign of weeping, and he didn't want to disturb the nice wrap job.

A slight throbbing in his head occurred as he sat up, and he clumsily inspected his scalp, finding a tender mass where that pommel had struck him. He felt somewhat dizzy, and combined with the aroma of the medicine and the wounded man beside him, as well as the stifling heat, the urge for fresh air was overpowering. He needed to exit the confines of the wagon. Contorting his body, he furtively cracked open the back flap to the canvas. The road behind them came into view, and he could see no other travellers. Sticking his head out all the way, he craned his neck to look around the side and forward. No signs of anyone else on the road at all. Pulling himself out, he could smell the freshness of the coast as he emerged from his den.

Kataris and Jacean sat on the bench, driving the wagon. Two of the horses, the ones that had belonged to the Sentinels, trotted alongside the coach, easily keeping pace with the mules that pulled it along. Walking along the running board, he made his way towards the two men who had their backs turned to him.

"Glad to see you up, Sentinel." The bandaged man said, not turning in the slightest to acknowledge him as he crept closer. Jacean turned suddenly, caught off guard by his approaching partner. The look on the young Sentinels face was one of weariness and pure exhaustion. Torbock clasped him on the shoulder, partly as a gesture of greetings, but also for a little extra balance. With a grimace, he lowered himself between the two men.

"Polemistius…" Torbock said, catching his breath. "He does not look good, he…"

"He is dying." Kataris said, little sympathy in his voice. "It will take a while longer, but the worst is ahead for him. The wound he received, I have seen many times."

"There is nothing we, I mean you, can do?" Torbock asked, holding onto hope. "He is a very important part of our mission. We need to keep him alive until we reach Millang'Sek."

"I do not think he will live that long." Kataris said, shaking his head. Chartreuse stains blotted through the bandages on his face, some small, some large. The unseen wounds underneath were weeping extra pus it appeared. "Even if we were to arrive today, he would be in no state to perform any task."

"How close to Petrichoro are we?" Torbock asked, knowing what the man said was true. A strange burning sensation was spreading through his chest, like a squeezing on his heart. He had felt these pains recently, but this was much more intense.

"A day and a half behind us." Kataris stated very matter-of-factly.

"A day and a half." Torbock repeated back. "That is not too… Wait? Behind us? What do you mean?"

"We passed through Petrichoro the day before yesterday." Jacean answered.

"How is that possible?" Torbock said, disbelief in his voice.

"You have been sleeping for several days." Kataris answered. "It should help with your healing process. We should reach Bridgegate in the late morning of tomorrow."

"How did I sleep through all of this?"

Torbock asked. "Even if I was exhausted beyond…"

"I drugged you." Kataris said. The little leper had a habit of cutting people off midsentence it appeared. "You needed it. We have been travelling the entire time, not making camp. The animals rest and find water every once in a while, but we have been on a steady pace the whole way. Jacean here had been awake for most of it. We both catch some naps while we can. Now that Torbock is up, why don't you get some real sleep boy, in the back."

Jacean didn't say a word, just nodded to them, and made his way to where Torbock had just come from. Exhaustion had overtaken any youthful defiance he may have had left. Torbock and Kataris were left alone on the bench, the bandaged side of the merchant's body facing towards his companion. With a glance that flashed the good side of his face, the man looked over at the Sentinel.

"You're healing very well, and very quickly." He mumbled. "Especially that knock you took on the head. You had a skull fracture, I'm certain of it. That was why I needed to put you to sleep. I apologize if you feel violated for that. Have you always healed quickly, like this?"

"You did not violate any trust. I have none in you to violate." Torbock said, almost meanly. For some reason, he did trust this man, and it bothered him deeply that he did. Why should he trust him so easily? "You are a trained healer, I take it? Expert work with the bandaging."

"The bandaging skills come from plenty of practice." Kataris said, waving his wrapped hand. "And I did some healing in the past, for a small part of my life. I was trained by the legions. I used to be a soldier, but was maimed badly in a fight. Then I became a Medicus with the legion since I couldn't fight any longer. Soon, I couldn't even do *that* any longer and I left. I couldn't exactly forget what I had learned."

"What legion did you serve with?" Torbock asked, automatically. It was a common inquiry amongst soldiers.

Kataris was silent for a moment. "The First." He managed to say after a while.

"In the capital? As a battle field Medicus?" Torbock was surprised. That was an unusual posting.

"Yes, in the capital, amongst other locale. Why don't you tell me about yourself, Dimidius Torbock?" Kataris asked. "Other than the fact you are a half-Homithan former slave turned Sentinel."

"Not much else to say." He grumbled. "That's my life summed up in a sentence."

"Why are you going to Akkedis? To Millang'Sek?" Kataris asked, rubbing the side of his face with his bandaged hand. "What was the nature of your mission with the ambassador?"

"I can't say." Torbock responded. "I'm

sorry." He added on the end.

"Hmmmm." Kataris hummed. "Are you bound to silence as part of your mission directive? Or is it you just do not trust me?"

"Sentinels do not commonly discuss the nature of their assignments with citizens. For security reasons amongst others." Torbock explained.

"Is that so? Even when there are so few of you on a long, distant duty?" Kataris looked at him with one good eye. "I was under the impression that it was a necessity at times to work with the local population. In fact, isn't that the reason you have that fancy medallion? So others recognize your authority and are required to aid you?"

Torbock shifted uneasily as he stared back at the man that was driving the carriage. That squeezing in his chest intensified, and so did the burning, radiating feeling.

"Perhaps. But this is a different matter entirely. It comes from Imperial high command, a matter of state, very important. I'm sorry." Torbock began to lock up, not wanting to say anymore.

"The Emperor?" Kataris attempted a grotesque impersonation of a whistle, his bandaged lips or lack thereof made it difficult to impossible. "From before he went into his coma? I thought that Morincian fellow who was calling himself a 'consul' was in charge nowadays. A consul of an Empire? I was told since I was a boy that an Empire needed a Emperor." He chuckled a bit, but Torbock didn't react and remained stone-faced.

"You must be going to reclaim that Legion stationed down on the Sout'l River. The Consul must feel it is time for them to be brought into this growing conflict. Smart move on his part; any force that can utterly destroy the Dutrigian army is a force to be reckoned with. So the Ambassador is the negotiator, and you two are his body guards?" The man slowly shook his head. "Times certainly have changed. Did you know that not too long ago, Sentinels themselves were the ambassadors, and they represented the Ebon Throne in diplomatic matters? Now you are just guards, mere security for the Upper Class. What do you know of the history of your Order?"

"What do you know? Since I'm sure you are going to tell me." Torbock said, intrigued yet slightly insulted. The opportunity to divert attention away from the details of their mission was enticing as well, and he steered the conversation that way.

"The Order of the Sentinels was founded a long time ago, even before the Forging." The man said with authority. "Back then, they say, anyone could become a Sentinel, as long as they swore to protect mankind in Domiterra. They were a powerful force, and even held sway over the old Kings at one point in history. As Calidia grew into an Empire and expanded, the Order of the Sentinels eventually were engulfed within its borders. The Order lost its autonomy, and lost touch with its original purpose. Where they once stood as a force for protection of human law, they soon stood as upholders of Imperial law and the Emperors will. They forgot the mystery of what they protected and they forgot what secrets they were founded under and for."

"Sounds like a very melodramatic saga. How did you come across this information, I have never heard it before?" Torbock asked.

"I consider myself a historical enthusiast." Kataris said. "Do you know what that symbol on your medallion stands for?"

Torbock just shook his head, and proffered a guess. "It's an old glyph, from the Age of Kings, that translates to 'Sentinel'. That's what I have always been told, at least."

"Not quite." And Kataris chuckled, which turned into a wet, chunky cough. "I will tell you, but not today. That's enough Sentinel talk for now. We have the rest of the journey to discuss such things; we don't want to run out of content so soon. The two of us still have a lot of time left."

"Very well. No more Sentinel talk. Why the bandages? What happened to you?" Torbock asked very forwardly.

"That is a long story." Kataris said.

"As you said, we have much time still." Torbock countered.

"I will give you the short story now, and

the long another day." And the man's face and mass of bandages contorted into a smile. "I was in the Boglands, past the neck to Akkedis. It's just beyond where the West River flows into the Bay of Dru. Have you ever been there?"

Torbock replied no.

"Good. Don't ever go there. Terrible place, its hell on earth. If the bogs themselves don't claim you, then the plant's and animals will. Insects, snakes, and beasts, and every type of poison you can imagine. Then there are the monsters; if you make it through everything else, there are still the monsters. Boglins, we call them. Clever I know, original. I made it out alive, but this..." He gestured towards his bandages. "This disease came back with me. It's been slowly killing me ever since."

"I'm sorry." Torbock said genuinely. "Is it..."

"No, it's not contagious, don't worry." Kataris cut him off.

"I was going to ask if it is painful." Torbock corrected.

"Yes. It is. I tell myself I've gotten used to it, but it still hurts. Some days it's worse than others." Kataris took in a deep breath and let it out, bandages stretching and fluttering as he did so.

"Do you ever have visions? Dreams?" Kataris blurted out, in the same directness he had just been asked about his disfigurement.

"I dream, yes." Torbock said. "Most

everyone does I understand."

"True." Kataris conceded. "But do yours seem very vivid, very strange? And do you ever dream while you are awake?"

Torbock didn't know how to answer that. After contemplating for what seemed to him a lot longer than it actually was, he said yes.

"I see." Kataris said. And that was the end of it. They remained silent for hours. When they spoke again next, it had nothing to do with their pasts or history lessons. They rumbled down the road, towards Bridgegate and Akkedis.

*   *   *

They stopped because they needed to rest. The animals deserved it, and so did the travellers. It had been over a day since they had passed through Bridgegate, and much longer since the wagon had stopped for more than an hour. The fortress of Bridgegate had been sealed up extremely tightly, word of the attack on and the fall of Dutrigi had only freshly reached the soldiers within, and tensions were high. Torbock knew that they would not be allowed to pass without some persuasion.

Even the Dutrigians, in such a state of civic disaster, their entire world turned upside down, recognized Torbock's authority as a Sentinel, and he was allowed conference with an officer. This had consisted of the Commander shouting from the battlements above, down to the lone figure on the far side of the moat below. After some identifying procedures and request for documents, they were allowed to pass through into Akkedis. Torbock presented the Dutrigian officer with both his official pass from Consul Macien, and also with the news about the fall of Dutrigi. The commander let on that they had found out not long before Torbocks arrival. They would continue to remain vigilant in their posting until someone who had left the fort returned with orders. Until then, they would hold Bridgegate.

Now, a days march later, the wagon they travelled upon was halted. They were all tired, but only Polemistius was dying. Kataris had told them he would not make it through the night. His health had taken a drastic downturn very suddenly. Up until a few hours earlier, Polemistius had been awake and talking. For the last several days, it actually seemed like his condition was improving. Torbock had held hours worth of conversation with the man as they lay in the back of the wagon. They had discussed matters of state, the relationship between Millangor and man, Millangor and the Empire, and the Millangor and the Hyerians.

They both knew he was dying, and it was Polemistius dying chance to ensure he did something right for the Gods to judge him by. Perhaps, before he crossed over, he could give someone the tools to make things better. His last words to Torbock before loosing consciousness had been; "This is it then. Just gray."

The Sentinel thought long and hard on those words, trying to keep this man in his mind as a sign of respect as he was about to perish. Torbock did not know the man well, did not even really care for him from what little he did know, but it was the right thing to do. Covered in blankets, by the fire, Vicaro Polemistius shivered and trembled, breathing in agonal, rasping gasps. Torbock had half a mind to slit the man's throat, to end his misery. It would also end their suffering through his suffering. As if he could read his mind, Kataris purposefully and quietly made his way towards the ambassador, with something that glimmered in the firelight held in his good hand. It was not steel or any kind of metal. It was glass. Carefully removing a cork stopper from the vile he carried, the man reverently poured a lilac colored syrup into the others gapping mouth.

Two very deep, loud breath and Polemistius stopped moving. He was gone. Kataris methodically sealed the tube and replaced it in his cloak.

"Gather rocks." The merchant said. "We will build him a cairn. That way, the animals won't get to him. While we forage for these stones, let's all eulogize this man in our own minds. Nothing needs to be spoken."

It took several hours for them to find enough rocks to make a respectable sized mound. When they were nearly done, and

Jacean was out looking for a good-sized stone, Kataris took the chance and beckoned for Torbock for a moment of conversation. Both men were sweating from the labor of moving the stones, breathing fast and deep.

"When this is all over, you will want to find me. Please, do so at your earliest convenience." Kataris dabbed at the bandaged side of his face, sweat and pus oozing through his now dirty wrapping.

"What do you mean?" Torbock pressed, confused.

"When the fighting is done, this war is over. Find me, I will have answers. I will be at the ruins outside Mt. Ikari. Do you know them?" The man asked.

"Yes, the ancient Ikaran ruins? You will just be there waiting for me? Indefinitely?" Torbock asked.

"Don't feel too special. I have a little trinket shop set up there. It turns a nice little profit." Kataris said. "You will find me there, don't forget it when the time comes."

"Ok. It may be many years before I find myself in that part of the Empire." Torbock said in an attempt to brace the man for the fact that he probably would never go.

"I will wait, I have nowhere to be. When I was bandaging you up at Dutrigi, I noticed that you had many scars. They were obviously made from different blades and different weapons. I noticed you had on your left side of your rib cage. It was kind of shaped like a cross or an 'X'." Kataris made a cross with a finger from each hand. "What weapon gave you that scar?"

"I don't know. I have a lot of scars, as you said. Maybe it was two different cuts overlapping." Torbock was perplexed by the question.

Just then, Jacean came crashing back into the small campsite, breathing hard and flustered. "Put out the fire! Put out the fire!" Frantically, his sandaled feet kicked sandy soil onto the campfire.

"Jacean! Tell me what's happening!" Torbock reached for his sword as he spoke.

"Saurians! Approaching from the south." He gasped and spat out. "The neck is narrow, they will find us!"

"We are in Akkedis, Jacean. Saurians will be out and about, not all are threats. We are here to talk with them after-all. What did you see?" Torbock relaxed a bit, realizing that his protégé was more likely than not getting riled up over nothing.

"Hyerians!" Jacean said, continuing to extinguish the fire. Torbock felt the bottom of his stomach drop out. "A whole army of them, marching north, towards us. Hyerians!"

"This far north?" Torbock said skeptically, and felt bad for not fully believing his partner. But this sounded unbelievable. "Show me."

"I will get everything here in order.

Return quickly." Kataris demanded, beginning to prepare his wagon and the beasts.

The two sentinels slowly made their way to the edge of the high ground they had been camping upon. Upon reaching the precipice, Torbock's heart sank down to where his stomach had lurched earlier. An Army of Hyerians was marching north, a column making its way past them and towards the direction of Bridgegate. The how and the why didn't matter at he moment, all that mattered was that it was true. Thousands of them, all armed and armored in their strange style. It was one of the most frightful sights he had ever laid eyes upon.

XXXIII
MACIEN

Hammering and pounding floated in from the background. Distant shouts of orders from officers and grunts of laborers wafted in through the semi closed tent flap. It was still daylight, and the army was averaging 25 miles a day, a fairly grueling pace, especially since the 1st Legion hadn't done that much marching in recent time. The fort was being erected around them, as the senior officers spilled over maps and intelligence. Macien felt a slight twinge of guilt and a pang of envy for the men outside. They were doing all the hard work, while these men toiled away in the confines of the command tent. Part of him yearned to walk outside, pick up a shovel or mattocks, and jump in to help with the construction. That was the easy way out, his job now was much more grueling and less rewarding.

Aides were compiling scrolls that had been filtering in from riders, men toiled away on tablets, updating figures. Secretary Amicus diligently filtered through the stacks, along with Tribunes and a small force of servants. The map had been unfurled, and all the pieces representing the forces were carefully placed in their spots. They were the same pieces that had adorned the map of the Imperial Chambers, but the map was different. They did not need a map of anything other than Domiterra and it's surrounding provinces; Homitha and the rest of the world would have to wait.

Legate Attius, in full armor, was conferring with a few of his staff. Pride was emanating from the old warrior, to be back on the campaigning field after being stuck in the Capital for so long. That same feeling was shared by most of the black clad soldiers that were marching west with the 1st. They were some of the best fighters the Empire had to offer, and they had earned their stripes in situations like this. Rather than have their skills atrophy and wither as a policing force, they were doing what they were meant to do. If Macien lived long enough, maybe he would make some changes to the way the 1st legion was staffed. He shook that thought from his mind, and returned to the task at hand.

"Let's begin. It will be a long night already." Macien said, and men began to get into position around the table. Aides and servants continued to feverously do their bookkeeping, knowing the Consul's request had nothing to do with them. Macien was still in his silver armor, minus his helm, the cerulean blue cloak of Jorbus hanging from his shoulders. Sword on his hip, his hand resting on the owl that was carved into the hilt guard, he gazed around expectantly.

Reading from the first scroll in a pile of them, Amicus started. "It appears that the initial intelligence of Silious marching south into Lacerterra have been confirmed. Multiple reports about a battle outside the walls of Dutrigi…" Amicus' face drained of color as he swallowed and pause. "According to this, my lord, Dutrigi has fallen." A silence filled the tent, even the aids slowed as the words were uttered. Only the din of construction from outside continued on without interruption.

"What do we know?" Macien asked, keeping his composure. The reality of the conflict had just been reaffirmed to him, and he felt sick. Kruegius filled his thoughts for a moment as Amicus reread the information on the scroll.

"Silious marched south, bypassing Trimontis and any of the towns in the foothills of the Vaus range. Dutrigi met him in the field, and they were crushed. Reports differ on how the battle played out, but all state it was an overwhelming victory for Silious and his Frontier Army. He holds the city, and apparently, the Dutrigian army was completely destroyed." Amicus set the scrolls down. "Petrichoro was taken at the same time, unknown what happened to the small garrison force the Dutrigians had within. Reports say he and his Frontier Army are beginning to head west now. "

"How long, do the scouts say, before he will arrive in Cortinum?" Macien asked, balling and un-balling his fists as he spoke. "And just to clarify, from this point on, this treasonous force lead by that man will be referred to as what they are, *rebels*. Nothing else."

"Very good, my lord." Amicus nodded. "The rebel army is slow moving, it appears. Depending on what route they take, and if they meet military resistance in Stathum, travel time will vary greatly for them. We have no solid evidence, and no way of knowing…"

"Extrapolate!" Macien said frustrated. "Look at all we have at our disposal. Make an educated guess, all of you. You all have great experience in this field, let's not let it go to waste."

"Initial reports say the Frontier Army force, excuse me my Lord, *the Rebel force*, is three legions strong." Amicus responded quickly. "That was just the force seen at Dutrigi. As you have indicated previously, they more than likely have a more sizeable army than that. If they are trying to move fast and not wait for reinforcements to marry up with them, and based on our own pace, I'd say we arrive in Cortinum just before they do."

"I concur with that, Consul." Attius chimed in. "Three legions moving together is a slow process, a long baggage train. We are only one Legion, we need less supply, smaller camps, and have greater mobility."

"At least we have a rough idea of our schedule and time constraints. It's a race to Cortinum, then." Macien nodded assent. "What of our other forces in the area? Our own troop movements and the proscription list?"

"Proscriptions went well, according to the reports. Most of those detained are being transported under escort back to the capital. As far as legion locations," And Amicus pointed to the map. "With plans under way to recall Legion VIII from Akkedis and Legion VI from it's garrison in Parym on Luctantum, as well as Legions we already have in the immediate theatre, including the 1st, we will have… five legions."

"Only three will make it to Cortinum in time. And we don't know how strong the full size of the enemy force is." This came from a senior Tribune. Ardermius was his name if Macien remembered correctly. "Our best bet, Consul, is if we are set on facing the enemy at Cortinum, will be to hunker down there until our reinforcements arrive. Five on three is better than three on three."

"Unless our waiting also brings *their* reinforcements into the field. Plus, we have the Cortinum reserve force to serve as extra manpower." This came from Attius. "We will need to hit them before they get their footing in the area."

"What of the other legions in Domiterra?" This came from Amicus. "The 3rd is being held back as a contingency. The 5th is in Aciem, and the 4th is stationed up by Arvum. If we start moving them now, they should be in position for our counter attack soon."

"They stay where they are, for the time being." Macien interjected. "If we move them around, we leave the capital and key cities unprotected from other attacks. Silious and his Rebels have a clean run up in the north, over through the Prau Valley. We need to maintain a presence in that region as a deterrent. The 3rd down by Kauvor will remain to protect the area until the Morincian Phalanxes arrive to support the capital lands."

"The 7th legion was ordered to march to Dutrigi prior to the battle that happened. Current projections put them in Stathum. They have been given orders to remain there, sir." Amicus read from a scroll. The secretary was doing a fine job of filling in for the vacant position of Master of Foot and Master of Troops until the replacements arrived. "What are your wishes for them now, sir?" The secretary stared at him coldly, awaiting a reply for his aids to scribble down and send with a runner.

"Hold on a second." This came from Attius. "Silious will be marching through that area soon, with the same army that obliterated the Dutrigians. Keeping that single Legion there would mean certain death for them. They need to fall back, and join the 9th in Cortinum. Along with the Cortinum Reserve force, and when we arrive, it's the only way we can field an army large enough to win this fight."

"I agree." This was from Ardermius. "Stringing our forces along, and allowing them to be picked off one by one is what Silious wants. Strength in numbers is what we excel at, remove that advantage, and we will fall just like Dutrigi."

"But," This came from Sonopius, the old Duke and cavalryman. "If they retreat, fall back from Stathum, Silious and the rebels will march unopposed all the way to Cortinum, with no resistance to slow them down. Then the fighting in Cortinum will begin before the 1st arrives, and the city may fall before we even get there. Perhaps the will be a necessary sacrifice."

"Sir!" This came from the Secretary, who was thumbing through a scroll midway through the pile, the others waving wildly in his other hand. "Sources also tell us that Petros has launched it's fleet."

"That's good news." Macien nodded. "With Duracee and our other fleets tied up with patrolling for pirates and keeping the Southern Sea safe, I sent a request to Archon Nerofides of Petros, requesting his fleet be utilized by us in this endeavor. They should be sailing west and to our location to assist with our efforts."

"These reports indicate that they are sailing north from Petros, towards Morincia. And it is an invasion fleet." Amicus finished. Macien had a terrible feeling bubble up inside.

Junæa and the children, Taraes and her kids, Jorbus, Morincia. It was all in danger. Betrayal by the Snakes of Petros, he should not have been surprised.

"Duracee, they need to be notified. Jorbus. Portopolis, Athyrtun. They are all targets, and they are the only ones who can do anything to defeat Petros now." Macien said, shocked.

"They are probably more aware of the situation than any of us by now." Attius said. "The Archons of the cities, they will know what to do. Princess Mallea and her advisors will send the appropriate relief forces."

"What else do you have, Amicus?" Macien said, almost going through the motions, still processing what he had just been told.

"I just received word that Vitruvian forces have been spotted along the west bank of the Brachus River, marching towards the North Jetori. And in what I had previously thought was unrelated, rumors of riots taking place in Enthaki, in both Sercylum and Æstus. There's nothing too credible to that, just a rumor. The Prefects of that area haven't sent any official word yet, my Lord."

Macien grimaced and ran a hand through his hair. It became clear what was going on now, so obvious once it was too late to prevent. "Silious is igniting a multi-front conflict. We can win in a single pitched campaign, and he knows that. He wants to divide and conquer. This was the same technique the insurgency used to overthrow the Cylathian Old Dynasty. Its easy to pick us apart from multiple fronts, and it will be testament if we can just hold everything together and keep it from crumbling. Like a pack of wolves taking down a giant Gray Bear, he hopes to wear us down. I expect more information of revolts and attacks will come trickling in soon."

Silence filled the room as Macien paused, placing his hands on the map. He watched as junior officers took down the Bull icon that represented Dutrigi, and the smaller one that represented Petrichoro. Only the small bull on Bridgegate remained. He watched as they slide the Snake of Petros north, it's destination unknown. He studied the board, and contemplated his next move.

XXXIV
ATHELTIADES

He had been dreaming of his father. Since
he had heard the news of the fall of Dutrigi, all
he could think about was his father, their last
time together, and that prophecy. While awake,
he thought of his fathers certain death. It played
out in different ways each time, a sword, a
spear, fire, or an arrow. Chances are he would
never know the truth behind how it happened.
When he slept however, he dreamed of his past,
of fond memories with the old man. These
dreams were more painful than the imaginary
truths of his death that acted out in his mind.

When they awoke him, it had almost
been a relief. By the awkward look on the
soldiers' faces that were standing in his sleeping
chambers, he was certain he had been thrashing
in his sleep. With a folded finger, he wiped
crusty sleep and the moist ghosts of tears that
had built up during his fitful slumber. They had
told him it was early morning, or very late at
night, depending on how you looked at it. Either
way, judging by how truly dark the sky was
through his small window, he knew Shaardon
ruled the Earth. Still not entirely awake, he
suited up his armor as the soldiers filled him in

on the situation. Movement had been spotted south of the fortress, and the Watch Captain had scrambled for a full call to arms.

Tension and emotions were running high since the shocking news of Dutrigi being taken by Silious and his forces. Hopefully, this was call to arms nothing more than a false alarm, some one being overly diligent when it game to their watch duty. The fortress had been completely closed since the news had arrived about the outbreak of civil war. The only exception had been those Sentinels and that ambassador, who were going to retrieve the 8th legion and bring them home, out of the bowels of Saurian country. Pulling his fingerless leather gloves on, he then reached for his arm guards. They were relics, made of actual bronze, not the Akkedan variety. Generations of his family had worn them, and his father passed them on to him as soon as he finished his March as a young man. With his helm under the crook of his arm, he strolled out to briefing.

The ramparts bustled with men. It seemed like every soldier in the fortress had arrived before he did. Scanning through the crowds, he looked for the black and white checkered crest of Commander Lysander. All around him men were occupied with tasks, the battlements an ocean of life and motion. Some men hastily carried bundles of spears and javelins to wrought iron caches that had long ago been installed for just this. Archers made their way to various locations, some running up the watch towers with huge quivers of arrows. A few teams were assembling scorpion ballista, and attaching them to bases that were affixed into the stonewalls. This was no mere false alarm, something credible had been spotted in the darkness beyond.

Lysander was conferring with some captains, pointing out into the night's landscape. They were huddle around a brazier, which lit them up like ghostly shades. Torches all along the battlements made it so the men could see what they were doing in preparation for whatever was coming.

"We have at least 3 hours until sunrise." The Commander was explaining. "What they are waiting for, I do not know. I want torches, lots of torches ready to be lit brought up here as soon as possible. Captain Rylikos, make that happen. Once they start against us, I want to light up the ground down there so we can see what we are dealing with." He spotted Atheltiades. "Commander, I will fill you in on the situation, walk with me." His voice was urgent and slightly frantic as he spoke.

"We sent a routine scouting party out just after dark last night. They never returned. This prompted further investigation, and a secondary scouting party discovered a large force of Hyerian Saurians lurking just beyond that knoll. The scouts said they were crouching, waiting, not making camp, but also not advancing. They estimated the size of the force as being in the thousands. Now that we are aware of them, we have spotted a few creeping closer and closer, spying on our situation. Any moment, they may rush us. What they are waiting for is anyone's guess."

"But it is giving us time to prepare," Atheltiades added. "So let them wait. The longer they do, the more efficient our bolstered defenses will be."

"Exactly." Lysander said. "Just our luck, not much moonlight tonight. These monsters can leap out of the dark and we wouldn't know until it was happening. You! Soldier, move that scorpion over to *that* base. This one only gives you half a field to fire on because of that tower."

There was no question to anyone on the battlements that Lysander was in charge. Everyone made way for him when he paced past, and when he shouted everyone looked at him expectantly. Even though he and Atheltiades were both the same rank, the way the man spoke, the way the man carried himself left no doubt that he was the leader. Just as Atheltiades was considering putting his own helmet on, since Lysander's was emanating command presence with his own crest, a hand fell on his shoulder.

"Atheltiades, I want you in the West Tower." Lysander said. "You will be my eyes above when the sun rises. I've placed archers and peltasts on both towers. Each tower is also equipped with one heavy scorpion. You have complete control over that operation. Down below, in the quad, we are getting the heavy Onagers into position. You will be calling down ranging and adjustments to them as they fire. Any questions?"

"Any word on reinforcements?" Atheltiades asked.

"Dutrigi has fallen. What reinforcements?" Lysander scoffed.

"We should send messengers as soon as possible. To the Empire, to Trimontis, to… to everywhere." He clarified.

"No. We need every man where they are, we can't. The Polemarch will return with his contingent of troops soon. Until then, we can't spare a single body." And with that, he turned and the conversation ended. Lysander began to shout orders down to the soldiers in the quad below, and then moved farther down the wall, making adjustments and corrections. With a deep breath, Atheltiades looked out into the darkness beyond, and saw only night. Blackness was everywhere and omnipresent. The torches were ruining their night vision. He then craned his neck and looked up at the top of the west tower. It was dauntingly high, appearing to be much taller at night than during the day. That would be his home for the next…day? How long could they hold out? He may even die up there, along with all these other men. Well, no use in stalling, he thought.

Starting his walk towards the portico entrance of the tower, the barking of Lysander in the background ceased, and a cacophony of shouts and screams broke the air. Spinning out of pure instinct, Atheltiades tried to see through the rush of men and the fluttering of red cloaks. A brief window parted amongst the men for a mere moment, and he could see what had happened. Lysander, and a few others close to him, had been riddled with spears. Nasty, roughhewn spears. Dozens of them protruded from the frame of the commander, who was instantly dead, lying in a pool of blood that reflected torchlight. Just as everyone manning the fort knew Lysander was in charge, so did everyone that was preparing to attack it, apparently.

Wide-eyed, Atheltiades didn't know what to do for a moment. All he could do was stare at the lifeless eyes of the other Commander, as he gazed down and away at nothing in particular. It did not take long for discipline to start and break down. Someone on the far end of the battlement gave the order to return fire. The twang of scorpions unloading, and the grunts of men as they threw javelins filled the air. Taking his eyes away from the dead Commander, the realization of what needed to be done dawned on him. He was the senior ranking officer now.

Even though he knew it would make him a target, he slammed his helmet on his head and began to move. With a final passing glance at the corpse of the previous commander, he started to give orders. There was nothing to lose, and nothing to gain; it just needed to get done.

"Cease fire! Cease fire!" He screamed, his voice thundering with authority that he rarely exercised. Even being a Training Commander, the need to use this voice had been infrequent. Conditions like this only came around on a battlefield.

Restraint took over as the soldiers ingrained discipline returned, and the javelin throwing and scorpion loading wound down to a trickle. Captains echoed his command down the line. Vigilantly, the Dutrigians with ranged weapons watched the darkness below, and the rest looked at their Commander intently. Now that he had *taken* command, responsibility for these men, he *needed* to command.

Instincts son, do not ignore them. They are the Gods way of speaking directly to you. Atheicles words from a long time ago resurfaced in his mind.

"Throw all the torches as far afield as you can. Dump the braziers over the edge! They make the enemy see us, but we can't see them. Now! Everyone else, form a shield wall, two deep. Protect from lobbed projectiles."

Torches streaked and cartwheeled across the night's sky like a close meteor shower. They landed in a patchwork of flame and embers. The ground below began to glow in pockets, and for the first time, they could clearly see the foe.

The red skinned Saurians scampered away as the flames came down and settled at their feet. They wore a hodgepodge collection of armor, some wearing no armor at all. Some had helmets, some had breastplates, and some wore what looked like Imperial legionary armor. Most carried spears and battle-axes, the weapon of choice for a Saurian. The occasional sword was seen glinting as the horde flowed across the ground. Some carried the flag of Hyeri, the black star inside an inverted yellow triangle, inside an upright black triangle. Just then, another volley of spears shot towards them, and it took Atheltiades a moment to comprehend what was happening. He had been so enamored with the surreal sight of a Hyerian army assaulting Bridgegate, he was slow to react and get his shield up. Multiple objects struck his round hoplon shield, careening off and jolting his entire body.

"Man the scorpions!" He yelled. "Provide a shield cover for those on the trigger! Shoot at what you can see, don't waste the ammunition otherwise!" The men did as they had been commanded.

"Archers!" He shouted up to the west tower. A junior officer peered down over the battlement up above. "Fire at will!" The officer acknowledged, and relayed the order across to the East Tower. Atheltiades made his way to the various battle stations, and made contact with the officers that were in charge of each one. Eventually, the torches that Lysander had ordered to the wall had arrived. Half of them were lit and thrown below, making the enemy targets that much more visible. Looking to the horizon, Atheltiades saw no sign whatsoever of the sun beginning its assent, not even a hint of dark gray.

Continuing to walk the fortification, the Commander saw that they were taking minimal casualties, while the Hyerian bodies were starting to pile up on the field beyond the trench. Slaves that usually worked within the fort on routine housekeeping tasks had been ordered to the walls. They were carrying off the dead or the maimed down to the quad beneath. Keeping the walkways clear of them made it better for maneuvering and for morale. Medicii were setting up a surgery station in the open quad down below.

The Hyerians continued to press on, relentless. Stockpiles of ancient weapons; spears, arrows and sling stones were all being pulled out of storage caches to finally be used. The shield wall held, the enemy spears occasionally finding a gap and the flesh behind. Saurians were incredibly strong beings, and the spears they threw, although crude by Dutrigian standards, were devastating when thrown by one of them. Rocks, which varied in size from a fist to a skull, were thrown or lobbed up into the ranks on the wall. Like the spears, they were thrown with great strength behind them and were deadly if they hit you. Some were thrown in a straight line, smashing into a shield or parapet with a crack or thud, while others were lobbed up, trying to reign down and brain the Dutrigians from above.

All in all, they were holding out well. Projectiles and ammunition were being burned through at a tremendous rate, but since the fort had accumulated such a massive stockpile over generations, that was acceptable. They had the trench between them and the enemy, and that meant the Hyerians couldn't get near the walls. The ancient fortress had never fallen, never been overrun. He remembered with a twinge of pain and irony that the same thing had always been said about Dutrigi itself.

Wiping sweat from his brow, he rechecked the horizon. Still dark, but he thought he could see the sky lightening a bit. That was a good sign. Down below, he watched the ground slowly disappear; it was being covered with dead and wounded Hyerians, their leaking ichor, and was peppered with spears, arrows, and scorpion bolts. From out of the edge of darkness, a wave of Saurians came sprinting across the field. They were almost completely covered in body armor, but carried no weapons. Saurians were impossibly fast when they ran, faster than any human. The enemy spearmen continued to throw volley after volley as this new wave of soldiers weaved between them.

Atheltiades watched as these armored Hyerians began to pick up the dead that littered the ground, and started to hurl them down into the moat at the base of the wall. His heart sank. They worked quickly and wantonly, throwing the corpses into the water below like cordwood into a fire. A few of the Saurians thrown in were still alive, only wounded, and struggled in vane as they were thrown to the crush below.

"Target the ones that are filling the ditch!" He ordered, and the men complied. As these scavengers started to die, their partners began to throw them in as well. Others flooded onto the field to replace those that were being killed. The more they killed the Saurians, the more these morbid engineers were given material to build their counter defenses. A shimmer of gold broke through in the east as the sun finally decided to rise. At least that was something.

XXXV
MIKUS DERRATA

It was late afternoon when they reached the palisades to the castra on the east side of Cortinum. The men were drained from days upon days of marching, but were still relatively fresh as far as today was concerned. Mikus Derrata waited in formation, full kit on his back, as contact was made with the 9th Legion that manned the fort. Mikus may have been new to the Legions, and he had yet to fight in real combat, but even he could realize the fort was on the wrong side of the city. Silious was coming from the west, where he had just smashed Dutrigi, a walled city. Cortinum was famously un-walled, and this castra was on the wrong side.

The 9th and the 7th Legions should have had the foresight to mitigate this problem by moving the fort already. But here it was, in the same spot it had been erected during recruitment for the Homithan campaign. The Legate was inside with his staff, conferring with the General and the Legate of the 9th. The 7th Legion had been making its way to Dutrigi prior to the crushing battle there, and apparently it was returning to Cortinum. Imperial High

Command had chosen this city as the next battlefield, and it was now a race to see who could field the strongest army, and be the first to do it.

After many hours of standing and waiting, hours that could have been spent building defenses, they received their orders. They were to spend the night in the current fort, and at first light, they would be notified of the plan for tomorrow. Setting up the tents within the half of the camp that was empty, vacated by the 7th when they went on the march, had been quick and easy. They didn't do a full set up, just tents and command posts. Each squad was on it's own for dinner since the mess hall was now a thing of the past. Fabian and Calvus were toiling over the meal, adding ingredients to the big cauldron hanging over the fire pit outside the tent.

Most of the men were gambling with dice, having finished set up and not yet fed and not on sentry duty tonight. Tilo was sitting by the cooking fire on a log, watching the game but not partaking in the action. Everyone else was playing, even Phenton and Strasa. Once they had their meal, Mikus had a suspicion that the duo would disappear from the rest of them. For now, the whole squad was together and having fun. Even Tilo was smiling at the banter that was being exchanged as the game unfolded.

"Fuckin' Dutrigi." Titus Vinius bellowed, arms crossed as someone else was rolling dice.

"I can't believe this is real. Silious smashed Dutrigi. It's a civil war."

"Dutrigi was one of the strongest forces in the entire Empire." Decanus Torantum said. "They must have put up a good fight regardless."

"They were fucking wiped out, gone." Phenton said. "Their entire army destroyed. And we are going up against that same enemy."

"With what, one, maybe two more Legions for reinforcements?" Strasa added. "It's suicide. They are just throwing us against them to try and slow them down from reaching the Capital. Dutrigi couldn't stop them, how can our handful of Legions?"

"My friend in the Legate's staff told me that Consul Macien is marching our way with the 1st Legion. He will be here in a few days to take command of the army and bolster our force." Vinius said.

"I'd feel better having him leading us than General Validus." Vinius said. "The old General is a fool."

"Don't speak such things, it's treason." Torantum ordered loudly. He then lowered his voice to a conspiratorial tone. "At least not that loud."

"What!" Vinius shouted. "We all know it. Look at some of the decisions he's made recently. Look at this camp! What good does it do here?"

"Legate Acadius has a good head on his

shoulders." Ferro said, dumping a cup full of dice down onto a wooden board. He cursed under his breath as he saw his roll, and picked them back up to roll once again. "Acadius will be trying to talk some sense into the General."

"In the meantime, I have a feeling we will all be doing some serious construction in the next few days." The Decanus spoke, picking up the dice for his roll. "Let's all try and be like old Tilo and get a good nights rest tonight." Tilo said nothing, just continued sharpening his dagger with a whetstone as if he had not heard the comment. The meal was just about to be served when the commotion started.

Sentries were shouting, groups of soldiers in full panoply running across the camp. Torantum ordered everyone to get battle ready. Mikus felt his heart hammer in his chest as he donned his mail shirt. It took several minutes for the squad to get fully geared up. Soon, the entire Century was together and making it's way to file in with the whole Cohort. It didn't take long for the rumors to begin floating down the line of what this was all about. A force had been seen approaching the city. Everyone was on edge. Men shivered from the chill in the air and from anticipation as well as the fear of the unknown.

After nearly an hour of stressful waiting, scouts returned with the information they had been holding out for. Apparently, the 7th had made it's way back into the city and was heading to the castra. What was left of the 7th that was. Either by choice or by force, they had engaged the Silious Army outside Stathum while withdrawing. They immediately realized it was a lost cause, and during the battle, they had fled. Forced to leave their baggage train and have their cavalry hold off any pursuers, they had marched here as fast as they could. They hadn't stopped to rest for several days. The men were ragged, bloody and bruised. The arriving force amassed outside the gates to the fortress, and after some conferring with Officers, they were allowed inside. The 2nd, which was fully geared and ready to fight, evacuated their own camp, giving up their tents to the exhausted men of the 7th.

The Legion was a little above half strength. Just over 3,000 men had made the march. Like drunken partygoers, the 7th filed in and collapsed on cots that were not their own. Blood, sweat and grim still clung to their fatigued flesh. Some slept in mail, other stripped naked and collapsed. All were asleep within an hour or less. The men of the second took shifts sleeping and being on active alert. They rotated in and out of the vacant tents that remained unused by the members of the 7th that had perished before arriving here tonight. Mikus and his Century had first watch, and spent the rest of the night attempting to sleep. For him, it did not come easy.

In the morning, the sun rose in a blood red light and everyone took it for an ominous

sign from the Gods. The 7th were allowed a day
of rest, so it fell on the 2nd and the 9th to start the
infrastructure project. The General had finalized
the details of the plan with input from the
Legates, and special attention had been paid to
the information the staff of the 7th had to offer
on the strength and abilities of the enemy. The
Cortinum Phalanx offered up whatever
assistance was needed by the Legions preparing
for the battle.

　　The plan was very straightforward; the
city had no walls, and it needed walls. It needed
ditches, it needed watchtowers, and it needed
defenses. Walls were the priority, along the west
and the north. The sea cliffs protected the south,
and if time permitted, perhaps the east could
also become walled. The fort in the mean time
will have to protect the east. Once the walls and
ditches were done, the next priority would be
construction of the defenses. They were unsure
on the timeframe, unsure how far they would
get before the enemy arrived, so construction
was fast and furious. Buildings were being
demolished to provide stone and timber for the
construction project.

　　Ten thousand plus military men, and
many civilian volunteers, diligently worked on
the walls and ditches. By the end of the day, it
was taking shape. When darkness fell, the men
were ordered to stop and finally rest. Work
would resume first thing in the morning, before
sunrise. Mikus and his squad returned to their

tent to eat a meal before passing out for the night. They weren't entirely surprised to find soldiers of the 7th already having prepared their meal for them. The two squads from different Legions shared a meal and exchanged stories with one another. The men of the 7th were eager to join the others tomorrow in the construction of the defenses.

Mikus had expected to hear that; the better the defenses, the better chance that they all had of surviving. What truly shocked Mikus, and the others in his squad for that matter, was the tale the 7th told of the enemy. Silence followed after they had finished describing what had been faced in battle. Mikus would have been nervous no matter what he had been told, since he had nothing to reference it against. It was the silence of the veterans in his squad, the dread in their body language that made Mikus afraid himself.

XXXVI
ADYPATUS EVENTUS

The Imperial Guard had picked up on his trail again. After spending time yesterday hiding in some low rent inn somewhere in the brackish area that was between the Operara and the Aliena District, they had sniffed him out. Sleep had not found him yesterday, his mind racing with thoughts of what to do next. Memories of Flaccus filled his mind, always followed by the sight of his severed head skidding to a halt of the floor before him. Adypatus Eventus knew that if he showed his face anywhere near a Cohort garrison, he would be apprehended on sight. The murder of his partner was on his hands. He had been framed for it, and the reason Flaccus had been killed was because Eventus had gone on some damn idealistic crusade against those who had did it.

But, he never had a choice; it had been the only thing a man in his position could have done. What made it worse, he realized, was Flaccus had been more than a partner. The kid had been a friend. Friends were rare things for Eventus, and that made the hurt and the guilt that much crueler. Ronio Flaccus may have been spying on Eventus, but that was inconsequential. He had still been a friend. Turning himself in to face the charges was possibly the only option he had left. If he were in custody, at least he could swear his findings under oath and have people around him that would listen to him. Even if he were killed for the crime he had been framed for, at least the truth would be told about the conspiracy.

His whole life he had been living for himself. Maybe it was time for him to sacrifice himself for the benefit of others. The other option was to run. Disappear. The corrupt members of the Guard would probably let him flee in exile. It would after all, accomplish what they wanted, him keeping his silence. But he would never be safe; he would always be looking over his shoulder. Desertion was also a capital offense to the Legions, and he would be put on the lists of bounty hunters who tracked down such men. The guilt and shame would still be there, no matter where he went or what he did. Even if he drank himself into oblivion each day he would still be himself after he reached the bottom of every bottle. But he would also still be alive. Those seemed to be his only options. Some farfetched schemes occasionally rose into the front of his thoughts, but his rational mind would stifle them.

With a recently full coin purse, he had set out south into the city, not sure which option he was going to choose. Before he made up his mind, he owed someone something, an explanation and a warning. He had cashed out all of his debts, collected coin he had stashed here and there for a situation when he desperately might need it. A situation like the one he found himself in now. The weight in the purse was substantial; enough to live comfortably in the far reaches of the Empire or beyond. To flee or to surrender? Flaccus would have turned himself in to get the truth out in the open; that was obvious enough. The young man was also dead, while Eventus was still alive.

Maybe if he fled for a little while, let the situation cool down, and then returned. Then he could root out and get justice against those who had done this. That bald Guardsman's face was burned into his memory, and when he thought of the man, he clenched his jaw and fists in pure hatred and anger. He swore he would kill that man, and he couldn't do that in some far corner of the world. He also couldn't accomplish it if he were executed. Perhaps he could stay in the city, in the criminal underground, and plan his move against those traitors.

All these thoughts had been distracting him as he made his way through the city. Avoiding the patrolling Guardsmen of the Urban Cohorts, he stayed hidden in crowds and shadows, with his cloak pulled up over his head. No doubt that his old friends in black were on the look out for him, as well as members of the Imperial Guard. Despite the 1st Legion mobilizing and leaving the city, there didn't seem to be any shortage of patrols through the streets from the half that remained behind. During a routine maneuver to shake anyone that might be trailing him, Eventus first discovered the Imperial Guardsman that was following him. He cursed to himself, and anger filled inside him. He was tired of this, he just wanted a drink and a good nights sleep.

"How did you find me?" Eventus said aloud to himself under his breath. Eventus leaned around a corner and watched the man, who was dressed the same as the ones who had raided Argentis' warehouse. He didn't recognize the man from that fight, but there was no doubt he was a member of the Imperial Guard. The tail began to look around casually, but if you watched him closely, you could tell he was frantically searching for the man he had just lost. Eventus realized he was instinctively squeezing the handle of his dagger. His knuckles were white, and part of him screamed at him to run out and murder this man very violently. With a deep breath, he relaxed his grip and slunk away into the alley he was hiding in. He would meander a bit in that direction before heading to where he wanted to go.

*   *   *

Two Imperial Guardsmen, dressed in civilian clothing, were loitering out front of Tassia's apartment building. One of them he recognized from the raid without a doubt. The others face he couldn't see since his back was turned and his hood was up. Eventus crouched in a shadowy corner of an archway, observing and planning his next move. He felt sick to his stomach thinking of what they might be going to do to Tassia. Perhaps they were here to wait for him to arrive, but he doubted it. The Imperial Guard, at least this branch of it, didn't operate like that. If they were trying to find you, they would threaten or hurt those you loved until you showed yourself. Somehow, these conspirators had found a connection between himself and Tassia, and he shuddered to think of the trail of blood that they created to get here. It dawned on him that his entire family would be a target, just like Tassia, if he were to go into self-exile. That option was becoming less and less enticing the more and more he thought about it.

Just then, a woman with a beautiful head of golden blond hair emerged from the apartment building. She had a vigorous and spirited gate to her step, which quickly slowed as she saw the two men gingerly approaching her from two sides. The men were saying something to her that Eventus couldn't hear, and Tassia took a step backwards. The one with his hood still on reached out and grabbed her arm. She tried to pull it away, to jerk it free, but only succeeded in slipping backwards and falling onto one knee. She screamed at them, and one of them backhanded her across the face.

Eventus snapped. He couldn't take any of this any longer. In a full sprint, he bolted from the shadows and across the street. Blade drawn, and silent except for his footfalls and snorts of angry breathing, he made his way towards the men in astonishing speed. The man with his back turned never saw him coming, and the second one made eye contact just before he collided with the first. A shoulder lowered into the man's back sent his sprawling to the stone street below with tremendous force. The flying man had no choice but to release his grip on Tassia. Eventus then lunged at the man who still remained standing, as he fumbled for his own dagger. Eventus grabbed him from behind, slid a hand around the corner of the man's jaw and pulled his head up and away, exposing his vulnerable neck. He stabbed the man multiple times in quick succession in the elongated neck and throat, blood splattering over them both.

The dying man was discarded, and Eventus leapt on the back of the other man who was starting to get to his feet. His body weight crashing onto the slowly rising man slammed him back down with a grunt to the street below. They both writhed, sandy beige dust accumulating on their clothes. The struggle was short, as Eventus opened the man's throat with a jagged yet deep slash from his dagger. Pulling back the hood revealed a man with a full head of hair. Disappointment mixed with relief as he realized it wasn't the shaven headed man he was hoping it would be. He was still out there for him to get.

Tassia looked horrified, a trickle of blood coming from the corner of her mouth where she had been struck. Eventus let his bloody dagger fall with a clank to the street below. He knelt on both knees, and held her. She pushed him away, and he noticed that he was covered with blood from the butchery he had just performed.

"Tassia, listen to me." He held her hands tenderly. "You are not safe. More of these men will be back. You need to leave, now. Go stay somewhere else for a week or two."

"Ady!" She shouted. "What is going on! Who were these men? How did they…You killed them!" She was in some sort of shock.

"They were going to kill you, trust me." He responded.

"Trust you?" she yelled back. "You don't show up for days at a time, and each time you have some excuse or another. Now this? I can't trust you, Ady."

"These are bad men." He said. "I've been working a case against them, and they have been trying to kill me. And now they were going to kill you to get to me."

"Who are they? One of your criminal friends?" She said accusatorily. He felt a stab of pain as she said that. How had she ever been able to figure that out about him? He had always been so careful to keep those two worlds separate.

"No." He shook his head. "They are members of the Imperial Guard. Look, the less you know the better."

"The Imperial Guard?" She scoffed. "And you won't give me an explanation and you expect me to trust you?"

He lowered his eyes, ashamed. "Tassia, I'm trying to protect you. I wanted to come here to give you a warning, and then to say goodbye. My plan was to see if you wanted to come with me, to run away from all this together, but I know now that it would never work. It wouldn't be fair to you." He reached into his pocket, and pulled out his pouch of coins. He hefted it a few times, and then placed it in her hands.

"What's this?" She asked, her face had a disgusted, insulted look on it.

"It's all my money. I was going to use it when I fled, but I'm not going to need it now." He nodded towards it.

"I don't want your coin, Ady. Your blood money..." She looked down at the two corpses.

"It's not blood money, Tassia. Take it and run, get far away from here for a while. Just go." He insisted, wrapping her hands around the coin purse.

"No." She dropped the money to the ground.

"Look!" He shouted, picking it back up. "I'm trying to make a selfless, heartfelt gesture here! I'm going to sacrifice myself for the safety of you and the rest of the Empire. I realize now that it's my only option. I'm doing it because I love you." His heart fluttered as he said it. He hadn't planned on saying it, but now he knew that he had been going to the entire time.

She didn't say anything in response.

"I'm going to be tried for a crime I did not commit, a murder of my friend that these men committed." He said solemnly. "I'm turning myself in to the Cohorts in order to get the truth out there. The safety of others depends on it, and they need to be brought to justice."

"Flaccus." She muttered. "Men came to the bar looking for you, other Enforcers. They said you did it, that you killed him."

"I did not." He shook his head, blood smeared on his cheek. "No matter what you hear, I promise you I'm innocent. I'm doing this for you. I love you." He said it again, just incase she hadn't heard him the first time.

"What... What do you..." She tried to choke back emotion, but failed. A tear began to well in her eyes, making them glimmer. She shook her head and swallowed hard.

"I have to go, Tassia. You need to go, too. It's not safe to wait... and damn it! I just said I loved you, and you can't say it back?" He was more frustrated than angry, more hurt than upset.

"I... I love you, too. But you're going to, you're leaving..." She said, and then reached in and embraced him. "Why did it take you so long to say this, to do this? Why wait until it's all over? Run away. I'll runaway with you. We can go north, we can go east, it doesn't matter. Let's go now, this second." and she began to climb to her feet. "I can grab some things and then…"

"No." he said. "I can't run from this. I need to do this. And you need to leave, too. Goodbye, Tassia." And he leaned in and kissed her long and hard. They both had tears in their eyes. The broke apart and then kissed again, just as long as the first time.

He held her a moment longer, and then he walked away.

*   *   *

The two Urban Guardsmen he approached looked shocked as he walked up to them. He was wearing a simple short tunic, splattered and stained with blood. His pugio dagger had been left with the bodies in front of Tassia's house, along with his cloak. The only thing he carried in his upraised hands was his Medallion. The two young men in black armor drew their blades and had ordered him to halt. He didn't recognize them. Calmly, he identified himself, and requested that he be brought to the Hold until he could speak with Lt. Grattus of the Enforcers, 6th garrison. After some convincing, they escorted him to the hold, and confiscated his Medallion as they locked him in the cell.

He knew that he was in no position to make any demands, but he requested Grattus come as soon as possible; it was of the utmost importance. They still moved in a deliberately slow pace, and it infuriated Eventus as he knew they were doing it out of spite. After explaining to them again that time was running out, and that the information he had was very imperative to the security of the Empire, they slowed down even more. They explained to him that they didn't take requests from people who murdered members of their order.

Now, he sat alone in the small stone nook, iron bars locked tight in front of him. Sitting in shadow, he looked across the hold and could see the empty cell that Gossum had sat in during his last visit here. The now dead criminal had said Eventus would make his way in here one day or another. Now he had to look at the cell and think of that terrible man he had sent to the afterlife, and hear echoes of that laugh.

Motion caught the corner of his eye, and when he realized what he was seeing, he shot to his feet. Taking a step backwards, he let the shadows consume his figure as he watched two purple clad Imperial Guardsmen enter the Hold. They were fully armed, capes flowing behind them as they made their way down the steps. Eventus felt his heart hammer in his chest, could feel the final line being written in his story in the Book of Fate. The two guards continued to walk down the steps, towards the Lower Hold and out of sight. Confusion filled him as several moments later, two different Imperial Guards walked back up the steps and out the only entrance to the Hold. After realizing they weren't here for him, it took minutes before his heart slowed and was able to relax and sat back down.

His mind racing, his anxiety high, all he could do was sit here and wait for Grattus. If Grattus even showed up, if he even gets the message. He tried to think of nothing, to clear his mind, but only wicked thoughts filled his brain.

XXXVII
DIMIDIUS TORBOCK

This was to be his first time inside a real Saurian building. Granted, he had been in his share of ramshackle thatched cottages and adobe huts that many Saurians lived in throughout the Empire's fringes. Never had he been in Akkedis, and never had he been in a Saurian city. As he had arrived earlier today, the Millangor capital of Millang'Sek was a place like nothing he had ever seen. Stone structures of good geometry, not the crude shapes he imagined he might find when he arrived, were everywhere. The buildings were made of natural stone, some plastered and painted, some not. Some had domed roofs, others flat with parapets. The streets were all dirt, acacia trees and palms sporadically growing throughout. Groves of eucalyptus were dotted here and there. It was a city that had a strange blend of permanency and yet also hasty, transitory construction throughout. Smells of bitter, pungent spice and a cloying aroma filled the land, with the underlying musty smell of Saurians.

As he had travelled down the street,

starring at the new sights that were everywhere, he had been surprised to see many *men* walking about. Green skinned Saurians dominated the crowds, but a fair amount of humans filled in the gaps. Some were soldiers to be certain by their garb, but most were civilians. If he had to guess, this was the new frontier of the Empire, and these men were hoping to strike a new business of find fortune in this place. Maybe some were driven by the urge to forge a strong new province for Calidia. Perhaps some had religious motivations rather than monetary or nationalism.

As Torbock examined the city more scrupulously, it dawned on him that Calidian Imperials were doing their fair share of infrastructure projects here. The familiar footprint of the architecture of the Empire was popping up everywhere. He even spotted what must have been the early stages of an aqueduct. The Saurians themselves even looked more Calidian than he had expected. The males wore tunics and some even wore jewelry, females wore palas and flowing dresses. He wouldn't be surprised if a group of Millangors came around the bend garbed in togas.

The Legion garrison building that they had stopped at was Calidian, no question about it. It was the standard footprint and design. The hues of the stone and tile roof were more subdued than normal, but blended in with the regional colors of the surrounding buildings.

The sentry at the gate, after being provided with Medallion and papers, claimed that the Legate of the 8th was stationed at the main castra to the south, along the Millangor-Hyerian border with the main body of the Legion. The senior Tribune in charge of this garrison, a man named Flametrius, was being summoned from within to speak with Torbock and company.

In the meantime, Torbock and Jacean were on their feet, mindlessly taking laps around the wagon while Kataris sat on the bench seat, still holding the reigns. The two Sentinels spoke to one another in quiet voices, pointing out features and buildings they felt needed to be commented on. Kataris deliberately cleared his throat, making a wet and chunky phlegm sound as he did, as if it dislodged a piece of his windpipe at the same time. He was obviously trying to get their attention. The two men approached the bandaged man with a slow curiosity in their step. The man starred at them, and then shrugged his shoulders.

"I guess I better be on my way, then." Kataris muttered.

"You are leaving?" Torbock asked, having grown a bit accustomed to the man's company recently. That intense feeling in his chest momentarily reemerged, and then it passed, leaving a slow burn as it went.

"I have business of my own to attend to, now." Kataris said. "I told you I was travelling as far as this, and I have brought you here. Safe and sound I might add. Minus that other fellow, but that wasn't my fault." He waved a quick moving dismissive hand.

"Where will you go now?" Jacean asked. "Is there anything we can do to repay you for your help?"

"I have merchant things to do." His answer was curt. "But you, you can finish this mission that is so important. That's how you can repay me."

"We will." Torbock said without any hesitation.

"I will be in the Ikaran ruins. Don't forget to find me there Dimidius Torbock, you gave me your word." Kataris saluted with a wrapped hand. "Take care of your business first. The arch holds up the pillar of man, and all that."

Torbock had no idea what that last part meant, but he saluted back. And with a snap of his reigns, the wagon lurched forward and left them standing there, watching the cart bumble down the bumpy dirt road. Not long after that, the gate opened and the two men were escorted inside the garrison. Flametrius was a strawberry-blonde man, whose eyebrows almost looked translucent white. He had a young round face and a sharp nose, but his features looked weathered. Piercing blue eyes stared at them, studying the two new arrivals as they entered his small office. He didn't bother rising from his desk and offered no greeting as they approached.

"What brings Sentinels to this part of the world?" The man opened with.

"Imperial business." Torbock said coldly, matching the Tribunes tone.

"Well, that's a shame." Flametrius stated, leaning forward and sitting upright. "Look around you, this isn't the Empire we are in. This is enemy territory."

"I'm sure, even being station out here in a backwater, you have been apprised of the current situation in the Capital?" Torbock's voice was more a statement than an inquiry. It was a condescending statement, but he had immediately disliked this man so it was ok with him.

"Yes. The Emperor is ill. A revolt from Frigiterra is a result. What does that have to do with you being here?" The Tribune asked, placing two extended fingers on his temple as his elbow rested on his desk.

"Our orders are to give our report only to the Legate. And to meet with the Millangor King." Torbock said, his eyes looking up and away, at a spot on the wall in the background.

"Well, the Legate isn't here, and I will not recall him in regards to such matters. You're only option will be to travel south to the edge of Millangor lands and to deliver your message directly to him." The man shrugged. "Sorry. I'm not putting my reputation on the line for *this*." He made a gesture towards the Sentinels as if he were discarding an unwanted apple core.

"Very well. And what of King Strank'lakon? How do I get an audience with him?" Torbock asked, already grasping that this man would be of no help whatsoever.

The Tribune threw a thumb at the wall to his left. "The Millangor palace is that way a little ways. Big spires, can't miss it. Anything else I can be of assistance of to aid you fine men?"

"No. You have done more than enough, Tribune Flamitrius. I will be sure to put your helpfulness in my report to the Consul and the Imperial Council." Torbock began to walk to the door without waiting for dismissal, just as the Tribune shot to his feet.

"Hold on. Before you go and…" Flametrius started, holding his hands up in a placating gesture.

"No, please. We will be fine on our own, like I said." Torbock turned and leaned back through the doorway. "By the way, we passed an army of Hyerians marching on the neck north towards Bridgegate. You might want to do something about that."

"What! That's impossible!" The Tribune bellowed from inside as Torbock gently shut the door. A few steps later the door burst open. "Hyerians?! How did they make it there without us seeing them here? They would have had to pass through the Wo'Styn Desert, and the jungles of The Wrede. Impossible."

Torbock and Jacean continued walking.

The 8th legion was going to be very difficult to mobilize out of this area. He had to come up with a way to convince the Millangor King to allow the Legion to leave, right when a Hyerian army was seen marching through his lands. The least he could do was ask.

*   *   *

The Millangor palace was built on a small rise in the middle of the city. The Tribune had been correct; the spires were big and made it hard to miss. He had noticed them as they had travelled through the city, but didn't know at the time that they were part of the palace. The twin towers that rose up and scraped the sky tapered to near points, and from a distance they resembled elongated anthills. They were the color of caked mud and appeared irregular. As they neared, he could tell that wasn't the case at all; they were symmetrical, mirror images of one another. The irregularities were intentional. The spires were almost insectoid looking, skeletal, almost vertebral. Ribbed arches and spines adorned the entire building. The Millangor flag; a field of half blue and half red, with a star of inverted colors in the center, flew in various spots, most noticeably the top of the spires.

Despite wearing very Calidian influenced armor and uniform, the sentries posted at the only gate in the surrounding walls spoke very little Domitian. Attempts to pantomime and communicate with a few loud, slow words didn't end how Torbock had hoped they would. Eventually, another Saurian appeared, this one dressed more like a commoner than a soldier. His mastery of the Calidian tongue was far better than the guards, and he was able to understand exactly what the Sentinels wanted. That didn't mean the request was to be granted.

After leaving to confer with unseen superiors several times, the pair was allowed to enter. As they walked through the gate, Torbock rested his hand casually on the hilt of his blade that was on his hip. It wasn't a threatening gesture, but a casual one, a natural one. It showed that he had no intentions to relinquish his weapon, and the Saurians made no qualms about him entering armed. During the wagon ride south, the dying Polemistius had bestowed tedious details about the nuances of Millangor and all Saurian society to him. The ambassador must have known he had no chance of surviving his wounds, and felt a duty to pass this knowledge on to Torbock so he could finish the mission. Noble.

The Millangor had a strong caste system. Soldiers were born to be soldiers, workers to be workers, farmers to be farmers, and so on. A soldier was defined by his weapon; to give it up to another was a sign of weakness and forfeiture of the right to bear it. So, he did not give it up, and no one asked him to do so. One of the guards gave a guttural, almost canine growl to Jacean as he passed by. The young man flinched slightly, startled mostly, but did not waver. When they had passed, the Saurian sentries continued to stare at them and conferred in their strange tongue to one another. Torbock was on edge, and he grasped his scroll tube tightly. This was his second time delivering scrolls to a palace in a short period. They were starkly different palaces however.

Inside, the citadel was almost cave-like, but not in the sense of it being a crude tunnel. The long passageways were dark but warm. The musty smell of reptile and smoke filled the air. Small oval windows high up on the walls let in minimal daylight and airflow; the Saurians preferred it hot and dim. Torches helped to keep some of the darkness away, but there weren't many of them. The floor was a highly polished brownish-gray stone, shimmering like water where the firelight danced off of it. The walls were made of rough stacked stone, irregular and fitting together like a puzzle. As they snaked their way through the long hallways, they occasionally passed guards, who paid them little mind once they noticed the Saurian whom had allowed them into the gates was escorting them.

Occasionally, the passed groups of similarly dressed non-military Millangor, who paid them no mind. They even spotted a human or two in the groups, probably an attaché or representative for some project or another. As they progressed deeper into the stronghold, they started to get challenged by guards, but the escort dismissed them with a snapping, cackle sound and a strong point with clawed hand. The guards immediately obeyed each time. The soldiers all wore chainmail and jerkins, and some wore helms and chest plate. Torbock noticed the weapon of choice was spear and battle axe, not a sword in sight. Blinking yellow and black eyes glared back at him when he caught their gaze. It was a surreal experience. His entire life he had pictured Saurians as living in holes in the ground and dressed as barbarians. These Millangor appeared more refined than he had ever imagined.

Finally, with no door or grand entranceway to announce they had arrived at their destination, they stepped into a vaulted room. The transition had been subtle, but the room they were in now was different than any they had passed through inside the palace. Columns that looked they twisted, braided pieces of stone held up the ceiling. Corrugated arches started along the base of the walls and tapered to the pinnacle of the room. They gave the appearance of having stepped inside a ribcage or into a giant mouth of needle like teeth.

Standing in two flanking rows were guards, all with giant double-headed battleaxes made of Akkedan Bronze. Various groups of Millangor were spread throughout the room, as if it were a formal Calidian banquet before the meal was being served. Torbock noticed no throne, no crown or scepter to denote a king. Truth was, he had no idea what clothes a Saurian King wore. Up until earlier today, he didn't have a clue what a Saurian building looked like. The aide that had guided them through the palace beckoned for the pair to follow him through the crowd.

They came upon a Saurian standing cross-armed as several others were explaining whatever it was they were saying in their language. By this ones posture, it was clear that he was their leader. The King was dressed in a tunic of red, and draped in a cloak of blue. A bright red stole hung down from his shoulders. The King was large, broad shouldered and covered in scars. One jagged scar ran down the side of his face, from the crown of his head, skipping over the eye and continuing down to the neck. In a strange way, he reminded Torbock of Kanion. The aide made his way to the king, and without apology, interrupted whoever was talking to converse with the monarch.

Torbock heard his own name, as well as those of Jacean and Polemistius, be uttered in the explanation. With a nod, the Millangor King made his way the few short steps to the Sentinels. This was a very important moment. Gestures from both parties upon introductions with a Saurian could dictate the course of the entire relationship. Vicaro had given him a crash course, but it was all very intricate and complex. Torbock hoped he was about to do what he had been coached to do correctly. Straight backed, and looking Strank'Lakon right in his eyes, Torbock raised his right hand slowly yet deliberately. This showed strength and confidence in your station. Torbock's hand remained palm up, inline with the wrist, fingers spread slightly apart. This was a sign of supplication and recognition of your inferiority to the one you are meeting. He brought it up to just below level with his shoulders; this showed also that you respected the one you were meeting, yet held a position of authority yourself. Jacean went through the same motions, yet did not raise his arm as high as Torbock had. This had been intentional, for it immediately put the younger just below his elder in social stature.

The King raised his own hand palm down, bringing it well above Torbock's before lowering it down to rest it atop the waiting hand. This was a sign of superiority, yes also showed respect. It had gone well so far. The green hand felt leathery, abrasive and warm as it tightened around his own.

"Strank'Lakon. Ut'Garok. Millang'Kral." The King introduced himself with a guttural rasping voice.

"Dimidius Torbock. Son of Ramzi. Sentinel." Torbock said, maintaining eye contact with the Saurian. They stared at one another for a long time. The King took in a few deep breaths through his green snout, opened and closed his mouth slowly as if tasting the air. Then with a grunt, the king turned the clasped hands ninety degrees, so they were perpendicular with the ground, and lowered them both down slightly, but not very far. With a reverent nod, he broke the gesture. It was a show of respect.

Then he turned his attention to Jacean, who had remained still through the whole exchange, hand hovering like a statue. With more much more force and much more speed than he had used with Torbock, Strank'Lakon grasped the young man's hand and squeezed tightly. With a grunt from the King and a grimace from Jacean, the arm of the Sentinel slowly lowered towards the ground, stopping about halfway.

"You heard my name. What is yours? Or should I ask your master?" Strank'lakon said in very clear Domitian. His eyes widened as he spoke, snout-like nostrils flaring.

Through clenched teeth, the young man replied. "Jacean Monodius. Son of Eosus. Sentinel." With pain in his face, he continued to stare defiantly at the King, never breaking the gaze. The Saurian leaned in, breathing hard through his nostrils as he did so.

"You have strength in you." The king said approvingly, taking another sniff. "You have His scent, His blood."

Jacean said nothing, but turned pale as the King spoke these words. The Saurian sense of smell was something of a myth amongst humans. They apparently could recognize anyone before they approached just by odor. They were also able to identify familiar members by the unique musk that they inherited. Torbock felt his stomach drop. Jacean had been smart to use his mother's name instead of his father's during introductions, based on the history. However, this twist might cause it to backfire and they would both be in a world of hurt. He had a suspicion they would root out the Dutrigian heritage, but had hoped to avoid it. If they discovered who his father was, this might not end well.

"I don't know what you mean." Jacean managed to say after a long awkward silent stand-off, hand still being held firm by the King.

"It is faint, but it is there." Strank'Lakon said. Others had made their way over and were forming up around the two Sentinels and the King. Some sniffed. "Dutrigius. You have his blood." And with that, the King raised the hands to just below level, and then broke the grasp.

The pale ashen face of Jacean regained its color; in fact, it may have even reddened a bit. He looked stunned and slightly embarrassed by the revelation.

"Dutrigius is the most reviled and the most respected human in our history. His descendants share that legacy here. I have smelled the old bones. You have his blood." The King said, and with that being said, the introductions were over.

"What do you wish of me, Sentinels?" Strank'Lakon asked, crossing his arms once again, standing tall and upright.

"We have been sent on behalf of the Empire, as ambassadors, to deliver this to you." Slowly, Torbock presented the leather scroll tube he had carried from the capital. With a gesture from the King, an aide took the scroll from the Sentinels hand and began to unroll it.

"Vicaro Polemistius, son of Vicaro, he was with you but now is dead?" Strank'Lakon asked as the aid read the scroll to himself.

"Yes." Torbock said. "Killed by a rebel force"

"I have heard of this new human rebellion." The King said. "And of the fall of Dutrigi. The Dutrigians are our old enemies. We should have been the ones to meet them in battle. We mourn their loss to the world."

"The history between the Millangors and the Bulls is long and tumultuous. That fight has come to an end for now, it seems." Torbock gave a slight bow of head as a sign of respect and of finality. "The Empire faces many threats, as you know. Homitha is one. This new rebellion is another. Akkedis is not viewed as enemy territory any longer. You are an ally of our nation, and we have need of the Legion garrisoned along the border in other theaters."

"You may not view the Millangor as a threat any longer…" Strank'Lakon started as he was handed the scroll to read. "…But the Hyerian threat is very real; to all of us. With Dutrigi gone, Bridgegate will soon follow."

"In regards to the Hyerians, *your eminence*," Torbock couldn't remember what honorific title to use with a Saurian King, "We witnessed a Hyerian force marching north along the neck towards the fort of Bridgegate. They had already passed by Utara'Sek. If they were sent to besiege the fort, they must have already begun."

Strank'Lakon made no sign of acknowledgement as he read the scroll. Once he had finished, he handed the scroll back to his aide, and grunted something in his native tongue. Then he turned to Torbock.

"We have known of this Hyerian force." He said in a flat voice. "They were spotted travelling north by scouts. They have already started to besiege the fort."

"How did they get past the 8th? Past your own army?" Torbock was letting anger slip into his voice. "Why have you done nothing?"

"Why?" The king sounded agitated as well. "Why would we do anything of the sorts for an ally that would ask to remove their protection in our greatest time of need!" He shot a finger towards the scroll the aide now clutched. "Our scouts spotted them heading north through the Wrede. You humans always thought it was impassable, to travel across the Wo'Styn desert and the jungles of the Wrede. It is not; there are ways. They camped a second force along the Sout"I to distract us this whole time."

"You just sat here and did nothing, then? What if they had decided to march south against your cities? And what if that second force decides to move across the river?" Torbock could feel any hope of this mission being completed with a successful outcome slipping away.

"This Macien," The King pronounced the name like 'Maw-see-awn' as he snatched the scroll back and held it up. "He has offered us rewards for allowing the 8th Legion to return to Domiterra. If we do that, then the Hyerians to the south will invade. Special rewards are nothing to dead peoples. I must refuse. It will take a long time to get them back as well."

"The fleet the Empire has anchored here, in this city; it is meant to bring the Legion back across the sea if we need them. We need them now." Torbock said.

"Your Legion is far from here, the ships do no good. Even if we had them march here to load on the ships, we would need to send our own warriors to guard the border first. We cannot leave the Sout'I unprotected at a time like this." The King shook his head.

"What if we used the fleet to ferry your force south to the border, replace the 8th, and then the Legion could sail back to Domiterra?" Torbock offered. "We know you have a large

force in Utara'Sek to the north... They could
make sure the Hyerians don't turn south and try
to invade here. The sooner we get our Legion
back, then we can put down this rebellion, you
can get your special rewards that Macien has
promised, and we can turn our attention back to
stabilizing Akkedis."

Strank'Lakon ruminated silently for a
while, rubbing his under bite jaw as he did.
Then he growled. "What can you tell me of the
rebels, the ones who defeated our old enemy?"
He rasped.

"Duke Silious is the leader of the
rebellion." Torbock said. "Dutrigi was destroyed
because of speed and surprise. If we have a
strong, prepared force, we can stop him. But the
Empire needs more men, they need the 8th."

"It would shame me to allow this man to
continue his war. He has stolen the valor we
have sought for generations of fighting the Red
Dutrigians." The king ruefully shook his head.
"Where will the next battle be?"

"More likely than not, Cortinum. And
soon. That is why we must hurry." Torbock
insisted. Just then an aide returned with a scroll
of Akkedan parchment. Strank'Lakon jotted a
quick scribble on it after giving it a cursory
glance, and the aide sealed it.

"Cortinum. They are a good people." The
King said. "Many of our people try to go there
for sanctuary. Many Millangor are in that city."
He then nodded.

"These are my terms, for you to accept as ambassador on behalf of Macien. First, we need this scroll brought to our force in Utara'Sek. He will carry it." The king handed the freshly sealed scroll tube to Jacean. The young Sentinel's mouth cracked to protest, but then he gave pause. The King then continued.

"Horse will be the fastest. We do not ride horse. Some of your people have horses they have trained to be not scared of our people and our lands. You will take one and ride to Utara'Sek as soon as possible." The king then turned to Torbock.

"My warriors will ride with you on the ships. You will be escorted and allowed to deliver your dispatch to the Legate of the 8th, you have my word as Millang'Kral. The force garrisoned here in Millang'Sek will remain, however. When your people end this rebellion, this Macien will hold true to his words he has written?" The king held up the scroll.

"I have met the Consul only once. But I believe he will do what he promises. He has the reputation of being a man of virtue." Torbock said honestly.

"Very well." Strank'Lakon nodded. "Let us go."

XXXVIII
TARAES KANTAUR

The dust stirred on the stone steps with each of her footfalls. The baked golden orange soil of the decomposed granite was sandy and got everywhere this time of year. Farther behind her with each step she took was the entrance to her family Tomb. Within, filling the urns and sarcophagi were generations of her ancestors. Some had been Dukes, some had not. Some even had been ancient Kings. A few were suspected of being demigods in family lore. Mt. Junas was filled with ancestral burial shrines like this for many families of Jorbus. These were common throughout all of Morincia. Her Father had been laid to rest and she had fulfilled her promise to him.

She had spent yesterday morning and early afternoon walking up the slopes to reach her family's mountain top chateau. The walk had been extraordinarily peaceful and spectacularly beautiful.

Her mother had not been there when Taraes arrived, and she would not return that night. She was probably staying with a friend at another chateau somewhere along the ridgeline.

Or she was out doing 'witch things', as the rumors would have you believe. The rest of the day had been spent preparing the clay for the effigy. She had brought the material with her, and for a good hour she watered and rolled it until it reached the consistency that she liked. Then she prepped it by smoothing it, cutting it to size, and shaping the borders.

Once the blank was ready for the carving, primed to have the profile of her father etched into its already drying surface, she closed her eyes. She remembered Duke Aedien Aktulus. She remembered her father. The beaming smile and the robust laughter that echoed through her mind was so real, so vivid. Upon opening her eyes, she made his face appear on the clay. Deliberate slicing motions, slow sweeping curves, and stabbing dabs all came together to create his image. She had stared at the image and realized it had come out starkly different than she had imagined or how she had practiced.

The face on the clay was her father to be certain, anyone who knew him could not deny that. The face *smiled*. That had never been the plan. Effigies of her ancestors had always had stoic, determined features, not smiles. However, her father had a wonderful smile, and this image looked like him. That was what the eyes had been missing this whole time. The small upturning of the mouth she gave him made his eyes sparkle with the authenticity that her father had possessed. A tear welled in Taraes' eyes and one fell onto the newly born forehead that had been carved into the clay.

That night, it was fired in a kiln that her mother kept outside the house for her pottery hobby. Taraes had started the fire that was used to heat it as soon as she had arrived, and by now it was the perfect temperature. In the morning, she had cradled the finished product and paraded it to the tomb. Once inside, she reverently placed it behind her father's urn that sat in it's own niche on the wall. Without lingering, she had left. No ceremony was necessary; that was over with a long time ago. The guards that had followed her did not enter the tomb, and they said nothing as she exited. They stayed far behind her now as she walked to the edge of the ridge.

Walking through the crimson red Manzanita, she found her way to the precipice. Below, the expanse of Jorbus was visible. She could see the city, see the Terraced Gardens, she the parks, the main streets. If she concentrated, she could make out the shapes of large wagons slowly lumbering along, but they were too far away to see people. Beyond the docks, she could see the turquoise waters of the Bay of Drakus as it mixed into the darker blues of the deeper Morincian Sea beyond that. The small islands that dotted the waters were ringed with lighter blues that turned to white as the gentle seas lapped upon them as waves.

The endless procession of ships of all different shapes and sizes, flying vibrant sails and different colored flags, continued to move in and out of the harbor. She thought she could see the trail of incoming ships grow larger as it reached the horizon, like they were trickling in from an armada floating far out at sea. But she couldn't focus that far out, and the image disappeared. She disregarded it as a trick of the eye, a mirage.

She took in everything: the mountain, the city below, and the sea. The smells, the colors, the breeze. This was home, it was in her blood, and she knew it was true. With a fulfilled smile on her face, joy replacing the sorrow that she had conjured back up earlier, she turned to head back to the main trail. As she did, she heard a commotion with the guards. She froze like a deer that heard a hunter on it's trail. The grumbling of voice, and the lack of screaming and steel on steel sounds put her at ease. She continued forward. The two guards had been joined by a third man, a youth who was heaving air and dripping sweat; a messenger.

"My lady Taraes!" The man gasped. "Your brother, Lord Darien, requests that you return to the palace immediately!" He stopped talking, placed his hands on his thighs as he crouched over and breathed heavily. He heart sank.

"What has happened?" She demanded, the Empress in her taking over.

"Portopolis." He spat out, putting himself upright again. "Invaded. Enemy has taken it over. Destroyed the fleet."

"What enemy? Homitha?" She asked. "Silious?" she threw out with an incredulous tone.

"No." The boy shook his head, curly brown, soaked hair flapping side to side. "Petros. Surprise attack. Petros did it."

"Petros?" She was dumbfounded, and then she began to quietly think aloud. "Why would they do that, they have no reason. They…" She stopped herself mid-thought, and then straightened up her posture with a snap. She began to run through the brush, snapping branches and tromping through shrubbery. Upon reaching the edge of the cliff once again, she could more clearly make out what she thought she had seen earlier. It *was* an armada. It was an invasion fleet. And it flew the colored sails and flags of the Snake of Petros.

"They are here!" She shouted as she ran back to the guards and the messenger. "Petros ships on the horizon." She burst onto the trail, and all three men shot upright as she did.

"Empress, we must get you to safety!" One of the guards said authoritatively.

"No." She stated. "The lookout on the peak, it must be told." She gestured to the highest point on Mt. Junas. The lookout was built on the top to spot ships that were coming towards the harbor. If an enemy fleet approached, it was supposed to raise a red flag and blow a horn. That would relay the message down to the forces below to prepare for the attack. They could see the structure, and see no flag flying, and they heard no horn. The sooner that flag went up, the better chance they had.

The runner, who was breathing like a blown horse, looked up the steep face of the peak and nodded. Before anyone could react, he gave a little crow hop and started to run up the hill. Taraes watched him in awe for a moment, and then turned her attention to the two guards. They both looked at her for direction.

"I am returning back down to the palace to find my Brother and Uncle, and to ensure my children and nieces and nephew are safe. Do not try and stop me, just try to protect me." And with that, she began her descent down the slopes of Mt. Junas. A queasy feeling was in her stomach and she had to fight back against the taste of bile in her mouth.

XXXIX
ATHELTIADES

It was the second day of the siege. Casualties had started to take their toll on the defenders. So had fatigue. The Hyerian barrage had come in waves, but it never truly stopped, only lulled. By late the first night, the men had been able to sleep in shifts, but the sleep had always been short, interrupted by some volley or another. Atheltiades was beyond exhausted, but he would not rest. Logistically, he was needed to ensure that the fort held. And in a brief respite from the fighting, he began to make calculations and replay key events in his mind. And he thought of the dead and dying. He thought of them not just as men and comrades, but as the gaps he needed to fill.

Pertinax, one of his most trusted Captains from the March, had died less than an hour ago during the last wave, a heavy stone having caved in his head, helmet and all. The body had just been removed from the battlements, and he had watched as the toneless arm flopped towards the stone below as he had been carried away. Captain Nikolos and Alkaios were the two remaining officers from his training cadre. The recruit leader of the training class, a youth named Diokles, had been appointed to fill the spot of Pertinax. Alexios, the Captain he had met at the gate when they first arrived, was in charge of the towers and the artillery. This was the same role that Lysander had given to Atheltiades when the siege started.

It had been a good idea to have someone supervising operations from above, so Atheltiades had delegated the role to Alexios. He did not agree, however, with Lysander's decision to withhold sending messengers for help. Four had been sent out to spread the word and ask for reinforcements. Since Dutrigi had fallen, who knew how many of the nearby cities were still standing, and if they could even send any aid at all. It was better than nothing, and had to be tried.

The fort was well defended, but a resupply of fresh soldiers and food and water would be welcomed. The water tanks were fully topped off from recent rains, the stores and larders were near fully stocked as well. They had no shortage of weapons and ammunition. But these supplies were not unlimited, and manpower was even more of a commodity. In the name of national security, slaves had been sent out to pilfer supplies from whatever merchants still remained camped on the northern side of the fort. These merchants were then ordered to go and spread the word about the siege.

Below Atheltiades, the broken and

bloodied bodies of Saurians were everywhere.
The moat below had been completely filled with
corpses, making the obstacle obsolete. The
Hyerians had attempted to break through the
drawbridge, to burn it, to hack it, to rip it down,
but it had been of no use. The Dutrigians had
back filled the doorway with stones incase the
invaders had made it through, but they never
did. The more they tried, the more the bodies
stacked up in front and wedged it shut even
tighter. Just two waves of attack ago, using their
own fallen as a bridge and footing, they had
tried using ladders to go over the top.
Bridgegate's walls had proven to be too tall for
the ladders they had made, and the maneuver
had been thwarted. If they kept piling up the
dead like this, they wouldn't have to wait too
long to try and reach again. They might even
make a ramp of bodies and charge right over the
top.

Sweat ran down his face, stinging as it
poured into his eyes. He grasped the hot-to-
touch metal of his helmet that had been warmed
by body heat and sunlight, and pulled it off. The
rag he had placed inside his helm to absorb the
sweat was saturated beyond the point of being
effective, and he wrung the cloth out. Black hair
was matted and caked with perspiration and
salt. A gentle breeze from the east cooled his
recently exposed head and made his crimson
cloak dance gently. Steam rose from his scalp,
and it wasn't even a cool day. Water bearers

were delivering dippers to the soldiers, and he accepted his eagerly, gulping and not caring that most of the drink ran down his chin.

What were they going to do next?

Historically, an enemy threw a hard first attack at an enemy fortification, and once repelled, laid a long siege. The Hyerians however, were not your typical enemy, and Bridgegate was not your typical fort.

Early the first day, the Saurians had tried hurling firebrands but they had been ineffective. Most of Bridgegate was made of noncombustible material for just that reason. One of the tents the Medicii had set up was lost, but no serious injuries had occurred. Hyerian strength was dependent on, well, their strength. Ingenuity and technology had always been a weakness to them. They lacked modern equipment, perpetuating violence and fearlessness instead. It was effective in open combat, but not in sieges against well built fortifications. The Hyerians weren't incapable of using technology, they just chose not to. It was part of their culture, to fight with strength and axe, bare-hands, up close and personal. Shields were rare, and siege weapons were even more of an anomaly.

That was why Atheltiades was so surprised to see a giant siege tower lumbering through the distant pass before him. At first, he attributed what he was seeing as a delusion of his exhaustion. Then he snapped out of that, and any illusion he had that it wasn't real dissipated immediately. Eight wheels, each larger than a man, ground forward. Dozens upon dozens of Hyerians pulled heavy Akkedan bronze chains, making the tower creep across the grounds.

Behind the tower, a fresh force of hundreds of Saurians marched, snarling and growling in anticipation of a fight. Spearmen began to fan out, sprinting in front of the tower and those who pulled it, getting ready to harass the Dutrigians if they attempted to halt the machines approach. Time was slipping away, and each moment the tower was allowed to advance, that made it that much more likely it was going to be successful.

"To arms!" The Commander shouted, helm slamming back onto his head. "Archers! Target those that are pulling the chains! Alexios, get that artillery firing! I want that thing toppled before it gets halfway here!"

The sound of bowstrings releasing and being drawn back once more filled the air around him. The heavy thud and snap of Scorpions and onagers unloading soon followed. Most missed their targets. One heavy stone however smashed into a row of the enemy pulling the chain, cutting them down like wheat at harvest. In a blink of the eye, their spots were filled with replacements. Hyerians came flooding in from the rear and enveloping the chain-pullers, throwing up shields and creating a protective barrier around them. They looked like an Imperial Legion when they went into their tortoise formation.

"Gods give us strength." Atheltiades muttered under his breath. He wiped the sweat from his eyes, as he thought of something they might do. Nothing came. The tower would slow as it ran into the piles upon piles of dead, but it would not stop. The onagers were dialing in under the scrupulous eye of Alexios, but so far the volleys were inadequate. It was too far away to burn, if it would even burn at all. The framework was covered with a patchwork of saturated animal hides and scales of metal dotted here and there. Flaming arrows would do nothing.

"Scorpions! Target the pullers of those chains, see if you can burst through those shields!" He shouted. "Have the slaves bring up the amphorae of oil and Wyrian Wine seized from those merchants! As fast as possible! Get those onagers firing, the closer that thing gets, the sooner it will be too close to be in their range."

He panted loudly when he had finished giving his orders, a combination of yelling, the exhaustion, and the nerves. This was going to be *very* close timeline wise. The tower was rolling at a steady, sluggish pace but was closing the gap. The onagers weren't hitting the structure, the artillery wasn't doing much to slow down the manpower. Just as he realized that, a heavy stone smashed into one corner of the siege engine. The dull thwack of the impact and the sound of splintering wood echoed back to the defenders on the wall. With a slight wobble, the tower tottered oh so briefly, and then settled back and resumed it's course.

"On mark!" Alexios bellowed back down to the two onager crews in the quad below. The men scrambled to reload the massive torsion arms that gave the devices their power. A rain of spears flew up and over the walls, catching some of the defenders on top unprepared. To be unprepared in this situation meant death. While they formed a shield wall and returned fire in coordinated strikes, the onagers once again unloaded. One went wide, missing the tower completely and hurtled into the marching Saurians behind, clearing out a good swath of them. The other hit dead center on the tower, punching a hole through the skin and buckling the frame slightly.

Atheltiades felt a flutter of hope in his chest. A few more strikes like that, and this tower wouldn't be able to continue. The scorpion bolts were starting to make progress on the Hyerians that were propelling the machine as well. They might have a chance. Then, his hope was displaced with despair as heard the shouts from below and behind. The onager that was right on target had snapped its arm, and with it damaged the sinew ropes that powered it. No way it could be put back in service in time, but the crew would try. The other reloaded, and Atheltiades hoped that they had made the correct adjustments to be of use this volley.

Hyerians were beginning to climb into the tower as it inched forward. Some appeared on the upper platform, and began hurling stones and spears onto the battlements they were about to besiege. They were within range, and many found their marks. They concentrated their attack on the area in front of them, and the Dutrigians held up shields or scattered behind more substantial cover.

"Target the spear throwers!" Atheltiades shouted from behind his own shield. If they had any chance at regaining cohesion, they had to give the enemy pause, and allow themselves to regroup. Spears rained down from above, and shot up from below. Stones careened of armor, flesh, and defenses. He could hear the enemy hissing and snarling, and his own men grunting and wincing.

"Regroup on me! Regroup on center!" The commander shouted. A stone, no bigger than a sling stone, clanged and ricocheted off of his helmet as he spoke. Inside, it had sounded like he had been struck with a massive hammer. The sensation of creased metal rubbing against his scalp let him know he had a nice dent, no need to check to verify.

Slowly, the soldiers made their way to a tight fitting formation around him, and they were able to pause a moment and reset, to come up with a plan. Archers continued to unleash volley after volley, some up into the Saurians on top of the tower, others shooting into the fields below. The tower drew closer. The one onager below was going to be out of effective range soon. The Scorpions fired bolt after bolt. Still, the tower came. That was when Atheltiades saw the oil and Wyrian wine being cached close to them.

The Commander turned to brief the men.

"When they get closer, we smash the oil and the Wyrian on the tower and the pullers below." He spoke loudly and clearly. "The Wyrian will burn hot. The oil will burn slow and make the fire last. We hit it everywhere, the base, the top, everywhere. Then we light it off with torches and flaming arrows. Then we throw more amphorae at it. That will hopefully halt it before it hits the walls, or burn it shortly after. In the meantime, javelins. Lots of Javelins. Gods give strength!" As soon as he finished his directions, the onager fired a final desperate shot before it was out of range. The speeding stone caught the top lip of the highest level of the tower right at the corner, and exploded the area it hit. Shards of wood, rock, hide, metal, and Saurian filled the air. Still, the tower moved forward.

Javelins took flight, finding empty ground or shield more often than Hyerian flesh. The Hyerian volleys continued back without end. The red skinned soldiers hissed and snarled, and the men could see the saliva dripping from their needlelike teeth and purple tongues as they opened their maws. Some of them had skin color that was almost brown, some were pigmented with more orange. Hundreds of shades of red filled the battlefield below, as well as the Black and Yellow flag of their nation. They were eager to fight, no doubt about it the way the horde writhed below.

With a deep inhale, Atheltiades gave the order to the unleash the incendiary attack. Dozens of ceramic jugs sailed through the air, and then dozens more, and then more. They smashed into the hull of the tower, they shattered into smithereens and sent liquid splashing everywhere. Jugs were thrown down at the base, down onto the shields that protected the pullers. Torches were lit and thrown at the tower and the soldiers. The fires started immediately. Flashes, conflagrations of intense flame, that soon receded. Small, less impressive fires remained, but those below that were pulling paused, and the tower slowed.

"Again!" He yelled. "Now!"

Once again, fully armed and armored hoplites threw jugs of cooking oil and imported alcohol. The flames grew once again, and soon engulfed the tower. But the tower did not stop. It was burning, but wasn't about to collapse. Soon, it was close enough that the gap between it and the walls was almost jumpable for a Saurian. It's progress had slowed, due to both the flames as well as the build up of bodies underneath it's massive, grinding wheels.

A few well placed javelins took out the Hyerians on the top of the tower, standing high above the walls of the fort. They were soon replaced with more Saurians. Then, the tower did stop. It could go no further; the fire and the bodies had taken their toll on forward progress. None-the-less, the main gangplank, located on the floor below the top of the tower dropped, and out of it poured smoke and flame. And then out poured Hyerians.

Screaming and baring blades, they emerged from the flaming conditions like demons crawling out of a doorway to Hades. Javelins caught several of them, but they continued spilling out. They slammed on top of and into the Dutrigians with blatant disregard for their own safety. With swords drawn, the soldiers in the front row began stabbing and hacking at the monsters that landed all about them. Bronze axes swung wildly, cleaving limbs or lodging deep into oaken shields. More and more leapt from the tower that was burning with greater intensity with each passing moment.

Snarling and snapping, screaming in a tongue that none of the humans knew, the Saurians flooded onto the walls. One that had lost it's axe grabbed the throat of a man next to Atheltiades and dug it's claws into the exposed flesh, squeezing. With a single motion, the Commander opened the beast's throat, purple ichor spraying across his blade and arm. It's final act in death was to continue to hold onto his victim as he jumped off the wall, both disappearing to their fates. A red blur slammed on top of Atheltiades, and instantly he was lying on his back on the floor of the battlements. Feet and legs blurred around him as the battle continued, but right on top of him was the face of death.

The Hyerian opened his mouth in a roar, sharp teeth spread wide, tongue flicking in and out. The golden yellow eyes were evil, like the eyes of a snake. They showed no signs of anything other than hatred and murder. The hot breath of the beast washed over his face and choked the own air from his lungs. The vile odor of hot putrefaction filled his lungs, and it made him feel queasy. Automatically, reflexively, the Dutrigians short sword stabbed into the flank of his attacker. Over and over, he stabbed. The Hyerian clawed at his face, gouging the helmet and cheek guards with his shiny black claws. Atheltiades continued to stab, and the Saurian continued to claw.

The commander felt his flesh open above his eye as a claw found its purchase. With a scream, he stabbed the attacker harder and deeper. The Saurian let out no death shriek, no sounds of pain or frustration. It just stopped moving, and collapsed on top of Atheltiades as dead weight. Gasping for air, he schlepped the Hyerian off to one side and tried to get to his feet. He needed to rejoin the fight. But the fight had stopped. The last of the Saurians on the walls had been killed of were in the process of dying. Purple blood and red blood was splattered everywhere. It took Atheltiades a moment to realize that the siege tower had collapsed. The structure had finally failed from the damage by the fire and the projectiles.

It had worked. They had won. As he looked around, at the horrors that filled his field of vision, he felt as though they were only delaying the inevitable. But they had to try, they had to do their best. Dutrigi may have fallen, but this fort still stood. And as long as Dutrigians still lived, then Dutrigi would never truly fall. He knelt down next to soldier that was trying to keep a massive gash on his thigh from bleeding. Tearing a cloth from the cloak of a dead soldier, he began the process of helping to heal the wounded. All the while, a shield wall stood tall to repel any attack that might be thrown their way. The wall was smaller, but still just as strong.

XL
ADYPATUS EVENTUS

Eventus had no concept of time in the perpetual darkness of his surroundings. Dim torchlight did nothing to illuminate the cave-like surroundings of the Hold. Occasionally, the entrance would open to allow guards in and out, but the light that came in from the outside was minimal. Time passed very slowly, and it was measured in changing of the guard and the growing scruffiness of his facial hair. The Imperial Guardsmen, dressed in purple, continued to file in on schedule and make their way down to the Lower Hold. He had a theory about what it was all about, one he pieced together early on. The mind of his that was always working out puzzles and mysteries was starved for exercise, and he began to draw conclusions about his surroundings and situation. His situation was dire.

The treasonous splinter cell of the Imperial Guard that was responsible for the murder of the Imperial Consul and the attempt on the life of the other, as well as the death of Flaccus and many, many others was hunting for him. And he was conveniently boxed up in a cell that they had access to, prepared like a sacrificial animal to the Gods, or wrapped up like a gift for exchange on the Festival of Kraseus. It was only a matter of time until they found him here, and then he would just be a dead, eviscerated corpse in a prison cell. The conspiracy would disappear then, lost into the annals of history. Maybe it would be brought to light by some historian generations from now, some future Meroditus uncovering the trails and strings that were there if you knew where to look. But they would get away with it.

What had this all been for? They had discovered the truth of what had happened, him and Flaccus, and now Flaccus was dead. They knew now that the Consul had been murdered by the Guard, and those who had wielded the blades were now just as dead as their victim. The assassin that had made his way into the Imperial Palace had been tracked down, and he had admitted to being assisted into the complex by the Imperial Guard. He could finger the man who hired him, but Sicarius had slipped away. The man who had hired him was more than likely working on behalf of Silious, who was now declared a traitor and a rebel anyways. If it were proven that he was the driving force behind the murders, perhaps it would sway public opinion of him towards the negative. But would it do anything more than he had already done by crushing Dutrigi?

Even if Eventus was given an opportunity to explain all of his findings to a judge or a hearing or the Consul, it wouldn't matter. He had no evidence, no living witnesses on hand. He was framed for murder, and it looked like he had done it. No one would believe him at all. Truth would pour from him with conviction and common sense points, but it would fall on deaf ears. He was like an oracle, a prophet, doomed to know the truth, the future, but have no one believe him, to be ignored. The memory of him desecrating that clamshell at the Temple of the Oracle flashed in his mind, and he cracked a smile. Irony, divine karma, Godly intervention. It was a cruel payback to be certain.

The man with the missing ear, the other man with the shaven head. If he found them, they would be the link he needed to prove his theory. But he was in a prison, and they could be anywhere. Stupid! Why had he turned himself in? He had no evidence, and no one would believe him. If only he had waited, unraveled another layer, then he could prove what was the truth and stop these traitors. He had signed his own death order when he had approached those Urban Guardsmen. And the conspirators were free to do what they wanted, continue with whatever their next wicked step was. Stupid!

Just then, commotion broke out from the Lower Hold. The dull and tormenting silence of the prison was disintegrated. The crack of the slamming open of the door reverberated through the cavern. Heavy, fast footfalls echoed as a lone Imperial Guardsman ran as fast as his armor would allow up the steps. Eventus watched as he stumbled once, deftly regained his balance, and didn't halt as he pushed the brim of his tipped-forward helmet up and out of his eyes. He shot through the door without hesitation. If the theory Eventus had developed was correct, this was either very good news or very bad news. Time would tell.

What felt like an eternity passed before someone reentered through the entrance. It was the same guard, this time with a Captain. The winded Subordinate was frantic, explaining what had happened. The superior was much more reserved and deliberate with his step, walking with patience.

"He just lifted his head, took a deep breath, and asked where he was!" The guard rattled. "Me and Paullus just looked at him, sir! Then I ran to get you, having heard you were right next-door at the Hall with that Judge! Paullus is down there with him right now, sir."

"Did he say anything else?" The Captain asked as he started down the stairs for the Lower Hold. Despite the dimness inside the space, his silver armor sparkled and gleamed. Eventus recognized the man as Pidaro. Instinctively, Adypatus melted back into the shadows.

"He asked for Duke Macien, and the Empress. And Water!" The guard said. "And he wanted the Imperial Council summoned at once."

"You did good by coming to me first, Guardsmen." Pidaro said as he bobbed out of view down the stairwell. Eventus craned his neck to watch until they completely disappeared from sight. "Now fetch the Medicii and the Priests. Go! I will have Guardsmen Paullus fetch the Imperial Council as the Emperor wishes."

"Yes sir!" an eager, excited voice boomed.

Eventus watched as the purple clad man ran up the steps once more, moving just as fast as last time, but no stumble the second time through.

The Enforcer forced himself to sit down. This would change everything if the Emperor were awake. The conspiracy against the succession government wouldn't mean a thing after all, the rightful Monarch restored to power. Silious and his rebels would lose momentum and support overnight. Emperor Greeth Kantaur would stabilize the Calidian Empire. Perhaps if Eventus requested an audience with the man, he would have all charges dropped and would allow the Enforcer to root out the unfaithful members behind the conspiracy. Then the bald man and the one-eared wonder would get what had been coming to them.

The second Guardsmen made his way up the steps, most likely going to fetch the remaining members of the Imperial Council. How quickly the scape of the world changed, life was so dynamic. This unforeseen twist had changed everything. No one thought that Emperor Kantaur would awaken again. The healers were being summoned right this second to wean him back to his usual self, the Council would convene to accept his rule once more. The dice had been loaded against Macien, but the Morincian had done a decent job of holding everything together as long as he did. Granted, civil war had ensued, but that was probably going to happen no matter who was sitting in the Imperial Chambers. Except the Emperor; if he were up and running like he was now, everything would be fine.

Why did he have a terrible feeling that something disastrous was about to happen, then? What was he not seeing? The Emperor had been moved to the Lower Hold for his safety. It had been done in secret obviously. And now, through some miracle, he had awoken from his coma. The guards summoned their Captain who had been visiting a Judge next door, which was strange. Why would Pidaro be at the Hall of Dikasta? The Judges there dealt with criminal cases in the city, not the Palace… like the murder case of an Enforcer, like Flaccus.

Something felt wrong. He did not trust Pidaro, and had felt that the man had been in on the conspiracy with no proof, just intuition. Pidaro had always given Adypatus a poor impression. Maybe he was projecting his personal views of the man on the current situation. Even before the encounter at the palace, the man had rubbed him the wrong way. Even back in their days when they were in the Legions, the man had been a prick. One time during a battle, when Pidaro had been an Optio of a Century in the same Cohort as Eventus, he had punched out Eventus' Decanus for not obeying one of his orders. The Decanus hadn't taken the man serious at first, since his helmet had been lost, and caked blood had covered his face. Pidaro's entire face was red, and Eventus vividly remembered being surprised at how much blood came from...

He gasped. Oh no. What could he do? Pidaro was alone with the Emperor. The urge to scream for help surged up inside him, but only a choking sound came out. Grabbing the bars of his cell, he began pulling and pushing, as if he could tear the iron from the stone with his bare hands. Just then, the front door to the hold swung open, and a steady stream of people began to flow in. Life Priests, Medicii, more Guards, all began to flood into the room and make their way down the stairs. They were meet halfway by the Captain in the silver helm, making his way back up.

Some ran past, around him like a rapid navigates a boulder, yet others slowed as they saw the look on Pidaro's face.

"The Emperor has passed. He is with the Gods now." Pidaro said solemnly.

"What!" shouted some. "Nooo!" Wailed

others.

"I watched the life go out of him. He is gone from this world." Pidaro said more sternly. Then reverently, he removed his helmet and placed it in the crook of his arm, head bowed slightly. Some stopped and stooped their heads as well, others pressed on to see for themselves. "I heard his last words, and they were 'Macien poisoned me.'" Anger and sadness followed this revelation. Wails came from the Lower Hold as people beheld the truth.

Soon, most went down to the Lower hold, some bringing the torches from the walls with them. This caused the hold to become darker, danker, and more isolated than ever. Pidaro continued up the steps, towards the exit. Muffled voices drifted up from below, but they sounded distant and quiet. The cavernous hold was quiet once again.

Except for two voices, that came from above towards the exit. Pidaro was one, the other sounded very familiar, yet Eventus could not place it.

"You are certain?" The recognizable yet unplaceable voice inquired.

"As certain as I can be." Pidaro stated. "He was awake. I had no choice."

"We all have choices." The first said. "Our master may not appreciate your going off the script. Although I'm sure he will not fault you."

"Silious ain't my master." Pidaro said in

an angry yet quiet tone. They were speaking at a level that would not normally have been able to be heard, except for the acoustics of the Hold.

"Silious is not who I speak of." The unknown man said. "But what is done is done. This may complicate matters, but it is a means to the end. Did he not have his ring?"

"What ring?" Pidaro said, annoyed.

"The Signet ring, his fathers ring. If he was not wearing it, that explains why he may have awoken." The man asked.

"You know, I didn't check. I had my hands full." Pidaro said.

Footsteps filled the room as the pair broke apart and headed different directions. Soon, Pidaro emerged into view once again, slowly heading back down the steps to the group assembled around the departed monarch below. As he walked, Eventus saw his close-cropped black hair, and couldn't help but notice the scar on the side of the face where his ear once had been. In the distance, through the thick stone walls, he could faintly hear the distant tolling of bells from the Temple of Calidius, the traditional heralding for the death of an Emperor.

XLI
MACIEN

There was just over a half moon, but it was unusually bright tonight. So were the stars. The cool, pale blue white of the moonlight and the warm glittering yellow stars filled the nights air like sparkling gems. The green star, Adelphos as it was called in Morincia, Phratis in Calidia, was surging and pulsing particularly remarkable tonight. The smaller but more intense red light in the sky, known as Sorohr, was a constant burning ember in the darkness. The air was clear, the stars amazingly vibrant and abundant. The huge cluster that formed the streaky band that ran across the heavens had a purplish hue to it. Macien had always called it "The Straw Thief's Path", from a tale his mother had told him as a boy, but it had many names, and he found few others that called it that whenever it was mentioned.

It was well after dark, and there was no chill to be found lingering in the atmosphere. Macien took a deep breath as he gazed upwards, and the air that filled his lungs was warm and stale with traces of fine dust. Around him, the camp was eerily quiet. This was the one of the first moments in recent memory where he had felt truly alone. Not only did he feel alone, but also he felt dwarfed by the epic firmament above him. It was refreshing, but he found himself not wanting to be alone. In fact, he wanted the opposite.

He wanted to be with his family. If that was impossible, he wanted his friends and trusted brother in arms around him. Greeth; he wished Greeth were here to make the hard decisions, to rule his own Empire. Kanion; If his Captain were here, he would know what to do and how to do it. Old Triaricles, Macien wished he were still alive. His father, Emperor Quel, Prince Quel. Prince Luqius, Gaius Versius. So many good men, wise men, all gone. He was all that remained. And to make it even worse, he didn't really want to be here in this situation. He found himself longing to be back on Luctantum, with Greeth being in charge, and Macien commanding his own phalanx against Homithans. Those were simpler times. Even better yet, he wished to be at home, without a sword in sight.

His entire world was slipping out of his grasp and out of his control. It was as if he was in a dream, one that he knew wasn't real, and nothing he could do would change how it played out. The predetermined moves on a giant Latrunculli board were unfolding, and he was just a pawn, while others made the major moves. But he was now also the most powerful piece on the board as well. Silious was determining so much, and Macien needed to deal with that right away. The head start he had in mobilizing the Legions and marching with the 1st hopefully would be the first step in doing so, but he still felt as if he were playing into some sort of trap or power play.

Macien gazed a final time at the heavens above, and returned his eyes and his mind to the earth and the world and situation around him. The 1st legion was camped all around him. They had marched hard today, and Macien had given the order that the construction of the usual Castra was to be forgone. Many of his advisors had recommended against such a blatant disregard for security so close to an enemy force, but he still gave the order. It wasn't as if he ignored what his staff had explained, they were advisors after all and that was their job, to advise. No, he realized exactly how dangerous it was, acknowledged it, and made a bold if not perilous decision. He took a chance.

Cortinum was close. Two days, maybe one if they drove hard. Hours of manual labor would exhaust the men even more for tomorrow's march, and he wanted them fresh and rested, so when they arrived at the battlefield, they would be ready to go and not be blown. If they started the march early, they might reach the city by tomorrow night, but they would be pushing it. An exhausted Legion was worth little when it came to a fight. If it turned out to be a siege, then they would be

behind the curve already and would never catch
up.

The outlines of the buttes beyond were
clearly delineated by the bright night.
Somewhere beyond the horizon, his enemy
waited. Silious had proved fast and ruthless,
striking like a viper. Dutrigi had been a major
blow to the Empire and the morale of the
soldiers and officers around him. No doubt it
had been a calculated move, to strike fear into
his enemy just as he was doing. The clever
bastard had also struck at Morincia, razed
Portopolis, and apparently was heading for
Jorbus next. That had been deliberately
personal, Macien knew, and also logistically
crippling. Many Morincian Phalanxes had been
summoned to help put down this rebellion of
Silious, but no doubt they were going to remain
at home, to deal with the threat from the Sea
Snakes. That meant his uncle Kyberien and the
Jorbus military would be staying behind to do
the same. Silious had cut the Empires
reinforcements off at the knees.

Enthaki was in upheaval. Vitruvian
invasion forces had been spotted in the Delta
Lands. A barbarian incursion, an Enthaki army
storming across the Dry Mountains, or a Saurian
attack would be the nail in the coffin, the Empire
would fracture. Anything was possible. But that
was all out of his control, he had to focus on
what he could affect immediately around
himself. He had a battle to win, which would

allow him a chance to win the war. If this battle were lost, so was any hope of winning this entire conflict. It was all up to him.

Why? Why was it all up to him? Why did Silious feel he had a right to call himself Emperor? Why was Greeth Emperor? Because this was how they were born? It seemed a preposterous idea. Macien was born to a certain family, so through a chain of events, the fate of the entire Empire fell upon his shoulders. What if Macien didn't want any of this? He didn't have a choice. What if he had never been born? Would *Darien* be leading the Imperial Military? What if Silious hadn't been born to be such a malevolent, entitled future tyrant? This was the way it was, and the way it always would be. Those in positions of power never gave up their power, never deprived their children of that power and the means to have their own memory and ego carry on in the form of a dynasty.

Once Greeth awoke, Macien would gladly relinquish his power and his burden. Let those who wanted to rule do just that. Once Greeth awoke, everything would be better. He had made an oath, a pledge to his friend, and it was one that he did not want to keep. Once Greeth awoke, that oath could be forgotten, invalidated. Once the Emperor was back on his feet, everything would be okay. In the meantime, he had a battle to fight so the Emperor could still have an Empire to awaken to.

XLII
QUINTUS VICTUS

The General had ridden ahead with his
forward party to get eyes on the battlefield for
himself. The main body of his army was a half-
day behind. Before him, in the valley below, the
city of Cortinum lay. It was a jumble of dark
shapes, most of the lights that normally brought
a city to life remained unlit. But there it was, his
next victory. The Imperial Legions that were
garrisoned here were doing exactly what he had
hoped they would do. Word of Dutrigi meeting
them in open battle had spread, and this was a
result he was hoping he would see because of
that. The Legions had built a large wall and
defenses around the city, probably out of fear.
They had changed their strategy based on
Victus' brilliant victory over the Bulls.

He had hoped they would burrow in like
this. The siege engines and artillery that they
would be utilizing would obliterate them behind
their makeshift walls and ditches. The unique
equipment they had used against the Dutrigians
had been left behind. Some of it could have been
very useful, but most had been specific to the
landscape outside that city. Brining any of it
would have slowed down the advance of the

Army immensely, so it had been abandoned.

That was fine, allies to the north had long ago been ordered to construct and transport engines to Cortinum. They should be arriving the same time as the brunt of the army would. Trivium had been given very explicit orders about timing and the importance or choreographing such an elaborate campaign with so many intricate moving parts. Once they arrived and got everything in position, they could start pounding the city with projectiles and fire. If the Legions hunkered within decided to stay where they were and ride it out, they would be obliterated. If they decided to try their luck on open battleground, they would be mopped up.

Everything would go according to plan. The face of warfare was changing, and it was starting to look more and more like him everyday. The old ways were as dead as Dutrigi. And soon, Cortinum, the abhorrent and weak "Free City" would be conquered. Calidia would fall next. Then Silious would be Emperor, and Victus would be Master of Troops of the entire Imperial military. Then they would conquer the world. The Kantaurians had weakened the fighting strength of Calidia for long enough. It was time for real men and real soldiers to step up and take the reigns.

Victus would be remembered in perpetuity as the greatest military mind of all time. The current administration would suffer immensely for the wrongs they had done to him. And Silious, well, one day he would realize the superiority of Victus, and by then it will be too late. The soldiers of the Empire would more than likely insist and contribute to his overthrow and replacement of Silious.

But that was the future, a ways down the road. This city before him lay in his way, between him and his destiny. From what he could make out in the bright moonlight, the walls that they were constructing below were made of stone. A lot of the material and supplies had most likely come from dismantling structures in the city, and then repurposing them as defenses. Judging by the camp size and array of tents, two Legions were garrisoned on the far side of the city. Excellent. One of those was probably the 7th, which they had given a thrashing as the disgraceful force had fled and retreated. This would go smoothly. Cortinum would be an even easier prize than Dutrigi. This speed-driven campaign would bring them to the capital at a rate where the legions being recalled would trickle in too late. Hopefully by then, the remaining forces would come to their senses and acknowledge Silious' claim to the throne, and all fighting will come to a halt. Then they could focus on Homitha and the rest of the world. First Cortinum, then the capital. That would be the war.

A few pockets of resistance would still hold out, but that could be dealt with later.

Morincia would be an issue; that would be certain. Petros was doing their part right now to destabilize that area, and it would need to be stabilized by Silious once everything else settled down. A smile crept across his face; it was grotesque and evil. His eyes were glimmering cold and calculating. They all matched his thoughts. He thought of the numbers, the angles, and the geometry of the battle that would unfold below in a few short days. The math was all there, he could see it.

Then he thought of the spoils of war, the broken and burning building, the broken and burning bodies. The screams, the blood. The pride, the undulations of victory cries. It all made him smile that much broader and more grotesquely. This was what he had been born to do.

XLIII
ATHELTIADES

The Commander had forced himself to sleep. It had been hard to admit he needed the rest, but easy to slumber once he stopped and closed his eyes. He sat and leaned his back against a stonewall, dipped his head forward, and instantly was unconscious. It would be dawn soon, and they had spent the night fighting, repelling the enemy. After the Hyerians had attempted to use that siege tower, the fighting had slowed slightly. The respite had been brief. The still smoldering husk of the toppled tower had fallen parallel to the great wall, and it made a convenient climbing structure for the Saurians to use. It served as a platform for the ladders, which reached much closer to the parapet when placed on the framework.

Ropes attached to dragonclaws had been thrown in abundance. At first they pulled the ropes tight, as if they were trying to tear down the walls. Then Saurians started to shimmy up the lines, hoping to climb up and secure a foothold for the rest of their brood. The ropes were easily slashed and the lines fell uselessly to the ground below. Like a disgusting imitation of a loaf of bread, the mound of bodies below grew and expanded, even starting to engulf the collapsed siege tower. The enemy was relentless. They were taking their toll on the defenders. More dead and wounded filled the quad below than were up on the battlements and towers. A day longer perhaps, that was all they had. Maybe two. That had been his last thought as he closed his eyes to the early morning darkness. He dreamt no dreams.

The horns awoke him with a start. The burning daylight blinded him. It took a few seconds for him to gather his wits and composure, and get to his feet. He was weary and his body ached. A sharp kink his neck had formed from sleeping slumped over like he was. Stretching his tight neck side to side, he placed his helm back atop his head. The padding within that had been dripping with cold, sloppy sweat when he had removed was now just mildly damp. The sun showed him that it was midmorning. He had slept hard, but felt more tired from it.

Finding a sentry, he was filled in on the situation. The enemy hadn't been what spurred the call to arms. An approaching group from the north road, the mainland, had been spotted. Climbing the tower, he could see it. Small. But they wore red. Reinforcements? Survivors from Petrichoro or Dutrigi? The Polemarch was overdue to be back, but Lysander said he had only taken a handful of soldiers with him. This force was several dozen strong; perhaps a half a hundred men. And they wore red. Whoever they were, if they were friends, they would be greatly welcomed.

As they drew closer, he could tell that they weren't exactly Dutrigian. Most of the red cloaks were brighter, more vibrant, and of a different cut than the regular army issue. Silvery armor shone where the Dutrigians would normally have been hued in bronze. The shields weren't exactly hoplons, either; they looked to be flat, and were smaller in size. Emblazoned on each was not an image of a bull, but a ram. Trimontis soldiers. And at the head of them was a Dutrigian Polemarch.

Atheltiades made his way down to the northern gate to meet the approaching party, leaving Alexios in charge of defending the walls in his brief absence. Polemarch Rhodenikos was short by Dutrigian standards, but exuded confidence and command presence. His deceptively youthful face and features disguised his age and experience. The Commander walked alone across the drawbridge to make his introduction and give his report to the Polemarch. They walked and talked, the Trimontis soldiers funneling in behind.

"I was still at the fort of Southpass when word of Dutrigi reached us. Captain Keratos and his men of the Trimontis garrison there personally escorted me here. Soon after we were underway, we received word of the siege going on here. Runners were sent to Trimontis to see if a larger force could be summoned to help support us. In the meantime, based on what you have said, this force I have with me now will be a great help in supporting the defense of the walls. Let me see these Hyerian bastards for myself, lets go up on the wall. Commander, I am relieving you of formal command of the fortress. Thank you for stepping up and holding it together. Damn shame about Lysander." And with a grunt, he began to bound up the steps, red cloak flowing behind. Atheltiades tried to keep up.

"Sir, the men that are still fighting have been doing so for days. Putting some fresh troops up there as soon as possible will-" Atheltiades began, but was cut off.

"Keratos! Have your men line out and relieve our men!" The Polemarch shouted, never turning or slowing as he made his way up the stone steps towards the defenses above. A sea of red followed up behind them as the Trimontis troops started up the steps.

After reviewing the damage and defenses, and seeing the horde of corpses and approaching belligerents below, Rhodenikos praised Atheltiades once more, shocked at what he saw but trying hard to keep that emotion from showing. As the Trimontis troops filed in the gaps along the wall, they were given pass downs and information from the Dutrigians they were relieving. Many of the ragged, bloodied soldiers refused to give up their post, and they were not refused that right. Some were ordered to get rest, and they did not disobey. A few Saurians harassed the wall, and the fresh Trimontis troops proved to be deadly accurate with javelin and spear.

The Trimontis men looked so similar yet were different from their Dutrigian brethren. They appeared scruffier, more rugged, more rough around the edges. They had broader frames and living in the mountains had made them muscular and strong. They wore their hair and beards long, in almost a barbarian fashion. Perhaps interbreeding and intermingling with the Vaus, the Greld, and the Deklar had taken it's affect on them. Perhaps they had needed to adapt some of the barbarian traits in order to survive and prosper in their lands. No one doubted their skill as warriors, and their appearance carried a certain air of intimidation.

Rhodenikos found Atheltiades after he had finished his initial inspection and size-up. "Commander Atheltiades, thank you again for your work here." The Polemarch nodded. "You're men have done a fantastic job. I knew your father, Atheicles, and you have made him proud, no doubt about that. Now I am ordering you to get some sleep. I can tell by looking at you that you need it. And find some food. A leader needs to keep rested and nourished whenever the possibility presents itself. These sieges may last a long time."

"Yes sir." Atheltiades said, his voice sounding far more tired than he felt. "One more thing, sir."

"What's that?" The Polemarch asked, cocking his head to one side.

"The March, the Oaths for my men. We never took them, we were…"Atheltiades started.

"They do not need to take the Oath. Look down there, look up here, and look into the quad." Rhodenikos gestured to each in turn. "They have acted more like Dutrigians than any spoken word could ever prove. You're men were initiated when they stood on these walls against *that*."

"Yes, sir." Atheltiades said, pride swelling within.

"Soldier, what are you doing here! You are disobeying an order. Dismissed!" And with that, the Polemarch turned and walked away.

Atheltiades went to find a place to sleep, feeling content with the Polemarch taking command of his fort once again. Sleep would come easy, and he hoped that he would again dream no dreams. If he did, they would surely be nightmares of monsters with sharp teeth and claws.

XLIV
ADYPATUS EVENTUS

The endless procession of people in and out of the Lower Hold kept Eventus from getting any rest. The bells tolled through the night, through sunrise, and still rang now at midmorning. They would do so until the sun set tonight, as was the tradition. The ringing was distant, muffled by the rock walls of the Hold, but still omnipresent in the background. The Death Priest had come not long ago, draped in the darkest black imaginable, the white skull face paint a stark contrast to their clothes. Eventus couldn't get the image out of his mind of them emerging from below, rising silently like inky smoke. On a bier, covered in a sheer purple sheet, was the body of Emperor Greeth Boldranus Kantaur, being carried away for funerary rites. The royal purple shroud did not move as he glided gently and evenly up the steps. Neither had the stiff cloaks of the Death priests; it was as if the cloth had been cast of stone.

The only noise that came from the procession had been the soft jangling of the armor of the Imperial Guardsmen, escorting the remains of the man they had sworn to protect with their own lives. Eventus wondered if any of these men he watched in the parade had been in on the conspiracy. But now, everyone was gone, and the Hold became just a prison once again, nothing more remarkable than that. The Enforcer slunk back into the shadows and waited. The chiming of the bells was the only thing he had to keep his mind occupied, to distract him from thinking of his fate, and all that he had seen unfold recently.

He was certain that the murderous, treasonous Pidaro knew he was here. The Captain had been visiting the Hall of Dikasta, no doubt checking the records of the Flaccus murder case and seeing if Adypatus had been found yet. The snake may have even of seen him after he had murdered the Emperor. Any moment now, he expected the doors to burst open, and watch as Pidaro or the bald Imperial Guardsman strode through, brandish a blade and gut him right here in the cell. Eventus patted his thigh, feeling the small stiletto blade that was still strapped securely out of sight. It had never occurred to those Urban Guardsmen to search him for weapons. If someone came to kill him, he'd get a cut of his own in first.

In the meantime, while he waited for death to come, he sat alone. A few coughs and sneezes came from other cells, but no one he could talk to. Talking between prisoners was strictly prohibited and punishable by beatings. Occasionally, a Dik would stroll by, but no words were ever exchanged. Just silence, dim light, and the distant bells. His partner had been murdered, so had members of the Imperial Guard, so had Consul Selygo, and now the Emperor. He was the only one other than the conspirators that knew the truth, and he couldn't tell anyone, for no one would listen.

The torchlight was brighter now than it had been earlier, extra lighting had been brought in to deal with the Emperor's death scene and extrication. With the added visibility, he could see the dark brown-black splotches caked on his skin and clothes. He was still covered in blood, and it had crusted over to the point where it was flaking off as he moved and flexed. It had all been for nothing, he had failed. He had let so many people down, especially himself. Adypatus Eventus rarely failed, and when he did, it stung.

A crack of light came from the entrance to the Hold as the door opened. The sound of the bells intensified as the outside was let in. A single figure filled the doorway; he was wearing full armor and was silhouetted against the bright sunlight. The crest on the helmet made Eventus' stomach churn. Pidaro had come. But wait... the crest wasn't transverse. As the man approached, he removed his helmet, and it was a recognizable face. It was a welcomed face. It was Lt. Grattus. Two Diks escorted him to Eventus' cell, and they were summarily dismissed.

No words were said for several heartbeats, as the Lieutenant allowed his eyes to adjust and take in the ghastly visage of the Enforcer.

"Talk." Grattus commanded with disdain and pity, a slight shake of his head following his words.

Eventus was suddenly at a loss for words. He swallowed a lump in his throat, and then his voice croaked out a few hoarse words. It was the first time he had talked in Gods knew how many days.

"I didn't kill Flaccus." He managed to rasp out.

Grattus lifted his chin at this, his facial expression showing conflict and struggling between different emotions, all while trying to remain poised.

"I swear it to the High Gods, I…" Eventus started.

"I know you did not." Grattus cut him off, narrowing his gaze. "You are not that kind of man. Explain what happened."

And Grattus listened as Eventus explained everything. He left out few details, even the ones that painted him in a poor light. The entire truth flowed out of him, and he said it in a manner that left little doubt every word of it was true. The Lieutenant said nothing, showed no emotion and stood stoically immobile as the tale unfolded. When the yarn was done, he let out a heavy sigh of resignation.

"I believe every word you have just said, Eventus." Grattus said. "And I owe you an apology. I should never have told Flaccus to report back to me if anything illegal or unbecoming of an Enforcer came up during your investigation. I betrayed the trust that you had in me, and in doing so, damaged my own that I had in you. However, you quite literally have blood on your hands, and no proof. Although I believe you, without solid evidence, a Judge and for that matter, no one else, will. You know as well as I that desperate men in a desperate situation like the one you are in, will say and do anything to avoid the fate that is in store for them. The Imperial Guardsmen you killed may very well be treasonous bastards, but without proof, it is just murder. I'm sorry you are in this situation Enforcer."

"Not as sorry as I am." Eventus responded as hope fled him.

"You put me in a very dire situation here." The Lieutenant sighed. "I can't in good conscience ignore what you have told me, especially since I believe you. But we need proof. And if you stay in here any longer, I'm certain you will die. And by knowing what I now know, I won't be far behind. Legally we are in quite a quandary, I'd say."

Eventus bowed his head.

"Sometimes, in order to serve the Goddess, you have to say fuck the law." And with that, Grattus removed a key from his belt pouch. "The laws of the Gods sometimes override the laws of man and especially the laws of the state. You have a week and a day, Eventus. One week and one day to get evidence, to find this assassin Sicarius, to do whatever you need to do. At noon on the 8th day, when Lucidus is at the height of his rule, we shall shine some light on this to a judge. Meet me at the Hall, I will be there with a Judge to hear your case. If I'm not there, the Judge will be, and I will be dead."

He slid the key into the lock and turned, and it unlocked with a deafening clank.

"You will be a criminal, an outlaw until you prove your innocence. Do you still have a blade on you?" He asked very nonchalantly as he swung open the door.

"Yes." Eventus was startled at what was happening. "Yes, I do."

"Perfect." Grattus said. "That will make a convenient excuse. I'll order the guards to stand down, and they will be my witnesses that you broke out."

The Lieutenant clasp him firmly yet gently on the shoulder.

"I am sorry, Adypatus. I owe you a favor, I know how much you like having those in waiting. I'm cashing it in for you now. If anyone can pull this off, it will be you. Gods give strength. Now put that knife of yours to my throat and lets get you out of here, son."

XLV

TARAES KANTAUR

Jorbus was burning. Black, oily smoke rose and billowed from buildings that were completely engulfed in flames. Ships were burning in the harbor. Dankoma Bay was a battlefield, warships ramming one another and debris was strewn about as if a storm had struck. The early warning signal they administered had given the Jorbus fleet time to react, but the Petros ships were like a plague. Landing crafts were stacking up on the shoreline, and enemy soldiers were making their way into the streets. Crashes and screams could be heard originating from out on the water and everywhere in between there and the fringes of the city. It was a nightmare, something Taraes had never imagined and hoped she would never see.

The few short hours it had taken her to make the way down the mountain had felt like an eternity. As she drew closer to the city, the carnage and destruction grew greater as the attack continued and intensified. Not knowing the fate of her children and family was making her sick. It was all she could do to keep from crying. But she did not cry, for she ran instead. Several times she had tripped, stumbled, but immediately got up and continued without bothering to dust herself off.

When her and her guards reached the heights of the upper city, they had to slow down due to the enemy troops in the area, but the urge to move even faster was so intense her heart felt it would thump out of her chest. In the distance, the not too distant distance, they had seen flashes of yellow and teal as the Petros raiders stormed across intersections and down streets. Still, she and her guards continued to make their way to the palace and the citadel within. The closer they got, they began to notice the bodies. Civilians made up most of the dead, but the occasional soldier lay where he had fallen. Women and children didn't seem to be granted any special immunities, and that made her more anxious to find her family.

The main gates were sealed, and both Jorbus regulars and waves of Petros soldiers clashed in the streets. It seemed more like a brawl or a riot than an actual battle. Without pausing, she made her way towards the rear of the complex. They dodged fighting men, leapt over obstacles, made way over the scattered dead and dying. She was heading towards a small doorway she knew that was hidden in the ivy on the north side of the walls. As a child she had used it to play, but now she understood finally after a lifetime why it existed. It had been her and her brothers secret, no one else in the palace had ever known about it, except father. That was for reasons like this. They may have need at some point in their life to secretly make way in and out of the walls, and the less people who knew about it, the better and safer it would be.

As they walked between the crumbling orange brown cut bank and the stone walls, Taraes searched through the thick creepers of ivy for the long ago remembered portal. It took some doing, and a few hacks of a sword, but they found the hatch, and dove into the other side. It was mere moments before a pair of cerulean clad Jorbus hoplites was on them, barking for compliance to their orders. Once the guards ascertained that it was the lady Taraes and two of their own brethren, they quickly whisked the newcomers to the safety of the citadel.

Inside the walls, it seemed more chaotic than what was going on in the surrounding city. Soldiers ran this way and that, the sounds of hobnailed sandals echoed throughout the halls. Women were huddling together, comforting one another, or running through the passages at a frantic pace, fear heavy on their features. Everyone was doing something, whether it was useful or not. Faint traces of smoke were laced in the air, slightly dissipating and permeating from the burning structures within the city.

She didn't need to think as she navigated

through the complex, knowing intimately every step and turn from her youth. She felt like a salmon swimming against the current, pushing through the flow of soldiers that were making their way to the fighting. The guards she had come with had fallen well behind; she was too nimble, too quick for them to keep up. The archway to the throne room came into view and the hoplites posted guard didn't think for a second about challenging her admittance as she approached.

As she blew into the room, she immediately caught sight of Darien, standing next to the throne, a concerned and frightened expression on his face as advisors and aides spat facts to him. In a strange contradictory way, he looked more like a man than he ever had to her, yet at the same time, so much the young boy she remembered him as. With a cursory glance, he acknowledged her coming through the door, but then adverted his eyes and returned his attention to his staff. Taraes scanned around the room for her children. She did not see them. She tried to find someone who would know where they were, but found no one available.

Finally, an old maid in a headdress, whom she recognized but could not place her name, told her the children were in the Duke's quarters with the Duchess and her children. Relief washed over her as she left the command post, left Darien and his ilk to take care of the defenses. Nothing mattered to her but seeing her children right now. As he was walking up a flight of steps, she had to pause a little more than halfway to catch her breath and subvert the urge to vomit. Collecting herself, she continued on.

When she came into the room, all the children were sitting on the floor together, as if playing a game, beautifully ignorant to the world crumbling around them. Junæa was sitting on a bench, watching them; stern consternation was on her face. Behind her, the hulking frame of Kanion and his partners hovered. The men were dirty and bloodied, so were their tunics, and they wore no armor. A servant had been bringing them a washing basin right as Taraes entered. It was clear that they had fought their way to the palace. Ladles of drinking water were passed around, and they feverously drank to slake the thirst she could sense from across the room. Andronikos and Tycho cleaned their weapons as Kanion made his way towards the Empress.

"Taraes, praise the Gods you are alright." He made no gesture, no bow of subordination as he sidled beside her. "We were away from the Palace when it started, past the harbor. The streets were filled with soldiers by the time we drew near, and we had to fight our way through to reach the gates. From now on, you go nowhere without at least one of *us* by your side."

She nodded, and knelt down to embrace

her children, her nieces and nephew. There was knocking at the door, as three young men of the kitchen staff came into the room, each carrying the familiar kit of a Hoplite of the Jorbus Honor Guard. The three soldiers, with assistance from the makeshift squires, began to gear up.

Cuirass were donned, pteruges were tied, greaves and arm guards, helms and shields. It took less time than Taraes would have thought; the deft, eager and experienced hands of the warriors made short work of it. Before her now stood three men transformed into mighty soldiers, soldiers without faces. The Morincian style helmets exposed very little of the facial features hidden beneath the metal. Kanion stepped forward, he was the only one with a crest adorned his skull, denoting his rank as captain.

"Empress." He began. "We have ordered more guards to be posted outside these doors. Tycho will remain here with you, Junæa and the children." He abruptly halted, as if something had just occurred to him.

"You are leaving us?" She asked, not surprised but merely curious.

"Taraes, yes." He nodded slowly. "I made a promise to your brother to protect you and the children. I'm going to do just that. Tycho will remain behind to make sure you are protected from any threat that may make its way here. Andronikos and myself are heading out to meet with Darien and assist with repelling the invaders. By doing so, we will be upholding our pledge to Macien. The best way to protect you will be by fighting these curs head on." He took a step forward, and placed a gentle arm on her shoulder. The weight of his massive hand reminded her of the strength yet delicacy of when Greeth touched her.

"I will die before I allow anyone who would harm you step foot within these walls, I swear it. Do not worry, we will protect you."

"Be careful, Kanion. We can't have people letting down Macien, now can we?" She asked bitterly, no playfulness was traceable in her voice, although they both knew it was there. She could tell he was smiling under her mask.

"I fight now for my Empress, not my Duke. Or Consul. Or whatever it is he calls himself these days. I will not fail her." And with that, he left. Andronikos was a step behind. After hugging and kissing the children once more, she stepped to the window. Jorbus was burning.

XLVI
DANQUIN ELKNAUT

The morning sun was burning like a white-hot orb in the sky. The pale blue expanse around it was cloudless and vast. The force that had recently arrived stood in stark contrast to the brightness of the day. Clad in dark cloth and armor, they had looked like ants as they had approached the field before Cortinum. The Frontier Army flew the orange flag of Akritus, and that was fine with Elknaut. That is what they were after all, auxiliary legions. However, they were now rebels against the Empire, and that was something he could not tolerate. Anyone who defied Calidian rule, even if they are Calidian themselves, defied the natural order of the world. These rebels were protesting against his own right and titles as a Golden Class citizen, and that was something else that he could not stand for.

Cortinum would not have been his first choice as a place to make a stand against the enemy, but it hadn't been his decision, and it really hadn't been his *side's* decision at all. Silious had picked it, and it was clear why. It had poor defenses. It didn't even have walls until they had built them in the last several days. The field in front of them was heavily favored for an invading force; it sloped downhill towards the city, one flank was anchored by coastline, and the city could easily be circumvented on 3 sides by outriders. Plus the rising sun would be in their eyes during a morning battle.

As far as strategic importance, Elknaut could care less. Yes, it was close to the Capital, but not extremely so. If it came to picking a battlefield site, he would pick the great walled city of Calidia over this place every time. And the fact that Cortinum had been chosen was a blow to him on a personal and political level. This bleeding heart community had despised people like him and his own people returned the favor. They hated the military, except in moments like this when their very existence depended on it. They didn't want walls because it sent the wrong message to the world, but in a moment like this, they needed them, and they were built at the expense and sweat of the very Legions they despised. The hated Golden Class status, they even felt slavery should be abolished throughout the Empire. But now, the privilege and training and preparation of the Golden Glass was how their city was to avoid destruction. Not a single slave or former slave would be seen preparing to attack the enemy.

This city disgusted him, but to him at this

point, it was now only a battlefield. It was only a site to fight for his Empire. It might do this city a world of good to have this battle here, to shatter the veil of the fantasy world that it had been living in. Some of the residences fled, packed up and headed east to the capital. Those people made him sick, they were cowards. Those that stayed behind however, he had much admiration for, especially those that were helping build the defenses and prepare for the siege that was to follow.

As he stood on the makeshift battlements, hasty yet sturdy concoctions of wood and stone built from disassembled buildings, he pondered the inevitable battle that lay ahead. If it came to a siege, himself and his cavalry would be useless. Granted, if it came to a pitched battle or a brawl behind the walls, his men and him could wield a sword better than most. But their talents and strengths on horseback would be wasted. And, best case scenario, if the did take to open combat on the field, they would be limited. The entire left flank was congested with coastal obstacles. Only the right flank would allow for proper cavalry maneuvering, and it looked deliciously open for such things. But Silious and his staff would recognize that and do whatever they could to limit such things and turn it to their own advantage.

The various Turma of his Wing had taken shifts riding and scouting, getting a feel for the lay of the land and trying to get eyes on any enemy troop movements they could spot. Pass downs of what information had been gathered by the various parties were disseminated to the junior officers, and a general idea of the size and timeframe of the approaching force had been mapped out. Approximately three legions, and this one that just arrived was the first. They were already beginning to dig in, and if Elknaut were in command, they would be running them down right now. The rest of the force was supposed to arrive later today or early tomorrow.

Scouting parties headed east had also informed them that Consul Macien and the 1st Legion should be arriving at the same time. Other than that, whatever other maneuvers were being performed by either side were unknown to the army garrisoned in Cortinum. Alarmingly, a very small amount of information about the Dutrigi battle had been filtering in. Rumors had it that strange artillery and tactics had been used, but most of the facts they heard directly contradicted others they had heard, or were so bizarre they must be fabrications. Solid, tangible intelligence on the force that was approaching was like gold to them, and it was just as scarce.

From what they could gather, the cavalry of the enemy used thoroughbred Greld horses, fine beasts that could outrun any Calidian mount. Calidian horses might be faster when it came to hard sprints, but the Grelds were bred for long distance. Both had advantages in a fight, but as time and the battle wore on, endurance was optimal. They needed to make sure that if it came to a pitched fight, it was to be short and ended before the scales of favor tipped to the enemy.

Elknaut watched as the enemy flowed in over the ridges, banners and flags flying like some long serpent winding its way to wounded prey. Whatever happened in the next few days, Lieutenant Danquin Elknaut would make sure he did everything he could do to bring honor to his name and his family. If the Gods decided he were to die, then he would face death like a Calidian noble, sword in hand with defiance in his eye and his heart. A real Calidian was not afraid to die when it came to protecting his beliefs and way of life. The only problem was his enemy would be doing the same thing as him tomorrow, for they were Calidian, too.

XLVII
MACIEN

Twilight was starting to come, and dark violet shaded the sky as they approached Cortinum. The first of the torches had started to be lit as they made their way to the city. The gambit had paid off, and the 1st Legion had arrived early, and they had arrived relatively fresh. Forgoing the construction of the castra had been a risk, but it had been the right move it looked like. As they marched into the city, they passed the abandoned fort of the 7th and the 9th. It had been left intact incase they needed to fall back to a secure contingency spot, he assumed. That had been smart. No one plans for failure, except for the wise and the cautious.

The city itself was eerily quiet. Purple Calidian flags of the Empire sat still and slack in the air, being just as flaccid as the emerald green griffin flags of the city. Windows were shuttered and boarded and few people were in the streets. A mandatory curfew had no doubt been enforced upon those who had decided to stay in the city. Light emitted from the cracks of a window from the occasional building, but most remained dark. The 1st had encountered droves of people fleeing east to find asylum in the capital or the lands beyond. If this battle did not go as Macien hoped, these refugees would find no such peace anywhere in the Empire. The sounds of boots marching on paved streets filled the air and broke the silence of the night.

When they arrived in the makeshift camp that had been set up on the northwest corner of the city, behind the clandestine walls, Consul Macien wasted no time. He called for a full meeting with the senior staff and ordered the 1st to set up their camp as he did so. The men would sleep well tonight, they had marched an unbelievable distance today, and the fact that they only needed to set up tents was another bonus for them. Who knew what tomorrow might bring, better to rest while they could.

The staff had little good news to provide. Cortinum had needed defenses, and the priority construction of those had consumed much time and energy from the men. The General in charge, Titus Validus, was formally relieved of command and thanked for his services to this point. The General was certain to have a lead role in the coming conflict, but Macien would hold ultimate imperium. Macien had fought alongside Validus in the past, and he was surprised the man had made as much progress as he had here recently. He had never been known for his tactical mind, so Macien guessed he had some bright junior officers under him. The Legates all seemed squared away, especially Acadius of the 2nd.

Intelligence on the enemy was scarce, and Macien made sure that the top priority for tomorrow would be to gather as much knowledge as they could about them. It appeared that three legions worth of soldiers, all wearing the colors of Silious had made camp outside the walls. It was unknown what their intentions were, if they were waiting for another force to arrive, or if they would begin their siege as quickly as possible, starting at any moment. The fact that they hadn't made a move yet made him think it was probably the former. That meant that the Imperial forces also had time to prepare against an attack, to further entrench themselves.

Rumors about the Dutrigi massacre were filtering in, and most were just hearsay. However, there were common threads between the tales. Everyone agrees the Dutrigians had unequivocally been killed, demolished, destroyed. They had faced Silious and his forces in open combat rather than weather the siege, and had been crushed as a result. That tidbit resonated strongly with the senior officers, and they were more inclined to burrow in and hold off the enemy through attrition rather than face them in pitched battle. The longer the Legions held out, the more likely reinforcements from across the empire would trickle in. It also meant that they could attempt to avoid the fate of the Bulls. Another common factor in all the stories had been machines of war that rebel army had used. Engines and projectiles, and giant contraptions that had laid down the Dutrigians like wheat being scythed.

In the light of the morning, he would walk the battlements, and get an idea of the battlefield before him, and the strength of the enemy force. Tonight his mind would run wild with speculations and scenarios, but tomorrow he would gather the facts and come up with a real decision. Tonight, he would sleep, but it would not be peaceful. Not only did he have a battle to contend with tomorrow, but also news had caught up with them of the invasion of Portopolis, as well as the imminent attacks on Jorbus and Athyrtun. That was personal, and that made him mad.

Images of his friends, visions of his family being hunted, tortured, murdered flashed before his eyes. In frustration he raked his fingers through his dark brown hair, and grasping clumps between his knuckles, he pulled. Blowing the air through his lips, he let the anger flow through him. He accepted it, acknowledged it, and then let it pass. With each breath and each flex of his tense muscles, the anger fled from him. He needed to keep a cool, level head. He prayed to the Gods before he slept that night, as he reverently fidgeted with the knucklebone of his father.

The night was powerful, the energy different than anything he had ever felt while on campaign in the past. This would be a pivotal moment not just in his life, but also in the history of the Empire. Whether he realized it or not, the entire world was watching him. Not just he modern world, but the entirety of the past was depending on this battle, and the whole future would study and scrutinize it for untold generations. Macien was about to be a major player in the histories of the world, and although he acknowledged it, no extra stressors were added because of it. If anything, it made Macien a little more comfortable, knowing that something crucial was about to happen. That validated his instincts about the movements and plans that he had made. He slept, but he dreamt no dreams.

XLVIII
DAHQUAL SILIOUS

Silious sat upon his horse, his black armor stood in stark contrast to the brightness of the day around him. Anger was welling up inside him, but he pushed it down. His anxiety of the situation was only compounding his fury and frustration, so he took a few deep breaths. Things were going well, but yet they were also not perfect. When he had arrived last night, he had expected to find General Victus already bombarding the city with artillery, crushing the force that was garrisoned within. However, Victus had done no such thing; the artillery had not yet arrived.

The General was just as frustrated as the Duke had been, explaining that the fault lay with Trivium, not himself. Victus had pulled off a stunning victory at Dutrigi, just as he had promised. The strategy for his success had been the perfect alignment of so many moving parts. All the siege weapons and artillery that they had used there had been abandoned as planned, left behind as to not slow down the speed of the next attack. A new batch of weapons had been constructed in Trivium to exact specifications, and those were supposed to have arrived

already. The Trivium force had yet to appear.
This was Victus' campaign, and any blame for
mistakes like this ultimately fell upon him. He
would be punished.

The element of surprise and the
advantage of speed had been taken from them.
They had lost that and they could never regain
it. If the attack had started as planned, Cortinum
would be theirs, the meager force would be
crushed, and they could march towards Calidia.
Take Calidia, and the war will end. Silious
would be Emperor. But they hadn't taken
Cortinum yet, and while they waited to begin,
Macien had arrived with reinforcements. The
more time they wasted, the stronger the
defenses got and the more bolstered the enemy
army became. Lourede's advice and prophetic
urging that he must make the first strike echoed
in his mind. He clenched his jaw as he thought
of this.

Silious had called for a parley with the
enemy high command. Victus had insisted that
his scouts had located the Trivium force, a half-
day march to the north. Silious was calling this
meeting to help drag things out and allow
Victus time to prepare his offensive. Silious had
half a mind to throw the whole plan out the
window, and just start laying siege with the
forces he had on hand. But a parley with the
enemy was necessary. Perhaps they would
surrender, accept the offer that Kruegius had so
foolishly rejected. The *soldiers* of the enemy at

least deserved the same proposal. They would be his soon anyways.

He saw the newly built gate to the hastily constructed wall open, and people on horseback emerge through the portal. Seven riders, a blend of colors. Jorbus Blue, the cobalt of the Legions, the purple of the Imperial Guard, the emerald green of Cortinum. A purple Calidian flag flying high above the group, only moving from the motion of riding, no wind was to be found today. It took all the composure and self-control he could muster to remain still and keep from fidgeting as he watched them draw nearer. Macien was unmistakable, his silver armor and cerulean cloak, mounted atop a gray-spotted brilliant white stallion. The Morincian style helm was pulled up atop his head, revealing his face, with the bottom rim of the cheek-guards resting on his forehead. The face of the man was flat, unreadable. A general in a purple cloak was beside him, doubtless Titus Validus from the intelligence he had been briefed on. One of the riders was a Jorbus Honor Guard, another an Imperial Guard, yet another a Cortinum City Officer, and the final two were blue clad guards for the General. Silious himself was flanked by four of his own Eagle Guards, standing like an orange wall atop black horses.

The approaching party stopped fifty yards or so from Silious' position on the small hill. After what appeared to be a very hushed and brief conference, Macien raised a hand to

Silious and slowly rode forward. As he moved towards him, he signaled Silious to approach, to meet him halfway. With a lift of his chin that feigned dignity, and rolling his shoulders back in a similar vein, he silently strode forward. His guards did not move, allowing their leader to meet the approaching magistrate on his own.

Duke Dahqual Silious IV, styling himself as the heir to the Calidian throne, made his way forward as his heart gently pounded in his head. So much was riding on this conference. Perhaps Macien would placate and offer up command of the forces within the city. That would bring control of the Empire as well. The war would be over, and just like that, he would have restored the valor and honor of his family and his ancestors. If he could talk sense into this Morincian, could show him the truth in his mission, the right he had to claim the throne, it could all be over. Generations of planning, just like that, coming to a head. It all depended on this initial exchange. What the introductions went like would dictate the course of the conversation, which would dictate the course of the negotiations, which would dictate this battle, and then the war, and then the dynasty, and then destiny.

Silently, Silious came to a halt, and awaited what Macien would say. So much rested on what he would say.

"Are you here to turn yourself in under the charges of treason?" Macien asked coldly.

Taking a deep breath, Silious gently shut his eyes and let it out slowly.

"*Duke* Macien," He started. "If you are acting in your capacity as Master of Troops, then I must inform you that you do not have the right to make such a declaration. Only the Emperor can do that, and last I heard, he still lives but cannot wake. Therefore, he has not issued such an edict against me."

"You know that the Emperor granted me Imperium, you were there. And you were there when we turned the interim government into a Consular government. Remember, you lost the vote?" Macien said, no pleasure in his voice as he spoke the slight. "Under that authority, I have declared you a traitor."

Anger was bubbling up inside Silious, and he gripped the reigns of his horse so tightly it strained his hand muscles. "I do not recognize this government, and I do not recognize your authority. I am speaking to you now as a fellow Calidian citizen, nothing more."

"You are not a Calidian citizen. You are a traitor and have been striped of all rights, Silious." Macien rebutted with determination in his voice.

"That is not true, but to appease your mind, then I shall say that I speak to you as a man." Dahqual's voice was dangerously low, words being spoken through clenched teeth.

"That too is debatable. After what you have done in Dutrigi, and everything leading up to it, I won't even grant you that title." Macien said. "But say your piece. Get it over with. I will not ask the traditional 'blood or water' bit, since you will have already made up your mind. But speak."

"I am the rightful heir to the Ebon Throne. The Kantuarians are pretenders, and you are a pretender to them. You don't want this; you don't want any of this. Allow me to be granted my birthright, and let's end all this. There doesn't have to be violence. All these men on this field will live on, to serve the Empire against real enemies." Dahqual allowed himself to crack his devious smile. "All I ask is that you surrender command of this force, and allow me to peacefully take my place as Emperor. It will be that easy. You can return to Morincia, to your family and your humble life. You can remain Duke if you like, but I have a feeling you won't even want that simple responsibility. The Empire is crumbling; everything is slipping away from you. By now you have doubtless heard that Jorbus is burning. Give me power, and it will all stop. I promise you all these things."

Macien set his jaw, and stared. "What of the Imperial family?"

"The Kantaurians?" He scoffed. "They will be exiled. Maybe to Frigiterra, that would be quite fitting. Except your sister; I will marry her to solidify my position. Her children will be sent away however, never to return to the capital."

"So in a few generations their offspring can start a rebellion against yours? I doubt it. I know you Silious. You will kill them all." Macien shook his head as he spoke. "Just like you hired the assassins to kill Selygo and myself in cold blood. I have people with me that made the connection. How will that affect your righteous claim to the throne, will it tarnish your image? More than Dutrigi?"

"I promise you this much, Morincian." Anger broke on Silious face, and vile hatred crept into his voice. "If you refuse my offer, they will die. I will kill the children violently. I will kill you, I will kill you're entire family. Your wife, your children, dead. Every officer in your army will be put to the sword. Every image of you that exists will be destroyed, every written record of your name will be erased. That goes for your entire family; it will be like you and yours never existed. Your ancestral tomb in Jorbus will be destroyed and desecrated with feces. I will evoke *condemnation of your memory*. This is a promise." He was almost frothing as he finished.

Macien said nothing, just slightly cocked his head quizzically to one side. Then he spoke. "You will not win. You will never win. Every advantage you had in this siege is already slipping away. You are stalling for something, for some strategic reason. The longer you stall, the more time you give us to prepare and to reinforce."

"No reinforcements will come for you, fool. This is it. Akkedis, Morincia, the northlands, Enthaki, they are revolting under my command. That will tie up your relief forces nicely. The force you have now is the only force you will get. It doesn't need to end like this. Don't have all this blood on your hands, Macien. Do the natural thing, the easy thing, the right thing."

A smile cracked on Macien's face. "The easy thing and the right thing are rarely the same thing."

"You will die. I promise. Just as I said, your name will be removed and it will be as if you never existed. No one will know who Macien was in a generation." And with that, Dahqual slammed his helm down. The thought of giving the order to have Macien killed by his Eagle Guard crossed his mind, but he dismissed it. He would enjoy destroying this man on the battlefield, enjoying having him know his world was slipping away and the truth behind Dahqual's threats would become a reality just before he died.

"When I win this fight, Silious, I will do the opposite. I will not condemn your memory; I will do the reverse of that. Your name will be in every history book, along with your image. Your actions in this life will be recorded for all of time with perfect accuracy. Not one word of it will be embellished. You will be remembered as one of the greatest traitors in the history of Calidia. That is already a fact." Macien lowered his head slightly, paused, and then lifted it back up with dignity. "I will also promise this. Your son will be raised to be healthy and strong. I will not punish a child for the grievous sins of his father. I give you my word on that."

"I would sooner my son die a terrible death than to be raised by likes of you." Silious said calmly, the anger subsiding that had risen so quickly earlier.

"You made your threats, these are mine." Macien said. "Very different from one another, just like you and I. As I said, you came only for blood, that is why I did not ask. I will look for you on the field, but I doubt you are man enough to take it yourself." And Silious watched as Macien turned his horse and headed back to his retinue. He would enjoy crushing the Morincian on the battlefield.

PART V

PINNACLES
&
PASSES

"IN WAR WE MUST ALWAYS LEAVE
ROOM FOR STROKES OF FORTUNE, AND
ACCIDENTS THAT CANNOT BE
FORESEEN."
-POLYBIUS

XLIX
ATHELTIADES

Since the Polemarch had returned and assumed command, the enemy had been uncharacteristically quiet. Perhaps the siege had reached the point where the attacks lulled and it was to become a stranglehold of attrition. Or, they were gathering strength to do another daring surge attack, a powerful offensive. Conventional siege tactics wouldn't work in this situation, since the fort was not encircled, and the mainland could resupply Bridgegate indefinitely. Therefore, Atheltiades was sure to be on the lookout for that next big offensive.

Sure, the Hyerians had continued to harass the walls, but the fresh Trimontis troops mixed in with the Dutrigians were making short work of them. It was almost as if the Hyerian attacks were done out of a sick tradition at this point, a show of presence rather than any real attempt at taking the walls. In the meantime, the Commander assisted with replenishing caches, repairing damaged infrastructure and weapons, and getting acquainted with their cousins that had come to join the fight.

The Dutrigians and the Trimontians were eerily similar but just as eerily different. A century or two apart from one another will change cultures and people. Interbreeding with the barbarians had caused the Rams to physically change as well. They had needed to adapt to the mountainous terrain of their new homeland. They grew beards and hair long, to stay warm in the snowy peaks. Their legs were thick, allowing them to move like the rams they wore on their shields and had emblazoned into the intricate designs of their armor. The clothes they wore reflected their new environment as well. Thicker wool, lighter armor, and shorter spears matched with longer swords.

The accents were the oddest thing, however. They spoke perfect Domitian, most of the officers still spoke Old Morincian as well, as was the tradition. But their accent was different, a slow drawl, and they used the occasional word that Atheltiades did not know. It was as if they were a strange barbarian version of his own people. But they could fight, and in the heat of battle and the darkness of night, the red cloaks they both wore looked the same. They were welcome, that was not up for debate.

Below, in the quad, the dead were being stacked like masonry. They would have to be dealt with soon, he realized with disgust. Disease would become an issue shortly, and the poison that exuded from the dead would run rampant through the fort. They hadn't had the time to deal with them. And they were running out of space, the dead encroaching on the area where the medici worked on the wounded. Someone suggested putting the dead on the northern side of the walls, but that would leave them open to carrion birds and looters. They would need to be burned or buried with proper ceremony; they deserved that much.

With the dead and wounded below, and the fresh contingent of Trimontis soldiers, the fort was crowded. Crowded with dead, dying, and more likely than not, the healthy but soon to be dead. Atheltiades rubbed his eyes. They stung bitterly from fatigue, and they screamed at him to shut them, allow them to rest. That was why he thought he had mistaken what he had seen. Perhaps his eyes and his brain, both exhausted, were playing tricks on him. From his position on the Western Tower, he thought he saw a cloud of dust coming from the north. Small, but it was growing. He rubbed his eyes once more, and the cloud was still there.

As if on queue, a horn bellowed from the sister tower to the east. The lookout had spotted it as well. Shortly thereafter, Rhodenikos made his way up to the top of the stone tower, and strode beside Atheltiades. Placing both hands firmly on the ledge, he narrowed his eyes and leaned forward.

"An army?" He asked more than stated to Atheltiades.

"It looks to be a large body of men, sir. In formation." The Commander offered.

"Maybe the Trimontis relief force? Or one

of the answers to the request for help you sent out?" The man stood up strait, and rubbed his cheek under his helm, and if checking for stubble growth. "It is a bit early for the Trimontis force, but it's possible. I will meet them at the northern gate. You have the fort until I return from that, in case anything happens with the Saurians. Hopefully this won't be too complex of a matter. If they are friends, they may need to camp on the other side of the walls, were getting a bit tight in here."

"And if they are not? If they are here for blood?" Atheltiades asked.

"If it's a rebel army, then it will be a short parley indeed." Rhodenikos said, no humor in his voice.

"If it is an Akritis force or one of Silious' allies, then…" The Commander trailed off, thinking of the implications.

"It will complicate matters. But we will not surrender the fort, not to a Saurian army, and definitely not to Silious." The gruff man stated. "Not while a single one of us is still alive to tell them what for. I must go prepare. Gods give strength, Commander."

"Gods give strength, Polemarch." Atheltiades said. And he watched as the man began his descent down the stairwell. He then turned his eyes back to the advancing cloud of dust and man. The day was bright, but he thought he could make out glimpse of orange flags. He swallowed hard, hoping he was mistaken. He decided to turn and look south instead. The dead littered the field before him, the ground barely visible. Outside of the range of arrows and slings, scavengers were reclaiming weapons and choice pieces of armor, to return and reequip the unseen army that was camped just beyond the rises to the south.

Something was about to happen; he could feel it in his soul, in his bones, and in his guts. Turning to face the north once more, he saw the unmistakable vibrant orange of the Akritus flag. So, that was that. Things were much more complicated now.

*   *   *

The army that bore down on them was smaller than he had first thought. Maybe three legion cohorts, about fifteen hundred men total. Small by army standards, but enormous when it came to sieging a small fortress that was already being attacked by another army. There was only one man on a horse in the entire force, and he was undoubtedly the officer in charge. His black armor and orange cap stood out against the rest of the men. In perfect formation, the Akritus soldiers were lined up a hundred or so yards behind the drawbridge, as the officer approached alone on horseback.

Atheltiades watched as the drawbridge lowered and the Polemarch walked across, alone. The two met twenty paces from where the drawbridge came to rest on the other side of the trench. The Commander stood atop the northern battlements, watching intently and hoping to hear the exchange between the two men. The most he could catch was the snorts and chortling of the horse, as it fought to stay still. The beast could smell the saurian stench that was wafting through from the other side of the walls. It wanted to bolt, but it was very well trained, and would remain, although reluctantly, where it's master ordered it to.

The Polemarch became infuriated at something, and raised his voice loud enough for those on the walls to hear. The words carried and echoed off the stone. "You slaughtered our people, then have the gall to order me to open the gates to this fort! Your Duke has made a deal with the Hyerians! You deserve everything that is coming to you!" and with that, he angrily swung about and started back to the drawbridge. Atheltiades watched as the enemy officer gave a slight, almost lazy gesture with his left hand. A half dozen arrows, long shafted and with little arc in their flight slammed into the back of Rhodenikos, bloodied metal heads bursting through the front of his chest plate. The man stumbled once, and then collapsed forward. The body tumbled into the ditch below, out of sight.

Atheltiades was stunned for only a moment. Then he broke into action.

"Raise the bridge! Raise it fast!" He screamed. "Send those men up here!"

He pointed down to the resting reserve force that was sleeping next to the dead and wounded in the quad below.

"Double time, to the top!" He yelled. "Archers and slingers!"

Just then, the horn blew on the towers above, signaling his call to arms. The fort sprang to life. Men stormed along the battlements, getting into position wherever they were needed. *The scorpions, they would be needed on this side as well.* He grabbed a Trimontis Captain, whose name he could not remember at the moment, and put him in charge of getting artillery set up on for the northern side. Briefly, he thought of getting at least one of the onagers turned, but dismissed that idea.

The Akritus longbow men were unleashing deadly volleys with accuracy that was frighteningly true along the walls. Arrows pierced shields, sticking into arms or bursting through to find softer flesh farther beneath. A tugging sensation was briefly on the top of his head, as he realized an arrow had flown through his horsehair crest, making a gap as it tore away the bristles. That damn helmet was making him a target, but it would stay. This was wrong, so wrong. The hope he had felt, the glimmer that they might be able to hold off the red-skinned horde, was gone.

The ancient enemy of his people was at the gates, and the fort that had stood strong through it all was the last hope to keep it at bay.

And they had been doing it. But now, now these traitorous excuses for men were ruining everything, betraying their own race. He could barely believe it, could not comprehend it.

The signal horn blew once again from up above. The ominous sound was like a demon wailing from hades. The men had already been roused, had taken their spots to protect the walls from the new threat. That menacing horn didn't needed to be blown, but once again it rang through the air, a constant backdrop to the din of battle. A thought went through his mind, an instinct more than a coherent notion. Atheltiades managed to tear his vision from the attacking men carrying the orange eagle flags, and give a look up to the towers. The men stationed in the vantage point high above were looking south, towards Akkedis.

Swallowing a lump in his throat, he hastily passed command of the northern defenses to Captain Nikolos, and rushed to make his way to the origin of the horn blasts. Winded, as he climbed across the battlements, he paused halfway up the internal stairs of the tower to look back at the Rebel soldiers. Archers were peppering the red cloaked men on the fortifications, but the shield wall was holding. He continued to the top, met with Captain Alexios, and peered over the precipice.

The Hyerian horde was advancing; in full force. Hundreds upon hundreds of them, thousands of them forming a sea of black cloth and red skin. Their yellow and black flags raised above the writhing mass, the black stars in the standards center made a perverse inverted version of a nights sky. They carried multiple ladders, and dragonsclaws that looked like they were attached to chains rather than ropes. This was the final push.

He turned to the north, and saw the dark armored lines of the Akritus troops preparing their assault. This was it, the moment of truth. If they were all going to die, then they would do it as Dutrigians. He accepted whatever fate the Gods had dealt them, and he would prove himself worthy of Elysium.

With a deep breath, he shouted. "Onagers!! Loose!" and then as the giant machines unloaded their stored energy and artillery, hopping as they did so, he turned down to the soldiers on the wall, and began to give orders. There was little need, the men knew exactly what to do, but they still wanted confidence in their leader. And, like it or not, Atheltiades was now the leader of the Dutrigian army, no matter how small it had become or how short his command would be.

L

ANTONEUS COMETA

A torch flickered in the small tent. That made Antoneus smile a bit. The irony was sweet as he noticed the dance of shifting shadow and light on the tent wall. With a slow, deliberate motion, he rubbed the black soot onto his forehead, and then smeared it down his cheek. Soon, his entire face was as dark as the night itself. The dark colored skull cap that was usually worn under a helmet sat atop his head. His clothing was a simple black tunic as well, and he rubbed the ash on the exposed flesh of his arms. With two fingers, he felt under his shirt at the wound on his side, and discovered it was ok. The stitches had been removed, and the scar tissue was beginning to form up nicely. It would not be an issue tonight.

Tonight was a realization of his life's ambition. He would be a member of the Imperial Guard, performing a field mission that only elite, hand selected individuals could pull off. The torchlight made him think of his days standing in a hallway as he dreamt of doing what he was about to do. His sica blades were darkened by flame soot and ash, to reduce any unwanted glare from torch or moonlight, and then sheathed on his belt. Those would be the only blades he needed tonight.

As the day had ended earlier, long after he had escorted Macien to the parley with Silious, the enemy equipment began to show up. It was being escorted by the burgundy cloaked soldiers of Trivium, and they protected it as if it were the entire Imperial family being touted in enemy territory. The raw timber beams and parts they carried looked like nothing much at first, but as workers began to assemble the components, it became clear that the material was prefabricated and then disassembled for transport. They began to take the shape of wicked, dangerous looking things. The big ones were some sort of massive catapult by the looks of it, powered by immense counterweights rather than the torsion devices you would find on an Onager. There were three being constructed, and seeing them sent a chill deep into the bones of Cometa. They looked of calculated death, of measured destruction, of murder.

Macien had explained that these machines where the entire reason for the delay by the enemy. That meant they served some far-reaching purpose in the strategy of the coming attack. *They probably were just powerful enough to smash the shit out of the enemy, us that is,* Cometa had surmised. After night fall, while the enemy was still in the process of constructing these catapults, Macien had decided it was worth the risk in trying to destroy them. Tonight. Before they were able to be used.

Cometa and Donovaus, the Jorbus Honor Guard leader, had been assigned with pulling off the task. Macien didn't give any other directives, just to take a small force and to make those three devices inoperable. And if any moments of opportunity arose, take out any other strategic advantages the enemy might have. They had come up with a rough plan, and now they were going to put it in motion.

He stepped out into the night of the camp, a bustling place that was full of soldiers on patrol and moving this way and that, even in the dead of night. The threat of the coming battle was looming, and everyone could sense it, everyone was on edge. The group he was to meet had already assembled, Donovaus talking to them in hushed tones. Most were dressed like Cometa, but some wore cloaks, some even wore metal armor. The armor was wrapped in a layer of hide to subdue its reflective quality and reduce noise. Some people really needed armor, if anything for mental reassurance rather than physical. Armor tended to slow you down and make you clumsy. If you were good with a blade, then you didn't need armor. He cringed as he thought of his recent failures. This would be a shot at redemption. No purple capes, no glitz and glamor. This was just him, him in his element.

The men had been briefed on the mission

and the roles they would have in it. A dozen men grabbed the special equipment, and slunk out into the night. The special equipment they carried were horse feed bags. Ordinary leather horse feed bags, six in total. Naturally, they had been coated with paraffin and waterproofed, as was the standard. But rather than grains and oats, these had been filled with pitch and naphtha. A highly reduced, thickened mixture, like a resin or a honey. They had been split into three teams, four men in each team. Donovaus lead one, Cometa a second, and a big man named Ajax lead the third. Each had been assigned one of the three engines to hit, and each carried two bags of the flammable concoction. They were going to burn these things to cinders, and kill anyone that got in their way.

The commandos crept through the shadows as the circumvented the enemy force, trying to find weaknesses in the rear of the enemy's column. The front was obviously too well protected, but the rear was relatively lightly guarded. At first, all three teams were together, but once the first team was in a spot they felt was prime, the other two left to get into their positions. This would have to be coordinated very tightly, and all three teams would move in at the same time once they were given a specific signal.

It felt like hours before Cometa heard the signal coming from Ajax and his unit, the last

and farthest of the three to get in position. The
sound was a whistle that sounded passable as a
bird song, but wasn't. Cometa's team repeated
the sound down towards Donovaus and the first
team, waited several heartbeats, and then
moved in. Torches rang the catapults, allowing
ample light for the soldiers that were assembling
them to work. The rest of the camp was
relatively dark, and the team was able to weave
through and avoid any spots they might have
been detected. The scale of the war machines
the closer they got became more and more
enormous.

Cometa was in the lead, the three men a
step or two behind him. He moved cautiously
but with purpose, one hand resting loosely on a
handle of one of his knives. The first man he had
killed that night had been taking a piss on a tent
post. Cometa came around the corner, and the
man was looking right at him as he emerged
from the shadows into the moonlight. The man
just stared, probably shocked, his brain trying to
process what he was seeing. Cometa didn't
hesitate. His knife was out and deep in the
man's wordless throat before he could utter a
sound. Without stopping even for a moment, the
foursome pressed on, towards the catapult.

A pair of soldiers had their backs turned
to Cometa as he came around another corner,
and both he and one of his men neutralized
them before they knew what was happening.
Another man had blundered out of a tent flap,

only in a tunic, probably on his way to the latrines. He stepped right in front of Cometa, almost colliding with him as he crept out of the shadows. Cometa already had his knife out, and the man's mouth was grabbed and he was being stabbed just as he realized someone was stepping next to him.

With the same speed and determination that they had used to make their way this far in the dark, the four man team pressed on into the light of the torches. It was a strategy that had worked well in history, and hopefully it paid off here as well. Cometa had both blades in his hands, and his eyes scanned for any threat that might come between his crew and their objective. At first, none of the enemy noticed. And when they did notice, they didn't understand. And by the time they understood, it was too late. Cometa went left, another went right, and two headed straight for the nearly complete catapult. A few screams and shouts of alarm were sounded, but that wasn't important now, not with the mark this close.

One of the bags was thrown hard against the wooden frame, the commando swinging it by the strap and slamming it down like a hammer throw from the track and field games. It exploded, splattering the incendiary substance all along the base. The torch was thrown in before the second bag was tossed on top much more gingerly. The whoosh of flames was instantaneous, and there was no doubt that the fire would catch.

Soon, the orange glow of the now burning tower illuminated a cache of barrels and casks that had been staged nearby. This was flammable ammunition that Silious and his goons had planned to use against Cortinum and the Imperial legions, from the very device they had just destroyed. Cometa paused for a second as his mind registered what it was, and then cut down a few men as he made his way towards it. He grabbed two nearby torches, and threw them both into the cache of barrels.

His three men had already started making their way back the way they had came, to the safety of the shadows, and he was right behind them. As they sprinted away, the conflagration of the barrels erupting behind them lit up the entire camp like it was noon, killing all the darkness they were using to escape. Cometa turned and saw a fountain of flame, at first dwarfing the burning catapult, but then engulfing it. Mission accomplished. He also noticed the burning structure that indicated the success of Donovaus and his team. When he turned to check on Ajax and the third team, he saw nothing; that part of the camp was dark.

Cometa briefly closed his eyes as he realized that the third team had failed. Ajax and his ilk were more than likely dead, caught and killed trying to make their way to the catapult. He frowned at their loss, and then he frowned at the next thought that crossed his mind. When they rendezvoused with Donovaus and his team, they would need to decide on whether or not they would try and destroy the third machine. It was, after all, their responsibility.

Security would be tight around it, and more likely than not it would be a suicide mission, but it was their onus, their burden. Perhaps there was a convenient cache of flammables nearby, from what he just saw that would be more than... A third pillar of flame shot up to the sky from the far end. Ajax and his team had pulled it off.

They met up with Donovaus and his two remaining men not too long afterwards in a dry creek bed under a willow bramble. They all were waiting for Ajax and his team to make it back to the rendezvous point before they were to return home to the rest of the army. The third team would never show up, however. The sacrifice they made was apparent and evident in their absence.

LI

DIMIDIUS TORBOCK

The swells were large, but the ship glided along the surface with such speed that the up and down didn't match up like it should. That was a good thing, since Torbock had a tendency to get seasick. But he felt good now. Even if he did get sick and retch, he was certain that it would be a dry heave. Food was abundant on board, but none if it looked too appetizing. The provisions that the Millangors had brought along for the voyage were mainly dried and smoked meats of an unknown origin. The thought of what they could have been originally in life was disturbing enough to overpower his hunger. A white, flakey fish of some kind was what he limited his meals too, since it was the only meat he was certain never walked on two legs. Unfortunately, the fish was sparse.

Darkness filled the sky, but a bright moon and torches showed him the rest of the fleet sprawled across the sea. They had favorable winds, and the Saurians that manned the oars propelled them along at speeds Torbock had never experienced before. Calidians were fairly notorious for not loving the sea, relying heavily on others to maintain that part of the Empire. Homithans however, could be described as being a seafaring, maritime power. As far as his mixed heritage went, in the case of the ocean, his Calidian side won the struggle for dominance. The sooner he was back on dry land, the better.

This rhythmic cadence of the rows of oars was something he had never seen with human crews. The ingenuity of human designed ships being powered by the raw strength of Saurian muscle was an amazing combination, and it caused him to have little reference for distance or time. Torbock watched the horizon continually, genuinely expecting a shoreline to appear at any potential moment. Still, his mind wandered as he watched the vast rolling expanse of the hypnotic dark waters around him. He thought of Jacean, hoping his partner and friend was safe and was successful in his own mission. It dawned on Torbock that the boy was no longer an apprentice, and in his first mission as a full-fledged Sentinel he was alone. Jacean was alone on a very important assignment, just as he was.

His own mission crept into his mind, and he couldn't help but shudder slightly and nervously rub his face and brow as it did. The mission was somewhat a success, somewhat a failure to date; everything was riding on what happened next. Concern that time was running out made it very nerve-racking. They had delivered the dispatches they were assigned to the appropriate personnel, however they were too late for Dutrigi. The Ambassador they were sworn to protect had been killed before he reached his destination. Torbock had taken it upon himself to negotiate on behalf of Calidia, and time would determine if he had done that well. Time was short, so he would know soon.

Then he thought of Rania. He thought of her, her smile, her touch, the way she scrunched her nose when he made her laugh. The stifled giggle that she tried so hard to keep from escaping. Torbock realized then that he had never had a reason to serve the Empire other than because it was what he was told he needed to do. Calidia did not care for him; he wasn't even an Iron class citizen. He had nothing to fight for, except to wear that iron ring one day. The family and friends he had known from the time before he joined the Order were all gone.

Rania however, she was something he could fight for. Maybe he was overthinking this, or rather over-feeling this. She may have only had a passing interest in him, and he was taking things way out of proportion. Still, the way he had felt around her, and the similar way he felt thinking of her, was very real. And it was something he had never felt before, so perhaps there was something there; a seed, a spark, a start.

Rania was in Cortinum, and that was where this fight was going to be, this battle, this line in the sand. That made him even more determined to make sure these reinforcements that Macien had recalled arrived. He just hoped they still had time, that he hadn't let it all slip away. If these damn ships arrived to a burned out husk of a city, like Dutrigi had been reduced to, part of him would die of shame, of loss. It wouldn't matter if he arrived with the 8th legion, and all the other Legions spread across Luctantum and the rest of the world. The war would be lost if Cortinum fell to Silious, he knew that was true. Time. It all came to time. Time and the Gods. It was out of his hands.

He grasped a thick hempen rope that was attached to a block and tackle, and it gave a creak and a jingle as he did. Leaning forward, looking beyond the bow as it broke through the inky waters, he saw land. A black sliver, darker than the sky and clouds, darker than the sea below, it began to emerge. The coastline was fairly dark, a few sporadic signs of life popping up here and there. It was then that he noticed the sun was beginning the earliest stages of its ascent. He wanted to believe they still had time, but something deep in his stomach told him he was a fool. Rania once again filled his mind, and strong determination and slight rage caused him to squeeze and twist the rope in his fist. Time. He hoped he had time.

LII
QUINTUS VICTUS

The blackened wood was still warm to touch as he held the charred beam in his hands. As if it were a beloved family pet, he held it with a gentle reverence and hesitant veneration. The new catapults had all been destroyed, and they were beyond repair. At first, he thought they could be made functional again. He knew however, that he was just being hopeful. Sorrow for not having these machines be utilized as they were designed filled him. They were glorious on the practice grounds, and he had longed to see them against the enemy. Now, they were useless. Perhaps one day soon, the plans would be used again to make more, but not today.

With a sigh, Victus set down the piece, and rose from his crouch near the rubble. It was still dark, and the torchlight illuminated the area. Anger flashed as he looked at the torches around him, the fire. Flames had taken away his machines, and for a second he entertained the thought of having all the fires in sight snuffed out as punishment. Gritting his teeth in a snarl, he shook away that foolish idea. He still had a battle to win, and soon he-

A flash of orange pushed it's way

through the men circled around the wreckage of the catapult. Members of the Eagle guard made their way towards him, followed closely by Silious. A very angry Silious. Quintus Victus saluted as his leader approached. Dahqual did not acknowledge the gesture, and began to speak without preamble.

"What is this? WHAT IS THIS!" the Duke bellowed. "These weapons, these precious weapons that we waited to be delivered have been destroyed? The enemy has been allowed to reinforce while we waited and now they are ruined! We sacrificed speed and numerical advantage for nothing!"

"Sir, its not my…" Victus started, refusing to allow the blame for this to fall on him. Silious cut him off since he had other thoughts on the matter.

"Do not tell me that this is not your fault. It is! You are the General here, and the security of this camp is your responsibility! The lack of planning on your part to get these machines here on time is also your fault!"

"Sir! Trivium was…" He protested.

"Trivium and its forces fall under your command! Their faults are your faults! If you truly believe they are responsible, then punish them. Put them on the front lines of the siege, hang their commanders for all I care! Give me Cortinum as you promised!"

"We still have plenty of artillery and siege engines, sir. Even without these," he firmly

kicked the wooden pile of wrecked equipment
with his heel, sending pieces tumbling and
stirring ash into the air, "we will still be able to
pound them with what we have. Tomorrow we
will reposition the-"

"No! Tonight. Now! The siege starts now.
We have nothing to wait for!" Silious was
shouting for all to hear. "We have the better
force, and they have juvenile defenses. We
attack tonight." As he finished, men began to
cheer nervously and shout fiercely. No doubt
the sound carried to the walls of the enemy
encampment.

Victus thought of numbers, of math, of
trajectories, of equations. The formulas were all
being erased, being wiped clean. The math was
slipping away, and the fog of war was creeping
in around him, darker than the night. The
geometry was dissolving as the shouting
intensified. This was not the way he had
planned it. The meticulous attention to details
was completely thrown away. It made his head
hurt, but at the same time, he felt enraged and
empowered. They *would* strike tonight, they
would crush the enemy. This was his army, these
were his men. They were superior in every way.

Math or no math, the battle was about to
begin, and the war was about to be won. Taking
a deep breath through his clenched teeth, he let
the cold air fill his lungs fully. Then Victus
himself yelled. It was a loud, crackling screech,
and it made his men cheer even louder. He

spread his arms wide, threw his head back, and yelled once more, his whole body gyrating.

"You heard our Duke! Prepare for battle, men!" The General shouted. "Officers, give the order to your men. I want full formation in ten minutes! The siege of Cortinum has begun!"

Like wind through a tree line, the camp came to life and became a mass of motion and tasks. Victus smiled to himself, and turned to Silious. The Duke was less amused than the General, but also less upset than he had been earlier.

"You have no room for error, Victus." Silious said, rather calmly and coolly. "I know you have not forgotten the terms of our agreement, General."

"No, my lord." Victus said. He knew too well what the Duke was referring to. When Victus had been sent to the Frontier Army as a disgraced officer, Silious had recognized the potential in the General. The Duke offered him complete control over the army as long as he promised never to fail. He needed to be perfect. One loss, one setback, and Silious would have him eliminated.

Wanting nothing more than to regain his glory and prestige, he had accepted. Death was not as horrible as shame and disgrace. But to be shamed and disgraced a second time, and then killed for it, would be unbearable. That was a powerful motivator for Victus to win this fight, and all future fights.

"Very good, General." Silious smiled his crooked smile. "Now go win me this city and then lets go get my throne."

Victus said nothing, just slammed on his helmet, and went to go win a battle.

LIII

MIKUS DERRATA

The booming sound made him cringe each time it crashed randomly into existence. *BOOM*. It was like a thunderclap, but more tangible. He flinched less and less as the bombardment went on, but he still flinched nonetheless. Along with prickly gooseflesh covering his skin, he had a constant, slight tremble and his teeth would chatter every once in a while. Mikus could smell feces and urine coming in wafts from down the line and all around him. He would be lying if he didn't admit that a few dribbles of piss had leaked out of his own bladder as he stood there waiting. He was in full armor, fully armed, just like every other man in this army. They were all lined up behind the walls they had built, ready for a battle. The rebel army was barraging those walls right now, and the artillery was striking in semi-predictable intervals.

He focused on the back of the helmet in front of him to both keep his nerves and to keep his mind from wandering. Occasionally, one of the projectiles would hit the wall directly in front of him, and the structure would lurch and send dust and debris out in all directions. It was still dark out, and most of the defenses and the grounds they were standing on where lit by torches. Sometimes, flames and embers exploded into the night as burning projectiles collided with the walls at tremendous speed. This fireworks show took place all along the walls, popping up here and there, sometimes in multiple places at once. Like rocketing fiery comets, some shots went long and streaked overhead into the city behind. Each time they passed, they lighted the world in a brief wash of an orange red glow.

It was the non-burning projectiles that flew past which were far more intimidating to Mikus. Each time his senses realized one had flown overhead, he slammed his eyes shut so tightly, his nose would crinkle. By the time you perceived the dark shape zipping above you, like some enormous bird, it had already passed you by. It was the humming sound and the concussive wave that was the early giveaway. WRRRRRRR. Even in the darkness of the early morning, the ambiguous projectiles were unfathomably darker in color. They were death incarnate.

No one knew exactly what the plan was, or what the enemy would do next. All that was certain was that the siege had started in earnest.

Several of the veterans had said that this bombardment would last a few days, to get them nice and weary and sleep deprived before the actual assault began. Others said that the makeshift walls wouldn't last that long, and that the real fighting would start sooner than expected. Some wanted to go back to sleep until the real battle began. Mikus didn't know if he could sleep through this, but he did know one thing; he was terrified. And the waiting made it worse. The walls protected them, but how long would they last, crude as they were? What if the enemy started with some other attack, like archers or some high-powered arcing device like the ones they had been assembling that would rain death down upon them? The wait was horrific, but he had no idea how terrifying it would be when the waiting was over. But, all agreed, the wait would last.

That was why everyone was astounded when they were given the order to prepare to sally forth. Men passed one another glances, perplexed and excited, anxious and fearful. People fidgeted, stretched out necks and arms, and shook out legs. Mental preparations were accelerated rapidly ahead of their natural schedule. Mikus looked up and down his own squad members, perhaps looking for inspiration on how he should be feeling and reacting.

The Decanus was eagerly looking at and receiving orders from the roving Centurion Alturas, who was making his own way back to his post, making sure the squads were all in order. Ferro was standing dispassionate and poised, eyes as glazed and face as placid as if he was hours into a boring sentry duty. Marcus was slowly nodding his head up and down, and tugging on his collar as his shield rested against his massive thigh. Phenton had a scowl on his face, firelight dancing off his piercing blue eyes and sweat-beaded face. He looked like he was a devilish creature from Hades, some diabolical minion of Shaardon. Vinius had traces of a smile on his face as he muttered some prayers to the gods under his breath. Perhaps the reason for the smile was because he was actually recanting tales of what he would do when the battle was over in some tavern somewhere. Strasa was pulling and gripping and yanking and twisting on his chinstrap. He just could not seem to get it positioned in the right spot, and had a frustrated, almost angry look on his face. Mikus had no doubt the expression came from the situation that was to come, not from the small piece of leather.

Then he looked at Tilo. The old warrior was staring right back at him. This may have been the first time in his existence he had ever been acknowledged by Legionary Gnaeus Tilo. The man gave him a slow nod, and Mikus felt his back straighten with this. The tremors, which had intensified in the last few moments, suddenly stopped. Peace and resolution washed over him. This was how it was going to be; the die had been cast. This was his squad, and they were going into battle in a few moments, and they would fight together as brother in arms.

Then the comfort he found in that was

washed away as Tilo spoke. The old veteran had a gravely voice, once that was not accustomed to speaking.

"This is going to be a rough one." He said, and all heads in the squad snapped their attention towards him as he spoke. "You two blue-hands, this will be a prime one to have as your first battle. If you make it through this, others may not seem as bad. Remember your training, and protect your squad-mates. They will protect you." And that was it, Tilo had spoken. It was both encouraging, but at the same time more discouraging than anything else. That was all. It was time. Toratum echoed the Centurion's order for 'shields up' to his squad, and the soldiers obeyed. The barrage continued, the streaks still flying overhead and the walls being pummeled. They were about to advance out into the open.

Mikus looked once more at Tilo, who now was facing forward with his usual calm indifference. Without thinking, without a thought in his mind, he hollowly asked the grizzled man a question. Even as the words spilled out, he had no control over what they were and no ability to stop them from coming.

"Do you think we are going to die?" Mikus asked in a quiet voice, higher than a whisper.

Tilo made no reaction to this, not even a flick of an eye or a blink. Mikus swallowed and felt relief come over him. That had been a stupid

question, and for a time he believed that the
man had simply not heard him. A few moments
later, without turning to face Mikus, Tilo
answered.

"Yes, I do." He rasped. "But I always
think I am going to die before *every* battle. You
will get used to it, it never fully goes away, but
sometimes it is more manageable than others.
Sometimes," he paused. "It is worse."

Mikus could tell that he meant right now,
it was worse.

The main gates to the wall opened.
Despite the fact that the entrance was huge, it
was dwarfed by the mass of thousands of men
waiting to run through it. It would take an
eternity to fit this army through these gates,
even in full sprint. Then, something very
unexpected happened. All along the length of
the walls, soldiers swung large hammers down
in near perfect unison, banging hard against
peculiar beams that were spaced out in even
intervals. With a rumble that rivaled the artillery
strikes, parts of the wall began to schlep off in
an avalanche of wood and stone.

When the scree and dust had settled,
dozens of portals emerged in the wall. Each was
wide enough to fit a Century through in
marching formation. The clandestine structure
now resembled some crudely constructed
aqueduct rather than a solid wall. It was still an
obstacle, still a fortification, but now it allowed
the Imperial Army to enter the field of battle.

And quickly if needed. For a moment, in the calmness of the early morning, the two armies were standing still and staring at one another completely for the first time.

Consul Macien could be heard giving the order to advance from the center of the line, near the back. There was a slight delay as the order was relayed down the line by the junior officers, filtering down to the legionaries. With a roar, the sea of blue and silver came to life in the darkness of the night and the brightness of the torchlight. Like spilled ink, they poured out into the dark of the field between them and the enemy.

The rebel army was stunned at first, completely surprised by the force emerging from the battlements. Then, they reacted, and the battle began. Flaming projectiles still shot in fiery streams overhead, allowing glimpses into the dark world that was unfolding before Mikus' eyes. The Legion was running, but not fast, it couldn't run fast. Armor was heavy and cumbersome, and the formation was awkward and constricting. But they did move quickly, even though it was not a dead sprint.

The middle of the line consisted of the 2nd legion just to the right of the 7th. On the left flank was the mighty 1st Legion, it's far side protected by the coastal bluffs. Over on the right flank were the ragged 9th and the Cortinum reserve force, augmenting one another. The entirety of the army's cavalry thundered out to the far right, utilizing the open area to fully maneuver and hopefully hammer the enemy against the sea. The enemy began to move forward as well, a wall of dark armor and orange flags. They moved slower, more cautious than the Imperial forces.

As the Legions approached the besieging enemy, men began to fall to archers. Arrows rained down, unseen until they found their mark. The screams and the men dropping were usually the only sign of where they struck. The artillery was slow to react to the approaching force, and was thereby effectively removed from the battle. If they couldn't adjust, then the enemy army was already out of range. The few that did get adjusted in time to be used were devastating. Huge divots of earth and gouges were carved out of the sea of men. The enemy scorpions and short-range devices hadn't yet been set up or manned; they had been caught unprepared. That had been the genius in the sudden and premature charge of the enemy; it had retarded the powerful artillery.

Mikus was breathing hard as they charged forward, his helmet slightly obscuring his view and giving him tunnel vision. The artillery striking the city and the walls did not slow much, and the occasional fireball was the main source of light for the men in the field. Each time one flared, he watched as a man here and a man there would stagger or fall. Still, the mass pushed forward. Men died, but the army advanced. He never saw the death of Tilo. At one point, he glanced over for a quick furtive peek, and the man was no longer there. It had to have been an arrow, since they had not yet entered sling or javelin range.

The rebel army had some very powerful and accurate longbow men. Shields and armor may possibly do some good against them, but it was unlikely. Those powerful shafts vectored right through most things a man carried, including the man himself. Your best defense was to march forward, and hope if they did draw down on you, it hit your shield. That didn't mean you were safe, but it was the best chance you had.

As they drew nearer, Centurions began to bark the order for tortoise formation. It required little thinking, instinct and training took over. Shields flew up high, interlocking and forming a ceiling for the men below.

Arrows pounded against the canopy of wood, metal and hide. Some found their mark, others missed. Some deflected, others lodged deep into the shields. One burst through the shield the Mikus held up, and he watched the wicked metal tip erupt through the wood, gnarly wood splinters blowing out in all angles. It had travelled a good foot after it had pierced. That would have easily gone through his arm… or neck.

As they advanced, Mikus watched through a tiny crack in the patchwork of shields as they drew close to the enemy. Once, he stumbled over a fallen man and almost fell himself. He regained his balance and marched on. The second time he tripped over a body, he recovered even more quickly. Soon, he learned how to walk to avoid the obstacles.

Then the javelins came. The front lines had transitioned past the bowmen and into the range of spears and slings. Like hail, sling bullets clanked down on the wooden covering. The javelin volley hit them with more power; like instead of small pieces of ice, the sky was dropping carp fish.

A man immediately behind him shrieked, almost directly into his ear. Mikus felt a warm spray washed across the back of his neck. Judging by the crimson spackling that appeared on his shield arm, it had been blood. With his right hand, he readjusted his grip on his pilum. Another peek through the crack in the shield wall, and another fireball overhead, and Mikus could see the faces, the eyes of the enemy. They were close. The light from the flaming projectiles was shorter in duration the closer they got, since a majority of its flight time was spent behind them now.

Toratum gave the order to loose their javelins. Mikus floundered for a moment, not quite comprehending the command, but mostly so infatuated with keeping his shield up and watching the enemy in front of him. Then he realized what he needed to do. He was so concerned about protecting himself and the formation with his shield, that the entire throwing process took but a mere heartbeat. He whipped his shield down, wound up and blindly threw the pilum up and away, and then slammed his shield back into position. His weapon may have flown to the sea, it may have gone strait up and was about to land on him any moment now, or he may have thrown it into the back of the man in front of him. He would never know.

The enemy returned a volley, and he felt several impacts on his own shield, jolting his entire body. Then the advance slowed as the very front lines of each force hit one another. Then the lines stopped completely. He noticed the men several rows in front of him had all drawn their gladii. This momentarily concerned him until he looked around at his own squad and his own row, and noticed that everyone still clutched their last pila. The din of the battle was overpowering, and he thought maybe he had missed the order for the second volley.

A gap was forming between the rows in front of him, and his own cluster of lines. It was a small gap, maybe several paces, and Mikus understood what it was. They were the second group, and the first group was about to switch out with them. The order came to unload the second volley, and Mikus took aim this time. He saw his target, and threw. He missed. But he did hit the man behind the one he had been aiming for. Ricocheting, the point went into the bicep of the man's sword arm; having found it's way through a gap in the enemy shield wall. A moment later, the struggling man was stabbed in the throat by a gladius.

The order to draw swords came soon after. Then the order came to move forward. Like two hands intertwining fingers, the second group slid up and in-between the front line, as the first recessed and dissolved to the back. There was one row in front of Mikus, and the man immediately in front of him was stabbing his sword like a mad man. In and out, in and out, vigorously, like he was sawing a log.

Mikus held his sword tightly, sweat making the pommel slippery. He was moist everywhere but his mouth; that was bone dry. Any second now, he would be face to face, shield to shield with a man that was trying to kill him. Something like that captures all of your awareness, and he didn't notice that the sun was beginning to rise. The whistle blew.

LIV
MACIEN

The two lines had collided and merged into one giant dark mass. Perhaps sending the men out in darkness had been the wrong tactic after all. Only under great strain could he tell which way the line was pushing and what forces belonged to what side. The fireballs flared and lit up the warzone, and certain linemen had been ordered to carry torches. Each Optio had been ordered to carry a torch, so they could get a general idea of the shape of the force and the contour of the frontline. That had failed. Torches were dropped when the fighting had started. It appeared to be chaos. But the sun would rise soon.

Macien had gambled much on this bold strategy, and time would tell if it had been worth it. Those massive siege engines, the sling-like catapults, had been destroyed in the raid; that could only of benefited the Imperial forces. The modifications to the walls, which allowed for the sudden expulsion of his forces by creating those portals, had worked. Rapidly getting the troops into battle and across the field had taken away the enemy advantage of their remaining artillery. They hadn't even yet bothered to set up, and suddenly didn't have time to prepare their short-range defenses. That had been a pleasant and welcomed side effect, a stroke of luck.

He had taken a chance on this tactic; he was trying to stay one step ahead of Silious and his sycophants on a psychological level. Hunkering down and waiting for the siege to come to them had been exactly what the enemy had hoped they would do. That was why they had crushed Dutrigi in the field, to set precedence. If Dutrigi had met them in open combat and been annihilated, why risk doing that again. They had brought machines of war to obliterate them as they burrowed into their defenses. They hadn't expected them to sally forth like this, at least that was what Macien had been betting on. And it appeared to be paying off.

Macien sat upon his horse, flanked by Generals, Legates, and a few senior Tribunes. Directly in front of him was his small contingent of honor guard, and the five hundred strong body of the Imperial Guard he had brought along. They were a reserve force, along with the Cortinum Phalanx position on the right flank behind the walls. Behind them was the city. That was it, this was the entire force. Cortinum and the rest of the Empire was behind them, and they were the last line of defense. The Free City was beginning to freely burn from the bombardments. Vigilant civilians that remained behind were trying desperately to quench the flames with bucket brigades.

The longer he watched, the more he could make out what he was seeing. Shadows became shapes as the sun began to crack into the sky. Everything was still a jumbled mess, but it was starting to become understandable and decipherable.

The 1st legion was heavily stacked to the far left, and slowly they were pushing the enemy line back, raking them along the coastal bluffs. On the right flank, the cavalry had done a great job of harassing the enemy archers and vulnerable side flanks of the enemy legions. But as he watched, he noticed the rebel cavalry was riding hard from the center rear to intercept the Imperial horsemen. And they were fast and powerful. The middle was gridlocked, as the two flanks tottered back and forth. If only he had another Legion, or his Jorbus Phalanx with just two contingents of Peltasts. If only the 8th had made it in time.

The Imperial archers were worthless at this range with the men so close together. The archers that Silious possessed were far more accurate and far more ranged than normal. He understood at once that they were essentially Wyrian longbow men, most likely trained by the northern islanders themselves.

Perhaps he should have held more horse in reserve. The right side was beginning to falter as the opposing cavalry clashed. It was becoming apparent that just as the left flank was pushing the enemy back, so was the enemy pushing the Imperial right flank back. Merseus favored the bold, and Balkree smiled upon the swift. What good was a reserve force if the main force was faltering?

"Gentlemen. It's time we went down to join our men in the fight. I'm going to the right flank. They need support. To your posts!" Macien informed his staff. They said nothing and he waited for no response. "Imperial Guard, follow me to the right flank!" And with that, Macien dug his heels in and took off down the gentle slope. Behind him, the Imperial Guard mobilized, and began their trek down to the front lines. The Legates all headed down to their respective Legions. General Validus remained on the hill briefly, and after a moment's hesitation, reluctantly headed down to the front lines.

Secretary Amicus and a small contingent of aides were left alone on the hill, to watch this historic moment unfold before their eyes. One way or another, the path of the Calidian Empire was about to be steered in an irreversible direction.

The wind beat against Macien's face as he picked up speed on his mount and propelled himself towards the front lines. His cerulean cape was stiffly pinned behind him as he gained more and more speed. He shouted out ahead for the Cortinum Hoplites to advance into the field of battle. With haste, they began to make their way through the makeshift holes in the makeshift wall even before Macien thundered through one himself.

As he emerged through the other side, not slowing his horse down in the slightest, a firebomb collided and exploded on the wall above his entryway. The early morning was turned to day as the fireball shattered above. Embers and sparks rained down, and Macien was fully visible to all that were watching. Their leader, emerging from the darkness, out of a ball of fire, and into the battlefield, did more for morale than he could have ever known.

With a yell and his sword raised above his head, he charged forward. Deftly he weaved through the green cloaks of the Cortinum Phalanx that was itself entering the fight. Everything else went away. It was just about this battle, this flank, this moment.

LV
DANQUIN ELKNAUT

Riding a horse in darkness was hard enough and dangerous in its own right. Riding it at full speed in such conditions was just reckless. Thundering in the dark as a herd with hundreds upon hundreds of other riders was near suicide. Charging into battle like they were, well that was magnificent, that was legendary. Lt. Danquin Elknaut's eyes had adjusted, and he saw the enemy; a ripe, juicy target that he could not resist. They enemy flank had been caught unaware and undefended.

Archers: deadly accurate and powerful archers that were firing upon his army, cutting down his men. He despised nothing more than an archer; they were the definition of cowardice. And in this case, they were damn effective. They needed to be eliminated.

The first few *Turma* ahead of him tore into them and began cutting them to shreds. The archers had been so focused on their tasks, and so shocked that the enemy cavalry was bounding down on them, that at first they did not react. Like docile slaves being punished by masters, they didn't break, they didn't run. Some were in the process of nocking a fresh arrow when they were cut down. Eventually, they broke, and the swords came down onto their fleeing backs. And eventually, the enemy legionaries formed up into a wedge to repel the charge. But not before a good chunk of them were taken out as well. It had been a mighty blow to the structure of the enemy line.

With his sword bloodied, Elknaut lead his men away from the front in a tight arc. They were preparing to loop back around with momentum and hit the flank once again, hopefully break them for the final time. The darkness obscured the rest of the cavalry fairly well, but he could see the general progress they were making and the direction they were headed. Like a river of flesh and steel, the cavalry relentlessly pounded the enemy. And the enemy was losing ground. This was a stroke of genius by Macien and his staff. This was the kind of boldness and aggressiveness that Elknaut could support. In short time, the battle would be theirs.

As his wing was realigning after finishing it's arc, hundreds of horsemen preparing to crash into the enemy once more, it happened. All he could hear at the time was horses, and the earth shook as they sprinted en force. The rumble filled his ears and body, shutting out anything else. He and the rest of his men were taken completely by surprise as the enemy cavalry cut right through the middle of his wing. Horses stalled, threw riders, were cut down, or knocked over. The momentum was hard to stop, and the result was catastrophic. In one blow, the enemy had ripped the heart out of the charge, and killed dozens upon dozens of horses and men. It momentarily crippled them. Then, he realized that it would take time to get the momentum back. That said momentum had shifted and was now possessed by the enemy.

"Circle back around! To the right!" Elknaut screamed as loud as he could, to whoever would listen. They needed room to pick up the speed and circle back around. The right was the only area they could do that in. His own Turma and many of the survivors of his own wing followed him. Others scattered, trying to reel in their mounts or find their disoriented squads. Danquin and his group galloped wide and he watched in the darkness as the enemy cavalry began to harass the Imperial lines. A brief assessment of his small force put it close to 200 horse, a little over a half of a Wing. The rest of the men were being pushed back towards the friendly line, or trying to circle back towards the small area between the legions and the wall.

The flank was faltering. He could see it as he drew closer. The enemy horse was eating it away like carrion birds to a corpse. Danquin gritted his teeth and urged on Polyneices. The horse responded with his characteristic burst of reserve speed. They had gone wide enough that the enemy had lost sight of them, and they had turned their back to do their dirty work. He had to choose between hitting the enemy legionaries, or the enemy horse. In a split second, he had made his decision; the enemy horse. He risked slamming into his own legionaries if he went after the foot soldiers. They closed the gap

The world erupted into a cacophony of human and beast screams. The enemy was hit harder than when they had cut through Danquin's wing not too long ago. As Elknaut and his men burst through the other side, he took a deep breath, realizing that he had been holding it for several heartbeats. His chest burned as he let out the hot air from his lungs and sharply inhaled the cold morning air. With out hesitation, he began to turn his horse to start another pass.

That was when he saw him. A ball of fire exploded on the battlement wall, and through the flames, clear as day, Consul Macien was charging towards them, towards the faltering line. A grin formed on Elknaut's face as his supreme commander, his Imperator, was joining the fight. His pride and his resolve surged. Around Macien, Cortinum regulars flooded the field of battle, making their way towards the line to reinforce it. And behind them, a wall of purple flooded through the holes in the partition. At first it was a trickle, but the Imperial Guard kept coming and coming.

Hundreds of them, moving faster than he thought any legionary could.

Macien was closing the distance between them, and soon he made his way to the cavalry force. Then he was riding in the middle of the pack. Then, he was leading it. Yells of excitement and battle cries filled the air. As the sun was starting to come up, Danquin saw that every Imperial soldier in the area was reinvigorated. Slowly, he watched as the right flank began to push the enemy back.

LVI
ATHELTIADES

Alexios had directed his men in the towers to fire at will. They didn't even need to aim; they couldn't miss if they tried. The enemy was flooding up the walls. Ladders were hooked into the parapets; the grappling hooks of the dragonsclaw's had found permanent purchase. The bodies of the dead enemy made a great stepping platform. Commander Atheltiades was dead center on the southern battlements, and he was the leader of the defenders. Right now, he was leading by example. Nothing else would have been effective. Nothing else would have mattered. He didn't have time to do anything else.

Hyerians landed on the platform, and he hacked at them. He cut them down. He would turn and another would be behind him. Archers fired, slingers slang, and artillery bombarded, and they all hit targets, but they still came. The commander screamed as he swung his sword, but his voice was hoarse and dying. His arms were sore, every fiber ached. He hacked at another, and then another. They kept coming.

Dutrigian and Trimontis reinforcements continued to funnel up the stairs and join the fight. Men died all around him; an axe to the belly, a claw to the throat.

Still, they fought, and still the enemy came.

He wanted nothing more than to check on the northern defenses, to see that they were faring better against the humans than they were doing against the Saurians. But he couldn't. Not even for a split second, his attention was needed here where he was. A slight distraction meant death. The men around him rallied, were invigorated by fighting alongside their Commander, the new Lord General technically.

A Hyerian had leapt over the wall like some kind of devilish version of an ape and one of the men next to him stabbed it right through the stomach. The blade went all the way through the back of the beast, bursting through the leather jerkin on the other side. In it's death throes, the Hyerian managed to slash his killer across the face, sending the man's brass helmet flying off, forever lost. The Dutrigian shoved the Saurian off his blade, pivoting as he did so, and sent it to it's death down to the stone patio in the quad below. As the man had his back turned to the southern wall, another enemy leaped upon it. This one wore a crudely made Akkedan bronze half helm. Atheltiades swung his sword down into the back of it's bare neck, and dragged the blade free, slicing deeper as he did. Then he turned his attention back to the wave of enemy coming over the wall. He was greeted with a wall of red cloaks, Dutrigians and Trimontis troops intermixed and forming a shield wall.

Thanking the Gods, he took advantage of the brief respite to look north. Half expecting to see Akritus troops making their way up the stairs right beside him, he was pleased that the walls were holding. But they were stretched thin. The enemy to the north was vast, and the defenses were weaker. Arrows were pelting the men that were atop the battlements, and slowly, they were succumbing. With a quick glance all around, he looked up, he looked down. They were holding, but they couldn't maintain this. At this point, he had accepted that. All they needed to do was hold out as long as possible, and to take as many of these bastards with them as they could. They would all be in Elysium soon, and he would have one hell of a story to tell his father. He turned, and took his place in the shield wall.

LVII
MIKUS DERRATA

He never knew what had given him the cut on his face. Whatever it had been, it had been small, or a small part of a much larger, deadlier weapon. All he knew was the only wound he had sustained so far was a small, almost superficial laceration just below his left eye. A bifurcated stream of nearly dried blood ran down his check, and around the corner of his mouth. Perhaps it had been a grazing by a sword or spear? Maybe a piece of splintered shield? A sling bullet? He would never know.

The sun was up now, and he was able to see everyone around him clearly; the enemy, his squad, as well as the dead. It was surreal. Only minutes earlier he had been in the front line, hacking and bashing against rebel soldiers. He had killed the enemy. He was a soldier now, no longer a blue-hands. This was about to be their *third*? No, *fourth* run in the front. They had taken the slight break to regroup and get a quick rest. The whole squad was breathing hard, and they all had blood on their blades.

Mikus broke off arrow shafts that protruded from his shield, and helped Vinius remove a pilum that had implanted itself in his shield and bent at an awkward angle. The spear was making the shield cumbersome and useless. Marcus had sustained a deep slice along the inside of his thigh the run before last. The original bandages had completely soaked through and rivulets of crimson gushed down his leg. Fresh linen was being applied to stop the bleeding. Marcus asked Phenton if he could help with the process, but the man had refused, cleaning his own sword instead.

Now, they were about to jump into the fight once again. Mikus was anxiously twitching his sword in anticipation. He was terrified, sure, but he was also eager. The sooner they won, the sooner the fight would be over and the danger with it. Together, his squad, his entire Legion shared in the danger. That made it that much easier to bare, and made them want to fight harder.

A whistle blew, Centurions bellowed orders down the line, and his group made their way to the front. Almost immediately, the man in the first row directly in front of Mikus went down, hamstrung. Without thinking, acting purely on instinct, Mikus stepped forward to fill the gap. He found himself quickly stabbing back at the rebel that had just wounded his fellow Legionary. Mikus watched for an opening in the enemy shield wall, but found none. The frenzied eyes of the enemy were seen well behind the barricade, but no other flesh was visible. Gritting his teeth, Mikus extended his sword up over the top rim of him own shield, and down below the eyes that were directly across from him.

The expression on those eyes changed, widened, as his gladius met resistance and it's forward progress slowed. Life surged into them; pain and surprise and expression and emotion. And then as rapidly as it had come on, all life left them, and the man collapsed. Mikus resumed his stance, locking shields with his new squad-mates. They took advantage of the kill Mikus had made, as well as a few other gaps that had been forged, and the Calidians pushed forward. They would take the line inch my inch, kill by kill. They had no idea what was happening on the flanks; all they were concerned about was their section of line.

The first row rotated to the back, and Mikus' squad stepped forward. He remained in order to rejoin his friends, as was the standard they trained on. A unique series of whistles blew down the line, and all the men on the front line knew exactly what it meant. They slammed their shields hard into the enemy, and then ground their feet and pushed forward. Unlike the unmovable posts that they trained on, these men they were pushing against *could* give. However, just like the posts, they *did not*. But that did not deter them from trying. The whistles continued to blow, giving them a cadence to pump their legs to. Slowly, and quite minutely, the enemy was being pushed back, inch by inch.

Noticing the enemy was now off balance, the whistle tone changed, and swords were to be used again. They stabbed, they sliced, and they dropped a few of the enemy.

Then another of the squad fell. Mikus thought at first that Marcus had lost his balance from his leg wound or loss of blood, or a combination of the two. From the corner of his eye, he watched the big man go down on a knee. A cursory glance showed a steady stream of blood flowing from a wound on his lower leg, the opposite leg of his other injury. He was also clutching his side, and Mikus saw blood seeping from between his clasped fingers. Then the man flopped down onto his ass, and lowered his head.

Mikus fought every urge he had to break from the line and run to his friend. Discipline and duty prevented him from doing just that, he couldn't leave his post in the line. Two other Legionaries came over from the back lines and dragged the still breathing big man away. Mikus returned to the task at hand, and saw that no one had stepped in to fill the gap that Marcus had left behind. Just as he realized this, someone did fill it. It was an enemy soldier, and he was about to impale the man that was beside him. That man happened to be Appius Phenton. Without giving it thought, Mikus rammed his blade into the man's torso, piercing right through the segmented armor that the Akritus troops wore. The man crumpled, falling to his knees.

Phenton caught sight of this, and flashed a contemptuous look at Derrata before returning his attention to the enemy in front of him. He was probably bothered more than pleased that some punk kid had just saved his life. Now shoulder-to-shoulder, the two continued to fight. Down the line, the Decanus Toratum was setting the tone by slowly pushing the enemy back. Next to him, Adamas Ferro was surgically finding chinks in the enemies armor and defenses. Quel Strasa was next, and he was yelling maniacally, his swordsmanship beginning to falter and get sloppy. Phenton grimaced as he did his dirty work. Mikus tried to keep pace with everyone else. Vinius was emitting an almost angry laugh as he anchored the right of the squad.

Farther down the line, Mikus caught glimpses of familiar faces, contorted and skewed in pain and rage and fear. Once of twice he spotted Davus or Dellan, along with other men he had taken the Sacramentum alongside. Men died on both sides, and fresh ones trickled in to fill the gaps. The line hadn't moved drastically one way or the other from what he could tell, but his picture was limited. And when he stopped fighting, rotated out to rest, that was when he realized he was getting tired.

The fighting felt like it would never end.

LVIII
MACIEN

The Cortinum Phalanx was far from an elite force, but they were helping weigh down the faltering right flank, and that was this battle needed. Truth be told, if looked at alongside the rest of the Morincian-stylized reserve forces, they were the least fierce. Generations of peaceful, open-minded policies had turned them into more an urban policing unit than one utilized in field combat. But this was their city, and they had shown up to fight. Plus, they had the might of the Imperial Guard around them to stiffen their resolve. If these reinforcements hadn't of showed up right when they did, the enemy cavalry would have folded the right side, and the entire battle may have been lost. It was holding now.

The left flank was faring far better. The 1st legion was steadily pushing the enemy back and putting them in real danger of breaking. Macien could tell that the black clad 1st Legion was doing such a good job of enveloping and moving the enemy, that the geographic barrier of the sea cliffs was becoming compromised. The farther they pushed, the wider the gap between the flank and the cliffs became.

Something about that concerned him deeply, but there was nothing he could do about it now; all the forces were in the field and he had no way to reinforce them. A shout by his side brought him back to the task at hand.

After a single pass, Macien had lead the forces back around this way, and now they were trapped. The rebel horsemen were hemming in the Imperial cavalry, and it was stifling them, eliminating their ability to maneuver and be effective. The Enemy line had closed around them like a gate, and they were trapped. Like a vice, they were being squeezed to the point destruction. They needed to burst through, they needed to charge and crack this box of men open. A small part of the cavalry was behind the enemy line, harassing them from their position, but the majority of the horsemen were crammed in around him, between the line and the walls. Macien was in the midst of them, as the horse idly pranced and rested.

Spotting a transverse crest of an Imperial Guard Captain, he ordered that half the force form up and make a wedge. The Imperial Guard was going to be the tip of the spear that busted this cavalry free and opened up the battlefield. Whistles blew, orders were shouted over the roar of the fighting, and the purple clad men sprang to life. Shields locked, and pike axe spears protruded at all angles, turning the tortoise formation into something more akin to an armored hedgehog. The enemy attempted to resist, and at first they were very determined to do so. But the intimidation of having the fabled Imperial Guard bearing down on them, as well as the deadly efficiency that justified that reputation came into play, the enemy parted. A small gap formed. And then it grew, was torn into.

Enemy horse tried to break the wedge, but the formation never faltered. Like a river hitting a boulder, man and beast crashed, sprayed this way and that, and was eventually forced to go around. Macien raised his sword, and gave the order to advance. The horsemen slowly came to life, picked up speed, and then began to propel through the gap. Not in a steady stream, but controlled, a Turma at a time. Hundreds of horses shot through, out into the open field.

Macien took a second to appraise the battle. To the south, along the coast, the left flank was still pushing the enemy back, turning them. That was good. The middle was stagnant. And this flank was still hotly contested. The enemy cavalry in front of them were starting to disengage even as he watched, pulling back a good size of their force to return deep behind their own lines. That was odd. He hoped that his own cavalry would not pursue, for that was foolish. His father, as well as many tutors in the Imperial Academy, had always said never to pursue a fleeing enemy. Chances are, that it would lead to nothing good. Besides, with the enemy horse gone, they now had the advantage on the right flank. Now would be the time to seize it.

Up on the slight hill to the far right, he saw a line of men appear. Had they always been there? Was he just noticing them now because of the light? They were garbed in a very dark red, almost a burgundy color, more brown than anything else. Their flags were gray with a red wildcat image, and they snapped and popped angrily in the wind. Trivium. Allies of Silious. They began to fire their ballista they had assembled on the hill down into the Imperial forces. Large bolts cut into the horsemen, and soon the arrows began to rain down from behind a protective shield wall. Macien opened his mouth to scream something, but no sound came out.

Then a thought occurred to him, and he craned his head to find the rebel cavalry. They hadn't withdrawn because they were being beaten; they were getting out of the kill zone that was about to be unleashed onto the Imperial horse. And they hadn't *withdrawn* at all. They were merely relocating to the other flank. In horror, the pieces fell into place in the Consuls mind. The unprotected flank of the 1st Legion, that gap that had been forming as the front turned. It hadn't been because of superior fighting… the enemy had calculated it. The enemy was feigning potential defeat to create that gap, to remove the protection that the terrain provided. And now, the enemy horse was circumventing around, and would be charging right in, to strike at the proverbial jugular.

Macien had been outmaneuvered, not the other way around.

LIX

MIKUS DERRATA

They were exhausted. The enemy was also. But they still fought, still continued with the crush of shields and the flash of steel. Mikus had a wound on his sword arm now, it stung, but it wasn't debilitating. It stopped bleeding on its own several times, but would reopen once he went back to using it. Sweat burned his eyes and chaffed his armpits and inner thighs. Muscles and sinews throughout his body began to weaken and tire. In a flash, he realized how grateful he was for old Cano Viberius and the training he had received. It was saving his life.

Commotion started far down to the left. New sounds and an undulating wave of disturbance washed down the swells on the sea of men. A dust cloud appeared to rise from the not so distant sea. That was strange. Vinius, the tallest of the squad, spoke first.

"Fuckin' flanked us." He said. "The enemy horse flanked us. They are hitting the exposed side of the 1st!" And as the realization of what was happening dawned on those in the line, the Imperial forces faltered. For just a moment, they faltered. Some didn't, some held strong, but pockets of the line faltered. And the enemy seized upon that opportunity. For a moment, Mikus was caught up in the fear and feeling of despair that was spiraling out of control and washing down the line. Part of him wanted to flee, to turn and run away. Some around him faltered, hesitantly took a step or two backwards, but not left.

Mikus was committed to standing his ground. The infectious fear that was spreading would only be countered by equally contagious shows of courage and resolve. Decanus Toratum was a great example of this, stoically standing strong and shouting encouragement. Ferro stood besides him, grim determination on his own face. Strasa timidly retreated a step or two, was shoved forward by the men he had bumped into behind him, and shouted and sneered angrily as he retook his place in the line.

Their time in the front was about to come, and the enemy was assaulting them with a renewed vigor. Mikus felt his legs weaken from a combination of fear and fatigue. The man in front of him had a dribble or liquid running down his leg. Everyone was showing fear this time, something had changed, something had shifted.

The whistle blew from the Centurions all along the front, and the rotation initiated. It was different this time; there was a slight hesitation. The enemy pressed particularly hard, and the transition had been sloppy. Two men in the front row, to Mikus' left, were cut down immediately. One fell forward, the other stumbled backwards into the row behind. This made the already edgy Strasa flail out of the way of the dying man, as if he were a flaming log hurtling towards him. That caused the man to let down his shield, and make himself vulnerable. The enemy capitalized on the opportunity. A sword jumped forward and rammed into Quel Strasa's stomach. Another plunged in a little higher, just below the ribcage. A weak scream died prematurely in his throat as thick, dark blood lurched out of his mouth.

Phenton wasted no time in killing the two men that had killed his friend. They both died before they had fully withdrawn their blades and long before Strasa sprawled onto his back. The continuity of their shield wall had been broken, and the enemy jumped at them. Phenton, who had turned to deal with the Strasa's killers, had left himself vulnerable to the attack. A gladius was making it's way for the exposed body, and Mikus threw his shield up and out, deflecting the blow. The force of the impact knocked him into Phenton, who grunted at the sudden blow. Ferro reached across and lashed out at the enemy that had gone in for the kill.

Off balance now, Mikus and Phenton collapsed to the ground in a heap. Two Akritus troops stepped forward, and began bashing at them with the heavy rim of their scutum. Mikus was taking the brunt of it, and felt his own shield begin to buckle, and perhaps a rib or two with it. Still, he held his shield up, protecting himself and Phenton. Then it stopped, and Mikus could feel the weight of the enemy lift. Ferro was standing over them, fresh blood splattered along his helm and face. He helped them up, and by they time they were all on their feet once again, the next row had stepped forward and remade the crumbling line. Breathing hard, Mikus reclaimed his weapons, and snuck a look at the gaping, wide-eyed face of the dead man that had been Quel Strasa.

"Thank you." Mikus heard Phenton say from behind.

"Don't thank me, *he* saved your life." Said Ferro.

Mikus turned to see both of them staring at him, each man ragged and disheveled, breathing hard.

Phenton gave him a slow nod of approval.

LX

DANQUIN ELKNAUT

They were trapped. They had blown out of one trap, only to be confined inside another, far more deadly trap. Death rained down on them from above in the form of arrows and ballista bolts. Troops from Trivium lined the upper ridgeline and they were loosing volley after volley upon the cavalry below. A shield wall protected the archers and the ballista launchers, and the thought of rushing up the slope in some suicidal charge crossed his mind. He dismissed it out of frustration and then became angry. He gritted his teeth, and they felt as if they might shatter under the force of his jaw.

These men, this situation made him furious. These worms dared to strike against them in such a manner. Lowly people, *rebels*, beneath even the Iron class, *traitors,* they dared to cowardly shoot at Calidian Citizens like this? *Golden* Class Citizens? Yet, there was nothing he could do. Except for retreat. But it wouldn't be retreat; it would be a withdrawal to safety. But if they withdrew now, they might lose the flank and lose the battle. If they didn't withdraw, then they would all be slaughtered, and then they would lose the line and lose the war.

A Wing Commander from the 9th had been impaled by a ballista in the first volley. Another had fallen not too far after. As he scanned the field, he watched men die, men crumple along with their mounts. Something needed to be done. Decurion Hostius, who was mounted right beside him, was at that moment struck by an arrow. It pierced his upper arm just below the shoulder, and pushed deep into his chest. Two more shafts hit him in quick succession, and the Decurion rolled out of his saddle, stone dead. That made it clear what he needed to do.

"Return to the rear! Back behind the line!" Elknaut shouted, and other officers gave the same command, echoing it down the ranks. They began to ride hard towards the spot where they had broken through with the help of the Imperial Guard. The hole was gone, sealed back up by men, friendly and hostile alike. They would push through, they had to. Hopefully the Imperial guard would recognize the cavalry thundering down on them and do something to help out. As they approached closer and closer, in a way the Imperial Guard did help them out. They themselves withdrew, leaving an area of line that was only enemy troops; enemy troops with their backs turned to the approaching storm of horse and men.

Elknaut was near the front, Wing
Commander Serepitus just in front of him
leading the charge. A burning feeling erupted in
his leg, and he felt Polyneices stagger for a brief
second. The burning feeling turned to a sharp
stinging sensation, and he glanced a look down
at his leg. An arrow shaft was sticking out at an
acute angle. Attempting to move his leg, he
realized that it was pinned into his horse flank.
It had gone through and through his thigh, and
still had enough force to sink into the horse.

Pulling on the shaft revealed it was
deeply lodged, and each time he investigated
and prodded, it caused Polyneices to whiny. The
enemy was coming up fast, and he would need
to do something soon. If his horse went down
from this wound or from an enemy weapon,
being stuck to it the way he was would surely be
a death sentence for both of them.

With his sword drawn, he hacked at the
shaft, holding the blade parallel to his leg. It was
an awkward angle, and the hardwood merely
chipped out a chunk. It took two more strikes
before the shaft split, leaving behind a barber-
chair as it broke in two. Still, they were rapidly
approaching the enemy. Danquin now needed
to slide his leg up and over the broken shaft. As
he tried, a wave of pain flooded his leg, making
its way to the rest of his body. Dark blood
pooled on the top of the wound, and streaks ran
down his horses flank.

Another attempt, and his leg lifted up a

bit higher, but not high enough. There wasn't time, the enemy was right in front of him. With a wet slapping sound, he slammed his leg firmly back onto the horse, and then prepared to cut down the enemy. If he was worried about getting de-horsed, then all he had to do was stay on his mount. He swung his spatha down, and killed an enemy. And then another. The horses that were in front of him never slowed, Commander Serepitus leading the way. As much as they were surprised to have the cavalry barreling down on them, the enemy still made way. They made way or they were trampled or cut down.

Once they had busted through, into the open space between the line and the defensive walls, Polyneices slowed. Serepitus, along with a few other Commanders and Lieutenants, was making his way towards Macien's position to regroup and receive new orders. Danquin tried to head that way, but his horse did not respond. It had stopped walking altogether now. Alarmed, he tried to dismount, but as the horse started to wobble, he realized he might not get off in time. This *might* not kill him, but if the beast went down, he was sure to have at least one of his legs shattered beneath its rolling girth.

With a stifled scream, he wrenched his injured leg free of the wooden shaft that had pinned him in place. Polyneices then gently, almost in a relaxed manner, collapsed to the trampled grass below. An awkward hop allowed the Lieutenant to avoid any serious damage. He then knelt by the head of the wounded animal. The large golden eyes looked at him in pain and in apology. The horse had a reddish froth in it's mouth, and it gently nudged it's head up and down. The eyes oozed with goopy tears and shame.

Danquin place a reverent hand on his horses head, and gave the ears a gentle scratch. "Thank you, friend. You saved my life." The horse snorted. "I am proud to have ridden you, and look forward to doing so again in the next life." A final nuzzle of his hand, a final snort, and the horse stopped breathing, and it's open eyes showed no life.

Rising to his feet, blood freely rolling down his trousers, he hobbled towards the command post. He already had a limp before this, but now it was going to be way worse. As he walked, he removed his *focale* scarf in a jerk, and then began bandaging his own leg to stop the bleeding. Macien was off of his horse as he approached, talking with Line officers and cavalry officers alike. Serepitus saw Elknaut approaching, and he walked over with deliberate steps to offer assistance. Elknaut waved him off, finishing the walk under his own power.

"We need to get you in the field as soon as possible." Macien was explaining, talking directly to the horsemen. "The Legionaries need your support, otherwise we will lose this flank, and then the battle. The right flank is faltering as you well know. If we don't do something soon, this war will be lost today."

"We will be no good out there!" Protested a Wing commander from a different Legion. "Those bastards on the hill are cutting us down, and we'd all be dead as soon as we got in range of them again. Send us to the other flank, we can do some good over there at least."

"I have a feeling that as soon as we head that way, they will double back the cavalry over here, and that will be the end of it. What we need to do is take out the Trivium forces on the hill." Macien said.

"Charging them will be a slaughter. All we would be doing is making their job easier by making better targets of ourselves the closer we get." Another officer offered.

"They have already eliminated all of you from the field of battle by making you squat here, living or not. You are already out of the fight." This came from a Tribune Danquin didn't recognize.

"We need to take out that force." Macien pointed. "And I think we can circumvent them, and hit them from their poorly defended rear. A small squad, maybe a single Turma. If they head back through the walls, and then north through the city streets, they will come out behind that hill, and then can come up the backside."

Danquin didn't hesitate in the slightest. "I'll go. My Turma will do it."

Everyone looked at him. No one spoke. Then Macien talked.

"Your name, officer?" He asked.

"Lieutenant Danquin Elknaut, 13th Turma, 1st wing, 2nd Legion."

"It looks like you are short a horse, Lieutenant. You weren't planning on running there, were you?" Macien said, a shadow of a smile on his face. Danquin thought of his horse, the one that had just died right in front of him. Before he could respond, Macien handed him the reigns to his own horse.

"Take mine." The Consul said. "Be quick, time is short. Gods give strength, Danquin Elknaut."

And after a moment, Danquin was on the mount, and then had found his Turma, and then they were underway. Sounds of horse hooves clanking rang down the paved streets as they picked up speed, running hard between buildings. Some were still standing; others had been damaged or destroyed by the attack. A few charred husks smoked, while still others were fully on fire. The wound in Danquin's leg throbbed as they rode, and it made him angry yet again. Those archers, those traitors on the hill would be repaid for what they had done.

LXI
MACIEN

The Archers and artillery on the right flank continued to harass and pelt the men below, causing them to slowly recede backwards. Mentally he attempted to envision where the young Lieutenant and his *Turma* might be, how far out they were from reaching the backside of the enemy. Once that happened, if it happened, then the cavalry could retake the field, and turn the tide on this flank. Then he looked towards the center of the line, and saw it too was steadily receding, slowly being overwhelmed. And to the far left, the situation was the worst off yet. The 1st legion was being smashed into by the full might of the enemy horse. They were faring well, but soon they would crumble. He saw it unfolding in his mind's eye.

Failure, defeat was soon at hand if nothing changed. They needed something, some shift in fortune to overcome this. But there would be none, for they had no reserve force. Reinforcements that had long ago been recalled were not coming in time, he understood that now. A small part of him had held out hope that fresh phalanxes or another Legion would arrive and join the fight. That would never happen.

To his left was Donovaus, and beside Donovaus was Antoneus Cometa. The rest of his Honor Guard made a semi circle around them. The fighting seemed distant now, removed, as if these men were watching waves crashing on the beach. They all knew it too, the imminent defeat, it was in the curve of their backs and the absence of talk or motion. Macien removed his silver helmet, and ran a dirty hand through his dark, slimy hair.

"Well." He said casually, as if getting ready to clean up and depart after a meal. "What do you men think we should do? You don't want to surrender, do you?"

"Never." Donovaus said firmly, not taking his eyes from the battle.

Antoneus said nothing, just a slow shake of the head.

"Then we have two options I guess." Macien continued. He sucked his teeth loudly.

"Option one; we retreat and take this fight into the streets behind us. I don't think that one would play out very well for our side. And the second option, the one I am more fond of, although it's not ideal, is this:" He slowly put his helmet on before continuing. "We head to the center, rally the troops into a wedge, and try to get to that bastard Silious over there before we all are cut down."

"Won't work." Donovaus said. "We'll die well before we get anywhere near him. Plus that coward would just ride away if we even got close." Then a smile broke his face. "Let's give it a try, though."

"Might give him a good scare at least, take some of his pride with us to the next world." Antoneus agreed.

Macien gently closed his eyes, feeling the warm sun on his face. That feeling of being back at the Lake of Spears bubbled up weakly, never taking full control of his emotions or thoughts. It was a shadow, and echo of a memory. And he knew why it had come to him, more than just the warmth on his face. It had been the last time he was able to open his own doors to his future, before this conflict that was. And now, the final door was in front of him, and he was choosing to open it willingly. The decision was all his, and he would seize it.

"Well, men." He said this louder, so his whole Honor Guard could hear him. "I thank you for your service. I could not ask for better men to have shared my life with, nor better men to cross into Elysium beside. I think we all know that our time has come; we can feel it in our bones, in our souls. Myself, I am going to meet it head on. You may come with me if you like. Gods give strength."

And he started forward, not slow yet not with haste, but with deliberate determination. Everyone followed him without hesitation. They would make it to the center, rally the men, and charge as hard as they could right towards the middle of the enemy camp. They would die, surely, as the flanks collapsed and the enemy swarmed them from all sides. But they would try, and go out with honor. A prayer was murmured under his breath

One final scan of the battlefield showed the situation deteriorating. The Left flank was starting it's inevitable disintegration. The right was slowly being bowed inward, despite the Imperial Guard anchoring it strongly. Idle and worthless, the cavalry was being penned behind the line, pushed towards the city walls. The Trivium forces on the hill were still firing, yet unmolested by Elknaut or any other force.

Macien Aktulus, Consul of the Imperial Empire, Duke of Morincia, Archon of Jorbus, unsheathed his sword, checked his shield's strapping, and tapped his blade against the owl beautifully painted on its front. The line was coming up fast, and so was his destiny.

A commotion started on the left flank. Macien could no longer see that far down the line, his vision being swallowed and narrowed the further he walked down into the masses. He did catch glimpses though, flashes of chaos, and it was enough to give him pause. The enemy horse appeared to be breaking off, disengaging for some reason. They weren't moving in a tactical maneuver, they were scattering, chaotically dissipating. It reminded him of when he had seen a mass of his Jorbus hoplites stir up a giant hornets nest during training exercises in his youth. And just like that, the left flank was given another opportunity to regroup. The enemy cavalry had completely broken, and some were not just leaving the flank, but deserting the field of battle altogether. The Gods had intervened in some way or another. If it wasn't the Gods, he was grateful for whatever it was. Fortune had shifted enough to give them hope, and that meant they had a chance.

LXII
ATHELTIADES

The sun was getting low, and the
shadows were growing long. Atheltiades was
covered in sweat and gore, human blood and
the purplish ichor of the Saurians. The Akritus
soldiers were ill prepared for a siege, bringing
with them only archers and some hastily
constructed ladders, but they were tenacious. If
they had brought proper siege engines with
them, this would have been over long ago.
Perhaps they were supposed to be a welcoming
party, an escort fort the Hyerian force that
should have already overtaken the
undermanned fort. The real threat was coming
from the Saurian side. The Hyerians rushed
relentlessly now, for what felt like days, but in
actuality was several long hours. At any
moment, Atheltiades wouldn't be surprised if
the defense broke for good. Still, his men held
the line.

Some of the men that had participated in
the March still lived, while others, most of them
actually, had died. Some were gravely
wounded, but continued to fight. They knew

that if they didn't, they would be shown no mercy if the defenses fell. Dutrigians and Trimontians blended together in a smear of red as they lined the walls, made indistinguishable from the same gore and muck that covered Atheltiades. Some were missing helms, some were wearing torn clothing, other were staggering from exhaustion and wounds. Still the enemy came, and still they held the line.

The square below was a sea of red cloaks and flesh. The dead were piled high, and the Medici tents were overflowing with the dying. Those that could still hold a sword or a shield had been recalled. The orderlies that came around to collect the dead and wounded had stopped coming around. There was no one really available to do that job, and there was nowhere to put them if there was. The dead remained where they fell, so did the wounded. And still, the enemy came. Hissing, snarling, the Hyerians continued to spill over the parapets. Atheltiades watched as a man who had lost his weapon bashed the rim of his shield over and over again onto the head of a Saurian that was sprawled on the stone underfoot, scrambling to escape the bludgeoning.

Sweat burned his eyes. He was thirsty, he was tired, and a very real part of him wanted to just stop. The futility of what they were doing was leaking into his mind, and that poisoned part of his brain wanted to let it all go. Drop your weapon, drop your shield, and dive off edge into the sea of red-skinned invaders. He physically shook his head as that thought surfaced, and it was flung away. Another Saurian appeared, and he stabbed it through the neck. Then he killed another.

A man next to him had his shield, which was firmly lashed to his arm, get enveloped by several sets of clawed hands. In the next instant, the man was gone, pulled up and over the wall. Atheltiades caught a glimpse of the sandaled feet as they were sucked away and out of sight. Then, the horn blew. It blew again.

He could think of nothing in the world that warranted a signal horn. They were all about to die. If more enemies were approaching, it didn't matter in the least. There was plenty here right now to finish them off. The horn blew again. And again. Reluctantly, the Commander broke away from the shield wall, panting. In deep rasping breaths, he sucked air. The thought of climbing the tower was daunting, but he knew he needed to. As he moved, his near numb arms began to shoot with pain; it was going to be a chore to start that hacking and slicing again, he never should have stopped. Up he climbed, not stopping at the windows in the tower, just focusing on putting one foot in front of the other. He leaned heavily against the rough stonewalls for support, pulling himself along like a drunk stumbling down an ally in the dead of night.

Up top, he made his way to the edge.

First, he gave a look north, and saw that the Akritus troops were making a hard push with the ladders, protecting the tips of them with concentrated arrow fire. In his brief look in that area, which lasted a heartbeat, he saw three of his men fall to the archers. Then his attention went to the southern defenses. The sight made his stomach drop. Hundreds upon hundreds of Saurians, making a writhing mass of red, were fighting to get to the wall, to climb over the top. It was like watching ants attack a food source, it was a swarm. There was no way they could hold them off. He had known that for some time, but now he truly accepted it.

He asked what had prompted the signal horn, and one of the men just pointed south, towards the area where the Hyerians had first been spotted. He saw nothing at first, expecting to see another wave of the red-skinned killers rushing towards them, several thousand more of them perhaps. Then, he saw something, and it took a moment for his mind to register what it exactly was he was looking at. A horse. It was a single horse, with a human rider. It was galloping north towards them, kicking up a fairly large dust cloud behind him as he went. Perhaps the Gods had sent some messenger to fetch them and bring them to the afterlife?

Then, from the rise behind the horseman, the dust that was growing gave way to shapes. Cresting the small dip, the shapes of men began to appear. Not men, no, man shaped, but not

men. And not Hyerians either. But they were
Saurians. Green skinned Saurians. The
Millangor. More and more of them came into
view. Hundreds and hundreds. An army. And
they were running. They were armed and
running.

They must have smelled the blood and
wanted a piece of the last of the Dutrigians, he
thought. Something told him that was wrong.
They were screaming, roaring as they closed the
gap between the fort and themselves. At first the
Hyerians didn't notice, they were so close to
their goal, to taking the fortress. Then, those that
were in the back of the horde realized what was
happening, and a commotion started. Like a
ripple, the panic spread through the Hyerian
ranks, and slowly, the steady stream of those
that had been coming over the wall subsided to
a manageable trickle.

Just as they men in the fort had been
forced to do, the invading Saurians were now
pigeonholed into a two front battle. And the
momentum that the Millangor brought against
them was devastating. With their backs against
the wall, the red skins got slammed hard. And
those that had been spilling over the top
completely stopped. Those defending the walls
welcomed the brief lull. Ladders were pushed
away, grappling hooks tossed back into the
crowd below. Javelins started to rain down on
the enemy again, that strategy had been
abandoned when those besieging started to

break through. Archers in the turrets loosed arrow after arrow, as fast as they could.

Below, the green was eating away at the red, axes and shields and even swords cutting deep into the Hyerian ranks. Sounds of monstrous anguish and anger filled the air. The men on the walls fought now with a renewed vigor, with anticipation that they might yet live, mixed with retribution for what these foes had bestowed upon them. The men relished it, unintelligently letting out primal screams as they fought now.

Atheltiades was captivated by the changing events unfolding before him. As much as he wanted to watch this from above, he knew he was need down below. The Hyerians were still a threat, and the Akritus invaders still needed to be dealt with. Perhaps he could divert some of the men to the northern end, to reinforce that wall since the southern attack had significantly been diminished.

A quick glance to the north revealed a faltering line, even a few Akritus troops on the battlements. His eyes darted beyond the wall to the distant horizon, and he had to do a double take. Another dust cloud, another approaching force. Silious reinforcements? Perhaps their siege craft?

Before he allowed his hope to flee from him once more, he noticed in the dying light of the day that this approaching force was garbed in red.

LXIII
TARAES KANTAUR

She was alone on the balcony, overlooking the unfolding scene below. The children were inside with Junæa, Tycho, and a few other nurses and servants. Taraes needed to see the fighting, to know what was coming. The Jorbus phalanx was doing the best they could to hold the palace, and they were doing it well. The enemy was everywhere, but she realized they were not strong enough to take the citadel. She also understood that taking the Citadel had probably never been their objective. Petros was notorious for being pirates, for being terrorists. They didn't want to control Jorbus, they wanted to loot it, to hurt them, to make them bleed. And they were doing it well.

Many citizens had made their way to the palace, filling the grounds with a large amount of people. If the Petros raiders wanted to hurt the palace, al they had to do was keep it under siege for about a week or two. Everyone here would starve to death, they didn't have provisions to feed all these mouths.

New fires popped up all across the city, from one end of the concavity of Dankoma bay to the other. The fleet had been routed. Resources were stretched thin. No one had spotted Kyberien and his force. Perhaps they were all dead as well. If Darien decided to go on the offensive into the streets, it would be disastrous. He would need thousands more men to properly clear the city; otherwise it would be a large game of cat and rat.

Gazing down in the quad below, she saw a large contingent of soldiers making it's way towards the gate, pushing through the refugees. All along the walls, Peltasts unleashed javelin and sling down on the harassing enemy. The group reached the doors, and she noticed that at the front was Kanion, turning to give a curt speech of encouragement to the men he was leading. His dusty blond hair and frame made him stick out in stark contrast to traditional Morincian features. She thought of Greeth.

That had made her feel guilty. It was the first time in a long while that she remembered thinking of her husband. And to be reminded of him because she was looking at another man, that was disgraceful. Thinking of Greeth also brought a twinge of nausea to her stomach, and that made it that much worse still. She actually felt like she might retch, and it took all of her composure and will power to keep herself from leaning over the railing and doing just that.

A few deep breaths through her nose did the trick, and the sensation passed. The scent of smoke on the air almost made it worse initially, but she overcame that. Then she thought of Macien, wondering where he was and if he were safe. Thoughts of mother came to her mind, up on the mountain and watching her home burn from far above. She thought of Mallea, of Linara, of all those people who had been such a part of her life for so long, and that she may never see again. She hadn't given any of them a proper farewell, including worse of all, her own husband.

The gates below opened under heavy cover fire from the men on the walls, and Kanion and his outfit flooded into the streets. She had no idea what he was doing or why he was doing it, but the enemy was being hacked away. The Hoplites of Jorbus moved towards some goal, laying waste to the teal and yellow clad marines and light infantry of Petros. The force was heading due east, parallel to the water and side hill. Her eyes followed their projected course, to try and find some objective, some reason for them heading that way. As her gaze scanned farther and farther, she saw a mass of blue soldiers fighting their own way towards the palace. Uncle Kyberien's force, no doubt. The sight of them sent a flutter of relief through her. *Something* was right in the world.

She watched as the two groups slowly drew closer and closer to one another until they eventually met, and then began to head back towards the Citadel. Distant crashing sounds and screams filled her ears, and she thought it was coming from Kanion or Kyberien's men at first. Then, she found the source. Out in the bay, ships were sinking. *Petros* ships were sinking. Some were burning. All of them were in danger, though.

Duracee ships had arrived and had immediately begun counterattacking the invaders. By the amount of ships she saw, Petros was greatly outnumbered. It was a sight to behold, and one she would be grateful to see for the rest of her life. The Petros marines in the streets saw the approaching enemy, and saw their own ships being ravaged, and all discipline broke. The invaders broke into a panic, and any semblance of organization that this raid once had disintegrated on the spot. Some fled to the harbor and docks, other ran into buildings to find some final loot or maybe to find shelter from what they knew was about to come. The stragglers that remained behind to fight Kanion and Kyberien's force were easily dealt with. Jorbus may be burning, but there was hope.

LXIV
MIKUS DERRATA

It was very hard for Mikus not to run. Even the threat of death, of his squad being decimated was trumped by his fear of the enemy right now. It was even the enemy he was truly afraid of; it was his own men that worried him. They were struggling to stay on point, faltering, and were showing a lack of cohesion. That made it seem like he was about to be cut down at any moment, that the slightest assault by the enemy would catch him unprotected by those he was supposed to depend on.

Thoughts of escaping the punishment for retreating passed by in a brief flash. Maybe the higher ups wouldn't know he had run? Maybe they would all be killed and would be unable to carry out the sentencing. All he knew was if he stayed here, he would die just as surely by the enemy than if he were to run and be killed for showing his back by his own people. If death was such a certainty, than perhaps he could make the inevitable end as briefly and hideously glorious as possible. When they found his body, he would have wounds in the front, not the back. And he would enter Elysium as a man, as a soldier, as a dutiful legionary.

It was his turn to step forward and into the front line. That rotation however had crumbled, and the lines now had become a giant smash. Men pushed other men in the back, hoping to drive the enemy back in a final desperate push. They were so tightly packed, that many men who had died were still propped upright. Mikus held his sword impotently, aggressively looking for an opening to stab it into, but they were few and far between. Enemy colors passed in quick glimpses between gaps in the blue wall, fleeting things like leaves in a strong wind.

To his right was Vinius, and just past him was his friend Davus. And beside Davus was Dellan. This was somewhat comforting to him as their fate was unfolding. As much as he would like to live, and if he couldn't, at least he'd want his friends to make it, it felt right to be next to them.

The enemy pressed hard, and he could feel his feet plowing backwards through the dirt as the line shifted against them. From the far left, the sound of the enemy horses intensified. They were losing ground, and even though this was Mikus' first fight, he knew it was lost; he knew the line was about to give. Like a child in swift water, he was being pushed in directions against his will, out of his control, and it was all he could do to keep from drowning. The enemy was standing taller with the momentum, like a wave they loomed over the Imperial forces, threatening to crash and spill over the top of them.

Mikus tried to hold his ground as the man in front of him was trampled to the dirt below. The enemy across from him, an old man, older than even his father, had locked eyes with him. The crazed eyes of a maniac, glazed over and shimmering beneath sharply angled eyebrows that sprouted from a glistening furrowed forehead were looking at him. But that wasn't true. The man wasn't looking at him as much as he was looking through him. The man had turned into a murdering killer that had spotted weakness on a victim and was finally closing in to finish the job. His sword sprang forward, stabbing and hacking over and over, beating Mikus back, beating him down.

Vinius stabbed the man in that soft little cup like depression just below the laryngeal prominence of the neck. Death was almost instantaneous, and the man's face showed no shock, no pain, in fact no change at all from his baseline crazed killer expression. Another enemy filled the spot, and Mikus took advantage of the transition by gashing open the man's quadriceps and crippling him. Phenton killed the next. More came each time, with renewed fervor. Everyone knew what was happening on both sides. This was the end, and all this fighting was just for personal achievement.

The commotion on the flank intensified,

and the world erupted into an accelerated chaotic scene. Dust flew, men screamed, and it sound as if horses were riding in all directions around them. This must be what it was like when a line folded. The rumble and the panic and the screams and the dust cloud were like a giant crowded building collapsing. Mikus swallowed, knowing that at any moment, this wave would... The enemy let up.

It was subtle at first, but then they ran. They turned and ran. The enemy officers could barely be heard over the din giving the orders to retreat. As if a powerful wind had swept in and blown them away, the enemy pulled back. Many were stabbed as the attempted to flee, and after a moment's hesitation, the Imperial forces advanced as a united front. Mikus was in the front row, and he caught a glimpse of what had caused the enemy to disengage and run for their lives. It was terrifying a sight for him to behold.

Hundreds and hundreds, thousands even, he could not see them all, a horde of green-skinned Saurians had crashed into the rear of the enemy flank. And they were tearing into the rebels, and ably running down those who had decided to escape. A roar came from the Millangor forces, something primal and terrifying. It began to catch on in the Imperial ranks as well. Mikus found his own mouth blaring out a guttural war cry as he and all those around him began to charge after the enemy.

LXV
DAHQUAL SILIOUS

A tremor went through his body. It started in his hands, and he gripped his reigns tightly as a result. It spread from there to his chest and his neck, where his airway shrank as it tightened. Audible wheezes could be heard as airflow surged through the contracted passageway. His head bobbled, and tears began to form in the corners of his eyes, as if a strong wind had pelted them. He wanted to scream, to yell, to do something, anything, but he could not.

The enemy had been of the brink of breaking, and he was about to be on the verge of total victory. Everything had gone right. Until now. From a narrow pass in the coastal cliffs, a flood of Saurians stormed onto the battlefield. They spilled in quick and deftly, and behind his own lines. The Horses had heard them or smelled them first, and they had been the first to break. Nothing could have kept them where they were; it was against their nature. First the horses broke, and then the rest went.

His forces were making a mass exodus, away from the battlefield, away from the Saurians. Perhaps they could reposition, make a stand, and take back the initiative. He had almost won, damn the Gods. He could almost feel that crown on his head, could almost feel the rough stubble of his scalp as he no longer needed to shave. It had been a matter of minutes. This was like a nightmare.

Surveying what was happening, he was still in shock, unable to move from his spot. His right flank, along with his cavalry, had been routed. And it was spreading down the line. His center was running now, and the enemy was pursuing. His left flank, with the critical support of the Trivium forces, was faring better. Perhaps if they all regrouped around the Trivium artillery, they could salvage victory from this. That was when he noticed the artillery, and the soldiers around it, were being smashed apart by a small contingent of enemy horse. They must have circumvented around and double-backed to the rear of them. The rest of the enemy horse was starting to make it's way up to them, and it was only a matter of time before the Trivium force was completely destroyed.

Running was the only option he had. As much as it hurt his pride to do so, he knew he needed to. But he was still frozen in place, and moving was something he couldn't do right now. Thoughts of his father, discontented and livid, were in his mind. His ancestors, like the great General Iroan Silious, surely had experienced defeat and had needed to regroup in their lifetimes. This was commonplace, he was sure of that. No, he would not run, he would not retreat. He would *regroup*. He would make a tactical withdrawal and gather his forces to strike again. That is all he would do. He had not lost, he had merely coma across a bump in the road. Tactics needed to be reworked and reassessed.

Thinking of General Victus finally broke his paralysis. This had not been Dahqual Silious IV's fault, no, the blame fully fell upon Victus. A quick scan showed the General, orange cape on black armor making him easy to spot, just below his current position. The General was barking orders to senior officers and orderlies, while back dropped by a mass of fleeing soldiers. A sharp inhale and a kick of his heels sent Dahqual thundering down to the General. His Eagle Guard was a step behind, being vigilant in the dangerous and dynamic situation that they all found themselves in. The Millangor force was steadily barreling down towards their position.

"Victus!" Dahqual screamed.

The General gave him a swift glance, eyes wide with fear. The venom in his commander's voice was making him as nervous as a spooked deer.

"Lord Silious, please, this is-" The General stammered, attempting to bargain for something that might save him from a terrible fate.

"Silence!" Silious demanded. Victus timidly and obediently nodded his assent.

A single finger jammed towards the General. No words came for a long time. Silious had so much to say, he just couldn't articulate it at the moment. He wanted to tell Victus that he was a huge failure. He had been the architect of this debacle. Sacrificing the speed they had made, giving up the element of surprise to wait for some stupid, worthless artillery; everything was his fault. Victus would try to blame it on someone else, blame Trivium perhaps, and that made Silious that much more furious. They man would never take responsibility for this mistake, or any that he had made in the past. Silious had been a fool to trust him.

Just then, he realized a truth. This wasn't the fault of Victus. No, this was his fault. He despised that Victus would blame this on his subordinates, because they were his responsibility. Silious was doing the same thing by blaming Victus. Ultimately, Victus was his General, therefore all the blame fell upon the Duke. Everything that he had wanted to say was forgotten in that moment of clarity. All that was left was to right some wrongs that he himself had committed.

His finger fell back to his side.

"You will stay behind and protect our withdrawal." Silious said calmly, having regained his composure. "If you try and run, you will be cut down were you stand by my men. Don't even look behind you. Face death like a man, Victus." The general was wide-eyed and open-mouthed. In the not so far away distance, the enemy was rapidly approaching.

And with that, Silious moved his horse away, turning to make his exit from the Battle of Cortinum.

LXVI
MACIEN

Macien watched as Silious turned and fled. His army had given way before he had. The Duke of Frigiterra had been as frozen as his native soil in the dead of winter, and watched as his army dissolved around him like that same soil come spring. Macien wanted to chase him, to catch the man, to wring his neck, to make him face justice. The rest of his army was feeling the same way right now, and were pursuing the enemy, running them down. It was wrong, it felt wrong.

He still had no idea how or why a Millangor army had appeared at the last moment, in the final stages of the battle, and had saved them from being crushed. Some things weren't meant to be contemplated as they appeared, especially favorable things. He would have the rest of his damn life to figure it out, and his life had just been greatly extended. Right now, he needed to lead this army, an army that's discipline was rapidly breaking down. It appeared a large number of Centurions and Optios had been killed during the fight, and that had caused severe damage to the chain of command. No doubt that had been a strategy of

Silious and his longbow men.

A wave of dark armor and orange and grey washed away from him, like a massive herd of wild horses. The thundering mass was only overshadowed by the sea of blue that was chasing after them, screaming for blood as they pursued. Bloodlust was setting in. Macien had seen this many times in the war against Homitha. It was disturbing, and ashamedly, he found himself participating in such emotionally driven furies a time or two. It was something that crept into you, slowly changing your psyche the longer you were in combat, until it altered your morals. War was made easier by dehumanizing your enemy, by separating yourself from them whenever possible. That made it easier to justify the things you did. The problem, however, was the greater divide you created, the easier it was to vindicate worse and worse things. Like slaughter.

Creating that separation was natural in war, but in a civil war like this, it was much more challenging. That was what made this bloodlust, battle craze that was unfolding that much more difficult to comprehend and that much more important to stop.

One of the fist things they teach you in the Imperial Academy is to never, under any circumstances, pursue a fleeing enemy. This held true for any size force; a few scouts or an entire invading army. It was usually a ploy, a set up for an ambush, or some way for the enemy to find some last desperate advantage to use against you. It was also dishonorable to do so. The enemy was meant to be faced head on, not stabbed in the back as they fled.

One thing was certain; this battle was over. And they had won. That was all that mattered right now. Tomorrow was another day, and new battles were still to be fought, but this one was done. Let them flee. The longer they ran, the farther they got, that was just so much more time the Imperial forces had to regroup and reinforce.

Run, he thought. Run far from here. Go where you will, but I will find you, Silious. You will be brought to justice, you will answer for all that you have wrought here today and in everything leading up to this. You will suffer in this life and the next. But for now, run away, while you still can.

"Give the order to halt the pursuit." Macien shouted to the officers around him. "All soldiers are to cease pursuit at once. I want the wounded tended to, from both sides. All enemy officers that we capture I want ready for interrogation. Then we begin burying the dead. I want the rebels buried alongside our own dead, with the same honors. That is our top priority today, and then we rest. Silious can run. We will see him again, soon enough, just not today."

LXVII
QUINTUS VICTUS

His breath echoed and surged inside his helmet. It was loud with the visor down, and it was loud outside, but the breathing inside the metal muffled and drowned out the outside world. His breathing not only resonated, but his heartbeat thrilled with a *whoosh-whoosh* upon each beat. Things had gone terribly wrong. The battle had gone wrong, it was all wrong. The equation had been altered, the math wasn't pure, the geometry was tilted, askew. The enemy was bearing down on him, and he just stood there, unarmed. He had a sword, but it was forgotten in it's sheath. He watched the battle through the sliver of panorama that his visor provided.

It had been beautiful, the victory he had calculated. It should have been here, unfolding before him, not this terrible nightmare. His math had been *perfect,* his vision of the future of warfare had been realized. He had crushed Dutrigi, and was about to crush the Imperial military as well. It was the dawn of a new age, all the math was there. What had happened?

He believed that his version of the future of war was the only possible way it could go.

Never had he contemplated that it may go another way. Yes, it must change, but did it have to go his way? He had thought so, but looking at it now, the answer was no. It always changed, true, just it didn't always take the best route. Perhaps his legacy, his contribution to the world of strategy and tactics and killing would carry on in a sense, in addition to whatever other changes were to happen.

Yes, he had changed the face of war. Granted, it was always changing, but he had left his imprint on it. And according to what his eyes saw, he could guess what the next step in this evolution would pertain. At least he had that clarity, that image of what may most likely come to be true to comfort him as he prepared to die.

Arrows began to land around him, wild shots by distant archers. The men that he had once commanded had almost all fled by now, but a few stragglers scampered around and away from the General. Quintus Victus did not turn, he did not flinch as the enemy approached. A seething wall of legionaries and Saurians would be upon him soon. An arrow hit his shoulder, and careened harmlessly off the armor. Another shaft landed right between his legs.

I will die a Calidian death, Quintus told himself as he drew his sword. An old death, the way of the ancestors. How ironic, how fitting. The man that tried to usher in a new era of combat, with ranged weapons and formations never before seen, was about to meet his death with a blade in his hand, and not even a shield to protect himself . It was going to be a heroic death, a single man against an army. An ironic death, for certain. Elysium would not be denied to him on this day. No scorpions, no catapults, no reapers, no Longbow men, none of that. No cavalry, not a horse to be seen. Sword in hand, and to be killed by a storm of similar weapons in a few moments, this was his fate. The old way.

Even he realized that he made a very tempting target, in his armor and orange cape. The faces of those baring down on him said it as well. But he was oblivious to certain things as he focused on his rapidly approaching demise. For one, the strikes of the sling bullets, *tinking* off the rigidium or making divots in the turf below his feet. Also, he couldn't see the arrow shafts that were appearing, striking into the ground closer and closer around him. One arrow even careened off his shoulder plate, and then another ricocheted off the top of his helmet. He took a deep breath. Before he could let it out, an arrowhead made its way though the eye-slit of his visor. It went deep, deep into his brain, and would have come out the backside of his helmet if the armor hadn't been so finely and strongly made. Death came but a moment later, and the General never knew how ironic his death had actually been.

LXVIII
MIKUS DERRATA

Thoughts were rare, incoherent things to him. Instincts were driving him, as if he were an animal. He did not *think* about swinging his weapon, he just swung it without thought. The enemy had shown it's back to him, and now he was killing them for it. Slicing down at legs, stabbing into soft torsos, cutting at anything he could find. They couldn't get away from him fast enough, and he couldn't cut them down fast enough. All around him, his fellow soldiers were doing the same thing.

All the tiredness that had permeated his body seemed to have been removed. He didn't feel tired or weak, simply because he didn't feel anything. All that mattered was killing theses men. They had tried to kill him, many times. They had killed his squad mates, they had killed his fellow soldiers. If the Imperial legions had broken like they had been about to, these rebels would be running him down and skewering him through and through. Why not do it himself, to them.

The enemy slowed, as the men in the front for various regions lost the fervor of the retreat. Some slowed from exhaustion, some slowed from obstacles, others slowed out of hesitation, shame, or a false sense of security. But they slowed and it caused those in the back that were in the most danger to come to a near dead stop as well, a crawl. This made them easy targets. Some tried to make a stand, but the cohesion was gone, and they fell with little effort.

The enemy screams were tremendous, enough for him to register them over the pounding and thudding, the metallic clang of weapons, his own heavy breathing and his fellow soldiers' war cries. The rebel's screams were of anguish and anger, yelling, pleading for those in front to move faster. A few were trying to grovel and beg mercy from the approaching Imperial forces. They were shown none.

Mikus killed and killed. Dozens of men, he killed on his own. Those around him killed the same. Blood must have splattered on his face, because hot streaks were running down his cheeks. It wasn't sweat, no his sweat had turned cold, and he could tell when it ran down from the brow of his helmet. This was different, warm. His vision blurred, and he thought he might pass out at any moment.

A heavy hand fell upon his shoulder, and then a second rested on his other. Upon feeling this, he knew he was done. He shut his eyes and took a deep breath, and shuddered as he did so. When he reopened them, the enemy had taken a good lead away from the Imperial lines. Mikus felt his sword clatter to the ground, and as he bent over clumsily pick it back up, he wretched. Nothing came out except a slimy stringer of saliva and bile. Fumbling for his blade, he vomited again, his whole body convulsing. This made his eyes water even more, and that was when he first realized he had been crying.

Reclaiming his gladius, he wiped his eyes with the back of his filthy, grimy hand and sheathed it. Those hands were still firmly clasping him, embracing him, holding him up. He turned to see that one of each hand belonged to Ferro and Vinius.

"I'm sorry." He said to them, not sure exactly what he was apologizing for. Was it for the crying? Vomiting? For the maniacal rampage he had just gone on, even though they had been there with him? For the deaths of those they knew? He didn't know, so he just said it again.

"I'm sorry too, boy." Vinius said, giving him a squeeze and a pat, before walking away. Ferro tapped Mikus on the helmet a few times, as if he was trying to mess the hair beneath like he was a child. Mikus remained stone-faced, the shock of the carnage before him setting in.

The battlefield that had once been filled with tens of thousands of men, all alive and strong with emotions, was now desolate with the scattered dead. Just moments ago, in front of them, had been a mass of men exuding anger, passion, fear, pain and strength. Now, empty husks devoid of life were lying motionless in heaps. The last of the enemy force was retreating from sight, leaving these dead and dying behind. Mikus just stared. Already the carrion birds, the scavengers, were circling and getting ready to feast. The dark birds of Shaardon, they were his eyes in the midst of pure daytime, scouting for him no doubt. All the Gods had been watching this battle, doubtless.

PART VI

PROMISES
&
PASS DOWNS

"EVERY NEW BEGINNING COMES
FROM SOME OTHER BEGINNING'S
END"
                -SENECA THE YOUNGER

LXIX
DIMIDIUS TORBOCK

The battle was over before he ever had a chance to use his weapon. Perhaps that was a good battle, then. He never was even in range of an enemy. The Millangors had landed on the shore, and in earnest and quick course started their attack. Those Saurians were fast and their endurance was unfathomable. Like a drove of wild horses, they thundered towards the enemy. Wild horses with arms and armor, claws and fangs, that is. The enemy never stood a chance, not at that point. Tyshae had smiled upon them, for the enemy cavalry had been on the coastal flank, and the horses had bolted upon smelling and seeing the Saurians bearing down on them.

Dimidius Torbock, glad to be on solid ground once again, had taken a long time to find his way to the Imperial command tent. When he did finally find it, it was empty. Well, it had been empty of those he needed to find, a few aides and servants were scurrying about inside. He made his way through the camp, through the perforated, crumbling crude wall, and back onto the battlefield. The purple of the Imperial guard caught his eye first. Then the Cerulean of the Jorbus honor guard. And then his eyes caught the glint of the silver armor. Macien, his helm off and heaped atop his cloak somewhere, was helping tend to and carry the wounded to the Medicus tent.

At first, this sight had taken Torbock aback; a major battle had been fought, and the leader of the victors was doing *this*. So much needed to be discussed, planned, assessed. For Macien to be doing this, with so many more pertinent and pressing matters at hand was negligence and recklessly irresponsible. But then, he noticed many senior officers doing the same, scouring the field beside him, and servants and scouts filtering in and informing the staff of intelligence and information. Macien *was* holding court, he just happened to be multitasking at the same time. His men were his top priority, and he was showing that.

Thousands of dead and dying were strewn about, and a large amount of survivors were assisting in tending to them. Torbock made his way down towards the Consul and his staff. In the distance, close to the coastal cliffs, the Millangor congregated, keeping their distance from the living and dead men alike. The Sentinel stood out drastically from those that were in the field, all in their matching uniforms. Torbock wore his travelling cloak and riding clothes, his chain mail obscured and his armor mismatched where it showed at all. His hand rested gently on the pommel of his spatha sword, the casualness and ease of it giving him all the permission he needed to approach unchallenged.

"In order to do that, it will take multiple graves, I think. *At least three.*" Macien was saying to a Tribune, pointing as he spoke. "You will make sure that they are dug, Thalian. Priests will be needed for the rites. I'm sure there are plenty inside the city that will be able to help."

"Yes, sir." The Tribune saluted. "Shall we bury the rebels in a separate grave?"

Macien slowly shook his head. "No. They are Calidian soldiers as well. They will receive the same rites and be laid to rest side by side with our own. That will please the Gods, and the historians. One day, we will be whole again, and we will need to heal. These men have family throughout the Empire, and we keep them from being disgraced any more than they already are."

"Yes, Sir!" The Tribune named Thalian saluted a final time, and went off to do his job. Macien began to go back to his own task, his retinue of followers behind him, when he spotted Torbock. At first it was a quick glance, a brief acknowledgement and then a look away, but once the Consul's mind processed what his eyes had just seen, he did a double take. A small grin came across Macien's face, and he gave a wave to the Sentinel, a beckon. Macien continued to search through the heaps as

Torbock drew nearer.

"Dimidius Torbock. I didn't know if I would ever see you again, Sentinel. But I am glad you are here." Macien said as he knelt down and reached for a wounded man's outstretched hand. "Where are you hurt?" This was gently directed towards the soldier on the ground. The Legionary responded in quiet tones, and Macien began to check where the man said. Torbock helped him lift the man up, who was grimacing, baring bloodstained teeth.

As they hobbled the man back to waiting assistants to take the man to the surgery tent, Macien talked. He filled Torbock in on what had happened since they had last seen one another. Then Torbock did the same. The story of seeing Dutrigi being sieged, about the death of Polemistius, about the Hyerian force marching north, about the meeting and negotiation with King Strank'Lakon. Macien nodded thoughtfully through the tale. When he got to this point, he spoke up.

"And you decided that you would bring the Saurians directly here, rather than down to the castra of the 8th for a swap."

"Yes, my lord." Torbock said. "It felt the right thing to do."

"You didn't think there was enough time." Macien furrowed his lip and nodded. "Well, I guess you were right. If you had showed up even *hours* later than you did, we would all be laying dead on this field rather than walking through it. When I saw that force of Millangor streaming into the fight, I didn't make the connection at first. Good work, you may have saved this Empire yet."

"The Saurians did that my lord, I just convinced them to come." Torbock said evenly. And I'd say your men can take a lot of the credit as well. They put up a spectacular fight from what I can see. After seeing what I saw in Dutrigi, I was concerned for whoever came next. Unfounded, apparently." The two men helped transfer the wounded soldier to a medicus orderly.

"Why did the Saurians come?" Macien asked frankly. "What did they want in return?"

"That's not something they told me directly, sir." Torbock said. It was true, after all. "Their King is here, or *Kral* as they call him. Strank'Lakon I believe wants to speak with you, to speak about the future. Generations of conflict and strife have made negotiations and relations between them and us strained and difficult to say the least. He knows that there is a new regime in the Empire, temporary or not. I'd say he is proving his loyalty and wanting to wash away the past, to start with something new. A modern day *Forging* of sorts. That's my guess at least."

Macien nodded. "I will speak with him. Thank you, Dimidius, for everything."

"It is my duty, Consul." And he gave a slight bow, which brought out the foreign

Homithan features in him.

"I fear that this war is far from over. I have another mission for you, if you will accept it. And also, I have that Iron ring I promised." Macien said.

"It can wait." Torbock said.

"The ring or the mission?" Macien asked.

"The ring." He said.

"You know, the mission can wait also. You have travelled many miles without rest. And we have all just fought an epic battle. Tomorrow, I will tell you of the mission. Get some rest, and get some relaxation. Talk to members of my staff for a tent, there unfortunately are plenty of vacancies."

"Thank you, sir." Torbock said. "I have a…a friend in the city here I will go and see. Hopefully my friends place, and hopefully my friend are unharmed from the attacks. I will check on her…My friend, that is."

Macien let out a stifled, snickering laugh. "I hope your friend is fine. And I hope you do *try* to get some rest. Dismissed, Sentinel."

Torbock turned away, and walked alone back towards the city, away from the dead and the soldiers that were wading through them. Huge holes had been started, hundreds of shovels breaking into the earth. Torbock only thought of her as the battlefield melted away and he emerged into city streets.

LXX
MIKUS DERRATA

Mikus and his squad hadn't been assigned to digging duty, although he very likely would have welcomed it. No, they had been assigned to body gathering and stripping. In twos they worked, carrying one body at a time to a pile that was close to one of the multiple mass gravesites. Anything that was valuable was to be taken from the dead. Helmets, armor, swords, shields, really anything that could be reused. It felt wrong to him, but he understood why it needed to be done. It was a reminder that although this battle was over, the war was not; no, far from it. And there would be other wars in the future.

The new segmented armor that rebels wore was rather difficult to remove, and looked like a very complicated process to don before a fight. Still, they removed it when they found it, and people came and took it away to stockpile. That had taken hours and hours, and they worked until sunset. The grizzly task would be done throughout the night by another shift, and he was certain they would resume again at daybreak.

Now, they were back in camp, eating

their first meal of the day. Calvus and Fabian had made a gruel of some kind in a single pot. Unknowingly, they had made too much, since there were far less mouths to feed. It didn't matter, they would eat it all. Combat made them this way. They were beyond famished, but didn't savor the food. There was an emptiness in them, one that no matter how much chow they forced down, they wouldn't be full. They also wouldn't feel hungry, just incomplete.

Mikus didn't talk, he just lay there in his bunk. Had it been a silent homage to the late Tilo? Was this why Tilo had always been so antisocial and withdrawn, had he experienced years and years of what they had just went through? Thoughts of the initial minutes after returning back from the lines filled his mind. Mikus had just gone through his emotional storm after the fighting had ended, and recovered enough to become human again. All he had wanted to do was to wash his hands and face. The sticky muck of the gore of war was caked onto him, staining his skin and marking his soul.

That was when he had seen Davus. His oldest friend, his best friend, was carrying the listless body of his brother Dellan. Del's head had been craned back in an impossible angle, his eyes mercifully shut. He was clearly dead, his pale skin and toneless body making it recognizable from a distance. Mikus made his way to his living and his dead friend, but stopped short. He realized he felt nothing, could show no emotion. The pain and sorrow had left him; his body and his mind had cruelly adapted to this new word, this new standard. If he went any closer, he may come across as heartless to his friend, when his friend might only want sympathy.

Mikus didn't need to see the tears on his friends face to know that he was weeping. Sniffles and sobs could be heard, as his friend gently but quickly rocked his brother's body back and forth. From underneath the rim of his helmet, the quivering form of Davus' mouth could be seen. Mikus stood there for a long while, hoping his friend would at some point look up and see him, relieving him of the awkwardness of him standing sentry over the sad scene. Davus did not see him, and eventually Mikus started to leave. Something made him stop. He turned, made his way over to Davus, and placed a hand on his friends shoulder. It was neither accepted nor refused, and after a few silent minutes, Mikus had left.

He had then scrubbed his skin. A large pool, one that had most likely been a water source for horses or aurochs or some sort of livestock, had been serving as a cleansing station. The water was a murky reddish brown by the time he got to it, and using it did make him more clean, but it made him feel dirtier at the same time. As his skin dried, it felt like a thin film had coated him everywhere he had washed.

Then he tended to his kit. He honed his sword, cleaned it, and replaced it. Any gross spots of blood that had been on his clothing or armor had been cleaned, but he did not polish. Polishing was something that could be done another time. His mind was wiped, and that kind of monotonous labor would drive him insane.

And now, after all that, he was just sitting on his bunk, doing nothing. If you were to ask him later what he was thinking, Mikus Derrata would not be able to tell you. His mind had been just empty, devoid of thought. It was like his brain was secretly replaying events from earlier, and removing memories that were too painful to keep.

Vinius at one point had come into the room and told Mikus that Marcus was alive and in the Surgery tent. Mikus thought the man had said something else, perhaps about going to visit him, but he didn't know for certain. He would see Marcus, perhaps tomorrow. He would let his friend rest, he told himself. That was it rationale, when in fact it was more true that Mikus wouldn't know what to say or if he could say anything at all if he had wanted to.

Not too much later, Ferro had made his way in, and sat on the bunk beside Mikus. Without any preamble, almost before he had finished sitting, Adamas began to talk.

"It's not easy." He said. "It's not something you can prepare for, either. But you did good today, I would fight alongside you anytime. It happens to most of us that make it through a first fight, and some still do it from time to time. The emotion, you know? It's nothing to be ashamed of. We're only mortals, and killing men shouldn't come easily to us."

Mikus nodded assent, but did not speak.

"I would like to say it gets easier, but that's not true. You just get harder."

"You saved my life today." Mikus croaked just above a whisper.

"And mine was saved by many others." Ferro said. "You saved many yourself. That's part of being on the line, being part of the shield wall. Sleep may not come easy, but you need it. For now, how about a drink by the fire with some of the guys? We will toast to the memory of Tilo and Strasa and Optio Trentis. We will drink to the health of Marcus Amintus."

"And my friend Del Ganno." Mikus added. He had come back around.

"And to Del Ganno. Come, tell us about Del." Ferro said, rising from his seat.

"Optio Trentis was killed?" Mikus asked.

"Yeah, early in the fight. Old Centurion Alturas picked Toratum to replace him, you know." Ferro added, reaching down to help Mikus get to his feet.

"Our Decanus? Good, he is a good man." Mikus said.

"Not like the new one." Ferro gave him a fearful look. Mikus had thoughts of Phenton as the new Decanus, and he felt his heart and stomach lurch.

"He may be handsome as the High Gods own bare asses, but at least he's a terrible soldier, and a rotten leader." Ferro added, with a smile

"You got promoted?" Mikus chuckled.

"Decanus Ferro." Adamas put an arm on his young friends shoulder. "It has a nice ring to it." And the two men walked outside, into the starless night.

LXXI
MACIEN

Drops of dirty water dripped down into the basin. It dripped from his hair, from the tip of his nose, from his chin. Each drop that fell took some of the grime, some of the salty sweat, some of the blood. But he knew it would be a long time before he was clean again. For a moment, he looked down at his distorted reflection, trying to catch a glimpse of himself between ripples. The now dirty water did not give him a clear image, and even if it did, he doubted he would recognize the man looking back at himself.

He plunged his hands in once more, and splashed his face, and scrubbed his arms. Patting himself dry, he allowed himself to take his first deep breath of the day. Alone in his tent after a long day of death, his exhaustion was finally able to safely bubble up. They had won the battle today, yes, but they had needed to. The enormity of this conflict was starting to set in. Silious would not be going away anytime soon. This war was going to be fought all across the Empire, and perhaps even farther than that.

A chilled flagon of wine was on a small table, and he overturned a ceramic cup and filled it to the brim. In a single draught, he drained it. Topping his cup off once more, he took a small, nobler sip this time and then set it down, forgotten. It was well past dark, and it had been a long day. He would rise early tomorrow and start another long one. All the known wounded had been brought to the Medici in the surgery tents. They had started to gather the dead and dig the graves. Tomorrow would be more of the same. It might take a week to get it all done.

Macien realized that as much as he wanted to be here for that, to see this thing through to the last shovelful of dirt, he couldn't. They were in a war, and he needed to get his force mobilized and prepared for what was going to happen next. And he had no idea what Silious' next move was going to be. He could guess, as could his staff, and they would discuss such things tomorrow. In his heart, he knew that no matter how many more battles they fought and won, Silious would escape, retreat farther and farther back until he made his way to Akritus once more. The bald belligerent may even go further than that, flee outside the borders of the Empire to some foreign enemy of the Imperial government.

Thoughts of the men he had watched die, on both sides, weighed heavy on his mind. The young faces of countless Legionaries, some just old enough to no longer be called boys, laying dead or dying on the field. Good men that he had known for a long time, some he had called friends, dead now. Brave men, like that young Lieutenant who had volunteered for the ill-fated mission against the Trivium forces, they were gone. Men like that, laying down their own lives so their fellow soldiers would have a chance. *Elknaut, that had been his name.* As much as it pained him, that was the past now, no matter how fresh the images were playing out before him. He had to deal with the present, and with the future, but he must never forget the sacrifices that had been made so he could do so.

Piles of unread dispatches and scrolls were on his desk, and he knew that he should be delving into them, but he couldn't bring himself to do that right now. Instead, he made plans to read them at first light. His schedule for tomorrow was already full, but he would make time. The staff meeting was first priority, and meeting and treating with Strank'Lakon was high up on the priority list. Supply requisitions, casualty reports, burials, promotions, capital business to be reviewed. His first priority should be to write to his family, but sadly that wasn't true. He would write to them, he had to, he realized.

Thinking of Junæa made him walk back over to the pile of scrolls and papers and tablets, and fumble through them looking for her seal. It wasn't there, and he frowned and walked away. Just then, as if someone had been reading his thoughts, a messenger announced himself at the tent flap. The Jorbus guards that were watching over the doorway didn't offer any challenge to the man, clearly an Imperial dispatcher. Sure enough, opening the flap revealed a man in a riding tunic, with the familiar purple and yellow hemming and cap denoting him as an official courier of the Imperial Palace.

It was a young man, and he nervously almost remorsefully held a scroll tube to Macien. "I'm sorry to bother you so late, Consul. This was marked as highly urgent."

Macien accepted it and said his thanks, filling the empty scroll tube up with communications of his own to go back to the palace. He dismissed the runner, who hesitantly hovered for a moment before reluctantly departing. It was as if the boy was going to say something, but couldn't find the nerve.

The tube had contained a single scroll. Purple wax kept it shut, and the seal of the Kantaur family was imprinted deeply into the glob. Mallea. He though of how late it was. No good news comes in this hour, especially under these circumstances. With a slide of his pinky finger, the wax crumbled and fell away. He couldn't unroll the paper enough to read it. The damn top kept folding back down as he read, and he thought he had seen something terrible, but it was curled over and he had to straighten it again. With a slight tremble he read:

Macien,

The Emperor has died. Per your arrangement
with him, you have been summoned back to the
capital to be made Interrex. The Consular
government is being dissolved. We have also just
received word that the insurgent forces from Petros
have been repelled from Jorbus. Gods give strength.
    -Mallea Kantaur.

Macien read it once more, and then again.
Greeth was dead. He grieved for him as both a
dead Emperor but mostly as a dead friend. And
a good friend at that, a lifelong friend. Then he
thought of Taraes, and what she must be going
through. He had died far from her, and he had
been the one who had sent her away as she
protested. She probably would have been safer
in the capital all along than back in Jorbus after
all that. Greeth was dead.

How could he return to Calidia right
now? He was in the middle of a campaign, a
crucial point of it, in fact. He did not want to be
Interrex. It had been a promise made to his
friend, a dying friend that also happened to be
the Emperor. He had sworn that if Greeth died,
he would be Interrex until his son proved
himself worthy to rule. That had been the
promise, the oath. Thoughts of the origin and
beginning of the Kantaurian dynasty, how it had
displaced the Siliousi in such a similar way ran
through his mind. The parallels were strikingly
obvious, and he doubted if it was a coincidence.
The Gods did strange things, and they liked to

reuse and cycle through similar situations with new players. Several of the players from the first act had been shuffled into fresh roles in this new act.

All eyes were on him. In this midnight hour, the entire pantheon of Gods were watching him, and everyone in the Empire and the world would be looking at him to see what he did, what choices he made. His father was there too, and all his ancestors, to see if he would make the right decision. It was a decision he would make tonight, how he would proceed with this. His family honor was on the line, and the easy thing to do would be to keep hi word and become Interrex. But as his father so oft said, 'The easy thing and the right thing are rarely the same thing.'

He had two options, and both were as difficult as they were correct in their own right. He could keep his oath, become Interrex, and try to hold the Empire together until Greeth Secundus was old enough to take the throne. Or, he could *not*. Breaking his oath to his now dead friend, he could continue down the path of this Consular government, a kind of Republic rather than an Empire. Perhaps he would remain as a Consul for several terms while the government took root, but he would see it through.

If Silious wanted to be Emperor so badly, it would be hard for him to continue this war if there was no Empire. An Empire needs an Emperor, but if it is a Republic, then *no one* could be Emperor. And the second part of his vow to Greeth, about his ruling until his son proved he was ready to lead, that fit in nicely to this scenario. What better way to prove you are ready to lead than to be voted into office by your peers? It was something to consider, a dream for another day. For now, he would continue with the fighting, and for the rest of the year at least, the government shall remain a consular government. If he was truly Interrex, then he had the authority to do that.

Sleep; that was what he needed right now. News of his friend's death and all the politics that it entailed made him even more exhausted than before. In the darkness of the night, with the lamps extinguished, he lay in his bed. Before he slipped off into the depths of his dreams, he heard an owl hooting outside his tent.

LXXII
DAHQUAL SILIOUS

Once it had been apparent that the enemy was no longer pursuing, Silious gave the order for them to make camp and to rest. He had called for a meeting with his staff, and instinctively had waited for Victus to arrive, forgetting that the man was now no longer with them. Silious was making all the major decisions now, like a true Emperor would from the old days. They needed to draft a new plan, a new strategy. They decided that they would fall back west, and then regroup.

They would then choose the next direction the campaign would take. Silious was inclined to take the north, the south was far too well defended and now they had lost the element of surprise and speed. They had lost the edge, and he needed to find it again. Vitruvian forces were making progress along the Northern Sea and deep into the Delta Lands. Perhaps they could use that momentum, spread east and then south, envelop the capital and force them to spread themselves too thin, and then sweep them up.

Gods, he had been so close. The throne was within reach, they had the battle but Victus had lost it. The eccentric strategist may have handed him Dutrigi on a silver platter, but he had bungled the real prize. Now it was up to Silious to *earn* his crown, like his ancestors. Victus had been a tool that he had chosen to give him an advantage, but it had been a bad choice it seemed. Now he needed to rely on himself, and new advisors. He had dismissed everyone from his hastily constructed command tent, and now he was alone.

Except he wasn't alone. Geneiada Lourede was lurking in a shadowy corner, he could feel the man's presence, could faintly hear the breathing.

"Speak, mystic. I command it." Silious said, pouring himself a glass of water.

"Very well, I speak." A voice said, and soon the image of the priest stepped from the shadow into the lamplight.

"Tell me about today." Silious demanded, turning to face the man. The torch and the heavy shadow danced on the priests face, distorting the features and turning it somewhat demonic.

"You were right to get rid of Quintus Victus. I had told you from the beginning that he was no help to you, my Lord." The man said, nodding slowly.

"Shut up! I don't want excuses, and I don't want you turning this matter around on me!" Duke Silious yelled. "You swore to me you had visions of a victory today, that we would triumphantly crush Macien and the rest of the pretenders. How do you explain this!" And then he threw his hands in an expansive gesture, around the dank war tent.

"The Gods had a hand in this, no doubt. They show me what they want to at the time, nothing is ever set in stone until it has passed, and even then it still isn't permanent." Lourede said. "I told you that you needed to strike first, did I not?"

"We were preparing to do just that. Macien sent that cursed raiding party. I should have you killed, you know? Like Victus, you have been a great disappointment." Silious seethed.

"You would be unwise to do so. To refuse a gift from the Gods is hubris and will surely be your downfall. I came to you because the Gods told me to. And they have their reasons. They are testing you, My lord. Do not fail that test."

Silious hummmfted in response to that.

"The Saurians, you told me that they would be taken care of. What happened with that? And where are the Hyerians we were supposed to unleash across the rural lands?" Silious demanded.

"The Gods do not have the same spiritual connection to the Saurians as they do with us, my Lord. Therefore, my understanding of them is very limited as well. They will be of no consequence if the Gods do not will it. Do not fear the Saurians." The priest lectured. "Also, I felt the presence of another Immortal today, during the battle." He added.

Silious was skeptical of this now as well. Was this man playing him, telling him things that he desired to hear?

"What good does that do me now? How can I obtain this immortality if I cannot even win a battle over mortals?" He said.

"I will track this being down, I know how to do so. Give me twenty of your finest soldiers, Eagle Guard preferably, and instruct them to obey me no matter what the order is. I will bring you your Immortality. I know how to unlock it, no one else can. Not many even know that Immortals still walk the earth like we do, my Lord."

This made the hairs on the back of his neck stand up. Silious wanted immortality, he dreamed of it, to be the Immortal Emperor that ruled over Calidia for all time. The anticipation was part of the reason he felt this prickling sensation. The other part was he suddenly, and very seriously, doubted his trust in this priest. To give him the command he wanted, well that could be very dangerous indeed. Twenty members of his Guard sworn to obey whatever this man wanted, could end in disaster for Silious.

As if reading his mind, the priest spoke.

"I will not use these men against you, My Lord. If I wanted you dead, a dagger here in this tent would be easy enough. I will use them to get this Immortal, maybe more than just this one. That is a promise." He stopped, but then added. "Order them to kill me if I say or do anything other than I have said I would, if that will reassure you."

Greed and desire won over Silious in the end. "You may have twenty." He allowed a wicked smile.

"Excellent. This will be a success, the Gods say it is so." The priest smiled, revealing incredibly white teeth. Silious was once again reminded of something his uncle had always said; *"Never trust a man with perfect teeth."* That advice made his own smile fade slightly.

"Priest, tell me, what should I do next?" Silious asked, genuinely interested in what the man with the leather skull cap would say.

"You must continue the war. That is all that matters." Lourede said.

"I know that, that goes without saying. But what have the Gods told you about what I should do *next*?" He asked.

"I have seen visions. What you should do next, they have not shown. But what I do see is clear. You must bring the Empire near the point of collapse. All across the land, you must fight. The people of Calidia will look to you as a savior. Crops will burn, roads will be blocked, and cities will crumble. They will blame the Emperor, they will blame Macien and everyone else for this, but they will not blame you. You will dam rivers, you will destroy bridges and collapse aqueducts. The land will be brought to the brink of chaos, and from that chaos you will rise! Like a phoenix you will rise!" A crazed glittering was in his eyes as he spoke.

"I will inherit a ruined Empire of crumbling infrastructure and starved people?" Silious scoffed.

"Not ruined, my lord. Shapeable. To your image." He corrected.

"They will not blame me, they will blame the Emperor, you say?" Silious asked, traces of counterfeit concern in his voice.

"Yes, the slumbering leader who allowed this to happen while he slept." Lourede offered.

"The Gods have not told you that the Emperor has died?" Silious raised an eyebrow.

Lourede had a rare flash of concern and confusion on his usual implacable face. Silious saw it. *So, you aren't as omnipotent as you make yourself appear to be?*

"My contacts in the Imperial Palace just informed me." Silious added.

"The Gods did not show me such things, My Lord. I am, after all, a mere mortal." And he bowed.

"You can have your twenty men. Bring me the immortality you have promised. Then perhaps I will heed your advice once more." And Silious dismissed him with a wave of the hand. "Find me when you are done."

"Where will you go next, My Lord?" Lourede asked.

"Won't the Gods will tell you that,

Priest?" Silious said sarcastically.

"Equium." Lourede said. "To harvest the fruit of your seeding there."

Silious did not respond, but that had been an interesting suggestion. Equium. Perhaps.

LXXIII
ANTONEUS COMETA

The edge of his knives had been honed to the sharpness that only someone like him could get them to. Sharp yes, but the angle was that so it would not chip or bend. The sica blades were sheathed after they had been oiled properly, not needing to be drawn again until they needed to be used. Cometa reverently placed the belt with the rest of his kit. His Gladius was impeccably sharp as well, but they were always easier to get an edge on, being made of such straight lines and a symmetrical point. He walked away from his kit in the barracks, away from his bunk, and out to the night air. Only it was no longer night outside. A brilliant orange-rose pink glow was blazoning in the sky. It had been a long day, day and a half.

He wore his purple tunic of the Imperial Guard, and a single dagger on his hip. The rest he left behind. Perhaps unwise in this case, being on the edge of what was a battlefield the last time the sun had shone upon it. He would take his chances; he would be going to sleep soon anyways, he had earned that. First, he needed to talk to Macien. The news of the Emperors death had spread like wildfire through the ranks of the Guard, and it was something the Consul would have taken very hard. But things needed to be said, and the future needed to be discussed.

The Consul was awake expectedly, and already going about his day with reading and writing dispatches at his desk. He surrendered his single dagger to his brothers that were guarding the tent, smiling as he did so. Antoneus was one of the last people that Macien needed protection from. He stood at attention until the Consul saw him and beckoned him over.

"Cometa, good to see you." Macien said, embracing him in a handshake. "Did you get any sleep, it is early."

"Not yet, sir. *Did you?*" He asked.

"Not much I'm afraid. I can sleep when I am dead. What do I owe the pleasure of this visit? Have you thought of what I offered you?" Macien asked, setting aside his scrolls and giving the Guardsman his undivided attention.

"Yes, sir. That's what I'm here to talk to you about, actually. *You being dead,* that is. They go hand in hand." Cometa said, no humor in his voice or on his face.

"Oh?" Macien asked, and rolled his hand in gesture that prompted him to continue.

"Sir, I know you requested that I undertake a new mission on your behalf. At first, I was thrilled. This very thing has been my ambition in joining the Imperial Guard. Even the sabotage of those machines the other night, well, that was exactly what I've always wanted to do. But now, with the death of Emperor Kantaur..." He paused. "I'm very sorry about that, sir, I know he was a good friend and you two were *very* close. I was there when he fell ill, in the room I mean. Anyways, I'm sorry."

"He was a good man. His death is a loss to us all. It's alright, go on." Macien nodded.

"You need people you can trust by your side right now." Antoneus jumped right into it. "The Imperial Guard, some of our members are corrupted by outside influences. I feel they were responsible for the Emperor's death, in fact I am certain of it. That is why I must respectfully decline your offer to undertake that mission at this time. I swore an oath to protect the Imperial family and the Emperor. Now, I will do everything I can to protect you, I swear it. I pledge to you, let me remain close to you, by your side, for I fear you will have many, many attempts on your life in the future. From both enemies without and enemies within. Allow me this honor, and I *will* protect you."

Macien walked over to him, and grasped his arm in embrace. "You will always be welcomed by my side. I too am deeply disturbed by the news of the Emperor's untimely death, and I fear a deeper conspiracy is lurking beneath it. You have had these suspicions for a long time, I remember you saying such things. It is my fault for not acting on them. If you keep me safe while I am here, who will keep everyone else safe back in the palace? Half the Guard is here, but the other half is back there."

"I say launch an investigation here, into the men that are on campaign. But I believe the biggest perpetrators are back in Calidia still. Remember those Enforcers, the ones I was working with when I got kidnapped and tortured?" Cometa asked.

"Yes. I met one of them. He's the one that told me of the conspiracy first. Flaccus, right?" Macien recalled.

"Those men know more about this case than I do. Use them; make them special investigators with powers of immunity and total jurisdiction. They will root out anyone that was tainted by this, and get the ring leaders." Cometa insisted.

"I will draft up a decree right now. If you remember, could you please give me their full names and titles?" Macien said. "And then get some sleep. I think you're on Guard duty tonight."

LXXIV
PUBLIUS NEUMON

The mess hall was as quiet as a tomb. That had been the spirit of the fort for days now. Terrible news had been filtering in, each more surprising and more ominous than the last. The only good news had been that after the last few watches, all the enemy campfires across the river had vanished. At first that had been good news, but now it seemed like some dark foreshadowing of things to come.

Initially, the dwindling campfires had been seen as a sign of enemy retreat, their withdrawal from the contested borders. Now it was known that the fires themselves had been a diversion of sorts, a kind of distraction to keep the Calidians and the Millangors alike from knowing the real movements of the Hyerians. All the while, while the multitude of fires burned, the Saurians had been marching a good majority of their forces north. Through what had been considered impassable terrain, the Wo'styn desert and the thick jungles of The Wrede, their strike force had marched, and eventually made it's way up the Neck to the fort of Bridgegate.

A siege had been started there, and the 8th

had no idea how that was faring. The size of the enemy force differed greatly depending on who the source was that had seen them, but it was large, that fact was not to be doubted. And who know how large the force across the river is, or was, rather. They had left, no longer burning the extra campfires to confuse the superiorly intelligent humans across the water. Maybe they were marching north right now, or were headed back down south to regroup. Perhaps they would appear north of the fort and encircle them. Maybe they hadn't left at all; perhaps it was all a feint.

The unknown was troubling enough, the fear and solemnity running rampant through the men. The known facts were just as troubling, if not more so. The enemy could be anywhere, yes, that was true. Also, the Millangor army had fled. Their allies, the ones they had been stationed out here to protect, had left without so much as a thank you. And when they did leave, they had taken the Legion's fleet with them. The 8th was completely stranded. And they had the mentality of men that were in such a situation. No one knew what they were going to do next.

Sure, there were rumors, suggestions floating around, but nothing was set in stone. And the uncertainty was causing dismay, which was contagious. Some wanted to march north, but that would be foolish. With the Millangor army fled, and an unknown Hyerian force terrorizing wherever they pleased, and a second lurking in the shadows, they might be marching into certain death. Even if they made it unscathed to the north peninsula, they had no ships to sail home on. And no one knew what was happening in Bridgegate, and rumors of the fall of Dutrigi had reached them recently.

Marching south into Hyeria would be even more foolish. Sitting here and waiting was foolish as well, but was the safest course. Plus, that had been the orders they had received from the Empire. If the Empire needed them, they would formally recall them.

The room was dimly lit, every other torch dark and unlit. Conservation of supplies was already starting. No need in wasting things like lamp oil in such a reckless fashion. That philosophy was apparently being used on the food supplies already. Grey, lukewarm lumpy gruel was slopped and sitting nearly untouched in Publius' tin. The watered-down wine that had turned to vinegar some time ago wasn't going down very quickly either.

He was grateful that the looming threat of death and destruction in the form of the invading horde across the river had ended. The stress that it had caused, seeing those fires burn each night had been tremendously tolling on him. In a way now, he wished that it were still there. For the state that he and the 8th were in was far more depressing and worrisome than when they had been certain death was just a stone's throw away.

LXXV
ATHELTIADES

The Hyerians had all died. Not a single one had been captured, they all died during the fighting. It had taken the green-skinned Millangor the better part of a day just to clear a hole in the pile of dead to reach the gate to the fort. Even now, they were working to clear the carcasses, tossing them irreverently out into the water. Shark fins were swarming in a feeding frenzy, hundreds of them. The water was turned a dark purple as the Saurian ichor churned into the blue sea. To the north, the arriving Trimontians had made short work of the Akritus forces, and a good number of them had been captured rather than fight to the last man.

Atheltiades was meeting now, on the southern walls of the fortress, with the commanders of the Saurian and human forces that had saved Bridgegate and it's defenders. As he would later discover, Grek'Laton was the Millangor General, and the Trimontis leader was Polemarch Korellius. Grek'Laton came alone, carrying a battle-axe on his back, and a curved short sword on his hip. It was strange seeing a Saurian casually walk along the battlements, armed, but after everything that had happened in recent days, not inconceivable. Especially considering what this Saurian and his army had just done. Polemarch Korellius brought a large contingent of his men inside the fort, and they immediately went to work tending to whatever needed to get done, aiding the wounded, and relieving the weary warriors on the walls.

A fourth man had climbed up to join them, and it was someone Atheltiades vaguely remembered seeing in the past, but couldn't place him. The man had Morincian features, Dutrigian features in fact, and was garbed and credentialed as an Imperial Sentinel. Atheltiades didn't realize how exhausted he was until he reached up to remove his helmet. A numbness shot through his arms, countered only by an ache in his shoulders. Suppressing tremors of weakness in his arms, he managed to slide it off in a controlled fashion. It was all he could do to keep it from plummeting out of his hands and clanging onto the walk below.

"My name is Commander Atheltiades, and I am commanding officer of this Fort. You all have my thanks, and I think I speak for the rest of my men when I say they are thankful for you as well. Please excuse me if I appear sluggish at all, it's been a long..." He tried to remember how many days they had been under siege, but abandoned trying to summon the answer, it was taking too long. "It's been hell. I'm tired because of it."

Polemarch Korellius spoke next, telling

the tale of how he and his men heard the story
from the messenger, and had mobilized as soon
as they could. It seemed that as soon as they
could was as fast as they needed to move,
arriving when they did. Grek'Laton and his
Sentinel companion told their tale next.
Monodius, that was the humans name, had
passed through Bridgegate not too long ago to
treat with the Millangor regarding troops station
in Akkedis. Atheltiades recollected something
about that, but couldn't evoke any specific
memory. It had been, after all, *hell,* and he was
tired because of it. When they spoke with the
Millangor King, he had sent Monodius north to
Utara'Sek on horseback. It must have been a
well trained Carpydian mount, to remain ride-
able in Akkedis. The Sentinel had made great
time to Utara'Sek, where a garrisoned force of
Millangor under the command of Grek'Laton
was waiting. With orders from his King, he gave
the command to have the Millangors mobilize
and head to Bridgegate. They too had
apparently arrived just in the nick of time.

    With the Akritus and Hyerians beaten,
the leaders were now meeting to discuss how to
proceed from here. A few of the captured
Akritus junior officers were confessing that they
had been sent with orders to take the fort and
allow the Hyerians into the lands of Lacerterra.
All but one was put to the sword following their
confessions for treason against the Empire. The
survivor would probably wish he had died with

the rest before too long. From the battlements, looking down onto the square, they watched as these men were executed. Atheltiades felt more akin to the hulking Grek'Laton than he did to these traitors below.

"What do we do now?" Atheltiades said to no one in particular. In fact, he was talking to himself if truth be told.

"This is your fort, Commander. That is your decision." The Polemarch said. "My men and I will remain for as long as you need us. Any way we can assist you, we will."

The Saurian and the Sentinel remained silent.

"What do you know of Dutrigi?" Atheltiades asked the group. Jacean Monodius spoke upon this matter.

"I was witness to the aftermath of the battle there, Commander." His voice was soft yet strained. "Dutrigi was completely overtaken by Silious and his forces. I believe the army was utterly destroyed. I'm sorry for your loss."

Atheltiades nodded.

"Petrichoro fell too, I'm afraid." This came from Korellius . "As far as I know, you here are the last of the Dutrigian army. Apparently the majority of your civilians still live, and rumor has it that a great number of them are barricaded inside the Old Walls. Silious didn't seem to care enough to try and crack into that one."

Atheltiades nodded again, more slowly

this time.

"And you, Grek'Laton," He spoke. "What will you do now?"

The Saurian spoke clear enough Domitian, slow and rough around the edges, but that was common for even the most fluent of his species.

"We are here to help, too. My people and yours have been at war for all of our time together. Now it must end. War never ends, we must end it. We are here as friends, and as the allies we have sworn to be in recent years. Hyerians will always hate us, and hate you. You will help us fight our enemies, and we will fight yours. We come as friends." He shut his under bitten jaw, with the two teeth that protruded upwards, and lifted his chin in a dignified manor. Extending his hand, palm upwards, he waited for Atheltiades to grasp it. With little reservation, the Dutrigian commander placed his hand atop of the green palm, and clutched it. It remained at the same height, neither rising nor falling. Equals.

"Thank you, all of you." Atheltiades said, breaking the embrace. "You are the reason this fort still stands and the reason I and my men still live. I have made a decision about what to do next."

Everyone looked at him expectantly, and he hesitated for a moment, unsure if the course he was about to take was the right one. It was a hard thing to do, but it also felt very right, very fitting, and very timely.

"We are abandoning the fortress." He blurted with finality.

No one said anything, and the conversation was quiet enough that none of the other soldiers in the area could hear.

"We have made incredible sacrifices here. For hundreds of years this fort has stood and never fallen, and countless have died to ensure that it still stood. But they did not fight and die and kill for these *stone walls*. No, they fought for what was behind them. They fought to protect their people, and to protect their Empire. Bridgegate is as much a symbol as it is a fortress. Today, it will be a symbol in a new way. We will leave the gates open, the bridges down. For those across the trenches, to the south, they are as much a friend to us now as those to the north." He gestured to Korellius as he said this. "The Hyerians will have to fight through our new friends the Millangors to get through to us now. You will hold Bridgegate, in the absence of Dutrigi." And now he gestured to the Saurian General.

"We will bury our dead here, beneath the soil inside these walls. They fought and died here, and this fort will serve as a memorial to them and all that died in the past. This will be a shrine to them and those who came before." He continued. "But I will not remain here, neither will my men. And I ask that you, both Trimontis and Millangor alike, join me."

Everyone was looking at him intently.

"I am marching to retake Dutrigi and to free my people. Then we will take the fight to those that have wronged us. You have already pledged your aide to me however you can. Will you join me in this endeavor?"

It was unanimous.

"We will follow you, Lord General Atheltiades." Korellius said.

"I am…" Atheltiades was going to protest this title, but he realized it was correct. He was the new Lord General, albeit by default for not dying with all the other officers there had been. "I am honored to have you by my side."

Korellius scoffed and looked around at the panorama of the battlefield below them. "Not as honored as we are, Lord General. I will follow any man that can pull of a defense like *this.*"

"Tonight, we bury and honor our dead. Tomorrow, we head for Dutrigi."

LXXVI
TARAES KANTAUR

A single tear rolled down each cheek as she let out at staggering breath. That was it. That was all she cried when she read that her husband was dead. Taraes Kantaur had known deep in her heart that he was dead before she had left the capital. She had already cried, already grieved for Greeth, for the father of her children and the husband she had always known she wanted. She dropped the scroll down onto a table, and went into the next room to tell her children. They cried for hours, for days. She comforted them the best she could, and she had cried again when they had cried, but those tears were for them, not for Greeth. Any parent knows how hard it is to see your children in such pain.

It was here they would stay, in Jorbus, to grieve for Greeth who was laying dead halfway across the Empire in the capital. She would stay here, like the old spinster that she was rapidly turning into, locked away in the upper rooms of a palace, under guard of her personal soldiers. These soldiers not only were here to guard her, but she knew they were also ordered not to allow her to leave. She was essentially a prisoner, banished to her home city. It could be worse, but it was far from ideal.

Macien was now to be Interrex. Darien and Kyberien had agreed to send soldiers like Macien had requested. Kyberien was to go with them and fill some roll in Macien's Imperial Council. Darien would now officially become Duke of Morincia. And Taraes, former Empress of Calidia, was confined to Jorbus. It seemed very unfair, the Gods had seen her happiness and had taken it from her in the cruel way they so often do. At least the city was safe for her and her family once again. For now, that was. The enemy was gone, and the fires were all but out, light wispy smoke rising here and there across the cityscape.

Petros had been repelled, largely in part due to the arrival of Duracee ships and marines. Duracee had been responsible for the colonies in Enthaki, and when they began to revolt, everyone had expected them to send most of their forces over that direction to stabilize the situation. No one, especially not Petros, had anticipated them arriving as quickly as they had in Jorbus. Perhaps something or someone had tipped them off. Either way, they had been welcomed, and after they had helped to liberate the city, they left a sizeable force behind to make sure it remained safe. Petros was far from being placated, however. Just the threat of them looming was enough to put every Morincian on edge. They would be causing trouble all along the Morincian and Crystal seas, pirating and pillaging.

She would help the city rebuild, the best she could. She was a priestess of Natori after all, and she would help heal the wounded. She would work with architects and builders to construct a city that the people who lived here would be proud of. Darien may now be Duke of Morincia, but she would be the Archon of Jorbus in all but title. She had left here along time ago, and made a home in the Imperial Palace. Now that she was back, she knew that this city had always been her home and she didn't care ever to return to Calidia to live. She would go back, she knew that. But this was her home once again.

She would see her mother. Up on the slopes of Mt. Junas, doing whatever it was her mother did up there. Perhaps her mother would come down to see her, but she doubted it. Just as Taraes had no desire to return to Calidia, her mother most likely had no desire to return here. She would make a point to go find her soon. They had much to talk about.

Her hand fell gently to her belly, and in that moment she knew a truth. Just as she had always known that Greeth was going to die in his slumber, and had only had that confirmed today, she now knew she was pregnant. She had thought it might be, suspected it, but in this moment, she knew it was true. Her husband's final piece of his legacy was swelling inside her. This child would never know its father, and that made her sad in so many ways. But Greeth would want her to raise it strong and with all the love she could give. She would. Taraes' mother would be excited to hear this, and see some sort of portents in the unborn child of a dead man.

In the palace, Junæa was taking everything very hard. She overindulged in wine, and wept frequently. Taraes found herself taking care of all the children more often than not. The Duchess, who wasn't quite a Duchess anymore since Darien was now the Duke, was deteriorating. It felt like if Macien came home soon, the wholeness of the family being back together, like it used to be before all this happened, would pull Junæa out from this well of sorrow. But that wouldn't happen anytime soon, and her sister-in-law was breaking down. Perhaps it would pass on it's own, but until then, Taraes would support her and help her as much as she could.

Kanion was here still, with Tycho and Andronikos, and that made things easier. When he was around, it felt as if things were going to be ok. He reminded her enough of Greeth to be comforting, but he was different enough in character and humor to not evoke sorrow or longing. He cared deeply for her, for the children, and for Junæa and her children. He was like a big brother, a protector that made everyone feel safe. She knew that if it came to it, the man would gladly lay down his life for any of them. She hoped it never came to that, but if a situation like that arose again, she felt comfort in knowing he was here.

Another touch to her belly, and she smiled. This child may never know it's father, but it would know love. And it would be safe.

LXXVII
NEROFIDES

A single burning light appeared on the horizon, bursting through the dark, starless night like a sun rising in the morning. The signal tower of Pterogines burned like a cinder, orange and hot. It was bringing them home, guiding them, a beacon to Petros. He took a long pull of wine from the amphora he held. The dark purplish liquid thinned and turned red as it ran down his face.

It was some Theiosian floral wine, and a single amphora cost more than your average peon made in a year. He did not care that it washed down his face, because he hadn't paid for it. He had taken it, like a man. They had raided the warehouses in Portopolis, and this had been part of the take. He had dozens more of them, and he could spare as much as he wanted. The one thing his people weren't going to have any shortage of in the future was… well, anything. They were free to take whatever they wanted now that Morincia was in chaos; the whole Empire was in chaos. Chaos was good state for the world to be in for Petros.

Jorbus would have been raided by now, that was something he wished he could have partaken in, but alas, he had not. Perhaps in the near future, he would sail there again and pillage and terrorize it once more. Just when those fools rebuilt their buildings and their hopes, he would come knock them down again. But that would wait. They would unload their bounty, celebrate a tad while they provisioned the fleet for another outing, and then find another jewel to pluck. Maybe Athyrtun? Or Gefyra? Perhaps they would sail up the Brellis River with those new longships they had designed and raid all the Morincian cities that were inland. The possibilities were endless.

Petros loomed, a negative image, darker that the darkness of the night. The walled harbor, the Caldera, was a welcomed sight. As much as any Petran loved the open sea, it was always pleasant to return to the homeport. If sailing and raiding was like a man in ecstasy with a woman, the safety of mooring your ship here was like a young child being embraced by a mother. Today he would drink, he would feast, and he would take many women to bed. He would shower them with gems and jewelry and his love and they would worship him for it.

The thoughts of watching Portopolis burn, and imagining Jorbus doing the same made him excited. He knew that his men had no desire to occupy these cities, or any other, for they had Petros. The Island was the only land they needed. They took from others goods and slaves and all the things that the rest of the world worked for. Land meant nothing. And razing cities was a waste of time and damaged these sources beyond repair. No, Nerofides and his ilk would only beat them up a bit, knock them down but not out. One did not kill the cow that gave them milk, or cut the head off the chicken that gave them eggs.

Jorbus and Portopolis would rebuild, true. That was the design. Then they would be harvested once more. And Petros grew stronger. As long as Silious kept his war going, Petros would be safe in doing whatever they wanted to do, for no one would oppose them. Duracee, those self righteous bastards, were occupied with those precious colonies in Enthaki. Jorbus was tied up in the civil war. Morincia was wide open for the taking. And take they shall.

He drank more of the wine. The burning signal fire pulsed and flared the closer they got. Home, for a moment at least. Then back out into the chaos to create more chaos. It was a glorious time to be alive, to be a Petran.

LXXVIII
LUCIUS TERTORUS

Lucius Tertorus scratched at his dark black beard. It was no easy task since his hands were tightly bound together at the wrists, but he had gotten used to it. He felt as though the gesture must make him look like some swooning maiden each time he did this, which was often. Since he had been captured, he had not been allowed to shave. No blade was brought near him. They had started feeding him meat not too long ago, but it always came precut or in a big hunk that he need to gnash at. At least his feet were no longer bound. Even the Deklar realized that him fleeing was impossible, just as he did. Still, he was not trusted to have his hands free.

The all sat in a large circle around the massive fire. Ugachekt, his original captor, was by his side. He in turn sat beside his father, Igachekt. Many chieftains from different tribes of the Deklar were gathered here, and all were watching the flames intently. Sparks and embers erupted upwards as the pitchy wood crackled and burst. Lucius scratched his itchy beard once again. He had recently asked for it to be shaven, but the only response he received was 'you will want it when the cold times come.'

Igacheckt was speaking to the group, and they were listening to the old man intently. His once reddish brown beard was now mostly gray, and his somewhat wrinkled and flabby visage betrayed a much bulkier, sturdier frame from his youth. Surprisingly, although the chief spoke in his native savage tongue, Lucius was able to discern most of what was said. Immersion in this culture, one that spoke little Domitian, allowed him to start to understand their speech.

The chief was talking about the wood that was being burned. It came from a life-tree of some long dead relative. It had fallen down, or part of it had. The people had then harvested the wood, and part of it was used tonight in this fire. The life-tree was a concept that Lucius found hard to fathom at first. At birth, a sapling was planted or claimed in your name by your father. It came from your ancestral grove. Somehow, it was determined where it was to be planted, by some vision or another. Usually it was close to the parent tree. Every member of your family came from the same family grove, maybe even your own father's tree. When it was planted or picked, the placenta and birth sack of your birth fertilized the tree. As your life went on and you grew, so did your tree. Every family member knew where their tree was, where their father's tree was, grandfathers, great-great uncles, and so on. When you died, you were buried under your tree.

This was an old tree, one that come down or had broken from age and girth. They were now honoring the spirit of whoevers life tree it was, and toasting with their drinks of beer and mead. He heard someone say that part of the tree was being turned into a drinking mug, a bowl, and a strong oak shield for the family to use. 'Chekt' was the Deklar word for oak, and that was the family root name of 'Ugachekt' and Igachekt. Different families had different species for their family trees. 'Rakt' was redwood he discovered, and 'Feirduk' was pine he thought he had heard.

After they had told the tale of Moachekt, as his tree wood burned, they began to discuss other matters. No one was allowed to stand until the meeting was adjourned, as was the custom. One time, in a previous meeting, Lucius had seen one man urinate while sitting, aiming his stream messily to the dirt beside him. Women brought more drinks as the meeting went on, for they could not partake but were here to serve.

That was when he saw her again. It was the second time he had seen her since arriving here in Estroe. She was stunning, and he couldn't help but stare at her. Black hair, icy blue eyes, she was like no woman he had ever seen. Thoughts of her lingered in his mind long after she had left the light of the circle. He drank the bitter beer in his cup to the last swallow, subconsciously hoping that she would be the one to bring him another cupful. She did not return that night.

The Deklar talked, but Lucius stumbled on the words as the night went on, and he lost complete track of the conversation. When the meeting had been called to a close, Ugachekt escorted him back to his quarters. The two men talked as they walked, the Deklar speaking in Domitian and Lucius attempting his mangled version of the Deklar tongue.

"She is not for you." Ugachekt stated. Lucius tried to feign ignorance, but it was useless. "Kallya. Cousin of mine. I see you looking. She is not for you, Kallya is for another."

Lucius abandoned his attempt at Deklar speech, and reverted back to Domitian. He kept the vocabulary simple and short when he spoke.

"Kallya is her name? She is very pretty." He said.

"Yes. She is pretty, she is also not for you." Ugachekt restated.

"I… I only looked." Lucius said.

"Look like *that*, that means other things." The blond barbarian said, a smile on his face that did not reach his eyes.

"Ok. I will no longer look at her." Lucius knew the words were false as he spoke them, and so did Ugachekt. To not look at her was as likely as not holding your breath underwater. Your body knew it would die if it tried.

"The Chiefs all spoke. After next snow, we will head east." Ugachekt shifted the conversation. "Your chief, Si-Las, he will be punished for what he has done."

"I don't think Silious has done what you say he has done, Ugachekt." Lucius protested. "He is not a kidnapper. Duke Silious is a good man. He would not steal away the families of the chiefs to keep them from attacking. We have armies for that."

"It is true, Loo-Sea-Us. And after next snow, we will fight against Si-Las and the Caldeens. Even if they kill the families, we will fight. Deklar are free, and no slaves. We will die free, you know?" The man said.

Lucius did know, and he had grown to admire these people in a strange way. He nodded. Then, pulling out a knife, Ugachekt reached out and firmly grasped the forearm of Lucius. The captive jerked away, but the barbarian was stronger and pulled the arm towards him. With a sawing motion, the ropes that bound the mans wrist fell away. Sheathing the blade, Ugachekt patted the man on the head like he was dog.

"See, Like I said, we are good friends now." Ugachekt stated, a beaming grin on his face. "You sleep now Caldeen." And the man left.

Absently rubbing his wrists, Lucius stood there for what felt like minutes but was only several heartbeats. His mind was reeling. The world had just been opened to him, and he looked east, back to where his distant home was. It was too far, a daunting undertaking. But he would be free, and just like the Deklar, he too would rather die free, on his terms, rather than to live a prisoner. But he wasn't a prisoner, he was free to decide what he wanted to do. And he chose the soft, pelt covered bed that he had been using lately. If he wanted to leave, he could do so at anytime. This was his decision. And he thought of Kallya as he crawled in under the blankets, and smiled as he drifted off to sleep, hands sprawled far apart like he was being crucified. That was wonderful, he hadn't been able to move his arms like that in months. The world would be different tomorrow.

LXXIX
DANQUIN ELKNAUT

He was freezing, cold sweat slathered across his body as his eyes slammed open and his lungs rattled for breath. Was he dead? Was this Hades? It was so dark and he hurt everywhere. Was he in a cave, in the bowels of some dark demonic place? Familiar sounds filled the air, sounds of men breathing, asleep like he had just been. His eyes adjusted as he struggled to sit up. Ultimately, he failed, his body would not obey. Sleep took him once more, and reluctantly he drifted away.

Again he awoke with a start, but the darkness was gone. It was bright, and he could hear voices. He was in a tent, laying upon a cot, like so many others around him. He was alive. An orderly was tending to the bandages on his leg and that must have been what had roused him from his sleep. The man casually glanced up at his patient, and noticed the man looking back at him. With slow understanding, he nearly jumped back with surprise, and then left abruptly.

He quickly assessed his own body, and

found that not only was he terribly week, but he was in tremendous pain. Each breath brought a wave of agony in his chest and abdomen. Tenderness and sharp jolts of agony radiated from multiple bandaged sites along his body. Again he tried to rise, but could not find the strength.

Soon, a man appeared in his field of vision. It was obviously a Medicus, and by the look on his face, he was happy to see Danquin awake.

"Ah, you are finally awake, soldier. That is good." The older man spoke. He was tall and slender, with a thinning crop of graying hair that had probably been brown at one point. The man had somewhat beady eyes that were too close together to pass as normal, and an axe head of a nose split the gap between them. Danquin tried to respond, but no noise came out at all.

"Do not speak yet, son. Give it time, rest now." The Medicus advised. "I am Medicus Titus Carrana, and you are lucky to be alive. *Very* lucky. The priests gave you the final rites several times since you have been here. Many thought you were dead even before you arrived." Another orderly came over with a ladle of water, and Danquin sloppily slurped it down. The man continued to speak.

"You were found on a remote part of the battlefield, an area where our sides scavengers went to investigate some enemy artillery.

Everyone else in the area was dead, well dead for the battle had been long over. They saw you move as they were combing the area, and brought you here. You had arrows enough in you to kill you, not to mention a nasty wound to your leg that had been previously bandaged, and some serious internal injuries. You had several broken ribs, as well as a broken left arm. Your breathing was extremely rapid and shallow, and you appeared to be just as low on air as you were on blood. We stopped the bleeding well past what should have killed you. Many times my staff urged me to stop working on you, to tend to others that had a better chance. Maybe it was my ego, or maybe the Gods saw fit to use me as an instrument to save your life, but I would not stop." He gave a brief smile, and it was a smile more or self-satisfaction than it was for genuine pleasure that Danquin Elknaut was still alive.

"We forced water down your throat through a device I personally designed. It gets inserted down into your stomach, and allows us to give you fluids without suffocating you. It then became apparent that the broken ribs weren't the only reason for your erratic and deteriorating respiratory cycle. If any other Medicus on this battlefield had been treating you, I swear you would be dead. But, the Gods saw fit for me to be your doctor, and you are here now."

"As a young man, I participated in some

experiments a local doctor had done on pigs. The animals were stabbed in the chest, through a lung. It was not a fatal wound, not at first. The more the animal breathed, the worse it got. You see, air would get into it's chest from the leaking lung and cause the animals lung to collapse under the increasing pressure. We had developed a device, a hollow tube that was inserted in between the animal's ribs and it allowed air and blood to escape, relieving the pressure and causing the lung to re-inflate." The doctor tapped a spot on Danquin's ribcage, and he jerked in response to the pain it caused.

"You were the first living human I had ever done it on. Lucky I still carry that tube with me in my kit. It saved your life. After that, you slept for days. Just as I had refused to give up on you, you refused to give up on yourself. The Gods have something in store for you, young man. You are here for a reason." The doctor smiled.

"My men." Danquin managed to speak. He remembered the raid now, thundering into the rear of the Trivium force that was pelting the Imperial soldiers far below. They had been spotted at the last possible moment, and the enemy archers had managed to unload a single volley before the cavalry crashed down upon them. Many of those arrows missed, but enough found their marks. One had gone into his upper arm, he remembered, through and through the tricep. They made short work of the enemy, but the enemy was numerous and eventually the Turma was being whittled down. Elknaut didn't remember the other arrows wounding him, or the one that killed his horses, and sent him flying, breaking his arm and ribs, and knocking him out cold in the process.

"No one that we know of survived. We have been asking around to try and figure out who you are, but we haven't gotten any responses back. You are most likely the only survivor. And it has been a remarkable recovery too, if I may say so again." The Medicus smiled.

"Elknaut." Danquin said under strain. "2nd Legion." He wanted to say more, but couldn't, he hadn't the strength.

"Elknaut." The Medicus repeated. "We will get in contact with the 2nd and let them know that you are alive. For now, get some rest, soldier."

Lt. Danquin Elknaut didn't argue with that order. As he drifted off to sleep once more, he dreamed. The dreams that he had that night he would never forget, they would haunt him and guide him for the rest of his life.

LXXX
ADYPATUS EVENTUS

The room was darkly lit, and that was exactly the environment that Eventus wanted. He could see the majority of the patrons, but they could not make him out too well. He had his hood up, which wasn't unusual considering it was a cooler night, and this bar was chilled like a cave. He sat in the same spot he was in the night before, and confirmed the man he was looking for frequented this spot nightly. Tonight he would act, time was getting short after all. He watched his mark, a squat man with dark hair styled in a military cut. He had a laugh like a jackal, and it irritated Eventus each time he heard it.

In the shadows, Adypatus Eventus sipped his wine and watched, as the man got more and more belligerent. The wine that he choked down was terrible, but he didn't care, he wasn't in a drinking mood. Strange, he usually was always in a drinking mood. But he thought of everything that was riding on this, and had limited himself to two cups, only as to not stand out as a guy in a bar by himself that wasn't drinking. After a while, the man paid his tab and was finishing his last cup, laughing that terrible laugh as he conversed with the old man he had been drinking beside.

Eventus walked across the room, weaving through large wooden beams that supported the floor above them. The man began to exit, and Eventus casually followed after him. After a short walk down an alley, the man decided that he needed to take a piss. Perfect. Sneaking up behind him, Eventus grabbed the man by the hair and slammed his head into the brick wall he was relieving himself on. The man collapsed into a snoring heap.

Eventus had dragged the man into an abandoned building not far away. He had awoken him with a bucket of old, putrid water that had been conveniently left in the vacant space by the previous tenants. With a gasp, the man sprung back to life. It took several long moments before the man put together the fact that he was hogtied and dripping wet in a strange place. He saw Eventus and swore at him.

"Let me go!" The man demanded. "You don't know who you are fucking with, man! Let me go right now!"

"Oh, I'm sorry, I must have made a mistake. Are you not Imperial Guardsman Marcus Bevellus?" Eventus asked, derision in his voice.

The man was taken aback slightly, fear on his face, in his eyes. That had been his trump card, and it held no value to his captor.

"I am a member of the Imperial Guard! You will die for this!" Bevellus tried to play it anyways in desperation, and just as he thought it failed.

"You don't recognize me, Marcus?" Eventus asked, leaning in closely so the man could get a good look at his face. Hatred was on the Imperial Guardsman's face, but no recognition. "You just tried to kill me a few days ago, back in that warehouse, and you've already forgotten who I am? Why did Pidaro pick an idiot like you to join his little team, anyways?"

"The Enforcer?" He managed to ask more than state. Then the flash of recognition flooded across his features, and then as quickly as it had come on, was replaced by fear once more. He suddenly became very, very afraid. "Look, I was just, you know, following orders. Please, it wasn't personal or anything. Please don't kill me, please."

"I don't want to kill you." Eventus tried to reassure the man. "But that's up to you, because I *will* kill you if you don't start talking. I want names, and I want locations. I want you to tell me everything you know about the death of Consul Selygo, the attempt on Macien, the murder of the Emperor, and the death of my friend Flaccus. I want to know about Pidaro, and I want the name of that fucking bald guy."

"Please." Bevellus' voice wavered, cracked, and he began to sob. "Please, I can't. I can't answer any of that, even if I knew something, which I don't, I can't. I couldn't, I can't."

"That's too bad for you, Bevellus." Eventus shook his head. "I will not kill you, I promise you that. But some things can be worse than death." He pulled out a dagger, and let it glint in the moonlight that was coming in the window.

"Noooooooooo!" The man screamed. Eventus shoved a dirty rag in the man's mouth, smothering his scream. Tears erratically rolled down the jerking face of the Imperial guardsman as he writhed on the ground.

*   *   *

Eventus wiped clean his dagger, and walked out of the building. He had left Bevellus alive as he had promised, but still securely tied up and in a spot where he could snatch him up and bring him to the Hold at a later time. That had been rather productive after all. Bevellus knew a lot more than he had let on at first, that little fibber.

Sextillius. That was the name of old baldy. Tomorrow he would find Sextillius, and that would be very rewarding. Hopefully he could keep himself from killing the bastard, that would be the hard part. Dragging him down to the Hall before the Judge and Grattus was the top priority. He would make sure he was there when he was executed. Might be he would request to swing the blade. As for now, he was ready for a drink. And sleep. His thoughts wandered to Tassia as he walked through the dark, empty streets.

She had left the city, just as he had urged her to do, and that made him feel assured inside. If she were safe, out in some country farm or wherever she had gone, then he didn't have to worry about his enemies using her to get to him. They would do anything they could to hurt him, and he needed every advantage he could in this situation. Still, he thought of her, and that was the driving force behind his determination to end this all. Her and Flaccus. They had both saved him in one way or another, and he owed it to them to see this thing through to the end.

Epilogue
THE OLD MAN

It was dark by the time they had made camp. The old man knew all the stops along this road, having travelled it most of his long life. This was the best one to stay at for this stretch of the road, so they had pushed on a little longer and harder to make it here. The fire was going, crackling and spitting embers up into a smoky trail that dissipated into the starry sky. The meal had been plain but filling, more impossibly fresh olive bread provided by the old man himself. Another wineskin had appeared, and tonight they drank it as it was, not heated.

"Is that all for the story today?" Jaimus asked, an exhausted look on his face.

"I think it is a good place to stop, I've been talking all day and you boys have been walking all day." The old man sipped his wine. "A good night's rest will be just what you need, especially if you are joining a legion tomorrow. They might have you marching and drilling all night long. Better rest while you can."

The boys said nothing, but wearily nodded in agreement.

"I've got a few questions." Cassius said. "How about you answer them instead of telling us more of the tale."

"Is that a demand?" The old man raised and eyebrow. "Or a polite request?"

"A request." The boy said, not daring to use a word like 'polite' to detract from his demeanor.

"Very well." The old man said. "But I won't clarify anything that might spoil the story. Many twists and turns are still ahead."

"Who are you?" Cassius blurted.

"That is for later." The man snapped back, smiling.

"Emperor Kantaur was murdered? That was never told to us by our teachers; they say he died from lung-rot fever." Cassius said.

"I ensure you, he was indeed killed." The man said. "All will be revealed, and why that fact was lost to history, too."

"Are you immortal?" Cassius snapped back.

"Philosophy this late at night?" The old man mused. "Are you immortal my young friend? Is anyone? What happens after death is between the dead and the hereafter, not for us to know."

"I mean, if you are an Immortal, how come you are old?" The boy asked.

"Yeah, in the myths, Immortals are always young and strong." Marcus chimed in. Jaimus nodded in agreement.

"Oh, you know all there is about Immortals, do you?" The man asked. "There are things in this world that people can't explain. Strange things. As of yesterday, you thought I was a crazy man. Maybe I am. But you think now, perhaps the old man is an Immortal. I will tell you this; I was. Once. Perhaps I still am. Or perhaps not, I can't be certain. Maybe I am just a crazy old man."

"How can you be Immortal and then not?" Cassius asked, throwing up his hands. "I don't believe any of this. I'm going to sleep. It's just a stupid story."

"Ah, true or not, you may decide. But it is a good story, is it not?"

Cassius said nothing, just glared. Then he turned and went to fetch his bedding.

The other two boys sat there looking at the old man, the fire casting their young faces in an orange glow.

"I believe you." Marcus said, standing. "I believe all that you have said. I look forward to hearing more of this tale; and figuring out some of these answers for myself. Good night, sir." And with that, he left the campfire.

The old man nodded. It was just him and Jaimius. The old man rose to his feet. "Goodnight, young man. I hope you sleep well." He said, stretching out his arms and groaning.

"If you were an Immortal, then you lost it." The boy asked. "Does that mean you are now cursed to die like the rest of us?"

The man stopped for a moment. His chest fluttered as the words sank in. It was only a heartbeat, but the thrumming brought back memories.

"I believe that I am to die, yes." He said.

"But I would not call it a curse. I have known curses, my boy. The cycle of life is no curse."

Jaimus nodded. "I wish I would never die. I wish I were immortal."

"I used to wish for that, too." The old man said, smiling. "Good night, Jaimus. Tomorrow, I will tell you more. Gods give strength."

Thank you for reading!

The story continues in ...
END OF EMPIRE: BOOK III

SCHISM

Please leave a review, and be sure to tell someone who might like this series where to get it!